Lucy's Children

A Salad bowl of Life Secrets
tumbling out of guarded Closets

Dr. Bhagbanprakash

VISHWAKARMA PUBLICATIONS VP®

Lucy's Children
A Salad bowl of Open Secrets tumbling out of guarded Closets

1st Edition–published by Vishwakarma Publications in India in Dec. 2016
Reprint–published by Vishwakarma Publications in India in Jan. 2017
© **Dr. Bhagbanprakash**

ISBN -978-93-85665-53-0

Published by:
Vishwakarma Publications
283, Budhwar Peth, Near City Post, Pune- 411 002.
Phone No: (020) 20261157 / 24448989
Email: info@vpindia.co.in
Website: www.vpindia.co.in

Cover :
Learnitude Technologies

Typeset and Layout :
Chaitali Nachnekar (Vishwakarma Publications)

'Proceeds from the royalty of the book would be used for the Odisha Nagarika Samaj ONAS'

This book is dedicated to the memory of 'Lucy',
believed to be the common grandmother of the humans, whose
2.8-million-year-old fossils were discovered in Ethiopia in 1974,
opening new windows to
understanding the origins and behavior
of her children today.

Note from the Author | vii

1   June Returns | 1

2   Caged Parrots and Super Citizens | 20

3   Waits, Worries and Wise Women | 38

4   Pushed Out to Unknown World | 52

5   Binny's Kitchen and Rituals in Tenjiku | 58

6   Apollo, Toilets & Vanishing 'Wives' | 74

7   Self, Sleeper Cells and Shaktiman | 83

8   From Innocence to Nonsense | 102

9   Moon's Mad Boy | 128

10 Migrant Seeds, Burnt Certificates | 142

11 Free Thinker in 'Fine City' | 155

12 How Big is Small? | 163

13 Suffering the Stupids | 174

14 Belief Bazaar & Conversation with Nina | 205

15 Shengnan, Shengu and Six 'T's | 225

16 Long Living Weaklings | 235

17 Second Fifty: 'Blues', Silver and Golden | 257

18 From Obituary to 'Woven Mat' | 281

Index | 299

Note from the Author

This book is a creative mixture of facts, fables and free thoughts based on the author's learnings from myriad real life events in multiple countries and cultures, the quintessence of which is captured in a 20hour air travel from San Francisco to New Delhi in June, that heralds the 'mega mating season of land and water'.

In 1951, when Eric Morley, father of the now famous Miss World contest staged the show for the first time, many had felicitated the winning beauty without knowing her ancestral connection with a 'beast'. Sixty five years later, in 2015, when tall Spanish beauty queen Mireia Lalaguna was decorated with the Miss World once again with a jewelled crown, many were still not aware of her maternal origins. Because it didn't matter now. The fact is, until 1974, the ancestral mother of all the beauties was sleeping under mounds of earth. It was a tiny African female chimpanzee, later on named as Lucy. The idea and inspiration for writing this book about her children, i.e, beauties and uglies, me, you and every one, came from her life and legacy. In a sense, she was the first real 'Miss World'.

The common name given to her was 'Lucy", which were actually several hundred pieces of bones, representing about 40% of her skeleton. The name was borrowed from the then popular song "Lucy in the Sky with Diamonds" known as LSD in the 70s, written primarily by John Lennon for the Beatles' 1967 album.

These bones had lain buried under layers of rock in a desolate region for close to three millennia, when anthropologist Donald Johanson first spotted the elbow and then the forearm. Within minutes, he knew he had stumbled onto a rare and real 'star'. The name stuck and soon became a part of the rich Lucy lore. Soon after, people started talking about Lucy, the "ape who stood up". Eventually, she emerged as the "holy grail of anthropology."

Lucy was classified as a hominid. The larger pelvic opening in her body proved that it was a female. The skeleton also showed a small skull that was similar to that of apes. Evidence of its bipedal upright walk was close to that of humans. This supported the view that bipedalism preceded the rise in brain size, leading to evolution of humans and their civilizations. It freed the forelegs of hominids enabling them to carry food, sharpening tree branches with teeth to make tools and weapons and change diet to a carnivorous one that eventually contributed to further brain growth. Female chimps were ahead of males in using the tools as weapon to fight and snatch food from male chimps, who refused to share it with their children. Interestingly, alongwith all these, Lucy is also believed to have developed the ability to prevaricate, pretend and evade, which were unusual attributes of animals at that time of history which they have rapidly refined.

In Ethiopia, her homeland, Lucy is fondly called Dinknesh, which means 'the wondrous one'. In 2007, the fossils and associated artifacts related to Lucy, were taken out for the first time, on a tour to the United States and remained there for six years. The exhibition, specially organized for the purpose was called Lucy's Legacy: The Hidden Treasures of Ethiopia. The author, who was present in USA during the exhibition, has used the title 'Lucy's Children', as a metaphor to remind the readers intermittently, about their real origin and how they have arrived at where they are today and to what extent they have carried forward her legacy. That long march and longer story will be worth a million more epics.

Keeping this as a back drop, the episodic, freewheeling contents of this book is embellished with recollections, reflections and illustrative examples of post-Lucy human nature and behaviour and presented with absolute honesty. Readers looking for a particular genre like fiction, non-fiction, memoir may be disappointed. For, it doesn't follow a conventional structure or logic as it is not about a single plot, person or place, nor is it about Lucy. Instead, the inclusive narrative, straddles multiple events, time zones and 'publics'; undertaking, both, outward and inward journeys and occasionally holding up a rear view mirror to Lucy's present day children like us, to stimulate self awareness. In this process, the writer has tried to tempt the readers to walk with him in a back and forth, 'local-to-global-to-local' journey as a social tourist.

In an unconventional way, the book dishes out the past, present and the personal on a platter through eighteen interwoven chapters and each one is replete with memories, moods, myths and anecdotes from different parts of the world. Each has a touch of reality and a tinge of reflection, minus overt prescription or presumption. Following a 'laugh-at-life-humour', the author observes how primordial Lucy's children have moved away from their ancestral mother to all the continents and changed themselves, as well as the world, beyond recognition.

Selected chapters of the first draft of this book were sent to some well-known writers and thinking readers for comments. Some didn't respond while a few obliged that included famous American Indologist Wendy Doniger and legendary BBC correspondent Mark Tully. Wendy was excited about the title but didn't have time to go through the contents. Tully said he was perplexed by certain facts presented. Another reader wrote: 'To me reading the book was like playing a snake and ladder game. Your narrative combines creatively the sensuous, serious and hilarious. In almost every second page I found pearls of common sense on how best to live a life and die a death. It nudged me to quickly climb up with you the ten critical stairs in the unfolding ladder of life, to learn its lessons and use these as utility tools in building a new 'society for all ages'.

A close friend picked up only one chapter titled–'Suffering the Stupids' and 20 minutes after shouted, 'Hey, I am one of them! Shakti Prasad, a young IIT faculty who had motivated me to write this book wrote: 'I found it to be an honest, authentic, and innovative portrayal. It has the potential to be the real soup for mind and heart besides being a lifelong learning partner.' And then asked 'Why have u dedicated this interesting book about affairs of women and men to a monkey? The book doesn't deserve it'. I told him that the answer to his question is there in the book itself. Three days later he withdrew the comments saying he had once again gone through the book, cover to cover and found the 'answer'. It was reassuring. I decided to go ahead.

I greatly appreciate the facilitating role played by the Book Bakers and particularly Suhail Mathur in bringing out this edition on time.

Bhagbanprakash
30.11.2016

1

June Returns

It was a warm, windy midnight in June, when summer arrives in Sanfrancisco and rains in India. Half conscious I was lost in the overcrowded memory lane for a while. The aircraft now took off, lifting up and dropping down a few times, and then confidently thrust forward, cutting into the layers of cotton wool clouds, climbing up and pushing through, leaving behind holes, channels and sound waves. Draped in a dark, wet saari, full of sound and fury, June, the soggy drencher had returned to India dutifully to keep its date despite bad 'boy', El Nino, playing spoil sport. Casting a green spell and thick undergrowth all around, June unites father heavens with mother earth in the tropics, under the shroud of clouds. The hot, humid affair goes on for months that melts mountains, fills rivers and swells seas. And for some, reviving undefined feelings of loss, trauma and pain, crowding and confusing memories with incidents and coincidences.

In 1947, India's bloodiest year of partition and freedom, empty June clouds had entered late and without rain. Trailed by a long spell of drought, it had crossed the sub-continent, hovering across river misguided souls had gone mad once again, forgetting their humanity. The incredible barbarity on both sides of the freshly drawn borders left a million dead and ten million displaced. As if the worst was not over; about a year later, Gandhi, the messenger of peace and non-violence, who led India to freedom, succumbed to three fatal shots of an assassin; one striking the chest and the other two piercing the abdomen. And that too, in an all religions prayer meeting. In minutes, the Mahatma breathed his last, with the name of God on his lips, paying with life for the sins of his insane children.

Hearing the news, mother was stunned and then wept inconsolably. Father burst into a bout of impotent anger, harshly and repeatedly cursing the killer. Grief and disbelief shook and gripped the whole country. The next day, our school was closed down in condolence. I was too young at the time to understand or imagine the reasons for such 'strange' reaction. I asked mother who Gandhi was and why he was killed, who killed him and what was the meaning of 'killing and death'? Eight decades later, this was what exactly an eight-year-old boy in Hyderabad had asked the police when questioned why he allegedly killed a six-year-old schoolmate after a scuffle over repeated bullying.

Mother said, "He was the father of our nation, who is now dead and gone for good, leaving all of us orphaned. About death, only people who are dead know. You would understand when you grow up." Like 'death', I also couldn't make out what she meant by 'nation'. However, the strange reactions to the incident lingered on deep in my psyche for long.

Each time June touches my skin on the terrace, with its soft, moist, playful fingers, much like delicate stroking of a lover, it rekindles feelings of old fears Fresh and raw in recent past, she had dazed me for days.

She had arrived with a rash of flash floods, hail storm and landslides, and snatched away two of my best friends, Mala and Yogesh, a loving couple in their 50s. They were on an excursion-cum pilgrimage with their children to the holy shrines on the Himalayan peaks. A week before, I had seen off the beaming family at the New Delhi railway station. They were so full of excitement and expectation.

A week later, we came to know that while trying to escape the nature's fury, Mala was pulled to death by another slipping, drowning man, who had desperately caught her by the hair for support. Her helpless husband met his end as soon as he was air-lifted, when his copter crashed, killing both, the rescued and the rescuers, ending the 'pilgrims' progress' in a double disaster. Earlier, helping and dragging each other, the harassed couple had trekked and trudged a long distance through rubble, water and ice without food for two days, in search of safety. The 'Abode of Gods' failed its devotees once again, reviving age old moral questions about death, destiny and the divine. The anti-gods ridiculed, referring to the event, as another example of the so called 'imaginary' God's 'cruelty' and failure to intervene and protect his own devotees. "God is dead... we have killed Him once again... there is no divine order nor rational morality, no meta physical world", they shouted echoing German philosopher Nietzsche. Then came the good news about the couple's two lost children. They were believed to have been buried and dead under the rubble when a land slide, triggered by heavy rains, had flattened the roof over their head. As the walls started cracking and collapsing, the escape routes were choked with debris. But they had survived miraculously, even as hundreds perished, and were now rescued to safety by locals after a week.

This time, the crestfallen faithfuls broke silence and celebrated the 'kindness' of the supernatural. There was nothing to blame or praise god for; it was the stupid climate and lack of preparedness that had caused the disaster. However, the first act of the rescued children was to perform the last rites of their parents. While dead Mala was found to be wearing a Tabiz gifted by her guru for protection from harm, Yogesh had tied round his waist the tiny statue of a deity for divine intervention during disaster. Rationalising the tragedy, a deeply religious friend said that the dead couple were 'damn lucky' for, their souls had gone from a 'holy place' straight to heaven, together.

In the late 90s, during a visit to the Emerald Buddha Temple in Lampang, northern Thailand, a Thai scholar had narrated to me an interesting real life incident in the history of Laos. Its King Setthatirtha had ordered three statues of Buddha to be crafted in emerald, diamond and gold, reflecting the images of his three daughters. Later on, in the 19th century, after attacking and razing the kingdom to dust, the invading Thai army had carried off in a big boat all the three statues named Phra Serm, Phra Sai and Phra Souk. However, unable to withstand an unexpected storm, the boat had suddenly sunk in the Mekong River.

In the subsequent search, that cost a few lives, two statues were recovered except that of Phra Souk, the most precious one. It was lost forever. The other two statues were placed in temples and are still being worshipped. Ironically, the meaning of the unlucky, sunken Phra Souk was 'Lucky Buddha'!!

Ancient Greeks used to call luck as 'destiny', and considered it bigger than the gods, who themselves are subjected to its invisible power. As an example, they cite how Oedipus, the ancient Greek hero, unknowingly killed his father and married his own mother. Later, after knowing the truth, he ended his life, unable to bear the immoral burden of incest and patricide. Soul, Divine and Destiny are the first three old ideas that continue to dominate the modern mind even today.

So, life on earth moved forward, leaving behind the likes of Mala, Yogesh and Phra Souk, swinging like a rope between despair and hope, with cruelty and kindness trailing behind every day reality and routine. The journey didn't stop, nor time stood still. Blazing through the rising sun and beaten down by falling rains, defiant June smiled once again, heralding the mega mating season of land and water in the tropics. As the sizzling summer slowed and cooled, the time for regeneration arrived. The nude trees, now clothed by mist drenched fresh leaves welcomed everyone. A strange mix of dusty winds, wet earth and green shoots joined in too. As the first rain-drops fell on the parched and parted surface, the top soil softened and swelled like the budding breasts of a growing girl; the soft flesh bulging on the hard pan of her bony chest, pushing and popping out like sprouts.

Springing back to life, the good earth reminds its children once again that she is the primordial mother of all mothers. So, one has the unique experience of seeing, both, life in death and death in life together at one point of time as if nature never believed in 'only one life'. She resurrects time and again and reproduces tirelessly. Like Prakriti, the feminine power of Nature, reviving Purusha, the masculine, kinetic energy, into procreation, unfolding into diverse forms. In parts of coastal India, June bears a biological symbolism. Farmers treat the rain induced moisture in the soil as an annual menstruation cycle of Bhudevi, the 'Earth goddess', filling and pumping with enough oestrogen, and reviving and recharging her for fresh productivity. The showers sink deeper to discover her hidden fertility where seeds would rest for a while to sprout, grow and reproduce.

During my brief visit to the 'Museum of Menstruation', a small private initiative of great historical value, on the outskirts of Washington D.C, I had come across interesting drawings, documents, stories and myths; almost as many as there are cultures. One was about Artemis, the Greek goddess who never attained puberty, had no menstruation and was childless. Ironically, she was being worshipped to prevent as well as facilitate birth, to help girls grow from maidenhood to motherhood!! In eastern India, I had the personal experience of witnessing a four day long 'festival of menstruation and fertility' called Rawja, which begins in mid June and ends with a ceremonial post-menstrual bath on the fourth day. During this 'period', no digging or ploughing of earth is permitted and all women in reproductive age are made to rest and relax.

While in some cultures menstrual blood is considered impure, in parts of Africa it is used as a charm to purify people. In ancient Rome, it was believed that a naked menstruating woman could scare away hailstorms, cyclone and lightening. And if she walks in the corn field without clothes, caterpillars, worms, pests and insects disappear. In parts of southern India, girls are given gifts on attaining the first menstruation. Freed from kitchen and other domestic chores, they sing, dance and swing. Reverberations in the skies and recreation on the ground compete with each other in a unique celebration of geology and gender, that returns year after year, to remind humankind how and why women matter.

As the aircraft was moving ahead, I stood up and walked around. Almost every third person looked to be different in terms of colour, culture and race. The plane itself was a mini flying earth in the sky. More than 2.8 million years old, the journey of the gene from female chimpanzee, Lucy, believed to be the common ancestral mother of humans, continues. I had seen Lucy for the first time in the American Museum of Natural History in Newyork city. She was silently observing her children and was probably trying to understand what has happened to them after a million genetic jumps!

A billion years before that, the common clay, mother of all mothers, had given birth to complex biochemicals that made life possible on planet earth. Since then, the endless and road less back and forth travel of life goes on, recycling 'from dust to dust', through 'life-to- death-to-life'. Mother earth has warmed up with life after coming out of the ice like deadly grip of harsh and hostile climes.

Hardwired to fall out of love and move on to new relationships, the meeting and mating of women and men from North and South, East and West, between black, brown, red, yellow and white, went on with differential speed through adventurous animals. About 65000 years ago, species like Nenderthals interbred with humans and emigrated to new lands. Sexually adventurous Homo Sapiens immensely contributed to the immune system that helped protection against pathogens. There is an interesting account in recent history as to how following the zig-zag genetic trail, the DNA of a Surat woman in India traveled for hundreds of years, covering half the planet, through a doomed love story, to finally enter into Prince Harry and William in Buckingham palace. How? Through another break up between Diana Spencer and Prince Charles. Diana had inherited it through the female line, from the Duke's great, great, great, grandmother, Eliza Kewark (1788-1820). Eliza herself was half Indian and half Armenian, product of another wild relationship between a white man and a brown woman, despite social barriers and attitudes.

Thanks to the dynamic gene, the wheel now has turned full circle, as an Indian origin would now be the King of England, whose British ancestors ruled over the Indian empire, for nearly two centuries. Taking it forward, another stream has entered into the White House, crossing continents, upturning the slave-master relationships on its head, once again. Nature, as usual, had the last laugh. A medieval poet-saint, Kabir, has described the process through a meaningful imagery from pottery. In a couplet, the 'Clay' tells the Potter: 'You are moulding and remoulding me with your fingers on the wheel today, but remember, I will do the same to you tomorrow'.

Conquests by Kings and Emperors, large harems and marching armies, millions of men and women attracted to new mates and falling into new relationships must have become carriers of the dynamic gene, spreading its further across race, religion and cultures. For instance, in China, pushed by the nomad raids, large populations moved southward attracted by profits from maritime trade with the South East Asian region. Afterwards, a political decision by the White colonialists disallowing officials to import their wives, forced many to take local girls as mistresses and avail sexual hospitality, further quickening the genetic mix. Later on, the process was repeated in Africa to Americas.

Gene is the real Janani (mother) and destiny, racing restlessly to unite humanity in myriad and mysterious ways, through colonialism, slave trade, wars, conquests and expansions. Through silk, spice, mountain and sea routes, through tours, travels, teaching and preaching, through love and hate, crossing countries and continents, were spanning the last four millennia. Nature has a unique way of defeating those who wanted to differentiate, divide, through its genetic conquests, resulting in shared and common chromosome, creating a melting pot with products called Khichdi in a local Indian lingo, a zig-zag juggernaut journeying towards homogeneity. The modern Chinese call it a 'hot pot', a large steel bowel in which a delicious chicken broth is brought to boiling point over a gas flame set in the centre of a revolving dining table. The diners sitting around it dip a wide variety of choicest meat, egg, roots and vegetables into the boiling broth and fish out the contents with their chopsticks, sharing with one another. After repeated stirring the contents lose their identity and the flavors their diversity, producing a unique taste. Individual ego has no place in nature.

As our plane was tearing through the rain clouds, I recollected how during bed time, my mother had narrated to me a story about Lord Krishna's adventurous adolescence and courage to challenge the ego of 'gods'. In order to remove a prevalent superstitious belief, he had asked co-villagers to stop praying and offering foods to egoistic Indra for rains as it was a blessing of nature only, and how a proud Indra, the great god of rains, tried to punish them for it. Almost similar to the arrogant Greek sky god, Zeus, who defeated the Titans and Typhon by always wielding lightning and thunder bolts to punish those who challenged his authority and the Roman god, Jupiter, the 'cloud bearer', is more like him. I once asked mother why some gods are so arrogant?

Another day she narrated an interesting small story-equally instructive. When demon Vritrásur stole all the waters of the world, Indra, the lord of heaven chased and defeated him in a big war and recovered the lost water. It was probably world's first recorded war to take control of the water resources. With full control over the rain clouds, Indra emerged as a powerful god of a rain -fed agricultural society on earth. Soon after, people started praising and praying to him for rains and protection from drought, famine, floods and cyclone.

This newly acquired power instantly went to Indra's head and inflated his ego. He started exploiting and harassing the people. Hearing this, Lord Vishnu and Shiva visited Indra in guise of hermits. They praised the extra ordinary beauty and grandeur of Indra's new palace, casually adding that 'no former Indra' had such a wonderful thing. A surprised and confused Indra wondered how there could be another 'former Indra'.

During this conversation, a procession of countless ants entered the royal hall. Pointing at them, Vishnu revealed that all these ants were actually former Indras. At this point, Shiva came. His wide open chest had a dense cluster of hair with a big gap in the middle. When Indra asked him about it, the hermit said that there are innumerable heavens and earths and each strand of his chest hair corresponds to the life cycle of one Indra in heaven. He told Indra that each time a hair falls, one Indra falls and another Indra takes over and on account of these fallen hairs, a gap had been created on his chest. Crestfallen, Indra's false pride dissolved.

When I narrated this story to an astronomer friend, he said Lord Shiva was nearer the truth. Because, astronomy believes that 20 percent of sun-like stars have earth-like planets. Assuming that the Milky Way has 200 billion stars, it is quite likely that there would be at least 10 billion potentially habitable 'earths', with equal number of 'heavens' with their rulers like Indra, in one galaxy alone.

Pride, power, arrogance and ignorance together are a dangerous cocktail. In such matters, many of Lucy's children are no less than Indra.

Tracing the socio-biological history of the humans is more than a thriller. There are umpteen stories to assume that perpetually in search of new land, food and water, people depending primarily on animals than crops for survival, might have trekked for months in different directions to escape the harsh climes and arid grass lands in their respective regions. They were migrating along with their prince, priests, hermits and cattle from both sides of the Caucasus Indicus, known as the Hindukush. The animals provided milk, butter and meat and their skins and hair was used as tent and clothing. No wonder then that in both the Indian epics, Ramayan and Mahabharat, there are stories narrating how, both, kings as well as seers had gone to wars over the cattle wealth called Godhan. The conflict between sage Vashistha and King Vishwamitra over super cow, Nandini, and the bloody fight between two kingdoms headed by Virata and Trigartha are two of the many such examples. Greek mythology describes how King Cadmus came from far away Lebanon, following the tracks of a wandering cow in search of his sister, Europa, who had been abducted by Zeus, who had disguised himself as a bull.

It was likely that the criss-crossing was taking place across the long winding mountain range during June, facilitated by melting snow. The travellers must have been delighted discovering new regions, more fertile flatlands and richer societies beyond their natural barriers and borders, culturally connecting the Himalayas to the Hindukush. The highest peaks between Europe and Asia have a history of dividing and uniting people, time and again.

As they trudged forward, the adventure buried many of them in slush and snow, on both sides. Hitchhiking on merchant caravans, long distance traders and knowledge seekers were also entering the sub continent. Hindukush in Parsi literally means 'Hindu Killer' mountains, a sad reminder of the era when generations of nomadic invaders, raiders and plunderers were killing and looting India- bound travellers and dragging captive Indians past these peaks of perpetual snow, to their side, as slaves. Unable to withstand the journey across a 800 km long range, in harsh, hostile weather, many of them used to succumb, lending the cruel name 'kush' or 'kill' to the high hills.

Some suspect, the other motive could have been an exploratory search across the hills and grasslands for the depleting Soma, the intoxicating shrub and herb that grew in dry and cool climes. Warriors used to drink extracts of this as elixir for instant energy, alertness and excitement before going to fight. Priests and sages used to take it for 'spiritual high' and 'Shiva', the destroyer god, for his cosmic dance, called Tandava. However, in the process, many adapted to the new clime and unlike the polar bears, who took about 300,000 years to adjust to the Arctic ice, they soon befriended the locals by sharing the Soma rasa, 'the sacred Vedic drink'. While the Vedas extol the greyish-brown king of shrub, Soma, as heavenly drops and food of gods; in Iranian language and Persian dialects, the stimulant is known as 'haoma' and 'homa'.

Then there were knowledge and information explorers like Marc Polo, Meghasthenes, Faxian and Hiuen Tsang, who moved on and on across mountains and deserts, cutting off themselves from family, friends and home lands. At times, people and knowledge travelled together on horse and camel backs on the knowledge highway at great risk. While crossing the northern mountains on the journey back to China from India, Hiuen Tsang was almost drowned in river Indus along with loads of rare manuscripts of knowledge that he had collected from ancient Indian schools of learning, but many were washed away forever. Despite the perilous nature of the journey, monks in large number crossed over central Asia and Tibet to reach India. There is a story about how ailing Emperor Gaozong, after hearing about India's highly sophisticated culture and advanced medical knowledge system, was excited and ordered a monk, who had just returned from India, to go back there again to procure longevity drugs and physicians to treat him. The tired monk accomplished the mission but died on way back to China.

Being constantly on the move, the explorers must have looked at the stars for direction and fire for protection from wild animals. Thus evolved astronomy, astrology and 'fire worship'. The Rigveda has over two hundred hymns dedicated to Agni, the sacred, healing and purifying Fire God and about a hundred hymns dedicated to Varuna, the Sea God. Thus the nomads and natives together sowed the seeds of a new culture and wisdom tradition that dominated the world of thought for the next three millennia. Most of the Vedas were written in forests, closer to snow clad mountains between Hindukush and Himalayas. Atharva Veda, the fourth one of the Vedic series, repeatedly refers to the 'woods and snow' while praying to mother Earth: 'O Earth, thy snow clad mountains and thy woods, thy brown, black, red, multicolour, protected by Indra. On this Earth, may we stand undefeated, unhurt, unstained.'

This was also the pre historic period, when many races and cultures were crossing the seas in South and rivers and mountains in the North and West. A branch of East Asians and another branch of western Eurasians, moving and mixing, created Native Americans, our newer relatives on the other side of the planet and settled down in the hospitable soil that assured them both bread and breeding, in relative safety, much like migratory birds.

Freed from forelegs and fed by large brains formed by continuous fish and flesh eating and consumption of cooked food, their urge to imagine and explore, became an irresistible and rewarding option. As level of sex hormone declined further, people became less aggressive and more creative, leading to more group living and social tolerance. The time thus saved, created tools, art, culture and mutation of language gene. The caves now looked more attractive with carvings. Beauty was born.

Armed with the defining marker of humanness, civilization now moved faster forward, enabled and inspired by increasing capacity of imagination, creative thinking and of course coincidence like long spells of warm weather caused by climate change, empowered Genghis Khan to conquer large parts of Asia and Eastern Europe, helped by nomadic horsemen. It is said that as grass grew rapidly following erratic unseasonal rains in the arid plain, an unforeseen thing happened. It provided the much needed fodder to sustain a growing number of horses. Consequently, this added more horse power to move soldiers on their back and gallop into unknown territories, establishing relationships with thousands of women and of course sowing wild oats in the process.

The process also witnessed a strange genetic attraction of the people for each other. Probably, by that time, the climate had baked the old Afro-Asian and indigenous Indo-Aryans into dark brown, red, yellow and black. In 'The Seven Daughters of Eve' (2001), Bryan Sykes refers to seven clan mothers with a common maternal ancestor, a common progenitor that sounds probable now, after discovery of Lucy's fossils. Dark skin, wavy hair and thick lips, travelling and covering continents faster. No other mammals were more mobile and more nomadic than these erect bipeds who had tamed the quadrupeds for company. So, humble Dingo, the wild dog and scavenger, whom ancient sea faring Indians brought to Australia, eventually became a cultural icon of the aborigines there. With them, travelled the new tools and technology, food production and processing skills. From the dwarf tiny brained hobbits to large elephants, a variety of other species, moved to distant places; mixing and pushing the genetic drift to faraway lands.

The genetic streams flowed in and out from all directions, mingling and merging with each other, creating seven seas of animals. Zebras, tigers and leopards, aided by nature developed black and white graphic stripes, to ward off biting and blood sucking flies. Barbary lions from North Africa and Asiatic lions from India mated, multiplied and improved their genetic stock. The Mongolian, Arabian and Indian horses mated to produce the famous Marwari war horses, which had an ambling gait, inward turning ears and exemplary valour that fascinated horse lovers for ages. Now, the botanical matched the biological with equal measure. Founder crops like wheat, rice and barley along with companion plants pea, lentils, chickpea, flax and their variants dispersed far and wide. The most recent ones are the mango mother, Dussheri, and father, Neelam, mating to produce Amrapali and Mallika, adding attractive colours to both skin and flesh of the king of fruits to become sweeter, firmer and fibreless. Rooted and unable to move; plants, through their colourful fruits with pulpy contents, have always been attracting birds and beasts to eat and carry their seeds to places where their young ones could grow in safety.

From wild Earth to Moon, Mars and the outer space, the humans continue to criss-cross the universe, using tools beyond imagination of early humans. Flat footed Lucy (AL-288-1), our famous ancestral mother, who was climbing, walking, jogging and running on this planet millions of years ago, would have been immensely pleased today, seeing the exploits of her ever adventurous children. The admixture of these ancestral populations and continuous conversation between cultures and genes gave birth to a riot of colours; each influencing the other. Unable to fight the full fury of the sun; many turned brown and their hair became black. In India, Lord Krishna's brown ancestors had surfaced; eventually converting the dark into the colour of the divine. The variety increased as people assimilated themselves into social frameworks to survive. Today, our response to such colours stems from deeper socio- biological roots.

Colour always attracts, often divides, and sometimes defines product of climate; white reflected lack of light as much as black having too much of it. Yet both have separated the world like no other colour, virtually becoming colours of pride and prejudice. Red, saffron, green have their own worlds with hoods, robes, flags and followers like highly visual and choosy mosquitoes, who are attracted towards their tasty targets wearing red, black or navy blue. For instance, pre human male primates are particularly drawn towards females displaying 'red'. Female baboons and chimpanzees redden conspicuously while nearing ovulation, sending a clear sexual signal, designed to attract their male counterparts like Virginia creeper turning copper red to welcome the arrival of autumn.

As humans forget their fundamental connections and fight on superficial differences, nature celebrates preferences and sustains differences. Interestingly, some belonging to one colour group feel and fancy the other colour to be more exotic, more wild and passionate and something very special. Umpteen male and females have confessed that they were wildly turned on by differences in skin, hairstyle, size and colour of eyes and lips as much as differences in music, food and climate. The story of dark skinned Krishna shows how the lighter skinned girls in his community were irresistibly gravitating towards him.

In human history, both great and small people have tried their best to make men and women colour bound. Nobel laureate and India born English writer, Rudyard Kipling (1885-1936), whom George Orwell used to call as the 'Prophet of British Empire', was consciously reminding his fellow countrymen not to cross the racial, social and sexual dividing line. The frequently used phrases were - half castes mixed with native blood, blackie white, half-baked breed, chi-chi, twelve annas or three quarter of a rupee, etc. Some of these were reflected in disdainful verses about white-black relationships. John Masters, another poet and novelist, reflects this colour prejudice in the film, 'Bhowani Junction' (1954):

'There was a young lady called Starkey,

Who had an affair with a darkie,

The result of her sins

Was an eightsome of twins:

Two black and two White and four Khaki.'

Many Indians were quick to internalize the colour prejudice. My sister, Manika, would always think she was not good looking as she was dark, despite my open disapproval of this attitude. Another lady in our area was contemplating suicide after delivering a child who was jet black although she and her husband were light skinned. She would go into a state of depression when she saw another child lighter than hers. Even the lighter ones were not free from this complex. In 17th century Europe, wealthy women and men, anxious to improve their complexion, used to rub their face with puppy urine. It is said some women of the day, including Queen Elizabeth, were applying this urine to further whiten the colour of their teeth. Some were covering dark spots as well as cuts on the face with fashionable patches designed as stars, moon and diamonds.

According to a legend, good looking Parbati, meaning 'daughter of the mountains', who was dark with unkempt hair, had married the Vedic god, Rudra (Shiva), who was white like 'camphor' and 'ice'.

Whenever the short tempered Shiva was angry, he would loudly call out to her, 'Hey, Kaali pahadi, meaning 'Hey, black woman of the hills'. As this continued, an embarrassed Parbati thought that probably her husband was mocking her dark skin. Feeling offended, she entered into a long spell of Tapasya, i.e., meditation and penance, until her skin turned white. After this, she was given a new name and called Gauri, the 'white skinned woman'. Although stripping a person's identity associated with name or colour leaves a lasting scar, this Aryan-aborigine pair survived the stress and turned out to be a greatly successful couple.

There is a view that it was an attempt to absorb a dark skinned aborigine into the fair skinned society of the day. Eventually, Shiva, known as Pashupati - meaning 'lover of animals', seems to have also adapted a lot many indigenous traits of the aborigines like wearing a tiger skin, riding a bull, wearing snakes around his neck, holding a trident in one hand and a damru or small drum in the other, with matted hair and body smeared with cremation ash and living in austerity without any property. He was probably the first communist before Karl Marx. The picture of a naked Kaali standing on the chest of this sleeping Shiva, holding the severed head of a demon king, who had a lustful evil eye on her lower body part, is now used as a mascot and symbol of women's liberation movements in modern India. This is another instance of using the images of the past to fight the prejudice of the present.

In a way, nature and evolution had conspired together in depriving humans of perfect perception of colours. If they had been gifted with a cat's sharp eye with a capacity to discriminate ten thousand colours or a pigeon's sight to distinguish ten billion, the world would have been culturally fragmented into trillion times by our visual computational device. Lucy would be happier than anyone else, as her colour conscious misguided children, including great poets and writers, would finally be liberated from skin based pride and prejudice.

From the window seat, I looked out; the sky was overcast with a canopy of dark clouds covering the sun. Colorful images of the earth had disappeared alongwith sounds of singing, fluttering birds. Incidentally, it was 6th June 2012. The day I was returning home, after attending a conference of Indo-Americans from colourful California, another cultural melting pot in the making. It was precisely the 157th day of the year, when Venus was on its last transit, passing directly between the Sun and the Earth, one of the most important celestial events in history and science of the 21st century. When the next 'transit' happens, more than a century later, in December 2117, none of the seven billion plus earthlings like us would be there to witness it, nor our children. But then, Lucy's children are immortal. At least eight plus billion of them would be there to witness the great event much better with more improved devices; maybe from another planet, as many would have already settled down there. People in the golden state were now getting ready to witness the historic event. The other exciting event was the six year long 'Lucy Exhibition' about which the whole country was obseesed. It was coming to an end as the Ethiopeans were making praparations to welcome her back. Throgh common grandmother Lucy' skeleton, culturally uprooted Americans were once again connecting to their common ancestry.

In USA, California is known to be the trend setter in science, astronomy, art, culture, life style and historically, the most attractive destination for the gold seekers, known as 'forty-niners'. They had rushed here in the year 1849 and afterwards, scouting for gold deposits in streams and river beds. Now, silicon chips have successfully replaced the yellow metal, but well before that, President Richard Nixon had ended the direct convertibility of dollar to gold on August 15, 1971.

It is a place full of young Indians. Bright young professionals and entrepreneurs from all over the world have made it the world's most high-tech state and most visible software centre. Indian netizens in their colourful sarees, kurtas, jeans and business suits are busy scripting the success story of a new California. I often tease them calling them 'ninety-niners', who like the 'forty niners', rushed to the Silicon Valley in 1999 in order to save it from a feared millennium computer crash in 2000 that didn't happen. Now considered America's best educated and model minority, earning twice the per capita income of an average American, their struggle to straddle two different cultures, wearing multiple identities every day and still survive with success, is worth another epic. The departure lounges of India's international airports are full of them with emotional scenes of tears, happiness and hugs. The Smithsonian Museum in Washington DC has chronicled the heritage of Indian immigrants and their contribution to the American melting pot in graphic details in an exhibition.

Centuries ago, their gold - loving great grandparents had already missed the free for all rush to exploit the yellow metal in abundance that had spurred a huge immigration. Strangely, Indians, world's largest consumers of gold, were nowhere to be seen in all the great gold rush that occurred in America, Australia, South Africa, Brazil and New Zealand in 18th and 19th century. One day, in an Indian community meeting in New Ark, a young software professional asked how India missed the 'golden' opportunity of '49'. I told him that it was partly by geography and partly by history and politics because the subcontinent was under colonial rule during this period, which had destroyed its indigenous free trade and discouraged voluntary crossing of borders. In the process, Indians slowly forgot their sea faring adventurous spirit.

Then, in a lighter vein, I said, 'But no regrets, although you failed the 'rush', the gold is rushing to your country anyway.'

'How?' Someone asked in surprise.

I said, 'About 3000 kg of gold is smuggled into the country every month to satiate the yellow appetite of brown Indians. Their women's irresistible weakness for gold, particularly in festive and wedding seasons, is legendary.'

To clarify the point, I explained how even ancient Roman Senators used to complain that India was draining the Roman Empire of its gold and silver in exchange of spices, silks and fine textiles that were preferred by the upper class ladies in Rome. In the 16th century, the Portuguese, along with many European countries, were also grudging that the hard earned gold they get from America is lost to the Indian 'sink', as their own citizens were too willing to exchange it for Indian luxuries'. In the 17th century, the British Parliament specifically asked East India Company to sell goods to the Indians rather than buy their goods paying in gold.

Then, I retold the famous explorer Vasco's da Gama and Indian King, Zamorin's, story. When Vasco's fleet arrived near Calicut's Kappad beach on May 1498, an excited Zamorin had sent 3000 Nair soldiers and courtiers to receive him. Overwhelmed by the gesture, Vasco sent a number of gifts for the king, seeking an early appointment with him. But looking at the ordinary nature of the gifts that included six hats, four branches of corals, some brass, vessels, sugar, honey and oil, the king was greatly disappointed. There was not a single piece of silver or gold. An infuriated Zamorin is reported to have declined to meet Vasco and cancelled the appointment. When Vasco reported this to King Dom Manuel of Portugal, the news spread like wild fire in European trade circles that the yellow metal was the only thing Indians valued in exchange of their goods. Since then, European traders always brought with them only gold and silver to buy Indian goods. The trend reversed only after the industrial revolution when machine made clothes replaced the handmade and alternative spice routes and sources were found.

The Indian obsession with gold is as old as the Indian story of creation. It describes how God deposited a cosmic seed out of his body in the water that turned into a bright, radiant golden egg, giving birth to Brahma, the creator of the universe. Brahma's other name is Hiranyagarva, which means the one born out of a golden belly. In Hindu mythology, all the gods and goddesses are either silver or golden hued. And in Indian culture buying gold is an auspicious act and selling it is always considered a bad omen. However, the weakness is not confined to India alone. Even Plato was measuring men and woman by metal, as Men of Iron, Men of Copper, Men of Silver and Men of Gold, the latest one representing the highest state of human evolution.

However, more than California's rainbow race and its gold, what impressed me most were its age old trees- claimed to be the largest and tallest in the world. The currently oldest living tree, 'Methuselah', is now aged 4845 years. Almost immortal. 'Prometheus', the second one, was cut down in 1964 when its age was 4844 years. However, the oldest living human-planted tree in the world with a known planting date is the historical Bodhi tree in Sri Lanka, still much younger to Methuselah. Its sapling was brought from India and planted in 288 BC. I love tall, towering trees as much as I hate to measure and map them like timber merchants. A short walk through flowering trees in peaceful serenity always lifts spirits to new high. The shade makes one feel like moving under the protective, cool and loving care of parents. In 2001, I was in Zimbabwe attending a conference, during which we had gone to see the great Victoria Falls. On the way, I was awestruck at seeing a number of majestic trees called Baobab, variously known as 'tree of life', 'upside down bottle', 'tree of hope' and 'monkey bread tree'.

Wow! Wow! Wow! - was my first reaction, when the guide drew our attention towards it.

The day before my departure on the 5th June, people were celebrating the World Environment Day. In the past, in one such celebration, the former President of India, Dr. Zakir Hussain, an erudite scholar and nature lover, was the Chief Speaker. It is said that after listening to tons of talks by tens of experts on why to take care of trees, he stood up and completed his key note address in just one sentence. He said, 'Trees take away what we give away, provide free food, shelter and shade, help everyone everywhere and yet always remain silent'. Then he sat down, amidst a thundering applause. He had made the point loud and clear. It reminded me of the story about a professor of poetry, who was to deliver a lecture to her students about songs. She had come prepared with a 3,000-word script, but as soon as she entered the class, a small, beautiful song bird, sitting on the window sill, started singing. The professor waited till the song was over and quietly left the class room; softly whispering to the students that there was no need now for her lecture on the subject. The song bird had done the job much better than a wordy lecture on poetry could ever hope to do.

It is said that when Einstein met Charlie Chaplin, the popular comedian of the silent movie era he had greeted him by saying, 'What I most admire about your art is that you don't say a word and still everyone understands you'. Witty Chaplin had answered smilingly, 'Sir, it is true, but your glory is even greater. The whole world admires you, even though most of them don't understand a word of what you say!' The Buddha, after attaining 'enlightenment' had declined to utter even a single word. He had just smiled and shown a lotus flower to the waiting people. Moving on from words to ideas and then to one's own experience and understanding is a quiet internal journey that cannot be expressed. Jesus Christ, too, needed just six words to express the essence of his faith: 'My Father and I are one'.

Moving far away from the Father, Lucy's children have converted the silent earth into a land of Babel with a continuous war of words.

2

Caged Parrots and Super Citizens

In our neighborhood, the nick name of an elderly widower was "Killer of Parrots", the legendary mimicking bird which appeared on earth about 68 million years ago. One day, he suddenly stopped feeding the pet, dragged it out of the cage and killed. Soon after, he went on a killing spree of parrots wherever he found them. It was found out that the real reason behind this eccentric behavior was that the unfortunate bird was mimicking the love words he was exchanging with another woman. Learning that he was cheating on her, his wife left him forever.

From early childhood, the silent and forgiving trees and the chirping, talkative birds had become my green companions. They were also my saviours from the village 'school of violence' and 'teacher tormentors'. Going to school was a dreadful journey every morning and, perhaps, the most exciting news then was to learn that the teacher was absent. For years, I felt like a 'caged parrot' inside the cruel class rooms controlled by cane holding teachers, who were bereft of any affection or empathy. Most of them used to bombard us every now and then with, both, verbal nonsense and physical abuse. For almost a decade, I had lost my identity inside this 'prison'. One of my classmates had lost his hearing and another his left eye vision on account of this. Quite a few dropped out for good. Two were withdrawn by panicky parents.

In primary school, once, when I failed to answer a question, the teacher beat me with a cane so hard that out of fear I stopped attending the classes for almost three weeks. Bunking the class, I used to sneak off into the forest on the edge of the village, climb up a leafy, shady tree and stay there for the whole day till the last period was over. Nestled in the foothills, it was the perfect setting for spending time, watching the birds, listening to their sweet songs and trying to make sense out of their twitter.

On the second day of hiding, I discovered two migratory swallows with tiny bills nesting next to my resting branch, in a natural cavity of the tree and trying to fill it with grass and thin twigs. Kissing each other frequently, the blue green male and the light green female were the perfect picture of a happy couple. Highly sociable, both were flying back and forth playing with friends, who were nesting on nearby trees, eating insects and fruits for survival. Then one day, one of them stopped flying and kept on sitting. I found out that she was laying eggs. The male bird flew down frequently, collecting dry twigs and soft grass, to cover the eggs and protect it from predators. A few days later, both started flying together back and forth from the nest to a fruit tree carrying piece after piece and putting it into the fledgling's half open mouths.

A little distance away, some other male birds were busy making visual and auditory displays–spectacular flights, singing intricate songs and doing elaborate dances, probably to win the heart of the lady bird. To seek further attention and impress the female, the male bird would show off his health and strength in different ways to convince her with the message that he was her best possible mate. It was almost like the male Kangaroos, who flex biceps to show off their muscular arms to impress and woo the opposite sex.

Another pair of bigger birds, one chasing the other, engaged my attention for a long time as their behaviour appeared to be very mysterious until I found out that one of them was a female. She would pick up a twig and fly back to a certain height in the sky and when the pursuing male bird would be near her, she would just let the twig fall. Now, the male bird would swiftly double its flying down speed to catch the fast falling twig before it reached the ground. Both of them would repeat this game for hours. Then, they would settle down on a branch or a high rock to kiss each other and mate. Seemed like the male bird had passed the test and proved his commitment to her. In retrospect, now I think it was most likely a simple and funny game before sex.

Watching projectile motions of birds, both horizontal and vertical, and the continuous velocity and acceleration, were, in a way, my first childhood lessons in physics. Now, I wonder how their heart and lungs muscles withstood the sudden fluctuation in speed from high oxygen sea level to low oxygen sky level. Another very interesting site was the termite mound very close to the tree that I was resting on. This attracted a variety of birds, bears and monkeys who were feeding on the termites inside. Once a black bear arrived and broke the mound open, causing millions of termites to come out of their tiny air cooled mud chambers.

The hiding continued for weeks and in between bird watching, I also finished reading the text books thrice over, in peace, and now understood these better without a cane holding teacher. I realise now that the forest is probably the most perfect and non-threatening setting for any serious reading, writing, learning and reflection. It is like a free open green school that gives students full control over their own experience based education. In ancient India, the best schools called Gurukul were set up in forests with the focus on learning to know, learning by doing and 'learning to be'.

No wonder then that jungles used to inspire and turn people creative, spiritual and philosophical. Brihad Aaranyak, (around 600 BCE) or the 'Great Forest of Knowledge', one of the oldest Upanishads, was written in the wilderness of forest and hills. Parts of it carries a conversation between a forest dwelling hermit, Yajnavalkya, and his wife and student, Maitreyi, about meditation and asceticism, self identity, nature of reality and duty towards God, guru, ancestors, fellow humans and animals. The universally acclaimed prayer-cum-mantra- 'Asato ma Sad gamaya…' is from this Upanishad Composed in the forest, the prayer says:

'Lead us from unreal to the Real, Lead us from darkness to Light, Lead us from death to Immortality,

Let there be Peace, Peace and Peace.'

Every day, I used to return home from the forest, mingling with school returning students of another class. Then finally, one day, my living with nature ended abruptly as I was caught by another classmate, who informed my mother 'Moon' about it. She was greatly worried as the jungle in which the tree stood was full of poisonous snakes and wild animals. On her insistence, I confessed to her about reasons behind this. The news spread and the teacher became angrier and unforgiving. To punish me for the long absence, the next day he hit me seven times so badly with a wooden rod that I almost fainted with unbearable pain. He was a strong believer in the principle of 'spare the rod and spoil the child'. The school, which many think to be a great social leveller, was for me an insecure place of violence, punishment, pain, torture, fear, and a veritable nightmare I always wished to avoid and forget.

Another day, the teacher asked a question on geography to everyone in the class. It was: Which country the river Nile passes through? When no one was able to answer, I raised my hand, stood up and said it was 'Egypot' or 'Misser' Desh.

'You fool, wetty pants, say it again', he shouted. I repeated. Now, he first watched me silently but sharply and then came near me menacingly, playfully shaking the ragged cane and thrashed me hard five times. Reeling under pain, I was shocked, firstly as I was expecting an appreciation since no one could answer that question and secondly, because that is how it was written in the text book. When I protested, saying I was correct, he thought it was a challenge to his uncontested authority. He became angrier. 'You are a stupid, good for nothing fellow', he shouted and punished me with three more lashes. Then he informed us that it was not Egyp'o't, as I had pronounced, but 'Egypt' and similarly it was not Misser but 'Misr' in Arabic. We had no idea what was Arabic. And I failed to understand why he had called me 'wetty pants' in front of everyone. Mother had told me that I had stopped bed wetting as soon as I had started crawling.

Groaning and grunting inwardly, I returned home and searched out the page in the text book and found out what I said was correct. If the teacher was correct, it must be a mistake of the printer. Next day, I showed the related portion in the book to the teacher. He started blaming my parents and abusing the publisher, but had no regrets for beating me black and blue and damaging my emotional and mental self, without any fault of mine. As blood rushed to my head with impotent anger, I tore off the relevant page and threw it away. The arrogant teacher lacked the basic intellectual humility-an important key to becoming a better person by simply recognizing that one might be wrong about what one thought, did, felt or believed.

Margaret Mead, well known cultural anthropologist (1901-1978), had said: 'My grandmother wanted me to have education, so she kept me out of school.' There is a saying that the Indian empire was actually lost in British public schools, as these schools turned out students, who later on were sent to the colony as arrogant, insensitive administrators with the strange mission of 'civilizing' the native Indians, the 'white man's burden'.

Like the caged parrots, often Romans too didn't have the full freedom of expression. So, aggrieved citizens of the Roman Empire used to write down their grievances and curses against the wrong doers on thin sheets of lead and bury it in tombs, as petition to the deity to punish. In my case, it remained buried and alive in my mind instead. Lashing a child for mispronouncing or missing an alphabet or a vowel, an accent or intonation, a dot or dash, is a cruelty and crime true teachers must avoid in order to learning joyful. In fact, this teacher, by his insensitive act, rewarded those who didn't know and punished the one who 'knew'.

My friend Raza was cleverer. Before the teacher asked a question, he would stand up raising one finger, which meant he needed a 'Shu shu break' or two fingers which meant 'Potty break', just to escape punishment. Once the teacher became suspicious and wanted him to hold off till the period was over. In minutes, he made the class room messy with both potty and shu-shu, embarrassing every one. After that, the teacher never asked him to hold off. However, after what happened to me, I had decided never to raise my hand ever again and say that 'I know' the answer and till today, I have not forgiven the teacher him.

Winston Churchill, who was frequently dropping out of school, had a slightly different experience. He used to complain that his teacher was never asking him questions to which he knew the answers, but always putting only those questions to him that he could not answer. Being curious, children everywhere have more questions than the world has answers. So, it is they who should ask questions more than the teachers.

Even Adolf Hitler thought most of his teachers had something wrong with them mentally, and quite a few of them ended their days as 'honest-to-God lunatics'. He later recalled how they had no sympathy with the students and their only object was to 'stuff our brains and turn us into erudite apes like themselves'. If any student showed the slightest sign of originality, they persecuted and harassed him relentlessly.

And then he said: 'The only model pupils whom I have ever known have all been failures in later-life.' Hitler himself was not a model student and proved to be a disaster. According to his teacher Edward Humer, he was 'wilful, arrogant and bad tempered' and always fancied himself in the role of a leader. But despite all that, there is a grain of truth in his assessment of teachers. Repeatedly humiliated by his debauch father and insensitive teachers, receiving no protection against mistreatment by others, without recognition, understanding or appreciation, he probably concluded that   right and justice were always on the side of the strong and mighty. That is how home and schools give birth to many little Hitlers.

About three millennia before, Gurus were following dialogue as the exclusive method of learning to stimulate the curiosity of the students (Sishyas). No snob, no abuse, no sticks. In Yajur Veda, the Guru asks: What is the name of the beautiful winged bird, who gives life and energy? Then he gives additional clues to get the right answer. Now the encouraged students debate among themselves and reply: 'It is Agni, the Fire.' Next question- 'What represents both earth and sky?' The answer comes after a free group discussion: 'cooking pot, cooking pot'. Then there are question–answer and quiz sessions, relating to mysteries of the universe, to promote collective learning and testing the knowledge of the priests, being trained to be spiritual teachers. For example, the Guru asks through four different questions:

'Who wanders lonely on his way? Who is constantly born anew? Who is the remedy for cold?

What is the great corn vessel called?

After brainstorming, the best answers are shortlisted and shared :

'The sun wanders lonely on its way. The moon is constantly born anew. The fire is remedy for cold.

The earth is the great corn vessel.' (Vaj. xxiii, 45-46, Trans. R.T.H Griffith)

However, in matters of language learning, what children need is friendly guidance, not punishment or reprimand. And each one of them has the right to be treated decently. Gandhi used to say that for students, a teacher is the real text book. The role of a teacher is to create a feeling of security and comfort so that instead of feeling inhibited, they feel elevated. In a real student- friendly learning environment, both the teacher and students are lifted to a higher plane of mind in which the giver as well as receiver of knowledge frequently interchange their roles and motivate each other. It is based more on human relations than the 'subject matter'. So, those who reminisce by saying that the most wonderful news for students in school was when 'the teacher was absent' are not entirely incorrect.

One of the reasons for lingering illiteracy in many parts of the developing world is unfriendly schools, merciless teachers and joyless learning. My father, Ramnath, withdrew me from my first village school for small children when he discovered that in two years I have just learnt two alphabets, i.e., A and B. At a tender age, many do not even understand the meaning of evaluation, exams, pass or fail. My younger brother, Sudam, in the third standard in our village school, came home one day and innocently announced with great pride that in his class he was the only boy who had 'failed', thinking that it was a unique achievement! He was a dynamic learner and instinctively hated rote learning. Another class mate of mine would be pulled by the ear because of his habit of tearing off and throwing away the page from the text book once he finished reading it. My image of a teacher was an angry person holding a cane, who would force me to memorize and rote one and the same alphabet day after day and never ask a question.

Long afterwards, I was in the Youth Ministry and part of a joint campaign in the late 80s that declared Kottayam in Kerala, as India's first fully literate city in 1989. My old friend, Thomas Abraham, Programme Coordinator of NSS, Mahatma Gandhi University, and myself had planned the strategy together sitting in a cubicle in Shastri Bhavan, in Delhi. We thought, if one city was made fully literate by mobilising teachers and student volunteers, it would give a big boost to the total literacy campaign in the country. Thomas, who had been trying to sell the idea, was quite confident and optimistic and assured emphatically, 'Yes, we can make it if you support us with some volunteers'. It took me five months to sell the idea to my senior colleagues, although the cost was nominal.

But there is an interesting sub- text behind this success story. That is, despite our best efforts and support from the District Collector, the city could not be declared 100% literate, because one illiterate Rickshaw puller, named Putappan (name changed), refused to attend the literacy class. A huge flag was ready to be hoisted on the day the city became free of illiteracy. But this would not be possible until Putappan became literate. The worried collector invited him to his residence for a cup of tea, and asked him why he was not cooperating. During the conversation, Putappan revealed that long ago he had taken a vow never to go to school. He was a seven-year-old child at the time.

When asked further, he informed that when he was in standard three, in an elementary school, a teacher had beaten him black and blue with a rugged cane, purely based on a wrong report. He didn't listen to Putappen's protestations of innocence. Unable to overcome the trauma, he ran away from the school, never to return again. The Collector, Kottayam, assured him that such a thing would never be repeated. Now, a convinced Putappen joined the literacy class and three months after, the flag of literacy was unfurled by the city's last literate, amidst much fanfare. The President of India sent a congratulatory message to the people of Kottayam. At personal level, I could feel Putappen's pain as my pain. After the 'Egypt' episode, the fear of physical punishment for telling the right thing remained in my sub conscious for a long time, deeply affecting my personality. Often in debates and seminars, I would feel diffident in speaking out my mind, fearing somebody would snob and humiliate me.

Lifeless, unfriendly and uninteresting classrooms often force intelligent and creative students to drop out. Steve Jobs was one of the celebrated drop outs who was early to discover the irrelevance of classroom education. Bill Gates of Microsoft dropped out of Harvard School and never returned to it to complete his studies. He rose to be world's wealthiest software innovator. In India, celebrities who failed to complete and missed the formal education, are cricket legends Kapil Dev and Sachin Tendukar and great actor director Amir Khan. In Japan, Honda Soichiro (1906-1991) dropped out of an engineering school finding its curriculum uninteresting. He worked instead as a garage mechanic to tune cars and rose to become world's number one car and automobile manufacturer that is the Honda Motor Company. A large number of students drop out from Indian primary schools. Surveys indicate, in USA, almost every 26 seconds a student drops out. Reasons are many and fear of punishment is one of them.

Corporal punishment in school is defined as 'striking the student a given number of times in a generally methodical and premeditated manner'. The punishment is usually administered either across the buttocks or on the hands and legs, with an implement specially kept for the purpose. Usually a rattan cane, wooden paddle or leather strap or yardsticks are used. All my teachers were coming to school proudly holding one of these. Less commonly, some of them would tweak the ear or smack the student in a deliberate manner on a specific part of the body with the open hand.

My 'hand writing' teacher used to hit my finger joints for any mistake. To further humiliate us, he would make us stand on a chair or kneel down on stony surface wearing a 'Dunce Cap'. Sometimes, he would force us to stand on one leg. Another betel nut chewing language teacher, oldest among his colleagues, would invariably come late, ask us for loud reading of the text and then sit on his chair holding the rattan cane, placing both his legs on the table and start snoring. The red paan juice would drool out through mouth corners, soiling his sleeveless shirt. One day, while sleeping with uplifted legs on the chair, his testicles dangled through the loose loin cloth, converting the class room into a field for spectator sports. As the loud reading was suddenly replaced by giggles, he woke up and discovering every one's gaze transfixed on his skin pouch, used the cane angrily to silence the bemused boys and embarrassed girls.

There is an old interesting story about the rote learning and how the wise and the caged live together. Young philosopher, Adi Shankara, (788-812), worried about increasing religious rituals in society, wanted to meet Pundit Mandan Mishra, a teacher and exponent of a branch of Indian philosophy called 'Purba Mimansa', known for promoting Vedic rituals. When Shankar reached Mandan's village and asked the people for the direction, he was guided in the following manner:

"It is very simple. You will find only one home in this village at whose gates there are a number of parrots inside a cage. They would be singing and repeating abstract questions like — 'Do the Vedas have self-validity? Are our actions capable of giving results directly or do they require divine intervention to do so? Is the world eternal or is it a mere appearance?' and so on. Where you find such a scene, know that you have reached the teacher- scholar Mandan's house."

Following the advice, Shankar reached the right place. But soon after, he could sense that the caged parrots were simply repeating sounds of the Vedic mantras being recited by Mandan's students inside the house, without understanding a letter or word of it. It was but natural, and not a miracle as the fellow villagers believed. Some tropical and sub tropical birds are good at the game of mechanically mimicking the sound or speech of the humans. Imaginative African-American poet, Maya Angelou, in her 'I know why the Caged Bird Sings' (1969) offers a different and empathetic interpretation: 'The parrot sings, because', the poet says, 'its wings are clipped and feet are tied, so it opens the throat and 'sings for freedom'.

But, like wise young Sankar, legendary Italian womanizer, Giocomo Casanova, knew the parrots mimicking tricks so well that he used the innocent birds cleverly against women resisting his sexual overtures. He used to buy a parrot and train it in shouting obscenities against his former mistresses who had fallen out. Then he would sell the bird to traders in the market just to embarrass the woman who dared to reject him.

Now, a disillusioned Shankar tapped Mandan's door. Another shock was in store. Typical of insensitive and arrogant teachers, Mandan first refused to open it and then declined to talk to him. Then, he started abusing Shankar harshly for trying to see him on an 'inauspicious' day! Shankar smiled, saying 'everyday is an auspicious day'. And then invited and defeated old Mandan in a formally organized scholarly debate.

My first college teaching assignment was in Puri, a temple town in coastal India. Within a week, I found out that in my class of 128 students, out of every 45 minutes assigned time, I was wasting close 18 minutes in just to record the attendance in a roll call. And the answer to each roll call was the same, in two words, 'Yes, sir'.

From the second week, I changed it, asking each student to respond to the roll call by uttering one word instead of two and be ready to explain its meaning if asked. We agreed to pick up one good idea behind the word and debate on it for five minutes. All the students agreed. Next day, the best word-cum-idea chosen was 'land' and we had an interesting discussion on land lords and landless. The following day, the best 'word' chosen was 'water', then 'truth', 'non- violence', 'honesty', 'morality', 'superstition', 'exploitation', 'compassion', 'empathy' and so on. Then, I reduced the roll call to just five students, picking them randomly, and used the time thus saved in discussing five 'ideas' in ten minutes.

The news reached the principal and he called me to his chamber to remind that I should follow the tradition and record attendance of each student and not deviate from the assigned subject. My second shock came during the examination when a student, unable to read a question, called me for help. I read it out and left the room. The next day the principal sent me a note asking me to explain why I was helping the boy in the exam. I failed to convince him that it was not so. At the year end, this was recorded negatively in my annual performance appraisal and confidential report and communicated to me. If questions and curiosity have still survived the formal education system, the credit goes more to the students than to the teachers and principals.

I always believed that teaching takes place only through 'reaching' the students and giving them an opportunity to question, enquire, reflect and question once again. Famous Brazilian teacher, Paolo Freire, used to call it conscientization or 'action-reflection-action' process in learning. Because, information cannot be put into long term memory if not blended with meaning and emotion.

Buddhist teachings ask a student to avoid four types of teachers, i.e., Wooden Millstone, Frog in the well, Mad and Blind Guide. The first category harbour false beliefs and always avoids study, reflection and meditation. The 'Frog in the well' types are unaware and have blind faith. The Mad ones have little knowledge, are never taught by a true teacher and are full of strong, negative emotions. The Blind Guide misguides and is unwise and without compassion. Padma Sambhav, a famous Buddhist teacher says, not examining a teacher is like drinking poison and not examining a student is like leaping from a cliff. The types are not restricted to teachers only.

My stay in USA was coming to an end. The Presidential primaries had reached its last leg in June. The political climate was getting hotter as the first Afro-American President was seeking a second term. My daughter, Gayatri, and son-in-law, Manoj, and many friends there were persuading me to stay back because June was also a month of festivity there. During this month, people love to hang loose, feast, drink and do merriment, visiting fire shows, sword juggling, concerts and wine testing tours. Being a tee-totaller and not a party animal, I had no interest in such things. It was also the month for the students to celebrate, before moving back to the rigors of academic life. For the non resident immigrants, it was time to revisit their parents and relations to refresh and reconnect with their roots.

In my case, elections had been announced and there were repeated calls from the Election Commission of India to me to return. While seeing me off at the airport, my children smothered me with hugs and kisses and I was in tears. For a moment, I thought I might not be able to see them again, given life's unpredictability. Once the children disappeared from my view at the airport, it was hard to be reconciled to being left behind and left alone. Overcoming the emotion, I went inside the sprawling San Francisco airport and entered the departure lounge after a thorough and irritating check-in.

Terrorists have only one success story to be proud of. They have enormously enhanced the inconvenience of ordinary citizens! The security frisked, x-rayed and examined every tiny part of my body, not even sparing the fly. Then all the zippers of the hand bag were pulled open and inspected inside out. It was another example of how for the mindless act of a few mad caps, a humanity of innocents suffers such indignity. However, when I heard that former U.S. Secretary of State, Henry Kissinger, was the latest to be subjected to such frisking along with many important men, I could understand the depth of the issue. Earlier, supermodel Bar Refaeli had complained on Twitter about a rough, sexual feel-up by an airport security person. Another model had complained that she had a feeling of getting manually raped by a guy who…was getting off on it.

Hearing this, a woman had commented that most of the people protesting the new body search procedures being men, now at last they're getting to see what it's like for a lady to be groped by someone who won't take no for an answer. Earlier, I had read about a funny incident involving John Malcolm, (name changed) who was stopped and frisked by the security at the San Francisco International Airport, because of a bulging package hidden inside his pants. Surely, this 41-year-old New Yorker wasn't packing an explosive device or a dirty bomb, or drug rolls, or jumbo sized- tube of toothpaste. The search found out that the protruding organic object was the world's largest recorded genital!

In an exclusive interview with the Huffington Post, Malcolm described his embarrassment and hard times with security guards after his extra large fly mistakenly became suspect. Precisely, it was 9 inches flaccid and 13.5 inches erect. Another co-traveler, as if enjoying the frisking, humorously commented with mischievous smile, 'When my dear girl friend insists on a test for sexually transmitted infections before a relationship, why I should worry?' Winston Churchill was more straight forward. Reacting wittily to a colleague's call attention that his fly was unbuttoned, he is reported to have said 'Don't worry, my dear, only dead birds drop out of a nest'.

On an earlier occasion, I had seen a distressed middle aged woman coming out of the frisking chamber with tears. Suspected to be carrying contraband, she was subjected to stripping and cavity searches. It involves thorough visual inspection and intrusion into the naked body and all its cavities including mouth, nostrils, ears, rectum and vagina by hand or a medical device. Funny and absurd stories about frisking galore, but the most absurd one was about a prisoner who tried to hide his cell phone in his rectum. He was caught when the gadget started ringing from the rear end of his body. Life continues to be an endless hide and seek game we loved to play in childhood years.

Now, post frisking, advancing forward, I could clearly see through the separating glass walls, the arriving passengers in troves and some in a hurry running even on the conveyer belt. Chatting, giggling, they were rushing towards the immigration counters, taking position for an early pass through. There was not a single known face, as if all were strangers descending from another planet not worried about departures. A co passenger joined me late and started blaming himself. A small scissor in the hand bag was the reason for delay. This is the fifth time he committed the same mistake. Every time he would tell himself 'I would transfer the scissor to check in bag at the airport' and then would forget. Recently he had received an award as the best manager of his company! A potter in my home town used to visit the temple everyday to deliver headload of earthen pots for the temple kitchen and would mutter 'God, I shall visit you tomorrow'. He missed hundrds of tomorrows and then one day passed away.

Life itself is long lesson if people care to learn. There is an interesting and educative story in the great epic Ramayan regarding Ravana, from whom his adversary Ram wanted to learn. Knowing that he was going to die, Ram came nearer to him to learn some important lessons of life. Kneeling at Ravan's feet and with folded palms, he asked, "O great king, you are known as an accomplished manager and ruler of Sri Lanka's golden era. Be my teacher and tell me, what made you so successful? I am an inexperienced son of a king who is no more and therefore I am quite eager to learn from you, the secrets of the state craft..."

Lying in a pool of blood and gasping, Raavan replied, "O Lord Rama, I really appreciate your humility. My success had many failures too. I had all the powers, authority and wealth and also powerful Lord Shiva's blessings. I had ten heads and twenty eyes, but I lacked foresight and commonsense. I could not overcome my 'ahankar'. My ego and arrogance defeated me.'

Ravan Samhita mentions about some useful feedback he gave to Ram and his brother, Laxman, based on his own experience of life events. Some of these were: 'Never antagonise your charioteer, your driver, your gatekeeper, your cook and more importantly, your brother; like I did in respect of my brother, Vibhishan. They can harm and weaken you badly anytime, at any place. Similarly, do not think you can always be a winner in future, because you have always won in the past. As a ruler, remember to trust your ministers and the advisers, who point out your mistakes and weaknesses, for they may have a valid point of view beneficial to you. And never underestimate or think your enemy is small or powerless, like I thought about Hanuman, as a mere monkey. Finally, do not think you can always outsmart your stars'.

Then he concluded by saying, 'O Rama, now listen more carefully. I had many dreams for my people which I couldn't implement for want of conscious planning. I wanted to bring down heaven on earth. I had also an alternative plan ready to build a ladder from earth to heaven, so that we all could straight climb up to there. But I had no time to put these plans to test to examine their achievability. I kept postponing all these plans to 'tomorrow'. And instead, I desired your wife and abducted her. Many of my actions were ill advised and priorities lopsided.' He finally told Ram, 'never ever to postpone things and neglect the importance of 'today'.'

A grateful Ram now requested Ravan's forgiveness for the great sin of killing a learned 'Brahmin'like him. And also asked brother Laxman to go near his feet and seek blessings.

Umapati, an old colleague of mine, was living in a city which I used to visit twice every year on official duty. Every time I was there in the city; unable to find time, I was telling myself that I must visit him next time. Then one day, a common friend, informed that he had already left the world two years ago. A similar thing happened in case of another dear colleague, Kewalia, who was living in Jaipur, a city about six hours drive away from Delhi. He was suffering from oral cancer. I talked to his wife, Krishna, who told me that he was now improving. I postponed my plan to the next day to go and see him. The following day, news came that he had passed away. Cheated by 'tomorrow', I have not yet forgiven myself for this lapse. When the heart looks forward to, the mind deceives by moving into backward mode. 'Tomorrow' waits for the 'day after' that creates more tomorrows as optimism yields to procrastination.

We all arrive in this world as tourists and strangers with temporary transit visa, and without knowing its actual expiry dates! Then we go on stamping our carbon footprints day after day. In a different context, Martin Luther King Jr used to say, 'We may have all come on different ships, but we are on the same boat now. At the airport you are made to forget the boat and remember the borders.'

And like me, all of them in the arrival lounge must have declared their 'yes' or 'no' in capitals in the visa form to a host of offensive, personal and loaded questions that puts you off - taking away the real spirit of the journey itself before it started. The visa form asks: Are you a terrorist? A fraud? A criminal, a burglar, a convict, a rapist, an outlaw? Are you coming to the USA to engage in prostitution or unlawful commercialized vice or have you been engaged in prostitution or procuring prostitutes within the past 10 years? Do you seek to engage in espionage, sabotage or any other illegal activity? Have you committed, ordered, incited, assisted, or otherwise participated in extrajudicial killings, political killings or other acts of violence?

And so on, as if the person would reply in the affirmative and they would cancel his travel papers! I still wonder why such offensive words are used. Particularly by a country whose citizens enjoy a lot of travel freedom and can visit as many as 172 countries without VISA!

Two words responsible for causing the self destructive, fratricidal Mahabharat war were: 'prostitute' in respect of Draupadi, daughter-in- law of queen mother, Kunti, and 'blind son of a blind father', referring to Duryodhan, son of the blind king, Dhritarastra. The other two words that added to the injury and hurt pride of the adversaries were Shakuni's constant taunting about the Pandav brothers' questionable paternity and his close friend, Karna, being openly ridiculed about his lowly parentage. Important national leaders were known to have wrongly mixed up words causing great embarrassment. George Bush Jr. was known for that. It is said that unable to find the right words, Nikita Khrushchev had once banged his shoe on the lectern. Diplomats say Vladimir Putin's tongue lashing and rash words often cut like sharp weapons. Stung by it, a French journalist once reacted by calling Putin repeatedly as 'Putaine, Putaine', which is a French synonym for 'prostitute'. Once freed from tongue, teeth and lips words pick up speed and work like bullets or buques. During my college days, our political science teacher once gave us a riddle: 'A 'little boy' killed 1,40,000 people and a 'fat man' killed 70,000, tell me who were they? We couldn't answer. Then he told that these were the code names for the two nuclear bombs that were dropped on Hiroshima and Nagasaki in Japan during Second World War. Then pausing for a while, he blurted out angrily, 'by some stupid bastards'.

The words and terms in the visa form were the least thoughtful and most hurtful. For a moment, I thought of cancelling the trip. I was to attend the graduation ceremony of my grandchild, Vanani, whom I loved so much, from a dance school. So, I decided to swallow my pride and move on. There was an announcement about flight delay as the plane had been hit by a big flying bird.

Birds in the sky, like fishes under water, are nature's super citizens. Every one envies the freedom of choice enjoyed by terrestrial birds and wild beasts that never needed a visa to fly above or move across borders. While countries and their coastguards quarrel over marine boundaries, the fish moves quietly and freely under water to reproduce in places of their choice. Birds also are used without their knowledge. In 2015, an ordinary pigeon caused quite a flutter among Gujarat (India) police, national coast guards, forest officials, and forensic experts and finally the home Ministry, when a chip was found tied to its claw with a number on the other claw and writings in Arabic across its wings. The poor winged suspect was detained for an entire day and subjected to a thorough strip search, like the one at the airport security. The system of visa was first imposed by Henry V in England to identify and enable its holder to travel abroad as a British citizen. Subsequently, it became mandatory for all trans-border travellers.

Instantly, the thought of Chilka Lake came to the mind. Asia's largest wetland in India, stretched over 1100 sq. kms is about 50 kms from my ancestral village. I never miss an opportunity to visit this lake. Free flying Siberian cranes come here crossing land and air borders of several countries to reach its warmer waters. Its beach and nearby trees are crowded and covered with coloured flamingos, grey legged geese and millions of migratory winged foreigners – all foreigners from north America, northwest Africa, Europe, Iceland, central Asia, without passport, visa and immigration clearance! On arrival, they would first claim the territory; strut around freely in search of prospective mates, followed by long courtship. Then they would make love with their foreign friends in the wild, lay eggs in peace and conceal the hatched chicks under the tall and thick grass. The annual 'honey moon' trips over they return home. No citizenship issues!

I had read somewhere that when an Ohio woman packed her bags for a Disney vacation, her tethered cat and a pet parrot in the cage didn't want to stay behind. They escaped from their place and found their way into her suitcase. Then unnoticed and undetected, they made it through screening at Port Columbus International Airport and were loaded into an airplane for a flight to Orlando. It is said that God loved the birds and created trees for them. Man loved the birds and created cage to control their wings. The cat didn't have to walk nor had the bird to fly. The pilot was doing their job. And this time, the bird and the beast, chose their cage, exercising freedom of choice! A loud announcement about the name of a missing passenger brought me back to the lounge from the lake. The waiting lounge was another interesting place where one's attention is drawn towards the departure chart, or the TV screen, with intermittent reminders for security checks, announcement about new arrivals and expected time of boarding and departure. No one talks to anyone. Each pair of eyes has a different kind of emotion and expectation, each minute of waiting has a different meaning and message, each person displays a patience and purpose, not known to the other.

Now a second announcement created a flutter. It said the departure would be delayed as the aircraft had been bird hit during landing and the runway was being cleared of bird carcass. The avian menace sent the flight schedule into a tizzy. Small birds have hit the big bird. The journey would now be delayed.

3

Waits, Worries and Wise Women

The airline expected us to report full three hours before departure. So even after the unpleasant and invasive security drill, there is still a lot of waiting time. Personally, I am used to it, as my life has been a series of waits; waiting in queues, at the counter, waiting for food, for trains, for the teacher, for friends and loved ones, waiting to do something, and of course waiting to go somewhere. In a serpentine queue, looking forward creates frustration while looking backward revives hope.

Through these, life teaches the power of hope and patience. Like Mary and Martha waiting for Jesus to arrive and save the life of Lazarus in the Biblical story. Or like the legendary Ahalya, who had to wait for ages for Lord Rama to arrive and liberate her from a curse. However, to kill the waiting time, I had carried some news papers, periodicals and other reading materials. I pulled out one with an unusual title that read "Don't put Expiry dates on People". It was about a recent medical discovery which claimed that based on certain biomarkers; it could now predict when one was going to die and who was at high risk of dying in five years. The editor had given equal space to both sides of the issue, arguments in favor and counter arguments about possible social consequences of this medical breakthrough. Some thought that medical science was about extending people's life spans, rather than telling them how long they have to live.

The new finding had claimed that a simple blood test like the one that estimates cholesterol, would tell patients about the rate at which they are ageing. When I shared this with a co passenger, he thought for a while and said that unless means were found for slowing down this rate, just coming to know how fast our biological clock was ticking - from the length of telomeres or protective chromosome caps in our cells - is hardly helpful.

A person's longevity is determined by several factors, some of which can hardly be measured. Overhearing our conversation, another fellow traveller butted in and reiterated that not knowing how long one lives is part of the glorious uncertainty of life. The new test, if true, has now threatened to take all that away by putting an expiry date on each person. 'When scientism induces such undue fatalism, it will be wise to discard it,' he said.

In this context, two real life incidents came to my mind. One was about a man, who after overhearing that he was going to die of a terminal ailment any day, became so restless that he stopped sleeping and eventually died of causes not related to his diagnosed disease. The other incident was related to a person called Pathani, who was a well known astrologer. After a thorough study, he had calculated the exact day of his death, which went wrong not once but three times. Every time, a few months before the predicted day, he would proceed to a holy town, hire a house and stay there waiting for the Angel of Death, who never came. Wishing to die in a holy place for an easy entry into heaven, he put the credibility of his profession into question.

So, even if taking the medical test for prior knowledge of the end can be a matter of individual choice, such a test could be put to Orwellian use- prone to mischief and misuse by manipulators, the critics feared. It could create a scenario when, insurance providers could deny a customer their service, based on result of such a test. Worse still will be a situation, when an organization could use the test as an excuse to fire its workers once the expiry dates of their lives are known. Matrimonial advertisers now could demand for the test and its results for deciding on prospective brides and grooms. Doctors and family members would find it easier to get rid of the incurable ones through euthanasia or mercy killing.

But the strongest argument against the death and departure test is that it would negate the healing power of hope. For, optimism is the ultimate tonic that sustains the human spirit. It can prompt and push people to achieve the impossible, allow them to celebrate life rather than brood over its finiteness. And then what is the fun of watching the game of life if the end results are already known? Life looks exciting because of the sequence of certain and uncertain expectations, events and acts. We sleep peacefully every night because of the hope of rising again in the morning.

Sometimes, it might also have a negative and fatal impact. I knew a professor of surgery in a medical college, who had suddenly fallen ill. After the diagnosis, it was found to be a case of terminal cancer in an advanced stage. Being a doctor, he insisted to know about the result of the diagnosis. Finally, he was informed and the next morning he was found dead in his bed after a severe heart attack. The prior knowledge itself killed him. Pulitzer Prize winner, renowned historian and famous writer of 'The Story of Civilization', Will Durant, who took 50 years to finish the 11 volume magnum opus, had been admitted to a hospital for surgery. Sometime after that, his wife and co-writer, Ariel, was also admitted to the same hospital on account of some heart problems. Although she came to the hospital much later than her husband, she died earlier, on Oct.25, 1981, while Will Durant was well on his way to recovery. His granddaughter, Monica Mehell tried her best to prevent the news of his wife's death from reaching him. But then, somehow, one day, the convalescing Will Durant came to know from another source that his wife Ariel was no more.

Within minutes his heart stopped beating. Forever!

And thus ended the story of the man who wrote the story of civilization.

Hope and life are sustained in four different ways. A feeling of intimate connectedness with someone you deeply love, a relational connectedness with everyday friends and relations, a social connectedness with the larger community and an individual commitment to a cause or spiritual goal.

The world does not stop with the stoppage of one's heart bits, howsoever great or powerful one is. It is a non-event. On July 20th 1969, when Apollo 11 was approaching its landing site, a computer overload alarm sounded. A young scientist in NASA control room was at a loss about what to do. The only other option was to abort and withdraw the mission. The decision was to be made in 15 seconds. This 26 year young, Steve Bales, the guidance officer of the mission, decided to do nothing. The alarm rang five times more. Steve stopped worrying and didn't change his mind. Finally, the crew in the lunar module managed the malfunction and landed on moon safely and made history, putting behind all worries and fears.

When flying a long haul, a passenger plane has always two pilots; one monitoring the screens while the other doing the paper work and talking to air traffic control, in addition to alerting the crew for landing and takeoff. Once the plane goes up above 500 feet, it is on auto piloting mode. A flying bird doesn't worry about falling from the sky. We do.

A week before my planned visit to London, an old friend of mine, who was working in the Indian High Commission, cautioned, "Be prepared, immigration counters have endlessly long queues and it might take at least four to five hours to get out of Heathrow."

"Why is it so?" I asked him, fearing the prospect of painful standing time.

"Any way out?" I enquired, possessed by panic.

"No way," he said. 'In fact, it might be worse. London Olympics is a few days away and there is already a visible rush, and the queue is likely to be longer."

During my nine hour long journey from Indira Gandhi International Airport to London- Heathrow, the worry never left me. How can I stand five hours in the queue? I might collapse... And lo and behold! When I landed and almost ran to the immigration counter to occupy my position ahead of others, the counter was almost empty! And it took me just five minutes to get out of the airport.

I remembered and realized how true and insightful was the golden words of Prentice Mulford, the farsighted teacher. "Create your day in advance, your life in advance; tell yourself, you are going to have a pleasant journey. By thinking in this manner, you are sending positive forces and vibrations which rush in advance to make your journey pleasant." Mulford explained it further by saying that if you are fearful, apprehensive, worried, angry and in a hurry, you release unseen forces ahead of you, who would translate your anxiety into reality. Our state of mind fixes things good or bad in advance. Repeating positive words creates positive spirits, injects energy vibrations. A half empty glass gives one a chance to fill it up with positive affirmation. Akin to this is another wise statement by Jack Canfield which said "Think of a car driving a long distance through the dark night, whereas the headlight has the capacity of showing the direction only for the first 100 meters." So, it is always wise to take the first step in faith.

I had an ingrained fear of the needle in an injection syringe and was always worried about the painful prick. I used to keep my eyes off it at the time of the piercing. One day, a psychologist friend told me that if I kept my eyes on it than off it, I would not feel any pain. And I realized later that he was correct! Thinking of pain is more painful than the real pain. During examination time, many students feel pain in parts of body because of the worry and anxiety. I had heard a story about Nobel Laureate for literature, Rabindranath Tagore, who, while undergoing a minor operation, had declined anaesthesia. Instead, he had fixed his attention on reading a book while the operation was on. It is said that Jesus endured the torment of crucifixion for some six hours without any apparent sign of pain. Feeling anxious or panicky about your pain or feeling that other people do not understand your chronic pain doesn't reduce it. Clinical psychologists say that pain management is a part of self management skills.

When I left the village for study at the age of thirteen at a place 70 kms away, my mother broke down and cried nonstop for hours. She was worried how I would manage life in an unknown faraway place. But I was more worried, not because I was going to an unknown place but more looking at her worry-worn face. Frankly, I was excited inside, for all my friends had gone to the town for higher schooling, leaving me behind. The feeling of being left out was festering inside and gnawing away at my spirit. Sometimes, I was weeping silently in the backyard of our house. So, this exit appeared to me like a stone of hope carved out of mountains of despair. In fact, this was like a god sent exit that enabled me eventually to see all the five continents of the world. Shakespeare was so right when he had said that if you had not left your habitat and not gone out, you have but read only the first page of the book of life. The prospect was liberating. My entire childhood, confined to a radius of one kilometer of the village, was eagerly looking beyond it to the world outside.

I had read a story about another mother, who was more worried than mine, about the safety of her little daughter trekking to school in an inclement weather. With each lightning and thunder, she was possessed by a terrible fear about the safety of her child. Full of worries, she now went out with an umbrella. After a while, she noticed her little daughter walking down the road very normally, without any worry, picking up nuts and fruits and eating with great pleasure. And at each flash of lightening, she would stop, look up and smile.

The puzzled mother ran after the unconcerned child and came in front of her yelling,

'What are you doing foolish girl? Why are you stopping at each flash of lightening, risking life? Are you not scared?'

'Why should I be, Mama?' She replied.

'Why do you look up and smile? Are you in your senses? The worried mother persisted.

'Oh, Mama, I am only trying to see the light of God. Aren't you happy that God above in the sky looks so bright, so good today? Have you seen how he keeps on taking my picture again and again with his flash light! And can't you see, he also talks to me through loud thunders, so that I can hear! He is so kind and compassionate. I am trying to understand him. Now, I feel he really loves me.' 'Oh, you mad girl. And why do you pick up and eat these soiled nuts,' she asked with a frown.

'O Mama, come on, I am not eating but swallowing only. You know, one day the seed would grow in my belly into a big tree, make me taller and walk with me. I feel bad that these trees are not able to move with me now,' she said with innocent optimism.

More or less, all mothers are worried about their children, particularly daughters, as much as the daughters lean more on mothers for help and advice. Moms all over the world make a lot of sacrifice for them. Although the world is changing, mothers in many countries remain mothers, always getting on children for not eating well, not dressing up on time for school and so on. Protective mother bird eagle builds its nest on high cliffs far away from potential predators. The instinct is wired into the brain of all mothers. They continue to give exaggerated attention to every bump and turn in their children's lives making them 'mother of worries'.

So, I often wonder if God had a gender, it would be feminine. The Mother, must be 'She', a real 'god' one can touch and feel. I started thinking seriously about it when my ten-year-old daughter asked one day why the God and the Prophets who represent and describe Him, are always males. Why is God the Father and God the son only? Why not God the Mother and God the daughter? Why the Hindu Trinity, i.e., Bramha (creator), Vishnu (preserver) and Shiva (destroyer) are all males? Although I tried to explain to her that God or 'Brahman', the fundamental life force, was neither male nor female and 'God is God', inside, I thought her innocent question was pertinent because in pre-literate and pre-historic societies, God was actually worshipped as a female figure and mother.

To be sure, I asked my teacher, Padma Charan, who was a reputed scholar and linguist and had influenced the direction of my life in many ways. Agreeing with the view, he told me about Artemis, the widely venerated ancient Greek and Roman Goddess, known as Diana. According to him her counterpart was Durga in India, both are lion- riders and mountain-dwellers and both were worshipped as creator. He explained how Alexander had come to the Artemis temple in Turkey on Mount Olympus, to pray and have her blessings before his conquest.

In fact, Artemis, with siblings Athena and Hastia, were the feminine Trinity, like Luxmi (goddess of prosperity), Parvati (power) and Saraswati (wisdom), the original Hindu feminine Trinity. As the world was more and more afflicted by conflicts and wars, the feminine god was replaced slowly by the masculine. Then he explained to me how in Genesis, it was not Adam but Eve, who was the real mover and shaker, exploring the garden, meeting and interrogating the snake, taking decisions and initiating change. No wonder, Krishna in Bhagwad Geeta, perceives himself as a woman when he says: 'Among women, I am the Goddess Luxmi, presiding over fame, prosperity, speech, memory, intelligence, steadfastness and forgiveness'.

Padma Charan was more than a teacher and extraordinary in many ways. It is said that an ordinary teacher tells, a good teacher explains, a great teacher demonstrates, but an extraordinary teacher involves and inspires each and every student. Pythagoras, the mathematician and Sir Isaac Newton, the famous scientist, were both extraordinary teachers. King Solomon and Buddha are the other examples. My teacher had a little bit of all these qualities. In addition, he used to instill morals and discipline into our minds. For many of us, he was a role model. Every day, in the morning he would do rigorous manual work which he used to call 'bread labor'. As an admirer of Gandhi, he believed that bread-labor helped to reduce the impurities within and dependency outside. It makes easier the practice of abstinence and self reliance. He believed that no food was free and one has to earn it by hard work. To prove his point, he once narrated to me an incident in Gandhi's ashram.

A man, with his wife and old mother, had come to the ashram to attend the prayer meeting and listen to Gandhi. Then both husband and wife joined others in cleaning the premises and tending to plants in the garden. When the lunch time came, an inmate came and invited him and his wife for the lunch, leaving out his mother. Thinking it was an unintended lapse, he asked his mother also to come along. To his shock, he was told that the mother was not invited as unlike them, she had not done the bread-labor.

"But she is very old," protested the son, feeling humiliated.

'We have easy work for the old also,' the inmate replied.

"She is not only old but blind also," said the man, expecting some understanding.

"We have work here for both old and blind," stated the inmate and quickly left the place to return with a basketful of cotton. Placing it near the blind old woman, he gently asked, "Aunty jee, can you pull out and separate the seeds from the cotton?" She readily agreed, finished the task in less than an hour and was invited to join others for lunch!

Padma Charan considered growing food with one's own hands as ideal for bread-labor and insisted that everybody should be his own scavenger as well as weaver, by spinning regularly and making his own cloth. After bread-labor, he would spend an hour reading religious texts and the next one hour in giving free coaching to students who were poor and weaker in study. In his study, a quote from Lord

Krishna in Gita was prominently displayed: "That person I love who is incapable of ill will and returns love for hatred, the person living beyond 'I and mine', beyond pain and pleasure, a person full of compassion, contentment and self control" (12: 18-19). Thus Gandhi and Gita were his twin guides in life. He is no more, but would live in my mind for ever as a role model.

And yet, he was constantly worried about three fears. One was what would happen to India, if and when Gandhi died? He would continuously ask himself, sure in his belief that heaven would fall. Then one day Gandhi was gone, assassinated by a fanatic, when he was on his way to an evening prayer for peace and harmony. Although earth was shaken a bit, heaven didn't fall. This reminds one of Mao Zedong's death when so many of his followers had cried bitterly before his portrait, wondering how could China survive without Chairman Mao? Today, China is an economic powerhouse. And Mao is peacefully asleep in one of those places housing all "indispensable" greats of the world. Followers of Mao and Gandhi have long forgotten their masters and mentors.

My teacher had lost his father when he was a kid and was deeply attached to and dependent upon his 80 year old mother, an assertive woman with tremendous mental strength. He would not take any decision in day to day life, personal and professional, without consulting her. Every night, before retiring to bed, he would massage her body to improve blood circulation and touch her feet in prayer and for her blessing. So, the second fear was-how could he live when his mother died? Then one day his mother passed away in sleep, suddenly making him feel like an orphan and emotionally shattered. He was 61. But then he overcame the grief in a week's time and became normal as his wife and children rallied around him.

The third fear had gripped him when he was very young. It was about the bridge over a river that connected his village to the Cuttack city nearby. Having seen earlier the collapse of a bamboo bridge over a canal, he would always avoid walking over the bridge to go to his city school and would, instead, cross the shallow river water. And when the water level swelled and rose, he would rather swim across. He was always worried that the bridge was not properly constructed and might collapse under his walking weight! My beloved teacher has already left the world, yet the bridge is still standing proud and strong over which thousands of heavy vehicles cross day and night. It is said that 50 percent of our worries and fears are related to things that are not likely to happen, another 25 percent are about past actions that could not be changed and another 10 percent about the opinion of other people that doesn't matter. About 10 percent is about health and wellbeing which could be resolved. And finally, only 5 percent of the worries could be real and worthy of attention.

Now coming back to the village, the period of pure, unadulterated joy with peers came to an end. The night before I was to leave the village, mom came to my bedside, wrapped a quilt over me and spent the entire night there, putting her hand on my head. I curled up in her warm comfort and felt instantly reassured. Earlier, on every birthday of mine, she would lull me into sleep telling a story connecting me to angels in heaven and earth, instantly enlarging my mindscape.

The first story is still fresh in my mind: 'Listen', she had started,

'when you were born, all wise women in the heaven celebrated the occasion and sent a beautiful gift for you through an Angel.'

'What was that?' I had asked in great excitement.

'Strength,' she replied.

'Where is that?' I had enquired.

'In your body and mind,' she said. 'That enabled you to crawl, to sit, stand, walk and run.'

I felt confused and mystified. 'But then, what was the gift on my second birth day?' I asked with more curiosity.

'They had sent two gifts, i.e. beauty and joy.' It was too abstract for me to comprehend.

She explained, 'You must keep your heart open and fill it with light and laughter, so that everyone likes you from outside and inside. It will also make you beautiful and joyful.'

On the next birthday she declared to me that this time the Angel had delivered two more magnificent gifts. Excited I asked her to tell me immediately.

'Intelligence and knowledge,' she replied. I was disappointed.

She explained what these meant: 'With these, you can now discover your own abilities and give it to everyone.' By this time, I had started going to the school.

'On your next birthday', she said, 'the Angel had brought for you a unique gift.'

'What was that?' I enquired, again with a lot of interest.

'It is called 'imagination'. With this you can attach wings to your dream and create new things.' The following year, according to mom, the Angel had delivered another two invisible gifts which she called 'faith and hope'. She explained and advised that I should never lose faith in myself and trust in goodness of others. She narrated further in her own earthy style how her 'hope' brought me to this world and how it sustained her through long periods of pain and suffering.

Then, after a brief silence, stroking my hair, she said, 'Look, knowing that you would not be here for your next birthday a couple of months away, this time the Angel has delivered in advance three more gifts as the last blessings of the wise women from heaven.' By then, I had lost interest in knowing what these could be and asked her why they were always sending gifts that I couldn't see. I asked her how and when could I see these wise women- the invisible donors of invisible gifts.

She said, 'Wait and listen to me first.' And then, she declared that 'this time the first one was 'respect', the second gift was 'wisdom' and the third was 'silence'. The first will humble your mind and illuminate your heart.' She advised me to respect the teachers, elders and all those who help me in life, even those who are different and do not agree with me.

About 'wisdom', she explained, 'It begins with humility' and asked me to always listen to the soft voice of conscience before taking any decision. 'Never barter your convictions for convenience.' Regarding 'silence', the third gift, she whispered into my ear, 'God loves it and you will be nearer to Him through silence only. All beautiful things he has created grow in silence. You can also touch the mind, heart and soul of the people through it. Break it only when you have to speak against injustice. In conversation, speak only when others are willing to listen to you. Avoid arguments but join discussion as arguments create confrontation but discussions generate solution. 'When you have these three,' she continued, 'you yourself will become a wise person and can send similar gifts to other children on their birthdays. Then, you can see concretely how these gifts are reflected in their behavior, character and action'.

Much later in life, I came across an old Egyptian proverb that was almost similar to what mom had said about the last set of gifts. 'Listen to your conviction, even if they seem absurd to your reason and listen to your reason even if they look absurd to your emotions.' Mom was always confident and full of courage, would never skip, jump, duck or dodge an issue. When I was about nine, a bad character of the village was regularly coming to our house and was trying to be friendly with her. One day, while talking to her, he touched her cheek with his finger. Mom looked at him straight and firmly in the eye, in silence. The man cowered down and walked away briskly like a thief, never to return again. That day I could feel what the power of silence is. For me, she was the real Angel, the dignified, wise woman whom I could see, touch and feel. Prophet Muhammad was so right when he said:

'Paradise lies beneath the feet of mothers.'

Sometime back, I had seen an unknown yet meaningful quote by a grateful child on the Mother's day, which said: 'On July 7, 1993, God sent me to the arms of an Angel. An angel whose arms are always open when I need a hug, whose heart always understands when I need a friend. An angel whose eyes are stern when I need a lesson, whose strength and love guides me and give me wings that enables me to fly. I am most fortunate to call this angel, my mother.' Absolutely true. I replaced the date with '14th November' 1942' and hung it on the wall in front of my living room to remember the great woman who had brought me to this wonderful world but left it and me quite early in life.

Our wait was over as boarding was announced and we rushed to take our place in the queue. And then suddenly, entered a middle aged woman weeping and wailing inconsolably, accompanied by her spouse and an airline staff. We couldn't guess what was happening; each one in the queue was trying to find out the reason. After a while, the person next to me whispered that the lady in distress has lost her son in an accident and was now taking the flight to her hometown for the funeral.

I had gone through such traumatic situations several times in life without knowing how to handle it. When my mentally retarded daughter was drowned in a bath tub and died instantly, my wife and I were dazed for months. It was early June and the day was extremely hot. Unable to bear the heat and also unable to talk, she came near the deep tub full with water and fell into it while trying to touch and feel the cold water for relief.

She was a normal child at birth and while four months old, had a fall from the bed. Soon after, she went into epileptic fits that remained with her, slowly turning her brain into vegetable. She had already become deficient in cognition, in adaptive behavior and in ordinary problem solving skills. All our efforts failed to make her normal. So, while one fall from bed made her mentally disabled, another fall into the tub drove her to death, a final farewell from our life. We lived with a sense grief and guilt for a long time, always thinking she could have been saved if we had been a little more careful and vigilant. Our text books and teachers were silent on how to face such life events.

By the time I was seventeen, I had already witnessed seven deaths in the family, in addition to two suicides and three accidental deaths in the village. My father had come to my village as an adopted child when most of its residents were wiped off by cholera. Five of my siblings died one after the other within one year of infancy and the sixth one succumbed to small pox. The first one was about four pounds and too thin to survive. The second one was less than a year and died suddenly in mother's arms for reasons no one knew.

The third one, a girl child, was four months young and died of choke during breast feeding. Tired of endless home work, mother had fallen asleep while the baby was still on her breast. When she woke up it was too late as the choked baby had stopped breathing. The next one was a victim of prescription and medication error and poor handwriting of the doctor. It was found out that the child was given the wrong medicine. The doctor had prescribed chloromycetin for typhoid to be given intravenously and the chemist, not being able to read the bad handwriting of the doctor, gave chloroquin instead. It reminds me of a saying that if you are not absolutely careful about reading books on health and medicine, it is quite likely you may die of a misprint.

The next one died of umbilical cord complications as the wound never healed. About two years after, she delivered a girl child, who survived for four years, died of dehydration from diarrhea. Simple solutions like life saving salt-sugar, oral rehydration therapy was unknown in those days. Now, it saves millions of children a year from death due to diarrhea, the second leading cause of death after pneumonia in children under five. The next one was also a girl child who survived up to her sixth birth day and succumbed to small pox infected by a cousin sister who was holidaying with us carrying the virus from someone else. Till today, I am not reconciled to this tragedy of not having a biological sister of my own. A thing common in respect of all the siblings was common destiny.

After each tragedy mother would write a long sorrowful poem in memory of the lost child, reading and pouring her heart out to others and cry. She was a natural poet without any formal education. This time, when her girl child was snatched away by fate, she was totally shattered and frequently fainted under the shock. Some sorrowful lines she composed I still remember are:

'My heart hurts all the time,

Where is my child, my life, my prime? Oh Angels, return my child,

Oh Gods, I will go wild,

Oh nights, she was my light, Oh days, return my sight......'

Suffering through years and ages, Lucy's children have learnt how to dip, drown and soften the sharp edges of their sorrow and wash away the grief and pain by anguished rivers of tears.

4

Pushed Out to Unknown World

Before I arrived in this world, mother had one miscarriage and another still born. So, in a way, I was her first living child. Following a local custom and belief, she had sold me to a deity in a temple for my protection during childhood and reclaimed me only at the age of 12 after a daylong prayer and paying a price to the priest. About the still born, I learnt from my uncle how she had refused to believe that it was actually dead and continued to hold it close to her chest because a year earlier, another new born baby that was thought to be still born and dead had been thrown into a garbage pit by a callous maternity assistant and it was only a little later when the baby started crying that it was rescued from the pit by a passerby.

Within a year, mother conceived once again and her body became swollen with rapid loss of iron and nutrition; it was another joyless and unwanted pregnancy. Unintended pregnancies are one of the primary causes of maternal and infant mortality. Those days, when contraceptives and vaccines were unknown, abortions were considered sinful and hospitals and maternity centers were distant and inaccessible. C- Section was an alien idea and assisted delivery meant another illiterate, elderly lady empowered by a metre long cotton cloth to tie round the belly to press and push the child out of the womb. The second instrument used to be an unsterilized sharp stone for cutting off the umbilical cord and the wound used to take months to heal and very often led to death by infection.

Another aunty in her forties and a relation of ours, living next to our house, had conceived for the first time about 25 years after her marriage. She was in labour for 40 hours but unable to deliver. By then, I was ten year old and couldn't understand why she was howling and wailing in pain. I entered her room to find her squatting without any cover, when two elderly ladies drove me out pulling me by the ear and threatening to inform my mother for the crime I committed. What is the crime, I demanded to know? There was no answer.

Next day, she was carried in a bullock cart 15 kms away to the nearest govt. Hospital but they didn't have C-Section facility, so while still in great pain, she was put into a public transport for a city centre hospital, another 50 kms away where she finally had a caesarean delivery and ten days hospitalization before returning home. Her child is now a grandmother. Gandhi's father, Karamchand, was widowed three times before marrying Putli Bai for the fourth time at age 40. All his three wives died of complications relating to child birth. So all of us, who are now alive in this world are great and fortunate survivors of infant mortality, under five mortality and, in the case of girls, sex selective mortality in male preferring societies.

Access to contraceptive, apart from providing sexual freedom, has empowered millions of women with an effective weapon of choice. One of the millions of beneficiaries was Melinda Gates, Microsoft fame Bill Gates' wife. She gives credit to the contraceptive for her rise in life and career. And says that she was able to go to college and then to business school and then pursue a rewarding career in Microsoft because of the contraceptive. She could decide how many children to have and when to have them because of this. It changed her future like many more millions before and after her, who wanted control over their fertility and freedom of the womb.

Neither Prabha, mother of India's famous revolutionary, Subhas Bose, nor Sharada Devi, who had given birth to Tagore, her 14th, nor my humble mother, Moon, had that freedom. Prabha delivered 14 children, Subhas being her 9th. 18th century's most prolific mother, the Russian Ms. Vassilyeva, must have cursed her fate in her grave for arriving in the world quite early and for undergoing the pangs of 27 confinements, during which she gave birth to 69 children including twins, triplets and quadruplets. Like all her eight children, my mother also 'pushed' me out after a daylong labour without any pain medication, obstetrician or nurse- midwife, which was really risky.

Like my mother, my wife, Binny, also pushed out all three of our children. Pushing is the final stage in labour. I remember when she felt that she was fully dilated and the time had come, she would ask me to call the midwife to help her with a castor oil shake before the contraction. She would then marshal all her energy and give two or three hard, long and painful pressure pushes as if she was moving her bowels. The baby would come out with the familiar cry that brings a smile to everyone present as it is a special time and special event. Our first child, Gayatri, was 7lb in weight and Binny remained without a tear. Stealing a glance at the baby, she had a great sense of achievement and seemed to have forgotten all her pain and pressure pushing for the moment. Two hours later, we returned home together and she walked to the bedroom without help, without effort and was feeding the baby herself. The total expenditure, including tips and sweets, was five dollars!

Years ago, while returning from the village school, I had seen a stout tribal woman confidently walking back from the forest with a head load of fire wood along with a newly born baby in her arms. She had delivered the baby there in the woods without any assistance. There is a grain of truth in the Japanese proverb that says: 'Giving birth to a baby is easier than worrying about it'. Hardworking women are known for this. The real challenge is the first delivery after which it becomes easier. In C-Sections, the recovery time lasts for at least a month whereas in natural vaginal birth, the pain is only during the birth itself. Therefore, I often wonder why there's such a preponderance of elective and planned C-Sections now. And how many hospital beds are occupied for weeks because of this and how many resources are wasted. It also undermines a pregnant woman's will power and confidence in pushing the baby out from the womb to the world. In fact, nature has designed the body of a woman in such a way that the compression of the birth canal automatically assists the child's natural journey out to the world without much wear and tear.

Recently, Reeti, a niece of mine, living in USA, naturally delivered her first child despite the doctor's advice to the contrary. She was very clear in her mind and had told the doctors well in advance that she would not like to deliver her first child in an operation theatre surrounded by machines, knives and blood bottles. When my younger daughter, Prakriti, reached the hospital after labour, they rushed her for C-Section without even informing or consulting her husband. But as Kate Middleton, the future queen of England, went into labour, Jesey Shore, the trashy TV star turned mother, led a campaign filling Twitter with a motivational messages to her: 'Push girl, pushhhhh…' And Kate did it, straining every muscle and nerve. The world joined the monarchy in welcoming the arrival of George Alexander Louis through the most direct natural route.

My mother-in-law, Bimla, who delivered all her six children naturally, would always tease her grand children as 'unborn'. One of them, taking her words seriously, would introduce herself saying, 'I am special, my mother is a virgin, I was not born; I am a C-Section baby. I was forcibly removed from the womb, my sleeping bed'! Many parents are not aware that Caesarean section (CS) is a major surgical procedure that increases the likelihood of different types of harm and risks for the delivering mothers and babies in comparison to natural vaginal birth. Short-term harms for mothers undergoing CS include increased risk of infection, surgical injury, blood clots, emergency hysterectomy, intense and longer-lasting pain coupled with repeated hospital visits. Babies born by caesarean section are more likely to have surgical cuts, breathing problems, difficulty getting breastfeeding, and asthma in childhood and beyond.

So, if there is no 'commercial' or 'medical' reason to perform one, vaginal delivery is the best option. Nature has blessed women with stronger butts and softer breasts, not to please men but to withstand the supine sexual pressure and to push out as well as protect the progeny. The pelvic opening of a female has been designed to be wider than male for easy delivery of larger brained babies. Generations after this region would lose its natural capacity for self delivery because of continued disuse, as the structure of teeth and jaws weakened after humans stopped eating raw meat and started using cutting tools instead.

Child birth is a beautiful experience for most mothers. Justly proud of being pregnant, some of them even love to flaunt the baby bump in public. So much so that a few even want to show it to the whole world like the young Indian actress, Shwetha Menon. She gave birth to her baby girl on camera. Three cameras were placed in her labour room and kept rolling for 45 minutes capturing every little detail of the delivery to demystify the 'conception to delivery' process and educate the people.

My father had lost his first wife and second child to postnatal complications. He was married, for the second time, to my mother when she was just 13 and lost her at 46, a year after she had delivered the ninth child. Multiple pregnancies at short intervals lead to repeated injuries to the reproductive system, giving it no time to heal. I recollect how two sexually active, good looking widows in my village, who were in their early thirties, had ended their lives to escape the social stigma after getting pregnant. One jumped into the well and the other used the rope to end her life. Such stigma persited for a long time and even in relatively open societies. For, when Margaret Sanger opened her first birth control clinic in USA, in order to provide information and skills on sex, conception and contraception, she was arrested. And in 1914, when she published the first issue of The Woman Rebel, a small feminist newspaper that advocated birth control, it could publish only seven issues before being shut down. Because the then federal law labeled any material relating to birth control, even if for academic discussion, was obscene.

In our extended family, there was an old woman whom we called 'Nanima'. One of her dreams was to be a mother with many children. As soon as she learnt about a woman in labor in her village, she would rush to the place to watch how the baby was being pushed out and feel very happy. Once a while she would ask her mother: 'Mama, why don't you push another baby? Now I can help you in that'. Nanima was married off at the age of nine. The following year, her 12 year old 'child husband' died of malaria, making her a child widow. Society desexualizes the widows, and forces them into a place above sex and pregnancy. Two years after this tragedy, she attained puberty and lived as a widow until her death at 93. The sun in her life had set before rising, making way for starless nights of darkness. She shaved off her head and left home wearing a borderless, coarse white saree to live in a 'holy city' of widows, eventually disappearing from our memory. How did Nanima live the rest of her four score lonely years can be the subject matter of another Greek tragedy.

The boarding had started by now and we went inside the aircraft, politely ushered in by smartly dressed, pretty and smiling airhostesses with a friendly welcome. As soon as we settled down, there was an announcement: 'Ladies and gentlemen, the captain has turned on the fasten seatbelt sign and if you have not done so, please stow your carry-on luggage underneath the seat in front of you or in the overhead bin. Please switch off the cell phones and also all electronic devices and make sure your seat and folding trays are in their full upright position.' Then a gentle reminder for the smokers, that it was a non-smoking flight that also included the lavatories, was played out.

But hardly anyone was listening; some co-passengers had lapsed into slumber and were snoring loudly. The next instruction was more important and was about the emergency exit and rescue instructions that you are asked to read carefully. It describes how you move towards the exit, how emergency doors are to be opened, how you wear the life jacket and place yourself on to it, slide and use it as a life raft. Then the captain asks the cabin crew to cross check door closure and declares the flight time in hours and minutes, the flying altitude, the ground speed followed by safety demonstration, both, live and on video screen.

Every time I listen to and see through this safety demonstration and drill, I have a mixed feeling of fear and hope. Particularly, when it tells you about the life vest, located under a pouch under the seat or between armrests. The instruction is to slip it over the head, pass the strap around the waist, inflate it, pull firmly on the red cord, and to remember that the seat bottom cushion could also be used as a floatation device if the plane came down on water. In my first air travel to Colombo, Sri Lanka, I had taken these announcements so seriously that I thought probably that was going to be my last journey, apprehending that the plane would crash into the sea any time! Otherwise, in air travels, boarding is like a soul leaving the old world below and entering a new body as the Indic religions believe.

5

Binny's Kitchen and Rituals in Tenjiku

From San Francisco to New Delhi via London, is a long 20 hour tiring journey, the distance of half a planet. This time, it seemed longer with the constant pain in my ear. I was looking for the ear plug which I always carry for protection against the air pressure discomfort but it was not there in the hand bag packed by Binny, my wife. Did she forget it? Quite likely, because she was busy with ten other things in preparing herself to manage life in my absence. I started worrying because to avoid pain it was to be inserted before the takeoff and removed when the plane reached the maximum altitude and then reinserted one hour before landing.

Then with a faint hope, I groped my body and discovered the gadget was well in place in my chest pocket. Binny has ensured that it remained close to my heart! Women are unique in this. They have sharper eyes for details and maybe, their brains are specially wired for multi tasking. I have seen her often stitching a torn blouse watching a TV serial, talking over the phone and cooking a new recipe while keeping an eye on the children and an ear for the doorbell all at the same time. In Indian mythology too there is a female deity called Katyayani, who has three eyes and four hands.

A day before leaving SFO, I had attended a lecture by a professor of psychology, specializing on gender, who was narrating the difference between women and men in processing information. Giving various examples, he was explaining how men's brain was designed to concentrate only on one work at a time. Many men cannot watch TV and talk over the phone simultaneously. Similarly, a woman can easily learn many languages but cannot find solutions to many problems. But a three year old girl has three times higher vocabulary than a three year old boy. On the other hand, a man's brain has lot of space for handling the analytical process and can easily analyze and find solutions. He is a fast driver and can see an object at long distance, his brain immediately classifies the nature of objects in front, and their direction and speed. Whenever I drove a car a little faster, Binny, sitting next to me, would be continuously shouting, 'go slow, be careful, take a turn, and look ahead…' My Sri Lankan friend, Sheila Ebert, was once narrating how one day her husband got out of the car in a huff, telling her 'You are interfering too much, so you better drive.' They stopped talking to each other over this for a week.

I have always found it difficult telling simple and harmless lies to Binny and was always caught easily. Lucy's male children are yet to perfect this act. Experts give the reason saying that a woman's super natural brain can observe 70% of the facial expression of men, 20% of their body language and 10% of the words coming from their mouth, so many a time, the man is easily caught while lying. Conversely, a man's brain does not have this special power. The professor narrated that this was why women can easily lie to men and get away while he gave several examples from real life. Continuing the talk, he said that at the end of day, men tend to identify problems one by one, and get irritated when disturbed with too many problems. But a woman is not bothered if the problems are solved; all she wants is someone to hear them. I have seen how Binny loved telling everything to me, many of which were not relevant to the context and then go happily to bed or repeat it to another friend or a family member.

Men love fame, status, success, and solutions whereas women want love, relationship, friends, family and children. If women are unhappy with their relations, they cannot focus on work but if men are unhappy with their work, they cannot concentrate on the relationships. 'Cross-cultural Research says a woman's brain is better wired for empathy, they are more prosocial, more concerned, better readers of emotional expressions and better providers of physical comfort. Women often use indirect language in speech. The professor finally concluded his presentation, drawing attention to a quote:

'Women talk a lot without thinking whereas men act a lot without thinking.'

A lady stood up and asked, 'Can you give one example, professor?'

'Yes, yes, why not? When you look around, you would find out that all over the world, most of the prisoners in jails are men,' he replied.

Former British Prime Minister, Margaret Thatcher is reported to have said in a meeting that 'When you want something to be said, call a man and when you want something to be done, call a woman.' All said and done, this is still an unresolved issue in human behaviour. But I had absolutely no doubt in my mind about the multi tasking skills of women as I have witnessed this amazing phenomena, both, in my mother, daughters and wife, almost every day.

Often I wonder why women have stopped evolving genetically. Millions of years of multitasking should have given them additional limbs or hands like the Dasabhuja, the ancient 'ten-handed' Indian goddess. Imaginative mythology was ahead of modern biology and anthropology in this respect. Have women reached the end point of natural selection and evolution courtesy contraceptives, abortions, slow reproduction and change of cultural traits and habits? If 'baby food' consuming and milk drinking adults could develop genes for lactose tolerance, surely, women by now could have developed multi tasking limbs with support of nature! Has evolution eluded our women?

Binny has had a love-hate relationship with the kitchen. It was her sovereign territory, a state within a state. Male intrusion was restricted up to the waterpoint only. She believed that no other species on earth except the humans had a kitchen and because of this, non-humans mostly live their full lives. 'God sends food and devil sends cooks to boil, oil and soil it with ice, spice and chilly', she would quote her Naturopath teacher, Dr Hiralal, and would narrate how women, more than men, continue to fight with fire and power, day and night inside narrow, claustrophobic, kitchen cubicles for ages since the Homo erectus controlled fire some 125,000 years ago. She also had a strange allergy to various types of kitchen appliances as she believed they make air in the kitchen three times more toxic than air in the street. She would caution about how kitchen pollutants penetrate into lungs, how gas cookers are a potent source of nitrogen oxide and so on. And if you ask her what the alternative was, she would say, 'don't cook, you don't need a kitchen.'

'Then what do we eat? How do we survive?'

'Very simple,' she would reply. 'Take natural foods cooked by mother Earth, sweetened by Sun, soaked by water and kissed by air and sweep clean your bowels by toothbrush foods like apple, orange, strawberry, cabbage, cauliflower and so many others. They also scrub, stimulate production of saliva and prevent plaque formation, giving you stronger teeth'.

To caution and convince about tinned food, she would quote George Orwell imperfectly, as to how such foods were 'deadlier weapons than the machine gun'. 'Feed human made food to the monkeys and their natural reproductive behaviour would change from seasonal to regular'-she would say.

'Imagine the Sun, our friendly cook-in-chief, is five billion years older than you, burns 4 million tons of fuel each second and takes just eight minutes covering a distance of 92,962,000 miles to reach the earth to serve you delicious pre-cooked foods and sweet juicy fruits! Don't you know that sunshine by itself is a nutritious food that protects the body from so many infections?' Then again to substantiate her point, she would now quote Napoleon Bonaparte, who had once said: 'If I had to choose a religion, the sun, as the universal giver of life, would be my god.' She would ask you to connect to the young rising sun every morning, which, she believed, widened and deepened one's inner wisdom. One is connected to a visible reality of the natural and spiritual. Half of the nights in a year, she would sleep on the floor on some pretext or other and in the morning walk in the park without any foot wear. To her, this was connecting to mother Earth, a kind of 'earthing' of the body for energy. 'We insulate our bare feet, rich with a network of nerve endings, from connecting with its natural mother, by wearing synthetic shoes and sleeping on elevated beds,' she would say.

Once, I tried to counter and convince her by quoting from Dr. Wrangham's 'Catching Fire: How Cooking Made us Human' (2010). 'Our ancestors were eating raw meat and tubers over two million years. For 1800 calories per day of such raw food for a person weighing 70 kg, the food collecting and eating time needed was about   18 hours a day. How production, storage and cooking provided early Homo-erectus with more time to think, reflect and recreate, how cooking made whole grains and cereals more digestible and killed pathogens in raw food, how it reduced the size of the digestive track and added billions of cells to the brain and so on so forth.'

But she rejected my argument outright telling, 'You are quoting from books, and I am telling from experience and close observation of nature. I suspect evolution of stronger teeth stopped since humans went in for soft cooked food because now they didn't need powerful teeth and jaws to crush raw plant materials. And our denture must have started weakening only after that. The consequence of which is an ever increasing number of dentists today.' Half convinced, I decided not to join issue and prolong the debate, which many a time, I had lost in the past.

Every morning, Binny would clean the room chanting 'Aum', wipe the walls and corners of room with a saltwater bowl to get rid of 'negative energy'. She would then softly sprinkle water on the spider plant she had placed in the kitchen and bath room corner and areca palm in the living room, while dusting off the Boston fern and English Ivy near the bed rooms, believing they would ward off the air pollutants. Then, she would burn incense of natural herbs that give out a fragrance which she believed would purify the energy level in the space inside the house. She would open all the windows and doors to flood the house with sunlight and fresh air for an hour and, finally, end the operation by switching on the music system for devotional songs for spiritual therapy.

After an early bath, Binny would go to our small back yard garden to pluck flowers for her gods, despite my reminders not to rob the poor innocent plants of their little colourful children. A tree smiles through its flowers and no one has the right to steal its happiness but she would not listen and even the leaves of some plants were not safe from her as she considered these to be dear to her gods. In the epic, Ramayan, the stories about Rishis or sages requesting Ram to protect their elaborate daily rituals from people, whom they called 'demons', may have to be understood in this context for it is reasonable to suspect that the so called 'demons' may have been greatly irritated by the strange and meaningless rituals and practices of the Rishis and that must have prompted them to prevent it. It was also, perhaps, a way of protest by the original inhabitants or the aborigines against the intrusion and 'defiling' of their habitat by outsiders.

One morning, to her shock, Binny found that all the flowers in the garden were gone and unable to accept the reality; she started cursing loudly at the unknown flower thief. I came out and after seeing her condition, tried to console and counsel her by asking her to forgive and forget and telling her that the trees would flower once again tomorrow.

'But then, how do I decorate my deities today?' She protested.

I said, 'You should be happy that your flowers have already gone to decorate the deities in the temple.'

She did not believe me and demanded to know how could I say that.

'By your 'flower thief' and in fact, you should appreciate that your gods will get the flowers a little earlier today.'

'But how?' She demanded to know once again, still unhappy and angry.

'Because, the thief's god and your god are one and the same,' I explained to an unconvinced Binny. The best thing in God, if he actually exists, is his eternal silence despite people shouting loudly about him from house tops and religious places and fighting in his 'name', as if he/she was deaf though religions and scriptures are always loud about interpreting god's silence.

Often force fed by a false diet of superstition, the rituals live longer than life itself and survive centuries by breeding more rituals through its passionate practitioners. In the early 90s, I was in Maldives attending the SAARC Ministers Conference In the afternoon, I went to a library to study more about this cute little country strategically located in the Indian Ocean and chanced upon a book on Maldivian folklore that explained how people suffered by following blind rituals.

The gist of the story was like this: The inhabitants of these islands were visited every month by a 'demon of the genie'. He came out of the sea and had the appearance of a ship full of lamps. People used to worship and pray him out of fear. It was customary with the islanders that when they saw him, they would take a virgin maid into a budkhana, an idol- house, which was built on the seashore. They would leave the girl there overnight and as they returned at daybreak, the poor, unfortunate girl would be found ravished and dead. Every month they would cast lots and whoever was chosen through this process had to offer his virgin daughter as a ritual offering to the genie.

Once, a trader named Abul Barakat came to know about this practice during his short stay in Maldives. He went to the idol house and killed the virgin eating genie who was actually another trader. Then he also threw the idol into sea. The news spread over all the islands like wild fire and people quickly abandoned the ritual and converted to Abul's faith, changing their belief for the fourth time. The Buddha was repeatedly disparaging rituals in several of his sermons. He was critical of the priests of his times, who were obsessed with performance of meaningless practices. He used to emphasize that the real path to Nirvana is better walked with mental discipline and ethical living than with rituals.

Our strange behaviors are often influenced by the way we think and perceive. During an earlier journey and halt in Hong Kong, I found a grown up girl repeatedly rushing to the wash room to vomit. Her mother told us that it was a reaction after she discovered a worm inside a cake. Sitting next to me was a middle aged person waiting to take the next flight and watching the incident. 'Yinduren?' He asked. I failed to understand.

'I mean from India?' He clarified.

When I nodded, he asked, 'From the land of Buddha?'

Another similar looking gentleman sitting next to us seemed suddenly interested and said, 'Tenjiku, Tenjiku.' Again not being able to understand, I asked curiously, 'Sorry, what did you say? 'Tenjiku,' he repeated. 'In Japan, we refer to ancient India as Tenjiku, which means 'the heavenly country.' I said 'No longer. The heaven is now locked in a fierce fight with the hell. We have all the religions and all the gods, holy ghosts and godmen and women, but the devils have outnumbered all of them. Maybe, only a new Buddha could help us out'.

He smiled, thinking I was not serious. Tenjiku is the Japanese pronunciation of the word Tianzhu, the old Chinese name for ancient India.

We had still some time to catch the next leg of the flight. As we entered into a conversation, looking at the vomiting girl, he narrated an interesting episode about two young Buddhist monks, who were travelling together on a pilgrimage. It was a long painful journey by road but on foot. As the sun set and the evening got darker, they decided to take rest at a small wayside monastery. An old monk living there offered them food and water before they retired to bed. One of them got up early in the morning and seeing his friend deep in sleep, resumed the journey, leaving a note for him, asking to follow him once he was ready.

When the second traveller got up two hours later, he felt thirsty and the old monk of the monastery offered him water in a bowl. As his vision slowly adjusted, he found it was a human skull. When he refused to take the water from the skull, he was gently reminded that the night before he had gladly accepted water from the same skull bowl twice. Hearing this, the young monk suddenly felt nauseous. His stomach reacted violently and he started vomiting without stop and died within twelve hours. While, his friend and co-traveller, who had also taken water several times from the same skull bowl reached his destination well on time. Psychologists call it 'contagion bias' when one is incapable of ignoring the feeling of contact with certain items that the mind had decided not to accept.

In Kurukshetra, Haryana, India, there is an old legendary Banyan tree. Many people believe that in the Mahabharat, Krishna motivated and counselled Arjuna under this tree to fight for rights and justice. On reaching the place at Jyotigar, I was shocked to see this last remaining relic from Mahabharat days was almost on the verge of extinction.

It was obvious the tree was fighting its marble pavement that was preventing it from drawing nutrients for support. Choked below by a ring of cement and concrete like a noose round its decaying body, it had lost contact with the anchorage of roots. Its branches were fitted with fancy lights and lamps with nails to hold, weakening and hurting it further.

Big and heavy bells were tied all over and lower branches were covered with 'holy' threads as wish fulfiller and chunks of branches had been chopped off. I came to know that all attempts by plant pathologists for its preservation were being resisted by the local priests. This legendary tree continues to tolerate in silence the mindless madness of its masters.

Back home, we had a similar sad experience in our own backyard in the group housing society inhabited by a highly educated middle class. Binny had a long desire to marry a Banyan and Peepal tree, which is considered a sacred and virtuous act. In south pacific religions including Buddhist, Jain and Hindu traditions, Banyan is called the tree of knowledge and life and believed to be sacred and one which always fulfils one's wishes. Its thick leaves, seeds and aerial roots nurture a variety of life forms. It is also the national tree of India. Thousands of people can take shelter under a fully grown and spread banyan tree. Similarly, Peepal (Ficus Religiosa) is the other famous tree under which Buddha had meditated and attained enlightenment. Both these trees have great medicinal value and emit lots of oxygen. Their seeds can germinate even in cracks and crevices. Both emit tons of oxygen and are ideal places for practice of meditation.

Binny had bought the saplings from a nearby nursery and planted them together along with wire-fencing for protection. Both the trees had a luxuriant growth and attained a respectable height. A year later, she organized a ritual marriage between them with Banyan as the groom and Peepal as bride that was followed by a feast. Some amused residents asked her about its significance. And here, she made the first and fatal mistake. Instead of explaining the contributions these plants make to enrich the environment, she told them how daily worship and prayer to the trees could bring prosperity. She quoted a Sanskrit shloka, which said: 'Every leaf is an abode of a deity and each branch equal to five deities'. But she herself didn't know that making tree a subject of veneration was the surest way to endanger its survival.

Sure enough, within a year, the 'tree -bride and groom' were burnt to death by an overdose of ritual worship and prayer. The residents, mostly women, would flock around the growing green duo with lighted candles, earthen oil lamps and burning incense sticks praying for prosperity and leave these materials there. The poor plants could no longer stand the heat of the ritual and overdose of religiosity and the dry grass and twigs catching fire from the holy candles precipitated the tragedy.

The 'bride and groom' eventually died of daily heat and burns that continued for one year. For some time, I was working as a Senior Adviser to India International Institute of Democracy and Election Management in the Election Commission of India, an independent constitutional authority conducting world's largest elections faultlessly for years.

There was a formidable chief ministerial candidate, who lost the elections in 2009 just by one vote. On his petition, the votes were recounted and recalculated and still the difference was one. Postal ballots, service ballots, and the NRI ballots were counted separately once again on his request to satisfy him. The difference was still one. At the end, he, reportedly, picked up the phone and saluted the Election Commission for the zero error.

The side story, as reported, is a sad commentary on rituals for ensuring good results. The fact is that on the day of election, the minister's wife, accompanied by her daughter and driver, had gone to the temple instead of going to the polling booth to cast their vote. She was there in the temple the whole day, organising an elaborate ritual and prayer to please God for her husband's victory!

Behaviour scientists say that rituals are basically anxiety ridden behaviour and future events that have uncertain, unknown and unpredictable outcomes are the ones where rituals are more likely to flourish.

In my village, there was a young, hard working farmer named Taria, who was a great devotee of elephant god, Ganesha, and was living happily with his wife and two children. That year, he had a good harvest and he kept the surplus paddy in his backyard for sale. In his house, he had hung pictures of the elephant in the prayer room. Members of his clan believed that the elephant was their common and original ancestor called 'Gotra', of which they were the descendants.

Once, early in the morning, his immediate neighbour informed that there were two jumbos standing in his backyard. Taria, through his half opened back door, could now see the huge animals and felt very happy. He considered it as an auspicious occasion and woke up his wife and children, telling that they must welcome their ancestors, who were now waiting in the backyard, with ritual and prayer. All of them rushed to the place with flowers, incence sticks, coconuts, candles, ripe bananas and prostrated before the two elephants. Feeling threatened, the jumbo duo, who was actually looking for food, trumpeted in anger. Taria's wife and children fled in fear but he stood up and prostrated before the animals once again. Now, an angry jumbo lifted him with its trunk and after swinging him like a puppet, threw him onto the ground and then proceeded to pound the well built and muscular Taria to pulp.

What was it, a black joke on life, supremacy of fate over fact or a lesson on how people both high and low are vulnerable to age old rituals and practices as a last resort to save hopeless hopes? Every religion has a fair amount of it but the older and the more privatised have more of it. Those who protested against it eventually ended with more rituals to prove their new identity. In Odisha, in eastern India, a new form of asceticism, called Mahima Dharma was founded against spread of Christianity and Hindu Vaishnavism. It conceived God as a 'void' called 'Shunya'. Then after some time, the followers of the new faith started constructing temples to pray the 'void' . And since a void can't be visible, they began worshipping the door of the temple. Buddha was against external rituals and silent about god but his followers started making his image and worshipping it as God. Each religion that started with new hope broke up into sects, cults, schools, branches and denominations with their own elaborate rituals. Christianity is reported to have the largest number of sects and sub-sects- i.e., more than twenty thousand denominations!

Coming back to Binny's kitchen, she slowly turned into a food fundamentalist and food separatist. Non-vegetarian or 'blood and flesh' foods were a clear 'no, no'- not even unfertilized eggs. Even onion, garlic were treated as untouchables, joined by drumsticks, egg plants, mushrooms, and tomatoes. On some fixed days, cabbage, cauliflower and broccoli were outcastes. To her, animal fats like clarified butter is vegetarian and vegetable oils from plants are non- vegetarian. A belief that I failed to change. Once, when I feebly reminded her that milk was actually non-vegetarian, she cut me short by telling how mother's milk protects millions of babies and how high milk consuming countries have more Nobel laureates and so on.

Binny's kitchen has separate utensils for different foods. As a hygiene freak, she would excel singer Jennifer Lopez by several counts. It is reported that Jennifer used to go out with her own toilet seat to have germ free droppings in the bathroom. I heard that on her birthday, her boyfriend presented her a gem-studded toilet seat consisting of rubies, sapphires, pearls and diamond set inside a plastic cover so that her behind wouldn't get scratched! However, unfortunately, Binny's poor husband was not so rich! If hygiene freaks could extend their habits just a few metres beyond their doors, the world would be free from filth and would be a much cleaner place. I had a glimpse of it at Changi before boarding for New Delhi. As soon as I entered the wash room, I faced a touch screen asking, 'Please Rate us After Use' followed by a five point scale of Excellent, Very Good, Good, Average and Dirty, so before leaving I touched the number one button. Soon after, another message popped up: 'Don't worry; this touch screen is sanitised for safety after every use.'

Binny would often try to convince an unwilling listener about how meat eating is an unsustainable habit, because to produce a kilogram of meat, an animal is to be fed with 18 kilograms of grain and cereals and all the energy and water needed to produce it. And how forty percent of food grains of the world are consumed by these 'meaty' animals and live stock, creating a food crisis. Once I reminded her that such animals are grass eating and we have pushed them into grain eating against their will. We had a big fight that day, thanks to both grass and grain.

In order to buttress her argument, she would cite from Gandhi to Hitler and refer to vegetarians like Milton, Newton and Bernard Shaw for additional support. When one entered into an argument with her about the lack of protein in a fully vegetarian diet, she would advise them to watch a 500 lb bull or the huge elephant or the ever agile and hard nut horse that provided the ultimate energy measure, i.e., the 'horse power'. She would assert that nature has programmed human body to live for 120 years which we reduce by pursuing wrong food habits and life styles. To those still not convinced, she would explain why meat eaters themselves do not like to eat the 'meat' of the 'meat eating animals' and prefer meat of vegetarian beasts and birds instead. She would explain how carnivores are born with long canine and wide open jaws and sharp claws to capture the prey and tear its flesh where as herbivores are born with grinder like teeth designed for eating and masticating plant food and how nature has made the tongue of a carnivore rough and acidic to be used for lapping blood and saliva whereas herbivores including humans have soft lips and tongues and their alkaline saliva acts on starches and carbohydrates. Carnivores have short intestine, smooth bowels, big livers and kidney that allows food to move along freely and throw out meat waste whereas herbivores have long intestine and small livers, wherein meat gets trapped and gets putrefied, putting too much uric acid in the blood that goes and gets deposited in the joints. Human body is a temple of god, why turn it into a grave yard by eating dead animals? Who has given you the right to kill them for food, for skin and fur, for experiment, entertainment, commerce and caging, she would ask.

She would insist as to how leafy vegetables, colourful fruits and food grains are actually preventive 'food- medicines' that provide twice as much energy compared to meat when consumed directly by humans. Only plant foods can provide sufficient, safe, sustainable and nutritious food security to everyone. To give it support from other religions, she would quote lines from the Bible: 'Then God said, I give you every seed bearing plant on the face of the whole earth and every tree that has fruit with seed in it. They will be yours for food. And to all the beasts of the earth and all the birds of the air and all the creatures that move on the ground-everything that has the breath of life in it-I give every green plant for food' (Genesis 1: 29: 30).

To convince further about the 'food medicine', she would pick up a full size ripe, red tomato from the vegetable basket, cut it in the middle to show how it has four chambers like the human heart and how it is the best food for the heart. Similarly, she would pick up a walnut kernel, telling how it not only looks like the human brain but also has the best brain food, enriching neurons. Red beans look like kidney and keep kidney active, figs grow in two, look like twin testicles and help in semen creation, egg plant and avocado look like uterus and when eaten by women, keep it in good condition, balancing hormone. Onion and garlic, when opened, look like blood cells and they actually cleanse blood! Round pieces of carrot not only look like an eye ball but also help in better sight. And finally, to floor the sceptics, she would quote health researchers, who say how vegetarians' post operative healing is quicker than the non-vegetarians.

Last year, she celebrated the day when she learnt that scientists from the Loma Linda University in California found out that vegetarian Adventist men lived about 9.5 year longer than the non-vegetarian. The study also found that vegans were, on average, 13 kilograms lighter than meat eaters and five units lighter on the Body Mass Index scale than meat eaters.

"See, I told you so,' she said with a lot of happiness and satisfaction. Coincidentally, the same evening, she called out me loudly to hear a spiritual discourse by saint Vaswani on her favourite TV channel. I understood the urgency.

The Guru was explaining: 'The 18th century opened the door for the rights of the ordinary people when in 1789, the French National Assembly passed the Bill of Rights. The 19th century gave rights to 'slaves', and the 20th century restored the rights of women. Now the 21st century will give rights to animals.' Binny was visibly happy and asked me if I agreed. Incidentally, we had a guest that day named Mallik, a non-vegetarian, who didn't agree. He quoted sources to say how fish and flesh had contributed to growth of human brain and how vegetarianism and agriculture have been relentlessly assaulting the planet, its topsoil, prairies, forests and the climate- the very basis of life itself. And how we feed our soil with fossil, blood and bones, how we eat a 'sentient' plant, destroy its children (seeds) and how a so called 'non-violent' plant also feeds on living soil with millions of micro organisms eating, excreting, reproducing, exchanging and communicating. The best thing we can do now is to start returning to the animals what we have snatched away from them during last ten thousand years, their wild food fields' he said. Then he narrated an event that ocurred in St. Mathew Islands, a 128 sq mile small area in the Bering Sea. Where, for want of predators, a population of 29 deers increased rapidly to an unsustainable peak of six thousand. Eventually most of them died of starvation caused by overgrazing and harsh winter.

While I was confused, Binny had decided not to be persuaded by such logic, but was unable to counter, partly because of her poor knowledge of botany and biology and world history. However, after this exposure to a different dimension, she would now ask people to take an informed decision. And that I consider was fair enough. One day, an environmentalist friend of mine visited our house and we talked about an hour on biodiversity and extinction of rare plant species. Overhearing our conversation, she came nearer and said, 'Your kitchen could save these plant foods only if you start eating these rice varieties, beans, roots and tubers and those which grew locally.' My friend agreed with her fully.

Binny practised what she preached. For instance, in the market, she would look for non leather, vegan foot wear and avoid crockery made of animal bones. The day I told her that an elegant silk sari is made by killing about 20,000 silkworms, she was shocked out of her senses and from that day she started wearing saris made of organic cotton only, now called Ahimsa cotton. Since then, any material made by harming an animal was off limits. She had great faith in the self healing powers of the 'body', which she called a moving pharmaceutical factory. Her backyard is full with healing herbs and plants that prevent her from hospital visits. While people take medicine after falling ill, Binny falls ill when she has to take medicine under pressure. She would begin and end her day with meditation, yoga and pranayam that helps her relieve all kinds of stress in addition to keeping her body and mind fit.

She would say meditation is not action; in a profound sense, it is doing absolutely nothing, just sitting still and kicking out the world out of the mind following three golden rules, i.e., be nothing, desire nothing, do nothing for fifteen minutes after which you can get up and get on with the world. Till now, Binny has no health insurance and has not visited the hospital for the last 30 years! It may sound too good to be true but it is very much true.

The captain started rattling off what seemed to be a well rehearsed, oft repeated announcement, "Flight attendants, prepare for takeoff please, Cabin crew, please take your seats for takeoff." He had ensured thorough checking of all vital parts of the aircraft as it is said that in 1995, little wood peckers had delayed a space shuttle by pecking tiny holes in the fuel tank! We were again reminded to fasten seat belt and the aircraft started moving forward on the runway for a while and then took off climbing towards its cruising altitude. The 'fasten seat belt' sign was tuned off, allowing passengers to move around in the cabin.

Like many, I always prefer a window seat, but for my own reasons. It gives me a real earth view. As you go up and look down the green and blue planet, you see how it floats like a plane as if on a restless journey to an unknown destination, constantly rotating and revolving. No one knows exactly when and from where it took off and how and when it was placed at the right distance from the sun to support life.

The trillions of living beings and hundreds of countries suddenly become invisible along with their racial, religious divisions and political borders, along with their endless controversies and conspiracies. Where are the powerful, the grand and the greats- the tall statues, the minars and memorials, the pyramids and pagodas, the high hills and great walls, the empires and dynasties, the life itself and all the hammers and nails to fix things permanently and where is the earth among the 1800 plus planets or among the 11 billion potentially habitable other earths among 200 billion stars in the Milky Way? And where are the people, who live, love, fear and fight each other? No trace, no existence. Just particles of dust!

6

Apollo, Toilets &
Vanishing 'Wives'

In Delhi, close to Shahjahan Road, is located the Union Public
Service Commission, a constitutional body, to examine, interview
and recruit different categories of civil servants. I was interviewed
twice by this body for different positions and later on, I occasionally
served as a ministry representative and observer to assist the interview
panel. During one such interview, an expert asked five candidates the
same question, i.e., to tell them the two most memorable dates in their
life. Normally, same questions are not repeated in an interview and the
Chairman didn't like it.

However, four of them replied to the question differently by
saying these were birth day or day of marriage, convocation, graduation
ceremony, first monthly salary, the first day in the university, first visit
to a cinema hall, first picnic, cricket world cup victory, etc. But the
fifth candidate had an unusual answer. Reflecting on the question
for a moment, he replied in five words: '16th June and 20th July'.
Mystified, one member asked, 'Can you explain why do you you think
so?' Then lifting the interview into cosmic plane, he explained how
they were so historic, so exciting, so breath taking, so unprecedented
and so inspiring. Both the dates were related to space travel.

On 16th June, 1963, Valentine Terescova was the first woman to
travel in space in the spacecraft, Vostok-6. Yuri Gagarin had done this
feat two years earlier but a woman in space was something very special

since during that time there was lots of reservation about a woman's ability to withstand the rigor of space travel.

Similarly, he said that when Apollo 11 landed on the Moon on 20th July, 1969 with Neil Armstrong and Buzz Aldrin, he had spent a sleepless night of excitement and wonder listening to the live radio broadcast. It is said that the then Indian Prime Minister, Ms. Indira Gandhi, had kept awake till 4:30 am to watch the landing on the moon. Another sixty million people were watching this historic event on television. Would u like to say anything special about it? Was the next question. 'Value of Time' he replied. Neil was extremely time conscious, so when President Richard Nixon talked to him for one minute, he replied to him in just 30 seconds.

When the space craft landed on the moon he did not hoop or cheer; he just commanded - 'Shut down', the two words to which, Aldrin responded in three words saying 'Ok, engine stop'. To the earth station, his entire message was in eight words - 'Houston, Tranquillity Base here. The Eagle has landed.' History is not made by words, but by people who live by it and after landing, Aldrin was in full control of his words and emotions.

The interviewee said further that he was just 13 year old child at that time and was mentally with them for the entire 22 hours on moon's surface consisting of fine talcum like dust that was strewn with pebbles and rocks.

During the journey, they had the unique opportunity of seeing the moon rising on earth's horizon and the earth rising on moon's horizon. Forty years after, today, the gadgets they had carried would look primitive. Apollo 11 had just 71k memory whereas now some small pocket sized calculators can store 500k.

Lucy's enterprising children have always been discovering the world with tools and gadgets that very soon start looking primitive and outdated to their successors and they then slowly meander their ways into the museums as relics of the past. During my first visit to the USA in 2002, I had seen the first space shuttle, a great wonder of modern science, preserved in a museum. It had outlived its utility.

When I had gone to London to face an interview for a job in the Commonwealth Secretariate, a member of the Selection board had asked me to mention one invention that had changed the world like no one else and never before. I had replied ' Printing Press'. 'And second one? Unsure, I said 'May be computer'. It was only partially correct as I found out later on. On the eve humanity was to enter the third Millennium, BBC Focus magazine had conducted an international survey to identify 100 far reaching, downright inspired ideas, inventions and gadgets that were history's eureka moments and had changed the face of the world for ever. The survey involved more than 1,000 researchers, science writers and common citizens who were asked to compile their lists of the most important inventions in the world impacting on development. The result provided interesting insights into the public mind and development priority of the planners. In this list of the 100 'Inventions that changed the world,' fire (590,000BC), wheel, and the steam energy occupied 4th, 5th and 31st positions respectively. And the modern toilet system with flush latrine was adjudged as number one. When I narrated this to my young artist friend Pradip Nayak in Mumbai, he instantly drew a beautiful cartoon depicting a man sitting on the toilet and working with a laptop . The caption says: How wonderful! I'm using world's first and second greatest inventions at the same time!!

Although every one may not agree, there is no doubt that the toilet system, with its sewage, drainage, sanitary latrines and flush lavatories, has been responsible to a very great extent in improving not only the quality of life but also liberating millions of women and men from demeaning health hazards on account of manual scavenging in some parts of the world. It has also prevented to a great extent fecal contamination of waterways, ground and drinking water and water borne diseases like cholera. In 1849, more than ten thousand people had died of cholera in London alone. It is said that even luxury palaces built by powerful nobles didn't have proper wash rooms and toilets. Everyday bath was unheard of and frowned upon and in France, perfumes were popular because of this reason only. So, the 'number one' among inventions was an example of how science could be used as an instrument for social behavior change for both rich and poor.

In my village, open air defecation was common. Once a middle-aged married lady in our locality fell victim to a rapist while she was returning home after relieving herself in the field. This married man grabbed her from behind and forced himself upon her despite her loud cry for help in the wilderness. Shocked, she didn't tell anyone about it for a long time out of shame and fear of social disapproval and stigma until the man himself started bragging about it and people began ridiculing her but there was no public outrage about the barbarous act. Abandoned by her husband as well as parents and unable to bear the weight of daily humiliation, one midnight she disappeared from the village for good and was soon forgotten, only to be occasionally remembered as a loose character who had shamed her family. There were no anti-rape laws in those days or an active media to highlight the plight of the woman. Lucy would have been aghast seeing the behavior of her children today. An old friend of mine, Prof. Rajendra Das, a German scientist of Indian origin, had forwarded to me a list of nine things that included the pocket calculator, post office, telegram, telephone, cheque book, music systems, TV, book, news paper and personal privacy which would disappear in 21st century itself and many during our life time.

I was particularly sad about the poor 'post office' and knowledge spreading 'book'. The 'post office' had launched the communication revolution in the world centuries ago. The first letter I had received in life was when I was 13. It was from Dena, my childhood girl friend, telling how my play mates missed me. She had to trek twice to the two km distant post office once to buy the post card and second time to drop it into the post box. This was my happiest day after leaving the village. I had preserved it as a treasure for a long time and was reading it repeatedly.

Like letter in personal life, telegram, the first magic leap in human communication, was a real game changer, liberating human communication from the constraints of time, space and limitations of body, delivering messages of birth, death, love, elopement and marriages. In 1857, the British colonists used telegram extensively to crush India's first war of Independence. My first telegram brought the saddest news of my mother's death when I was away from home. It had also enabled me to rush back, catching the earliest train to be at her funeral. Recently, India has closed down its 162 years old telegram services, following many other countries.

The most important one in the line of fire would be the all

important 'book', till now my best personal friend and an eternal companion of knowledge workers, with all its ideas and wisdom written on paper in black and white. It has already started yielding to the ubiquitous CD- the compact disk. In the early 70s, I had travelled 400 Kms by a passenger train to buy just three books, i.e., 'Pedagogy of the Oppressed' by Paolo Freire, 'The Deschooling Society' by Evan Illich and 'My Experiments with Truth' by Gandhi, from a particular street in distant Kolkata city. Within a month the first one was stolen and another colleague lifted the book 'Deschooling Society' from my study promising to return it in a week and forgot it for good. There was a teacher in my college, who would borrow a rare book from the library, tear off important pages and chapters from inside for his use before returning it quietly to an unsuspecting library assistant. Writing, along with speech and agriculture, was one of the three critical things that had defined the direction of human civilization. In Guten Berg's printing press, the first typeset printed book was the Bible. Afterwards, world religions had travelled faster riding on it, but not without resistance. Mass production of books was opposed by the 'copyists' for taking away the source of their livelihood, by aristocrats for mechanical vulgarization of knowledge, by politicians for empowering the people and by the clergy and custodians of social order for fear of spreading subversive ideas and heresy.

It is said that both the Chinese pilgrim-scholars,,Faxian (337-422 Ad) and Xuanzang (602-664), had carried from India loads of hand written Sanskrit texts and spent the rest of their lives in copying and translating them. The same book which had spread reading of religious texts, philosophy, history, science and literature and disseminated new ideas for many revolutions finally ended clerical monopoly of learning. Books also had changed men and women in no small measure. Gandhi has confessed in his autobiography (part IV) about the 'magic spell of a small book' titled 'Unto This Last', by John Ruskin, that changed his entire attitude to life and work. The superstructure of Gandhian philosophy was built on three simple ideas contained in this book: that the good of the individual is contained in the good of all, the lawyer's work has the same value as the barber's and a life of labourer is the life worth living. Sadly, the long journey from palm leaf to papyrus to paddy straw and then to the power of the printed word would soon be over. My authentic companion, the Oxford Dictionary, is already gasping to survive. The information overload is just too big to print and carry or keep in shelf.

I wrote back to Prof. Das, adding two more things likely to disappear- i.e., the 'humble house wife' and the institution of marriage itself. The word 'wife' around which myths and mythologies were created and on which traditional husbands hung up for long, would be the next victim as 'married' people would no longer like to use it as an 'honour badge'. The pleasure or pain or even pride of calling one 'my husband' or 'my wife' may not last beyond the 21st century. Pema, a Malaysian Muslim lady colleague of mine, would often come to the office very late and one day, when I asked her gently about the reason, she told me, 'Because, I don't have a 'wife' and because I am somebody's wife.' I understood what she wanted to convey.

Dozens of once dazzling inventions have already disappeared without a whimper that includes the large steam engine and the small fountain pen. Antibiotics may overcome mortality for one more century. A few unforgettable ones have pushed civilization fast forward from violent hunter food gatherer stage to the present era of human rights. Humans through millions of years, have self domesticated and tamed their aggressive behavior, using both tools and tolerance through group living in early middle and later stone ages. Yet their fighting instincts continue in different forms. My Kashmiri friend, Kapil Kaul, a highly reputed social marketing expert, once narrated to me an interesting story about the fighting habits of some boat dwellers of famous Dal Lake. In Kashmir, a number of families, traditionally live in boats which they call 'donga'. The lake has hundreds of them. People living in the donga always avoid a physical fight despite provocations and when a domestic fight looks unavoidable, they sail out to the shore and vent out their pent up anger against each other that often converts into a street fight. Passersby enjoy the sight and intensity of the fight that is often joined by folks from the neighbourhood. Why do they control and suppress their anger inside the boat and let it loose in the street?

Kapil explained, 'First, because they are aware that the boat has visiting guests, who would feel offended, and second, the donga cannot bear the burden of their violent behavior and might lose balance, shake or sink.'

Often contextual constraints compel us to control the inner demon. There is a related joke about human behaviour and carbon footprints. Once two planets accidentally met in the cosmos and the first one asked: "How are you, my dear?" "Not so well," the second one answered. 'What is the problem?' 'I've got plenty of Homo sapiens on my body. They are killing fellow humans and all other life forms through highly irresponsible behavior and are also always digging me left and right, stealing all my treasures besides polluting the air and the water" The first one smiled and said, "Don't worry, I had the similar ones also, who signed their own death warrants long ago and have led themselves into oblivion. Now, I am peaceful. If your ones are similar species, I assure you, they won't last long."

Moon man, Neil Armstrong, is no more. He passed away when I was in USA and now, visitors laugh at the primitive look of the calculator he was using in his historic mission. During our life time, we have seen many new things which nowadays arouse no curiosity. For instance, our village school had declared a special holiday to show the students a radio, an automobile and an earth mover and I was excited beyond imagination. A talking box? How was it possible? There was no one to explain. Since, the audio box was over sized, I thought someone inside must be speaking. Father had told me once how in his childhood, he had travelled 20 kms to see a bicycle. I had spent three days traveling in bullock cart to have a glimpse of Jawaharlal Nehru, India's first Prime Minister. Ten years later, I had cycled 47 kms to see and listen to Vinoba Bhave, the Sarvoday leader, of the famous and innovative land gift movement.

This 'King of Kindness' and India's 'walking saint', walked on foot for 13 years covering 40 thousand miles and collected about 40 million acres of land gift by changing the heart and minds of the land owning class. He redistributed these to the poor and landless. He had been chosen by Gandhi as the first soldier of non-violence.

Although young, I was greatly impressed by the moral strength of Vinoba's argument when he said that mother earth belonged not only to humans but to all living beings, from bacteria to elephant. The assassination of Gandhi on 30th January, 1948, had shattered him. He was doubly shaken watching the 'second assassination' of Gandhi on the following day, i.e. 31st January. On this day, the dead body of the apostle of peace and non-violence was placed on a military vehicle being pulled by 200 army men surrounded by another thousand police and security while three air force planes were flying above during the 5.5 hour journey to Rajghat where his body was cremated with gun salute and full military 'honour'. Gandhi himself would have been horrified looking at this scenario.

The flight attendants duo, one male and another female in their twenties, were now walking around the cabin, offering snacks, water and beverages in customized trolleys. The plane and its passengers, though 30000 feet above from the earth, had not forgotten anything. Together, they were still carrying high on the sky the decadent class structure, the privileges, patronages and deprivations. The seats were also different and hierarchically arranged as business class, club class and economy class which self critical passengers refer to as cattle class in jest. The quality of care, attention and choice of foods also vary accordingly. However, fed up of that food on ground, people don't mind it up above in the sky.

By now, the aircraft had gained further speed and stabilized. I pushed up the window shutter to have another view of the divided world we had left behind. The mighty mountains, the large oceans, the great wall of China, the tall imposing Qutab Minar, the grandiose Egyptian pyramids and the sky high Empire State building, had all disappeared from the view of our lonely plane and along with it, all our artificial differences. Like in the mental plane, as one rises higher, many so called big problems of life look smaller and smaller and then disappear altogether.

Up above, the nearest galaxy, large Magellanic Cloud, was 1,63000 light years away, equal to about 10 trillion kms, from where it would look as if the earth didn't exist and humans tinier than a bacteria, I thought to myself. With its surface soil looking red with rich iron, Mars was now appearing a bit larger. After recent discovery of its frozen water and thin atmosphere, mother earth was no longer the only and lonely living planet and forever surrounded by radio waves, those living on it are not alone either. The bacteria under Martian surface and other unknown planets in the multi-verse may be laughing at our limited self centric vision. I remembered Nicolas Copernicus, who spent a life time convincing the conservatives that earth was not the centre of the universe. Following up this further, Sigmund Freud reiterated that humans are also not the centre nor the purpose of the earth. Someone asked David Foster what was the purpose of this intelligent universe, if it was not stupid?

He replied, "To become more intelligent."

7

Self, Sleeper Cells and Shaktiman

'Sunita Williams heads off to space with Ganesh, Gita and Samosa,' screamed the media when she first went to space in 2006. It is reported that her father, Deepak Pandya, had gifted her the famous Bhagvad Gita, the song Divine as a spiritual companion. This holy book, for the first time in history, had described in detail, the existence of multiple universes or 'multiverse'. It is said that, after going through it, Sunita had more questions in her mind than the holy book could answer. So, well before she took off from the Baikonur cosmodrome in Kazakhstan, for the second time, she was given copies of the Upanishads, a collection of philosophical texts that explore the meaning of life. This being the origin of the Gita, she was advised to find out the answers by herself. Etymologically, Upanishad means sitting near a teacher to receive wisdom. It combines cosmology, theology and psychology and describes the Brahman or the 'universal spirit' and the Atman or 'individual self', as one and the same.

While cosmology enables one to look outward to the multiverse, psychology aims at looking into the world inside the mind. Theology looks around, up and in, to discover and feel the presence of the 'divine'. It believes 'self' as, both, primary and ultimate reality. It and subordinates the world and God to self, to be realized through awareness, introspection and meditation. Another related story says that to felicitate Yuri Gagarin, the then Soviet Communist Party General Secretary Nikita Khrushchev had called a big meeting. There he declared with pride: "Look, Gagarin flew into sky and space, but failed to find any god there." He was using Gagarin to validate the atheistic foundation of communism. Until around age 8, children see God as the 'man in the sky'. Even elders point their fingers towards the sky, while referring to the God almighty as the sky always looks larger than all of us, distant, unknown and all pervading.

My thoughts derailed as there was a sudden commotion inside the plane. A young boy, sitting in the same row as mine, was trying to break open the window, inspired by an onscreen video violence. Assisted by the mother, he was immediately overpowered by the cabin crew and was made to change his seat with a mild warning to the parents to be more watchful. We heaved a sigh of relief that reminded me of the movie 'Airforce One'. Windows are very vulnerable parts of a commercial aircraft, which are zealously guarded. If broken open, it leads to depressurization for a few seconds followed by a rush of air from the cockpit towards the damaged window, along with the debris. It is quite likely that the persons sitting next to the window, if not properly strapped in, would get sucked out. We had escaped a fatal accident, thanks to an alert crew. They proved to be our real gods in the sky, whom Yuri Gagarin missed in space! And of whom Nikita Khruschev was not aware of.

The other day, while opening the mail box, I had chanced upon an unsought mail posted by an unknown mothers' forum with a title 'Why Boys Need Mothers'. It showed a number of funny but meaningful pictures of small boys uprooting flower plants, competition jet- pissing to demonstrate whose penis can throw it faster to a longer range, taking off girls under wears to find out genital differences, sticking and holding big round fruits onto their chests to mimic mama's milky breasts, throwing pillows up to the ceiling fans, inserting fingers into power plucks, igniting fire with flint rocks, etc. Like boys, girls also need strong, protective, affectionate fathers as a daughter's first understanding and exposure to a man begins with the father.

I had a close and fiercely independent cousin called Manika, who was more than a sister in many ways. Always close to her father, she was blessed with extra sensory receptors in her nerve cells. For, she was always quick to feel the suffering and pain of others. And then, she would sacrifice all her comforts and go beyond her limitations to make others happy. And she would do all this, while looking after her chronically ailing husband. One needs a brain to feel one's own pain but an empathetic, intelligent heart is needed to feel the pain of others. Obviously, she had a habit of thinking more from the heart than from head. An act of goodness always made Manika feel happy and even in great difficulty, she would not forget to smile. And when a friend or relative would appear, her face would light up, eyes would sparkle in excitement and a wave of joy would overtake her cheeks. Her arched eye brows would dance with happiness and she would instantly forget all struggle and pain in her personal life. When the dominant social value is about attaining wealth, comfort, competition and survival, not to speak of glamour and fame, Manika was both an exception and aberration.

In Srilanka, there is a popular saying that a kind hearted woman gets pregnant repeatedly. Like that, people used to exploit Manika for her kindness and 'ready to help' attitude and inability to say no. Abraham Lincoln had this weakness too, which he realized very late. 'If I have one vice...,' he is reported to have confessed, '...it is my inability to say no'. Manika was the proverbial 'agony aunt', before whom people are comfortable to bare and share all their worries. Anybody, anywhere in distress and Manika would be there to help out, even if she had to beg or borrow. Helping others is the other name of humanity, without wearing the heart on the sleeve. Obviously, because of her helpful nature, she has a large, unmatchable circle of friends and wide social network.

There are innumerable examples of women being not only 'giving' but also 'forgiving' and merciful even after grievous hurt and humiliation. One of them was Sita, consort of lord Rama and the real heroine of the epic, Ramayana. The story goes like this: Once a tired Rama had fallen asleep on wife, Sita's lap. Kakasura, a devil with evil intention and disguised as a large crow, flew close and pecked at Sita's bosom. When the bird repeated the act, Sita tried to shoo it away by throwing a few twigs but after stopping for a while, the bird resumed pecking her bosom again and injured Sita. As she started bleeding with pain, Rama also became aware of the unforgivable offence committed by the crow. He just picked up a straw and after converting it into a deadly arrow, sent it after the immodest bird to kill it. Chased by the arrow and fully exhausted, the crow finally fell at Rama's feet, seeking mercy. Pacified and persuaded by a kind hearted Sita, Rama withdrew the arrow and let off the crow.

Manika was no Sita but no less forgiving. Cheated left and right, even by friends and relations, she has forgiven and forgotten, and never let down a friend. Our lives are interconnected and friends are a valuable commodity and social capital, which sustains social entrepreneurs and social relations. Now, management experts say that a major key to longer life and better performance in office is, how well one is socially integrated. In an organization, people who have good 'peer to peer' relationship and social support , have lower mortality risk than those who didn't chime well with their co-workers.

While I was attending a seminar on Social Work practices in Tagore's Sriniketan at Viawa Bharti University, our facilitator, Prof. Rao, narrated a story about a famous American poet, who had once come to England to meet his old writer friend in London city. Both the friends spent the whole night talking and recollecting sweet memories about their past association and relationships with the other friends and school mates. In the morning, the American poet had to travel back to his country by ship. When he reached the port, it was over crowded- not by the travellers but by their friends and relatives who had gathered there to see them off.

The poet suddenly felt lonely when he realized that there was no one there to see him off. He approached a porter boy and gave him one pound, requesting him to do a simple job and the job was that as soon as the poet boarded the ship, he would turn back towards the waiting crowd and from there the porter should look at the poet with a smile and wave his hands, bidding him a happy goodbye. The porter did exactly that and the poet's spirits lifted up and sustained him through the rigours of a month long lonely journey! Rich or poor, desire for attention, thirst for care and hunger for love are in the DNA of the humans.

But need for help, support, empathy is often not limited to humans only. There are umpteen instances of dolphins and whales protecting swimmers against sharks. In the seas and water bodies, all the fishes band together to protect their partners and friends by confusing the predators. Adult musk oxen stand together and build a horned wall to save their children from wolves. In reproductive preparation, a penguin consumes large amount of food to store body fat so that when her single egg comes out, she can take care of it with full attention without bothering to go out for food because she has to stand on her egg for three long months in order to keep it warm and save it from being frozen to death. When a chimpanzee becomes old and arthritic, younger chimps come forward to help her out. Baboons provide vocal consolation to their distressed infants through gentle grunting. Birds sing, chirp and give regular contact calls to reassure their eggs before they hatch. When the weather is hot or the end of incubation period is near Zebra finches sing to their eggs. But the most empathetic and cooperative are the elephants as they take care of their blind, orphans and the infirm. Ants stop during their long journeys to stroke one another and when a piece of food is too large for an ant to carry, others come together to help out. And when one of them is injured, all of them carry it back to the nest. Spiders die to save their young and butterflies train their young on how to eat honey drops from the trap line of flowers. Long before the arrival of humans on the scene, many animal species had already understood the value of collaboration, cooperation and advantages of working as a team and helping each other for survival. Mencius, a devout follower of the famous Chinese philosopher, Confucius, used to say that each one of us is born with a mind that can't withstand the suffering of others. This may be the eason why a child Siddharth's (Buddha) heart bled looking at an injured bird and a schoolboy Abraham Lincoln stopped other children from squashing the insects in the campus corner. Indian sage Valmiki's inspiration to write the great epic Ramayan came after he observed the painful separation of two birds in love, when one of them was killed by a forest dweller.

I had a lurking fear that like Florence Nightingale, Manika too would not find time to marry but she did and was blessed with two wonderful children. Soft hearted Manika was a strong mother too, giving continuous support to her children almost like female bonobos that made them more peaceful, friendly and disciplined adults. Evolutionary anthropologists believe that, unlike chimpanzees, male bonobo's behavior is influenced as much by elevated thyroid hormone as by their mother's support. As a matter of fact, all successful American

Presidents had strong mothers.

George Washington used to say: 'All I am, I owe to my mother, Nancy.' Gandhi's personality and philosophy of life were greatly influenced by his mother, Putlibai, who apart from teaching him the importance of self discipline and self purification, made him promise, in the presence of a Jain monk before he left for higher studies in London, to abstain from three things, namely - meat, alcohol and sex. In Indian mythology, the mothers are always strong characters. The most famous was Yashoda, who had raised a difficult child, Krishna, with a strong hand with no indulgence towards his pranks on milkmaids, stealing butter and other adventures. Consequently, Krishna emerged as the most successful hero of Mahabharat and his words became the Gita, the song divine.

Both the children also inherited from Manika, the altruistic gene in abundance. One of them, Shaktiman, was a precocious child and grown up before his time. This self motivated young man had wide range of interests in life. Among peers, he was the ultimate and authentic encyclopedia and among elders, he was the proverbial Man Friday, who never failed to deliver. Like his mother, Manika, he was also very special and it would be difficult to straight jacket him into any defined psychographic segmentation, like 'actualiser', 'achiever' 'maker' or 'fulfiller'. He represented a bit of each. Like love at first sight, he would instantly infect you with his innate simplicity, naturalness and lack of artificiality. With a wonderful capacity to appreciate the smallest good things in others, he is least interested in honours, status, rewards, popularity and prestige; his only focus is on self- development and inner growth.

Never afraid of sticking his neck out to tell the truth that the 'emperor is naked', in a crowd of his age group, he would always stand out for his brilliance. His friends describe him as 'cool' but not the 'Papa don't preach' type and miles away from the raw, rebellious, drug loving, girl chasing, rock 'n' roll brand. To me, he is the new age 'super cool', who are real, authentic, calm, friendly and warm and always comfortable in their skin and who do what they like to do out of conviction without regrets or hesitation. He is ever willing to be part of solution than problem, as against the prevalent habits of finding a problem for every solution. For instance, if he overhears or even suspects that you are in difficulty, he would quietly overwork to bail you out, before you are even aware of it. In order to save a friend, he would not mind putting his own neck on the line and take all risks. Such souls can be compared to the unique leadership element in 'water' for water never moves forward without filling in the cracks, crannies and craters. But then, water also has a desire, an aspiration to move further in its long journey even if it means continuous perseverance to overcome obstinate resistance from rocks and mountains.

So the hardworking and intelligent, Shaktiman, being human, once in a while felt robbed when his genuine and merited aspirations were thwarted repeatedly, particularly, his strong intent to enter the civil service. Undeserved failures occasionally sent him to bouts of depression which he wouldn't show or share. Yet, like a sore thumb, it remained in his heart, refusing to heal. The saying that you are lucky only when you work harder, somehow was not working in his case. The path to reach life's goal is not always straight as I had experienced it myself in my zig zag career graph.

Being too much attached to this young man, I was a bit concerned. Once I had tried to explain to him that a failure was not the final defeat and how world renowned mathematical wizard, S.Ramanujan, 'The Man Who Knew Infinity' (Robert Kanigel), had failed four times in his Intermediate exams (1907) and the Madras University had found him unworthy for a certificate. Still he didn't lose heart and within years, Cambridge and Royal Society elected him as Fellow, a rare honour. Famous bestselling author, J.K.Rowling's Harry Potter manuscript was rejected more than dozen times by literary agents and publishers and an assistant had tossed it into a rejection pile, thinking it wouldn't make money. Bollywood's legendary actor, Amitabh Bachchan too, well known for his deep baritone, was rejected by All India Radio as a radio jockey and narrator. This eventually turned out to be a blessing for him and Bollywood. Then I told Shaktiman about the ageless perseverence of river Colorado at Grand Canyon which I had visited some years ago. What struck me was how it took nearly two billion years of the Earth's geological history to make way for the river. Colorado and its tributaries continued cutting their channels through layer after layer of hard rock to finally establish only a curved course but in the process, the beautiful configuration and unintended architecture they left behind, captured the imagination of the whole world. Together, they also imprisoned both the pain and pleasure of almost a timeless struggle that enabled them to reach the final goal. In his Study of History (1939), Arnold Toynbe has described how Nature had always rewarded those who take on the challenge and struggle to move forward despite harsh environmental conditions and where there was no challenge, evolution has always slowed down

India born M.S Swaminathan and Verghese Kurien (1921-2012) became legends in their life time, one as father of Green Revolution and another as father of White Revolution. None had planned for nor dreamt about it. One's parents wanted him to be a police man and the other was to fulfill his parents' desire to be a mechanical engineer. Just like my father, who was training me to become a traditional priest but that never fascinated me. Bill Clinton, in his younger days, had wanted to be a full time saxophone player in a funky jazz band. He, instead, landed up in the White House, as President of United States of America! Hitler's father Alois wanted his son to follow his footsteps and join the civil service as a customs officer but he wanted to be a painter and fought with his father to allow him to join a classical art school. Neither the father's expectations nor the son's wish was fulfilled and the world suffered the consequence.

Beethoven's teacher thought he was a hopeless composer. Henry Ford refused to accept defeat despite repeated failures and ultimately reached his goal of becoming world's most successful car maker. Darwin's father considered his son as low in intellect while Einstein's teacher had described his student 'mentally slow' cherishing 'foolish dreams'. Both the parent and teacher were proved to be terribly wrong. Ramakant Achrekar, coach of cricket legend, Sachin Tendulkar, had rejected Sachin's admission into the cricket academy for failing the test. Eventually, Sachin emerged as one of the greatest cricketers of the world.

A.P.J Abdul Kalam wanted to be a pilot but failed. He couldn't qualify as his rank in the merit list for pilots was one behind the last successful candidate but for him it was not the end of his world or dreams. Instead, he rose to become the father of missile technology in the country and then the most popular President of India, the world's largest democracy.

One doesn't know what is waiting out there and hence should not lose faith in oneself. Catching and plucking low hanging fruits is always an easier option than cracking hard nuts and Shaktiman had chosen the latter as a natural instinct like the load bearing and brave Sherpas, who habitually set their sights on no less than Himalayan heights and accept the associated rigour in their stride.

On 29th May, 1953, it was Tenzing, the hard nut Sherpa, who was the first to reach the top of Mount Everest (29.028 ft), the highest summit on earth. And from there he dragged half unconscious Hillary; hand over hand, by rope to the top, risking his own safety. But then, it was Edmund Hillary who was knighted for the glory by Queen Elizabeth II and the last razor sharp step to the top was named as the 'Hillary Step'. Tenzing lost out as people were not certain about his nationality. Afterwards, the apology for an award came in form of petty gifts that consisted of an electric stove, a wrist watch, a radio, a small piece of land, supplemented by the then Prime Minister, Nehru's old clothes! He didn't mind nor was he overjoyed with glory, because for a Sherpa, mountaineering was so normal, like fish in water.

But then, due reward came, although a little late. Six years later, he was awarded the Padma Bhusan, the third highest civilian award in India and the Time magazine named him as one of the hundred most influential people of the 20th century. It is not known to many that Tenzing had dropped out of the monastery thrice and that his father actually wanted him to be a monk, not a mountaineer. I had an opportunity of meeting Edmund Hillary in March 1987 in the Asia Centre at Chandigarh when he was High Commissioner of New Zealand in India and had come there to address us as a Guest of Honour. During tea time, I gently asked him whether the story I had heard about Tenzing's last minute help to him was true. Ever jovial, Hillary gave a hearty laugh saying, ' It is an awkward question you are putting very late. Tenzing was a great guide'. He didn't elaborate and I didn't persue.

One day, seeing Monika upset after the civil services results of her son were out, I shared with her an interesting conversation I had with a senior colleague, Prof. Mohapatra, a college teacher, long ago. Otherwise a jovial person, Mohapatra was as upset as Monica, but for a different reason. When I asked him, what he said was beyond my imagination, particularly coming from a teacher. He elaborated, 'Look, I have two sons, but I am really worried about the second one because he is doing so well in studies which means that he would end up either as a poor academic like me or as a 'Babu' (bureaucrat), living far away from us, sitting in a cubicle with a limited salary and spending the rest of his life trying to please his boss and political masters for a few crumbs of power and privileges. Poor fellow! And if he tries to make money and be rich, he would land up in jail. But look at my first son. He failed repeatedly in exams, was apprehended twice for rash driving and road accidents and dropped out of school but he is now an independent and successful entrepreneur, earning twenty times my salary and creating jobs for many! He also looks after us.' Monika was also a teacher but didn't like Mohapatra's purely utilitarian view of education. Her secret desire was to see her son rise in life and career. I told her that life, though full of unpredictability and surprises, never disappoints the deserving in the long run. 'Patience' is not always ungrateful to its practitioner. And, there is always a place larger than our self constructed 'dream world' and in the long fight between perseverance and resistance, the former has repeatedly proved to be the ultimate winner. As river Colorado has shown to the world. But then, even after winning all that one wanted, life might still look unfulfilled, no matter what you have or achieve.

A very precious part of my life was spent in promoting volunteerism among the young students belonging to 'National Study Service' (NSS) in universities. This three and half million strong organization eventually became world's largest study-service outfit. The popular motto of the organization was 'Not Me, But You" which meant 'you', the other person, is more important than 'I' and 'me'. We were taking students from campus to the community and from the college to the village to understand and appreciate the value of giving and helping others. It was the time when Ayn Rand's 'The Virtue of Selfishness: the New Concept of Egoism' (1964) was being debated in many parts of the world.

Rand was promoting the morality of 'rational self interest', denouncing the destructive character of altruism but the intellectual world was sharply divided on the issue. One view was that each one of us would pass through this world only once, so any good thing to be done, any kindness to be shown, any help to be given must be done now as one may not pass through this world again. The other view was that since one has only one life, one must enjoy it fully, partially reflecting the old maxim 'Do what you love and love what you do.' Rand's fans and followers were so full of the 'I' and 'Me' that they had no space for 'You' and 'We'- critical factors to sustain a relationship. It is said that when some of her supporters married, they even didn't like to share the bed and literally became 'strange bed fellows' because each one was possessed with the idea of a personal 'orgasm', without thinking of the other partner's happiness, failing to realise that all love was 'expansion' of the self where as selfishness was 'contraction' only. Jean Jacques Russeau, the legendary political philosopher of "Man is born free" fame had a long affair with a shopkeeper's wife, sired five children during the relationship but consigned all five of them to an orphanage to enjoy his 'personal freedom'. When asked, he replied by saying that they would grow up as better workers in an orphanage. In any society, increase of self centric persons leads to decreased understanding of what others like or dislike. Therefore, three millennia before Ayn Rand, the Upanishads had asked individuals to move from 'self' to 'self inquiry', from 'I' to 'Who am I'.

I thought back to 1971, during my short stay in Sriniketan, a social laboratory near Shantiniketan, where the great poet –philosopher, Rabindranath Tagore, was doing his educational experiments. There I had seen a quote written in bold letters on the wall inside the training hall, with three inspiring short sentences from Tagore that cleared many of my self - doubts and dilemmas after reading Ayn Rand. These were:

'I slept and dreamt that life was joy.

I awoke and saw that life was service. I acted and found, service was joy.'

So, one day, while watching TV, I was delighted by the answer that Barack Obama gave to an Indian audience during his second visit to the country in Jan' 2015. Asked 'What makes him smile after a bad day', he aptly said, 'To hear that I made a difference in someone's life...' I stood up and clapped.

After joining as a college teacher, I had started taking students from the campus to the nearby community, mostly villages, during holidays and vacations, to work with people, understand their problems and learn from them. We used to walk the entire distance, with halts after every two kms, squatting under the shade of a tree, discussing local and. global issues related to poverty and development, war and peace, mercy killing and death sentence and so on. In order to motivate them, a few slogans were coined. Like 'Connect the college to the village, university to society, knowledge to action, book to broom or kitab to kudal and text to context' etc and offer a helping hand to the people, as and when needed. We did many experiments to awaken the sleeping empathy among them. One such experiment that really changed the attitude and behaviour of many was called 'Living with the Poor'. Those were the days when political leaders and planners were busy giving long lectures, endlessly, about poverty in India. I called a group of students and asked them, 'Look, there are tons of talks and loads of books on poverty, but how many of you had actual experience of 'living in poverty?'

There was none. Then, I proposed whether they would be ready to experience it, first hand. Most of them seemed to be excited. We selected seven and explained to them that each one of them has to live for seven days in seven poorest families. They would do exactly what their host-parents do every day for a living. Then, we selected seven poorest families in a cluster of seven small villages and hamlets and discussed the proposal with the identified family heads. They were also equally excited, although reluctant to engage the college boys in the daily wage work that was mostly manual.

While selecting the families, we applied five conditions. One was, the house should not be in a dilapidated and collapsible condition. Second, there should not be a grown up girl in the house, an extra caution just to eliminate possibility of a scandal. Third, the boy should not be an economic burden on the family and hence must carry basic ration for the period of stay. Fourth, no one in the family should be suffering from any seriously contagious disease. Fifth, whatever he earns by working, he would give to his host parents as economic support and if there are senior citizens among them, he would process their application for old age pension and other welfare schemes.

Each student was given a pocket diary with one dozen questions, the answer to which he has to find out during the stay. Some of these included: What were the frequently used words and idioms used by the poorest persons during conversations? What were their dreams and aspirations? What was the quality of their food, garments and, of course, literacy levels? Are their children going to school? Do they have any cultivable land? Any premature death, suicide in the family? How many times had they seen the local development officer and the doctor visiting their village? Had they taken any loan and how much interest they pay on that? How much do they earn every day and how much out of this they spend on non-food items, did they have money to cremate or bury their dead family members,etc.?

Out of the seven host families, two were stone cutters, three were agricultural labourers, one was a firewood collector and one was an unskilled construction worker. During the one week experiment, one student left mid way, not being able to withstand the rigour. The experiment became a subject of heated debate in the entire village cluster and was thought to be a kind of "disruptive innovation". Smartly dressed, educated college boys from rich families, living in ultra poverty, carrying head loads of firewood, cutting stones, digging and carrying earth for the village roads, cutting rows of paddy with crescent shaped sickles, were the kind of scenes that had never happened before. Local media reported the event with excitement. Some schools of Social work used it as a case study and learning material.

Emotionally, the most shattering event was the eighth day when each boy bid farewell to the host parents after handing over his earning. The departure was unusually surcharged with a lot of fluid emotions from both sides. In one particular case, the couple were pretty old and had lost all their three children- to malaria and one to snake bite. They almost virtually prevented the boy from leaving them. In seven days, this boy had won their heart and become a part of the childless family.

The same evening, we invited all the host parents and all other student volunteers for a community dinner, preceded by sharing of experiences by the seven boys including the one who defected. It turned out to be a second farewell and was equally emotional. I left the place with a heavy heart and feeling a lump in my throat. Next month, I quit the University for another assignment in the national capital. But the experiment did not end there. A few years after, I was surprised to find out that six out of the seven students who had gone through this process had, on their own, decided to become social entrepreneurs and community change makers. Three of them shifted to a remote tribal area, set up voluntary organizations and are still living and working there with the poor.

Looking at poverty from a safe, comfortable distance, tall talking and romanticizing about it, is a much easier option than the experience, rigour and reality of living through it. One's social self and sense of empathy gets stronger by such tough and challenging experiences. However, objectivists, like Narcissists, love to love themselves - a kind of masturbation. They think that they owe the world nothing except their own glorious presence. But their opponents cite umpteen examples from animal and plant worlds, showing how they help each other by sacrificing personal time and energy.

For instance, Dolphins nurture one another constantly and share their concerns with their community. Considered masters of relationships and communication, they are always supportive of each other. Once a while, it is reassuring to see a monkey cleaning a hippo's huge mouth and dangerous teeth without fear. A female mosquito undertakes a life risking mission of blood sucking to ensure that all its 150 eggs are well nourished and gives her life after delivering them! Interestingly it also injects the person with a special painkiller fluid before drawing blood. The most recent (2017) real life incident was about how a hairy dog named Kesley saved her master "Bob", a stranded Michigan man, from freezing to death. She kept Bob awake by lying on top of him, by licking his hands and face while continuously howling throughout the cold nights for help from the neighbours that came at last. Plants process information from the environment and transmit to other plants to help them grow, reproduce and prosper together. Every tiny cell in the human body, about one hundred trillion in number, love and help one another.

My village was located in the foothills and was surrounded by a thin forest. The incident happened years ago, while the rainy season was withdrawing. A tigress stealthily entered the village and killed a healthy calf and was trying to drag it into the forest to share the catch and feed her two babies hungry for days. Unable to carry the calf, she gave herself a good meal and ran away having been noticed by some of our villagers, who raised an alarm. After an hour or so, she returned to the same spot with her two hungry children. While trying to help them to feed on the prey, she was now surrounded by angry villagers and killed. The frightened and orphaned cubs fled back to the woods, leaving behind the bleeding, dead mother. Decades after, I still wonder who was selfish, the calf owner, the killers, the hungry cubs or the caring mother tigress? And for what, for whom and why?

To Ayn Rand, 'I' was a dear word, but not 'You' and 'we,' which were the words of serfdom, of plunder, of misery and falsehood. In one of the Upanishads, there is a dialogue between a sage and his female student, about the psychological roots of selfishness.

The 'Shishya' or student, Maitreyi, asks of her Guru as to why parents always liked their children.

'For their own happiness, as they are created out of them,' the Guru replies and explains why they also look alike.

To the question 'Who is free?' The guru says that when one goes beyond self, when streams merge into river and the rivers into the sea.

About three millennia before the great American dream of 'Life, Liberty and Pursuit of happiness', the Upanishads in ancient India, rising above the individual self, had spelt out a more inclusive and super socialistic dream of- 'Sarve bhabantu sukhinah...', i.e., 'a happy, healthy, life of peace and goodwill 'for one and all', free from pain and suffering'. Subsequently, Buddhism emphasized 'Anatman' as opposed to 'Aatman' and defined that there is no 'self' independent of others' self. Even the subtle mind can't be considered as 'my mind', independent of universal mind and consciousness.

Writer Arthur Young (1741-1820), explained it in a much simpler way when he said, 'God sleeps in the minerals, awakens in plants, walks in animals and thinks in humans.' I am tempted to add god also 'flies in birds, flows in water, and smiles in flowers.' However, psychology can only help in understanding the mind. It can't decide social values and norms. If Oedipus complex had been allowed its full play, the world would have become full of incestuous monsters. Baser instincts, evolved through millions of years of insecurity and fights and fears of and for survival, would have overtaken all finer intentions. Thus, selfishness and selflessness have many shades.

It is said that once Alexander was returning home through the

Arabian Desert with his battered, bruised and tired army. Then the water stock carried on the camels' back ran out and, soon after, the soldiers started feeling thirsty, including Alexander. His worried body guards went around and collected a small pot of water and offered it to their leader. Alexander lifted the earthen pot, looked at it for a moment and threw it away to the shock and surprise of every one. He said, 'As long as my soldiers are thirsty, I cannot accept even a drop of water.' This gesture of the leader electrified the army and boosted their moral instantly. They rallied together, marshaled their residual energy and started digging the ground deep and found water for everyone. Leadership is not front loading oneself for selfish gains. An oft quoted statement on leadership says: 'Don't follow me, I can't lead you, don't lead me, I can't follow you. Let us walk hand in hand to reach the goal faster and together.' Leadership is basically an attitude, an epitome of social desirability, a prerequisite to influence individuals, groups, communities and organizations.

Looking at the attitude and habits of persons like Manika and Shaktiman, one is reminded of the famous behavior psychologist Abraham Maslow and his popular theory of the 'Hierarchy of Human Needs'. Long after he propagated this theory with five sets of human needs in shape of a pyramid, critics questioned his wisdom because they thought his need pyramid was incomplete. It begins with physiological need like food and water at the base, followed by safety and security needs after which comes the need for love, belonging, self esteem, recognition and appreciation and finally self actualization.

Critics said that a strong desire for self actualization can't be the ultimate need, as it might sometimes degenerate into selfishness. And hence, the need pyramid should be revisited as sometimes even needs do not follow a hierarchy. It is said that Maslow thought over the issue and added three more 'needs' after a lot of research, reality check and reflection. Two of these were placed before self actualization, namely 'cognitive need', i.e., the need to know, understand, explore. The second one was the 'aesthetic need' or the need for symmetry, order and beauty that everyone loves, feels good and happy about.

The third one, which Maslow added later on, after a long debate, was 'Transcendence'. It is the need to go beyond one's self to help others for their own self actualization and fulfill their own potential like a mentor and guide. What is the secret desire of a true teacher and mentor? -'Shisyat ichhet parajayam,' replies the scriptures. It means - a true teacher is one who secretly desires to be excelled by his students. Helping others adds to happiness of both and makes one feel like 'walking on holy ground'. Manika was doing it as a part of her second nature. In her house, one always finds boys and girls from poor families whom she helps stand on their own feet and fulfill their full potential.

A popular and oft quoted side story from the ancient Indian epic Ramayana, which my mother once narrated to me, was about a small brown squirrel with three white stripes on its hairy back. While Lord Rama was busy building a bridge to Sri Lanka on the deep sea with the help of an army of monkeys and bears in order to reach and rescue his wife, Sita, who had been abducted by demon king, Ravana, this little squirrel was watching the process from its burrow and wanting to be a part of this great effort and help Rama, it went up and down carrying tiny twigs and pebbles in its mouth to add value to the construction work.

The monkeys and bears that were carrying bigger stones and larger logs of wood started mocking, teasing and chasing the tiny squirrel, until a watchful and impressed Rama intervened. Appreciating its tireless and selfless efforts in helping a stranger like him, he gently caressed the squirrel's back with his three fingers that became permanent white stripes, enhancing the creature's beauty and appeal further. Recognition and appreciation is a human need that the little squirrel was not waiting for nor was it daunted by its small size and limitations. When a melting heart maiden named Sujata, spotted an emaciated and enervated Gautama, meditating under a Peepal tree at Uruvela, near Gaya, she immediately rushed back home, prepared and offered the ascetic a bowl of milk rice. Gratefully accepting the nourishment, a reinvigorated Gautama went into deeper meditation and became Buddha, the Enlightened One and Buddhism was born. Such little gestures sustain the world and, probably, are its last hope. As I grew up, the message became clearer.

Not everyone could be like the squirrel. Famous Indian cricketer, Sachin Tendulkar, had been drowned with medals, awards and honours including the Bharat Ratna, the highest and rarest civilian honour of the country. Yet, in his heart of hearts, he was still craving for an appreciation from his coach, Achreker. The last time I watched him on TV in Nov. 2013, taking final farewell from Cricket, he openly mentioned how intensely he yearned for Achrekar's appreciation.

"Sir has never told me 'well played'. Sir, you can say it now." The appreciation did come from Achrekar the following day but at the end of Sachin's 24 years long illustrious career.

Now, scientists say that there are 'sleeping selfless stem cells' in people and human altruistic behavior is natural and is visible when these cells become active. Stem cell experts say that there is also altruism in bacteria which is why they are great survivors as they help each other. Probably, it is these cells which prodded Warren Buffet, the second wealthiest American, to donate 99 percent of his fortune amounting to 47 billion dollars to charity, to be spent for health care of the poor in developing countries. When asked about the share of his children, he said he didn't believe in dynastic wealth. He was ridiculing the dynastic, acquisitive and wealthy as 'members of the lucky sperm club'. Both Gandhi and Lincoln were clear givers, combining greatness with goodness plagued by pathological giving, but ultimately dominating the top of popularity and success ladder. This instinct made Lincoln to invite his arch rivals to join his cabinet while Gandhi declined to accept the highest position of power, giving credit to others.

Among the feminine Trinity in Hindu scriptures, there is a deity representing prosperity and good fortune called Laxmi. Like her, another male deity in the Hindu pantheon for wealth is Kuber, who like an over- intelligent dog burying bones in the sand for future, was hiding wealth and possessions. So, while wealth amassing Kuber is described as pot bellied and ugly, prosperity bestowing Laxmi is presented as beautiful. She is worshipped in million homes and temples as a generous 'Giving Goddess', whose blessing spreads and cascades. The more you give, the more you get back. Like when you give love, you get more love. Significantly, there is not a single temple dedicated to the god of wealth Kuber. The metaphor and message is loud and clear. Anyone who gives is beautiful and the one who only takes and acquires is ugly. The greedy think, giving is anti-economics, for, by giving something one will be left with less of it. Referring to the human greed, Sir Isaac Newton had once commented: 'I can unravel the complex laws of motion and calculate the movement of stars, but not the madness of men on earth.'

It is said that even human embryonic stem cells under duress produce molecules that not only benefit themselves but help in the survival of nearby cells. Similarly, one's brain size also determines how good one is at helping and keeping friends and social capital creation. The orbital prefrontal cortex above one's eyes is believed to be the link between number of friends and size of the brain because in order to retain a large circle of friends and relations, one has to mentalize and develop mind reading skills.

When Lucy's mother became old and unable to walk and collect food, her children must have been there with her to help out. Today, many of them have left their parents and habitat in search of greener pastures. Yet some of them are still around carrying the old magnets in their hearts. This magnet of selflessness pulls people who need their help and this magnet again makes them think of and live for others. And enjoy giving without asking. Shaktiman is one of them. With a larger magnetic field, which he has not yet allowed to turn wooden.

8

From Innocence to Nonsense

The third time Binny and I visited New Ark in California, our eight year old grand daughter, Deegha , a highly talented girl with a creative mind, had innocently started imitating a famous fashion model. While wearing a red Indian lehenga, she would see to it that the upper part of her left shoulder and chest remained half exposed. Then she would strip off the salwar a little down the navel displaying a part of her under belly. And brush and gather the hair into a pony, adding some waves and curls to it, trying to follow the back and front hairdo styles of a particular Bollywood film actor. Slowly, she also developed a desire to look thin with elevated levels of body dissatisfaction.

Media, ads, movies, peers and the new society, continuously send out messages suggesting it was extremely important for 'modern, new age girls' to burn the bra, wear revealing clothes, display body parts and look sexy, that they would be judged more by their looks than by achievements. The innocent victims begin to believe they are what and how they wear and bare. Adding to this, music videos and pop shows dish out toxic mixtures of sexualized, lewd lyrics and violence, which youngsters first repeat without understanding and then become all too aware of its meaning and message and innocent children like Deegha get easily influenced.

Girls much older to her are first made to develop 'body shame' and feel inadequate, which undermines their social and emotional well being. Consequently, many of them indulge in self surveillance of the body and spend a lot of time looking for right type of lipsticks, berets, conditioners and other cosmetics. They start watching sentimental serials, reading movie and life style magazines, looking for trendy dresses, and dancing to the tune of Bollywood item numbers. The innocent nursery morality and school girl conscience goes for a six. Sex shouts loudly from cyber café, cinema halls, bill boards, music and porn with explicit erotic materials. Sexualised images of women are on display almost everywhere, mainly targeting the men.

Men showing off their muscles and women showing their skin to attract each other is so common these days. Cyber stalking, following ex- boy friends on the web, hitch hiking to 'hot' chicks and 'flirty friends' no longer shocks any one. There are more than a thousand sites on 'same- sex' relationships alone. Other sites feed adolescents with scenes of rape, molestation, incest and nudity, that depersonalizes finer elements of sexual relations, reducing it to a mechanical function devoid of sensitivity. The more of tops and bottoms one exposes, the more fame it bestows. Peers encourage boys for sexual exploration to attain a new identity and freedom. Not surprisingly, forced intercourse and unwanted sex are on the rise, often shattering the inner self of girls in their teens.

I vividly remember, until I was nine, living in nude was so normal. Our peer group consisted of five, namely, Raza, Rani, Panchi and Dena-two boys and three girls 'next-door', including myself. We had free access to each other's family. Often we were eating together in each other's houses.All this has disappeared now in the age of refrigeration. By the time the food was ready, my friends, particularly, the girls would be already there, crowding around the country oven without waiting to be invited. Then mother would over feed us with great affection. In fact, our parents were so much like each other and so loving that for a long time, for an outsider, it was difficult to distinguish who were whose biological parents. There was actually no difference or discrimination in their behaviour towards any one of us. The families looked so similar. Happy families everywhere are all alike and it was as if the whole village was rearing and raising us, in a way. In case of girls, the feeling of belonging was much stronger as they were considered the daughters of the whole village, in fact, the whole region. It is said that when the people of Mithila came to know about their daughter Sita's suffering, repeated humiliation and tragic end, they had decided collectively never ever to give in marriage any daughter of their area to any boy from the Avadh region, where Ram was born. Salma Noor, an academic hailing from this region told me recently that even today, thousands of years after the Ramayana days, such hurt feelings persist.

In the village, one of our favorite pastimes was to play the 'spouse game', called 'Bohu bohuka', mostly imitating what parents do to each other. This probably was an early initiation to family living. We were all nude and quite familiar with each other's body. Our pubic and pelvic zones used to be in full public view. Parents and grand parents often used to call it 'candy' touch it and give flying kiss to show their affection. There was absolutely no curiosity, no embarrassment, no sense of shame or offence.

But then, times changed, during our time itself. Once my sister-in- law had come from USA with her two daughters - one was about ten and the other eight year old. On our way to Konark, the sun temple, known as black pagoda, we visited a relative in a nearby village. As soon as we entered the house, both the girls started shouting in excitement pointing fingers at the two boys standing completely nude with their dangling genitals. 'What is this, mama?' They asked still giggling. Initially, the mother didn't know how to respond, but soon, gathering her wits, she said - 'This is real India, the India you wanted to see.' The girls had a hearty laugh, the little boys also joined in the fun, innocently.

Sensing the mother's discomfort, I told her in jest, 'Get ready, the really real India is waiting to welcome you. You would see more such scenes carved out and captured in stone on the temple walls of Konark you are going to visit now depicting the whole lot of LGBT (lesbians, gay, bisexual, transgender) at one place in all their erotic abandon. They would depict in graphic details how liberal and modern was the 12th century India in matters of sexuality, the primal force in all living beings, from bacteria to the great gods. You will also see how, day after day, the heritage of yesterday mocks at the hypocrisy of today, the prudent past titillating the prudish present.' I saw in her face a melting pot of emotions - excitement, curiosity and fear.

When Michaelangelo's masterpiece 'David's Carrot and Two

Vegetables' was flown down from a Florence museum for display in an exhibition in another country, it created a storm as the customs declared it as 'porn' material. Many devout Hindus offer prayer to female and male genitals of a particular God and Goddess in temples as spiritual symbols of creative power and energy and no one feels awkward or embarrassed.

Feelings of embarrassment are more or less a cultural orientation. There are different points of view. Recently, an Ohio girl, dating a well attired Indian Muslim boy on student visa in USA, was narrating appreciatively in her blog as to how her boy friend was expecting her to properly cover up vital parts of her body and how during the dating and subsequent marriage, her 'skirts became longer and neck lines higher.' She also wrote about how she was made to view the relationship as sacred and her body as a temple only to be shared with the person she loved and vice versa. Responding to the blog, a friend said lightly, 'If people don't cover, what is there to discover?'

I had an interesting experience in the early 80s while undergoing training in a cross cultural setting. One of my co-trainees was a young man from the Carribean region named Roberts. Eventually, we became very friendly. Whenever we met, I used to either hug him or put my hand around his shoulders affectionately as he was about ten years younger to me. Then the three month long training came to an end and it was time for departure. There were participants from 18 countries and after the formal farewell meeting, Roberts came up to me and asked: 'If you don't mind, shall I ask you a personal question?' I said, 'Come on, we are friends and you are free to ask any question.' Then with a sense of seriousness, he asked, 'Are you gay?' For a while, I felt a little embarrassed as I was not expecting a too personal question like this. However, quickly gathering my wits, I said – 'No, I am not; I'm married with two children. But then, what made you think so about me?' I asked. He explained that in his culture when two males hug each other too much, too close and too frequently and walk hand in hand, they are perceived to be gay. In India holding hands is not a sign of sexual orientation.

Sensing my embarrassment, Roberts said, 'No, nothing unnatural, I am also gay and there are innumerable greats who were gay and lesbians including Britain's Queen, Anne, and she had a long term relationship with her lady in waiting, Sarah Churchill.'Seeing my new interest, he reeled out names of many celebrities for my benefit.. 'What is there? Sometimes, I like noodle, some other times I like rice and sometimes both,' he said casually. 'Have you read scholar Aristophane's narration in Plato's Symposium? He asked. I expressed my ignorance. 'Then listen. He says that in the beginning men and women were one - round shaped with four arms, legs, two faces and two privates. They were too strong and threatened the power of God, so God split the humans down the middle, leaving each half with a desperate desire to be united with the other. The women, who had a slice of the original female, developed sexual weakness for women and are the ones who we call lesbians today, and the man, who had a slice of original male, was drawn towards male and is now called homosexual.' It was an old story he was quoting to justify his preference.

Roberts would have called me a 'bisexual' if he had seen my bedroom two years after marriage. By that time Binny had joined me at my work place in Puri and soon after, her younger brother Balu also came to stay with us for higher study. He was a brilliant boy with a good sense of humor, but was always afraid of darkness and reluctant to sleep alone in his room. At night, he would get up from bed every now and then, become tense with rising palpitations, particularly after lights were off and was persistently worried and suspicious of the presence of an imaginary ghost inside or a peeping thief outside the window.

One midnight, he shouted loudly and woke us up telling that a thief was trying to break open his bedroom door. We found out it was actually the flapping sounds of two pigeons making love in the sky light, but we asked him to shift to our room. There was no space for a second bed and three of us slept together on the same bed – Binny on my right and Balu on my left. After it had continued for more than a year, I started teasing Binny, telling her, 'Look, now I have two wives - a female and a male, one I married to and the other one I got free. 'Buy one and get one free' used to be the popular ad in those days on garments on 'Sale.' Displaying a rare mix of wit, humor and mischief, she retorted, 'No, not free, he is my protector from predators like you.' Three of us had a hearty laugh over that. However, Roberts' first suspicion and feedback about my sexual orientation, I never forgot afterwards in cross- cultural working situations. Now, I became more conscious about my innocent 'back slapping' informality, for, Lucy's children behave in strange, divergent ways, based on where they stay. Unlike Roberts, Arab men love to walk hand in hand and hate to see someone sitting with both the exposed feet on the ground. Egyptians come physically closer to talk to each other. North Americans like the opposite. Kenyans show respect by grasping the right wrist with left hand. Many Indians touch the feet of the elders for the same reason. African women show affection by hugging and kissing each other on each cheek. In some other cultures people love to be hugged and consider distance distasteful and so on.

Raka Rashid, a highly cultured Muslim Bangladeshi woman colleague of mine in the Commonwealth Asia Centre, would almost run for cover or hide from my westernized Singaporean friend, Seri, everytime they happen to meet. Seri used to give a tight hug to everyone he met. Culturally, women in many civilized communities don't like to be publicly and physically touched. Public display of affection like cuddling and kissing is offending to many in some cultures. Now, it is scarier, for, one deep kiss is reported to transfer ten million bacteria. My wife, Binny, had complained to me bitterly, when a Minister embraced and parked a peck on her cheek in a Colombo conference. Then a lady delegate did the same to me, infuriating her further. How can these women touch you like that, she asked me repeatedly. During a short stay in Bangkok, I happened to meet a Thai gentleman called Pramoj in a Bangkok Indian restaurant and was a bit amused to learn from him as to how Luang Phibun, one of their great rulers had endorsed a legislation exclusively aimed at reforming Thai manners. One of these rules wanted all husbands to openly kiss their wives before leaving the house and again on returning from work. Many Indian and Japanese women do not like to discuss sexuality nor take the lead in physical intimacy in bedroom.

Kissing and hugging in public is a strict no-no in many traditional Asian societies. Depending on social values, women are perceived to be either sexy or sexless and men as henpecked or unromantic, cold and insensitive, shy of making the first move. Culture has covered as many women in the world as there are coverless, representing different attitude and outlook. In 2002, we were in Honiara, the capital city of Solomon Islands, in connection with a Commonwealth Ministers Conference. It was an unusually memorable event because on the first day of the event we were given a grand welcome in the presence of the Prime Minister and on the final day there was a coup that deposed him. I had taken the return flight just two hours before that happened but at the grand opening ceremony, 54 countries were present and on both my sides, the representatives happened to be ladies.

We were being treated with the choicest cultural shows when finally 500 grown up girls in two rows entered the podium, dancing and singing, and all of them were topless! It looked as if the daring breasts were competing with their bare legs in full vigour and for a moment, we didn't know how to react. Two South Asian ladies, one from a Muslim country, standing beside me, lowered their heads and looked other way in embarrassment, pretending as if they have not seen anything. Earlier, when I was in Maldives, another island country with similar climate, foreigners were put up in isolated island hotels as they didn't follow 'beach decency.'

During my first visit to Indonesia, another country with a humid climate, a troupe of beautiful Javanese women, well known for their courteous smiles, had also greeted us with a colorful dance in front of Campong houses that looked like temples but they were wearing clean Batic sarongs with brightly colored blouses and heads covered. The difference was probably on account of Islamic dress code. In Kuwati society, wearing bikini is not a matter of personal choice or individual freedom for women as it is perceived to be an assault on local values and sense of decency and modesty. Seeing Solomon topless girls, conservative Victorians would have been outraged. They used to cover up even legs of chairs and tables, because these looked like bare 'natural legs'. Perspectives vary by place, values, time and clime. However, the topless teens of the tropics were the least conscious and were in their elements, entertaining everyone with their dancing skills. A secret side of me also enjoyed watching this unusual dance.

Inhabited by Melanesian people and other tribes, Solomon Islands is a small country consisting of large number of islands. Here many aborigines worship their ancestors in 'skull houses' and don't hesitate even to kill those who dare enter it. Minus the violence, I had seen something similar in traditional Japanese homes called Butsudan, or altar, where the memory of the ancestors is preserved and worshipped. Once a year, a ceremony popularly known as Bon is organized to remember the dead family members, something similar to Sraddha or death anniversary in India. When a member of the family dies, a tablet bearing the posthumous name of the departed soul is kept in the family altar after the funeral. Some tribes in other islands, after killing their enemies, proudly wear their skull and bones as garlands and live naked. There are some similar practices elsewhere in the world, of drinking blood and eating bones of the dead. As many in these societies consider funeral as an unnecessary and extravagant ritual and instead prefer roasting and eating the dead body as more practical.

The climate in South Pacific region including Solomon Islands remains extremely humid throughout the year. This renders clothing or covering the bodies unnatural and inconvenient. The minimum temperature is 27.c or 80.f and the coolest climate appears in June and lingers on for some time only. May be, because of this, nude dance in traditional costume is popular there. In the Indian Ocean, the Andaman Nicober Islands were earlier called 'nude islands', as in some of them nude living was very natural. Here tops and tits have no sexual connotation. People think that nature provides it for storing milk for babies. Thus, animals that give birth to multiple babies have up to dozen udders and tits. Cultural values are often intertwined with the climate- smart life style of the regions.

On return to India, Binny and I were invited to the opening ceremony of a new Digambar Jain temple in our locality in Dwarka. Being unaware of the complete nudity practiced by the Jain saints, Binny was greatly embarrassed by the two dozen monks standing on the dais fully naked. Digambar, which means 'sky-clad', believe that a true monk must throw off his monastic robes and practice ascetic nudity, just as he had arrived in this world, without even a loin cloth. He must renounce all material possessions and live a life freed from social considerations of pride, fame and shame. He can eat only once a day and that too as much as his two palms cupped together as a bowl, could carry. While the spiritual discourse was going on, I found some curious girls stealing glances and staring at the lower body parts of the naked monks with more interest than listening to their religious discourse. In comparison, the topless Solomon girls were relatively better dressed with fully covered belly and bottoms.

However, during my childhood up to eleven years, the only occasion on which I was wearing something was while going to school or attending a ceremony and, of course, in winter. As soon as I returned from school, an elderly aunty would be waiting at the entrance of the house to take off my dress, which, according to her, became impure, having been touched by others. For the next school going time she ensured my full nudity to keep the house 'pure'. Even when I came home for my mid day meal, she would repeat the same drill. She would not allow me ever to take meals with clothing on. If I insisted, she would give me to wear a very dirty piece of silk cloth not washed for months. She believed that a clean cotton cloth became impure in one use while a silken one, even if dirty, unhygienic and used unwashed for months, remained always 'pure'. She would also insist that I urinate outside before entering. Much later in life, during my visit to Japan, I found out it was similar to the old practice they called Uchi and Soto, which roughly meant clean inside the house and dirty outside the world. It is not Soto if the child urinates just outside the front door. Corresponding to this, they use another two words- Tatemae and Honne or front and rear, meaning public and personal behavior. Parents think that a child gets dirt and germs if it visits a neighbour's house. Neighbour in Japan means two households on both sides and three in front. But Japan has left India way behind. Recently (March 2017), an angry female Warden of an Indian Girls hostel forced 70 girls to strip naked in the class room in order to find out who was menstruating, after she had spotted blood stains in the wash rooms that made the hostel 'impure'.

One day, Shankar, a non resident uncle, working in Kolkata city, had come to meet my mother and had a big laugh when he saw me and Dena sitting fully naked and eating from the same plate. 'Hey, what do I see, and how ugly? Are you not ashamed of sitting naked like this and that too in front of another naked girl? Have you forgotten your age?' Then he called my mother to convey his displeasure. Now that nudity has emerged as a cult, the sense of shame is much less.

Similarly all the innocently naked girls playing with me didn't have any sense of shame or guilt. They were young enough to understand the connection between nudity and obscenity. Today, if somebody would show them the grainy pictures of 30 year old Kate Middleton, now Duchess of Cambridge and future queen of England, in the celebrity magazine 'Closer', they probably would feel more relaxed and less embarrassed about their childhood nudity.

There was a female saint in India who was always moving naked. Once someone asked her how she could do that among so many males. Without batting an eyelid, she replied, 'I don't find any male in this world'. There are many tribes, where women display no sense of shame by baring their bosom. They rather feel awkward and ashamed to cover the body. When David Livingston (1813-1873), the legendary explorer, requested his naked black African hosts to put on some clothing before arrival of his wife, everyone present there started laughing. He was further shocked to see the queen of Balonda, sitting naked on her throne while holding court for Livingston. Sexual morality and modesty varies from culture to culture reflected in their dress code. Just about a century ago, a Chinese woman was ashamed of showing her feet, an Arab woman her face, a Tureg woman her mouth and an Indian woman her bare head.

However, after being ridiculed by the uncle from the city, I decided not to allow my uncompromising aunty to take off my clothes after the school, despite her threats. But after hearing the comments of the city retuned uncle, Dena seemed to have felt more ashamed as she now started wearing her country bikini that covered the lower part. Then, within a year, she stopped coming to play with us. Next year, Rani and Panchi also disappeared from the group. We were wondering what had happened, until one day Raza informed us that they had now 'grown up'. Still, I could not make out what did it mean until one day, Prema, another girl from our batch in the school, left the class room suddenly and rushed towards her home. All boys, like peeping toms, were looking at her through the window railings and seemed to be fully enjoying the scene. I also joined them out of curiosity. Prema was walking briskly with her back towards us, which was splattered all over with the first menstrual blood. Before this, several girls had been withdrawn from the school, one after the other and I kept wondering why.

Then after returning home in the evening, I could hear sounds of drum beat continuing the whole night. I couldn't sleep properly that night. In the morning I innocently asked mother about it. She said Prema had 'grown up'. She was a topper in our class but stopped coming to the school. A similar incident had happened to my 11 year old sister- in- law, Renuka, a bright girl, when she attained puberty a year after my marriage. Soon after, she was withdrawn from the school. Earlier, for the same reason, my wife, Binny, Renuka's elder sister, had also been withdrawn from the school. It took me almost a month to convince Renuka's grandmother to send her back to the school. She is now a Professor of Mathematics in a prestigious American University after doing her M.Sc and Ph.D from the reputed IIT, Kharagpur, in India. It is also here that a self confident Renuka chose her spouse from another ethnic group, ignoring resistence from parents. This is the hidden potential of each and every girl child! Societies and cultures respond differently to this new feminine status of girls. Often this is reflected in mutilation of body, tattooing the face, legs, arms and the back, piercing the earlobe and nasal septum. In some cultures, the hymen of girls is perforated to facilitate sexual relation and the penis of the boys circumcised by cutting off the foreskin.

When I was attending a Commonwealth Women Ministers conference, a Minister, while making a presentation, was narrating the practice of 'breast ironing' in some West and Central African societies. She further elaborated that there was a time when all of Cameroon's 200 ethnic groups followed this strange and cruel method which had no relationship with religion, socio economic status or any other marker. The practice is carried out mostly by the girls' mother who pounds and massages the pubescent girl's breasts using hard or heated objects like grinding stone, wooden pestle, ladles, etc to make them disappear or stop growing. Her sole intention is to protect her girl child from sexual harassment, rape and premarital pregnancy. Its main motive is to deceive the boys, who, looking at the growing breast of the girls, conclude that she was now ready for sex. My Cameroonian colleague, Pamela, told me that she herself was a victim of this practice and later on faced a lot of problem while trying to breast feed her baby.

In traditional societies, menstruation separates girls from the asexual world of infancy. They were bound to domestic sphere and boys were initiated to outdoor tasks leading to traditional role stereotypes, which is fortunately breaking down. This is what happened to Rani, Dena and Panchi- three girls with three different characters. While Rani was alternatively cool and emotional and more focused on her goal, Dena was more open and loved every one's attention. Her secondary sexual characteristics were becoming more visible. Her breasts were now bigger in comparison to her height and attracted unusual attention. Once Raza, a compulsive flirt, teased her on her physicality, shouting obscenity in front of everyone, telling, 'Look, how the small walking tree has such big fruits.'Then he would ridicule her triangular face, hooked nose and bushy hair calling it both a bird's nest and a boy's bed. Feeling offended, Dena ran back home weeping. We were all embarrassed not knowing how to react. From that day Dena avoided the peer group.

Later in life, Dena lost her proud pair and feminine marker to mastectomy in her fight against breast cancer. Women, who strip off and use breasts for big business, find it difficult to reconcile with the new reality. It doesn't make one less woman though.With much persuasion by us, Dena now rejoined our group but was quieter. One day, her mother came screaming and forcefully pulled her away yelling how dare she play with the boys now that she had 'grown up', an euphemism for her 'post puberty' home bound status. She being my first crush, I missed her a lot. It takes a moment to have a crush on someone in the innocence of childhood. For some the memory stays for life and for many it lasts until one meets another favoured person.

For both, girls as well as boys, growing up years are a bubbling cauldron of hormone-laden emotion, ready to explode at any moment, into full-blown crisis. I recall how my childhood friend Raza, with roving glad eyes, was obsessed with girls. He would not even spare our lady teachers in the class room and would continuously stare at their curves. Some people attribute this to a perennial male weakness for female body. Some call it voyeurism, spying on women when they undress or engage in intimate behavior. Cashing in on this weakness, now film and television serials also entertain audience with intimate scenes to make money.

Recently, the management of several private schools in Kerala, a state in India with high human development indicators and higher social status of women, wanted lady teachers to adopt a particular dress code and cover themselves properly to avoid preying eyes of male students in classrooms as many lady teachers noticed students continuously staring and secretly taking pictures of their bosom with mobile cameras while the teachers were busy writing on the blackboard. Subsequently, most of the images found their way to popular social networking sites. Such incidents forced many schools in the state to ask lady teachers to wear an overcoat or apron on top of their sarees or kurtee. 'Drape yourself in nine yards, cover yourself from head to toe,' advised another circular for girls against provocative clothing, proscribing jeans, and designer blouses that expose cleavage peeks or are held by noodle straps, strings and knots. Men are prescribed shirts and trousers or kurta pyjama and women, saree or salwar-kameez to look dignified and serious at the work place.

As for Raza; he eventually came to be a sex addict which is now proven as a mental disorder. I could not make out the reasons behind his relentless pursuit of women. Now, in retrospect, I think he was more like what I hear now about super star golfer, Tiger Woods. Once he slipped into a girls' hostel at night and was caught and severely beaten. Still, he didn't change a bit and had no regrets and the moment he saw a girl, he would turn giddy, hot, nervous, unstable, ridiculous and irrational, as if possessed by a spirit. But for his untimely death, he would have become a second Casanova, the great Italian seducer of the 18th century, who is reported to have slept with more than ten thousand women. But unlike Raza, Casanova had a difficult childhood. He had lost his father at age eight and his mother had no time for his son as she was in theatre and constantly travelling. So, he was shifted to a boarding school at age nine and then to his teacher, Abbe Gozzi's house, where he met Gozzi's eleven year old daughter, Bettina. His first experience with the opposite sex was when Bettina fondled him in privacy. 'And little by little,' confessed Casanova, 'she kindled in my heart the first sparks of feelings, which later became my ruling passion. Cultivating whatever gave pleasure to the senses is the chief business of my life,' he had declared and would reinforce it by saying that men were born to have sex with women, as if it is a birth right.

I didn't realize that women also could be like this, until I met one such lady in the clinic of a psychiatrist friend. It was in early 80s when she barged into his consulting chamber and told him: 'Doctor, I want to sleep with you, let us go to your bedroom.' Without showing any embarrassment he told her "Ok, Ok, we will surely go together but I have a friend, so just wait and relax and come after some time'. 'No, I can't wait,' she insisted.

Later on, I asked him how a woman could be so open. He said she had a problem called 'anxiety neurosis' that rejects socially enforced sexual modesty like 'good women don't express sexual desire'. The incident made me think further on the issue. Is it because we are yet to recognize the biological reality of female sexual desire and continue to be guided by the social construct that women can't have higher libido than men? And that they can't or shouldn't even chase men! Despite the fact that much of sage Vatsyayana's Kama Sutra - 'Human Love Skills', deals with proactive female sexuality only. The fact is that there are 8000 nerve endings in the clitoris dedicated exclusively to enhancing female sexual pleasure whereas the penis has only 4000.

In one of our gender and sexual health training programme in 2001 in the Asia Youth Centre, we had invited Kothari, a well known sexologist. There was a game in which participants were asked to frankly convey in writing through anonymous slips, about how women were proactive in sex. One slip said: 'I like frequent sex as also my boy friend, so I don't have to ask for it.' Another male participant wrote: 'Whenever she needs it , she tells me directly, invites me to bed, touches me, kisses me on the chest, caressess me, puts her naked leg over me, does some mischief to arouse me and she always succeeds. I also feel happy.'

Three women in epics, victims of social and sexual stereotyping, come into mind. One was called Srupanakha (woman with sharp, long nails), who's real name was Meenakshi, the 'fish eyed'. She was the sister of Raavana, Rama's main antagonist in the epic. A pivotal character and variously named in South-East Asian Ramayan stories, as Sarpakenaka (Indonesia), Sammanakkha (Thai), Surapandaki (Malay) and Surpanakhar (Khmer), she was a liberated feminist and humiliated for expressing openly her love before men. She first proposes to marry Rama and being spurned by him, proposes to his brother, Luxman, who, non-chivalrously chops off her nose. Writer Valmiki, not only changes her name in the epic but also describes her as ugly, pot bellied, cross eyed with a grating voice, oversized breasts and a heart full of wickedness.

The second one, who suffered the most for a single episode of sexual freedom was Ahalya, which literally meant 'one who has not been ploughed', meaning a virgin. An unparalleled beauty of her time, she was married off to sage Gautama, who was old enough to be her father and was always busy with his vedic rituals in forest, smearing his hirsuit body and face with ashes. Neglected and sex starved, young Ahalya grants the wish of Indra, the king of gods, to have a union with her. As Indra, in the guise of a hermit, was leaving her room after the union, Gautama finds him. Enraged, he first curses Ahalya to turn into a 'stone' and Indra to have a thousand 'vulvas' all over his body. The third one was princess Lopamudra, sage Agastya's scholarly, young and beautiful wife, who moves from a palace to the hermitage of her old husband. Feeling tired of Agastya's austere, sexless life, she openly sends a poem to him asking for love, which makes the sage realize his conjugal duties. A hymn in Rigveda is attributed to her.

Interestingly, Indian mythology has given young Ahalya the status as one of the five great 'virtuous women', daily remembering and uttering whose sacred names, is believed to destroy great sins – 'mahapataka nasanam'. The other four women are Draupadi, Tara, Kunti and Mandodari, all powerful characters. All of them were in full command of their sexual and social lives, asserting their womanhood with conviction and courage, a clear contrast to submissive, self effacing, and suffering, Seeta, whose chastity was repeatedly challenged in public and unable to bear frequent embarrassment and humiliation, she asks mother earth to break open and swallow her back. In Greek mythology, Zeus, the ruler of gods, asks Tiresias, who has experience of love making as both male and female, as to who gets more pleasure from intimacy. Tiresias reveals that it was the woman, who enjoys sex ten times more than man. Zeus's wife, Hera, who was present during the conversation strikes Tiresias blind for divulging this well kept secret of women. But Zeus immediately compensates by giving him the power of foresight that makes him a prophet.

Experts say, once women are liberated from the social construct around female sexuality, they would enjoy sex more than men. The meekest of them could be the wildest in bed. During my daily travel route to the Election Commission of India in Delhi, near Parliament Street via Sardar Patel Marg, alongside the forest belt, I often noticed very interesting animal behavior, particularly in case of Langurs and Baboons. In the animal world, the female Langur, like many other primates, is always first to signal the male that she was ready to mate. In order to make it more explicit, she would shudder the head, lower the tail and would repeatedly show her anogenital region in the body to the male. A female baboon is always the first to initiate mating by presenting her swollen rump to the male's face. Birds are known to be the most over the top in matters of courtship. The female night frog enters the male frog territory when it is time for to mate. Another type is more proactive and would hoist the male she likes onto her back for mating. Even plants and flowers try to optimize their chances of reproduction in divergent ways. Flashy, fragrant flowers attract wind and insects to move the pollen between male and female parts. However, today, with sex positive feminism spreading, female sexual hysteria has waned to a great extent. The latest evidence of it was when twenty six women openly declaring that they were in love with Roman Catholic priests wrote to Pope Francis, urging to make vow of celibacy optional for the priests. They said further, how denial of sexuality was tearing their souls and how they were undergoing 'devastated suffering', caused by the church's age old ban on priests' having sex , marrying and leading a normal life (Vatican Insider).

In retrospect, it is now easier to understand my friend, Raza's mysterious habits and weaknesses. A few years ago, when I was travelling in a bus on a busy road in Delhi, the young driver was going round and round at the same traffic crossing instead of going ahead, until confused passengers protested against his strange behavior. He stopped the bus and asked the young woman sitting behind him to go back to the rear row and sit there. When the young lady protested, he told her: 'Madam, you are not properly dressed and my attention gets diverted looking at your reflection in the mirror, I am sorry.'

In 16th century India, there was a blind saint named Surdas who was a great poet and musician, known for his devotional songs. It is said that he composed 100,000 songs and wrote a magnum opus called Sursagar or Ocean of Melody, out of which only 8000 are extant. Mughal Emperor, Akbar (1542-1605) also was a great admirer of Surdas. There is an interesting story about how Surdas lost his sight. During his early life he was a beggar. One day, he knocked at a door and the woman opening it was very beautiful. For a moment Surdas was totally enchanted by her beauty and developed a desire for her body. Soon after, he came back to his sense and felt so guilty that he instantly destroyed his two eyes blaming it on the 'evil desire'.

Much later in life, I had a chance meeting with a socio biologist who told me that this was a common trend among many men. The real culprit is the gene, he said. Sex is the individual gene's way of multiplying... Just before this, the frontal cortex, vital to judgement, shuts down. According to him the brain behaves in this way for higher biological purposes, to facilitate reproduction and once a while it also creates rapists, who not only assault a woman's body but also destroy her soul. Late Khuswant Singh, one of India's courageous columnist and writer, was known for his famous admission that the first thought that enters his mind seeing a woman is how she would be in bed. His friends used to call him in jest a 'lecherous' and 'dirty old man', but that is the way his brain was pushing its envelope. Explaining it further, he said once the social norms and culturally acceptable behavior weaken and sense of judgement is deactivated and pushed back, the most unlikely pair of man and woman can get together, mate and reproduce. A female is more careful in this matter as her ovum is rarer and the persistent fear of possible maternal investment in time and energy she has to make.

Thus while an average female can reproduce about 12 times before menopause at around fifty, a promiscuous male, in freewheeling sex, can sow thousands of wild oats. But the female is a careful, selective shopper and keen to ensure her genetic continuum. Maybe, that is the reason why women are better and safer drivers and less likely to cause accidents where as men tend to speed drive, crash and die behind the wheels. Another reason why a male is more afraid of dying than a female is, most of his seeds also die during orgasm. So, his genetic success lies in winning as many bets as possible. In medieval India, this option was available to a privileged few in form of 'Swayamvar', a kind of mutual selection of the best breeds. Male aspirants used to move from event to event to be a part of as many bets as possible within social constraints of marriage. Subsequently, the process and privilege was limited to royalty only. A male is instinctively more aggressive, as historically he has been competing with other males for female attention. Females are less liable to indiscriminate sexual advances for want of a need for that. Thus, the institution of marriage evolved as society's response to discipline sexual behavior and change the brutish image of human relationships. With this evolved, living that provided parental protection to the children from the other males.

In addition to the genetic urge for seed selection, both male and female are keenly interested to know the difference in their anatomy. But early in life, girls and boys develop tremendous interest in the anatomy of each other. Children are more curious to know and to confirm whether their body parts are similar to the adults. Curiosity gives birth to interest that develops into desire. Raza was beaten for the second time for this reason when he sneaked into the girls' hostel and was peeping through a bathroom window. When the girls raised alarm, he shamelessly showed them his 'fly', just to mock at them or maybe, thinking that they would be interested in it. Angered and outraged by his absurd behavior, they surrounded and overpowered him while another girl was attempting to bobbitize and chop off his genital with her laboratory knife, when panicking, he pushed them and ran for life. I recalled this event instantly when recently (2012), I saw girls in Delhi in a procession against rapists, holding placard boldly declaring: 'If You Rape, We Chop'.

When I narrated this episode to my friend, S D Sharma, a senior civil servant and State Election Commissioner from Bihar, he had his own story about a girl who was more daring in defending her modesty. It was an incident of attempted rape of a tribal girl in 1986-87, by a lustful local politician, in the Indo-Nepalese border area. When the man abducted, by force, a poor tribal girl from a paddy field, she didn't raise any alarm nor put up a fight or resistence. Encouraged, the man now came upon her, when the girl suddenly caught his erect penis and violently bit it off from its base and fled from the field holding it as a trophy. Bleeding profusely, the rapist ran in pain and panic, to the nearest hospital, but refused to reveal how it all happened. The brave girl had the last laugh. The following day the Chinese media dished out gory details of the story of a man called Fan, whose penis was cut off by his wife as a payback for his adulterous affairs with other women and after hearing that doctors had sewn back and reattached the penis, she crept into the surgical ward and repeated the feat once again and threw the penis into the drain.

My seven year young grand child would often follow me to the wash room to find out how I piss and asked repeatedly to show him where my 'pee' comes from. For some time I was in a dilemma but finally decided to address it head on, by allowing him to find out for himself. Since then, he has stopped asking me about it His next query was about where babies came from and all that stuff that all children innocently ask of their parents but the answer to which they don't get from their embarrassed parents. These are frequently asked questions that need convincing answers. Avoiding and hiding would only enhance curiosity of innocent inquisitive children. Often illustrated books or medical anatomy videos are more helpful if carefully chosen because some of these are diagrams and some are medical procedures while some videos are geared toward kids, some to medical students and some to patients.

Almost twelve hundred years after Vatsyayan, it was Wendy Doniger (1940), a scholarly lady professor and Indologist in the Divinity School of Chicago University, who addressed the forbidden sexuality question upfront. Interpreting and educating the world about the perpetual conflict in the traditional Indian society about human, sexual desires and religious, spiritual aspirations, Wendy, whom I call the Ubhay Bharti of our times, analyses the issue thoughtfully in her book ' Siva: The Ascetic Erotic' (1981).

It is said that in 8th century, Adi Shankar, India's ascetic philosopher- cum Vedic scholar extraordinary, had to concede defeat before an erudite woman like Ubhay Bharti, wife of another thought leader of the time, Pundit Mandan Mishra. Because of his absolute ignorance of Kama Shastras, a subject of study, dealing with 'sex-love science' and rules of marital life, Shankar failed to answer a single question of her on the subject. According to legend, he begged of her a month's time to study the subject. And left his own body and entered into the body of a youthful prince, who had just passed away minutes before. He spent enough time with the princess to have full knowledge and experience of the intricate aspects of human sexuality. Then he returned to his own body, to challenge Ubhay Bharti once again and now defeated her. Both she and her husband became his disciples. It was probably the first attempt in human history by a woman sexologist to establish the primacy of 'human sexuality' as an academic discipline.

The fact was that young Sankara, who was initiated into spiritual order in early childhood, didn't have any exposure to or interaction with the opposite sex. Thus his education remained incomplete, as he realized after his defeat. The message is loud and clear. In early childhood, boys and girls identify with the same sex and prefer to play with children of their own sex. But after sometime, they also feel naturally attracted to the opposite sex. While we were playing the 'spouse game', my childhood playmate once told me 'Let us have babies'.

I asked, 'But how?'

'Simple, by sleeping together,'she replied.

'Are you sure?' I asked, not knowing what to do.

Pat came her answer. 'Mama and Papa are sleeping together and had babies like you and me, so why can't we?'

Popular actor Chris Hemsworth has recently revealed on the EllenDegeneres Show as to how his daughter, India Rose, one day confessed and complained to him about why she didn't have one of those things her twin brothers Sasha and Tristan have between their legs. When he told her that girls had two breasts that boys didn't have, she said : 'I don't want breasts. I want to be a boy.' Chris didn't know how to handle the question. Often female anatomy is used for social discrimination. In our village an uncle would always serve more food to his son than to the daughter. Both were twins. One day when the daughter questioned this practice and wanted to know the reason for it, she was curtly told that the boy had a penis!

In our Gole Market flat in Delhi, we had a neighbor who was a doctor in community medicine and public health. One day, I was really impressed hearing him explain to his five year young child how boys and girls, like all of us, have so many cracks and holes in the body, like our mouth, nose and ears. Similarly, there is a hole in the penis of boys and one in the vagina of girls for pee to come out. Just like that there is also a 'hole' in our butt for dropping the 'poop'.

In the same way, to the innocent questions like 'where babies come from', or 'how I came to the world', he explained matter of factly to the children that 'just like plants grow on earth from small seeds, children also come from small seeds that grow inside mom's tummy. These seeds come from dad, who plants it inside mommy, where it stays warm and safe for more than nine months. That is how I also came to this world' he explained. That's all that children needed to know at that age and they feel happy if it was shown with the picture. They can be told how love creates life on earth in the form of babies. If parents don't make a fuss out of it, children won't. If parents themselves hush, hush and view the topic as dirty or taboo and keep it from them, children would try to find it out by themselves from elsewhere anyway, mostly from their ignorant peers in a distorted manner and are quite likely to be misguided by others. Unfortunately, many parents have also a poor knowledge of anatomy.

A survey on 1000 women of all ages conducted by British Women's Cancer Charity Appeal has revealed that 50 percent of women didn't know where exactly the vagina was. This most intimate body part is always wrapped in mystery and euphemism. Vaginal health itself is a taboo. Very often, during vacations, I used to visit our close relatives. On one such occasion, a man whom I used to respect as an uncle, called me to his room and came physically very close to me. Then, while talking to me, he put his hand inside my pocket and tried to run his fingers groping deeper and was trying to pull down my pant. I couldn't understand what he was trying to do. Feeling confused, embarrassed, scared and awkward, I extricated myself and started running.

Next day, I returned home and innocently narrated the whole episode to mother. She looked extremely upset by my narrative, her eyes dilated in anger, anguish, anxiety and shock; as if a great disaster had befallen her child. With a stern look, she asked me never to go near that man. She called out father and together they went into a huddle. From that day, the man's access to our house was restricted and a protective barrier was built between us but it left me more confused. Years later, some other incidents of different nature confirmed that the man had also a proclivity towards same sex relationship. Once, he was even caught sodomising a junior boy in the school hostel. Probably, he needed more help than censure to come to terms with his sexual orientation. Sexual minorities have their own problems and being maligned and misunderstood, often go underground.

Our school had a residential wing for both teachers and students. One senior teacher, staying in the hostel, was a paedophile and used to sexually exploit the children. In fact, as soon as he saw a young boy, his brain used to be over activated with sexual desire. This came to light when a boy started crying and ran out of the hostel never to return again, accusing the teacher of forcing him to oral and anal sex but we were too young to understand it then. A few years later, when I moved to a city hostel, a batch mate confided in me how inmates were being exploited by the monk of a local mission hostel in perverse ways. There are stories galore about sexual exploitation by monks, in missions and monasteries of different religious orders. Erasmus had termed these as public brothels wherein lusty priests were deep in debauchery to the extent of seeking sexual favours even from female penitents, promising to absolve them from the guilt of sin and punishment in purgatory. The unrealistic, unnatural rule of celibacy had ensured that. And unfortunately, it still continues.

Children come to the world with predetermined proclivity, ability and temperament. All my three children are different from each other. While one is cool and controlled, the second one is combative and confident, and the third one is cooperative and compassionate. While one loved only Barbies, the other one was fond of teddy bears and the third one loved toy cars and aeroplanes during her childhood. A cousin sister of mine, now over sixty, still has a Barbie near her bed. Each one of my brothers was different from the other in attitude, outlook and temperament. Similarly, sexual curiosity and preferences of some individuals also vary.

There was a highly erudite yet equally highly perverted professor of political science in my university, who was 60 plus. While interviewing girls for admission into post graduate courses that he taught, he would ask each one to show her lower anatomy. Those not cooperating would be disqualified on some ground or the other. In those days, sexual harassment laws were very weak and no one dared challenge him because of his control over the admission and evaluation process, clout in the campus academia and the university syndicate. Finally, one infuriated brave girl confronted and taught him a lesson by taking off her saree and the inner and pissing straight on him. This was enough to bring the shocked, shameless man back to his senses.

In Indian mythology, there is an oppressive, proud and perverted character named Mahishasur, son of a demon and a female buffalo. This two horned demon was always harassing the Devas or godlings. So they created a powerful and beautiful woman called Durga, who could control and kill him. When Durga challenged him for a fight, the demon was so attracted by her physical beauty that leaving all arms he stooped down and started staring through her underwear. An embarrassed and angry Durga now killed the demon instantly with a sharp spear. Today, in India, the punishment for each sexual harassment is three years imprisonment plus fine and demands for harsher punishment are rising.

Male and female are eternally curious about each other. It is a part of their genetic make up. Being visual creatures, males are more attracted to the female body. Realizing this, in many societies females are advised to properly cover up the erogenous zones in the body like hair, breasts, buttocks, nape, nipple, thighs, knees, etc which are likely to attract undue attention of a male and trigger latent sexual desire and fantasies. Even among children, such curiosity is innocently natural. Pointing to her genitalia, a small girl asked her mother: What is this called Mama? After worrying and wondering for a moment how to respond, the mother said: 'Oh, it is your cute "po po." You must always keep it clean.' She seemed to be happy hoping to have satisfied her. But then, pointing towards her perineum and anal area, the little girl again asked the same question. The mother went dumb for a while groping for a name and then told her 'Oh, it is your "pu pu"dear', I also have one like yours.' The matter didn't end here as the child asked once again 'And what do you call that dangling thing of boys? "Little chick" and "little eggs" –she replied casually, not feeling sure.

Lower body parts have different names invented by different societies like 'little flower', 'vulva', 'fanny' and in some parts of India sanskritised terms like 'yoni' for girls and 'ling' for boys of all age groups. Trying to avoid clinical as well as slangs, some people prefer the more generic and umbrella terms like 'privates' or 'private parts'. 'Teaching on touching' counselors of child sexual abuse sometimes use these terms. I always conclude my sexuality training sessions with a statement: 'Everybody and anybody is somebody because she or he has a body without which you are nobody.' All children have a right to know about all parts of their body. Sexual hygiene is as important as oral and anal hygiene. This helps them in their later years- particularly during growing up years when they are sweetly innocent and confused and need advice, guidance and value clarification to overcome personal dilemmas related to their sexuality.

In ancient India, worship of male and female genitals was a common practice which can be seen in the innumerable Shiva temples where stone phallus or lingams with several stylized varieties are found. In Greek mythology, Hermes, with an exaggerated phallus is depicted as a fertility god. Another Greek god, Priapus, son of Aphrodite and Dionysus, whose symbol is also a phallus, is described as the protector of lives stock, fruit plants, gardens and male genitalia. Phallus worship was also prevalent in ancient Roman culture.

In ancient Egyptian religion, there is a reference to phallus in the life story of Osiris and his wife Isis, who like Shiva and his consort, Parvati, were worshipped as god of regeneration and rebirth as well as god of afterlife, underworld and the dead. Legend says that when Osiris's body was cut into fourteen pieces, his wife could retrieve all of them except one, i.e. his penis, which had been swallowed by a cat fish. From all these stories of the past, it is evident that sex was never considered as dirty but respected and worshipped in temple as gods of birth and regeneration. Nature itself is more sexy than the myriad creature who live in it.

During one of my visits to USA, I had come across an interesting counseling column in a newspaper which began with a 'request-for-advice' letter from a confused young woman that read:

"I am a 23 year old virgin by choice. I am not necessarily holding out for marriage and I'm not a prude either, but I think it is important to wait until I am in a trusting relationship. The problem is, in my recent dating, I have come across two things. One is that the man has found out that I'm a virgin but he is too horny and impatient to wait for me to feel comfortable. Two, he has found out that I'm a virgin and he sees it as a challenge and now tries everything to persuade me to lose it to him. Thus my problem lies in the fact that I can't seem to be staying in a relationship long enough to feel comfortable having sex before the guy loses interest in me because we are not having sex. What can I do to get past the sex barrier with guys? Please help."

In response to this, the gist of what the lady counselor replied was like this:

'No, my brave girl, don't get past the sex barrier. Embrace it, adore it, feel proud of it and worship it... how lucky you are to have a wall between you and some untested wonderful thing. You are pure, rare and virginal, innocent and still untouched since you have been avoiding casual flings. Boys see such girls as more attractive, unattainable and sexy. I will say there is some ugly beep on the other side of the virginity wall...It is definitely tough, but when the right guy shows up, he won't mind. Stick to your principle, but don't let yourself get so paranoid of opportunists that you end up untouched by life.... The unmistaken message is – wait for the right guy who'll be willing to wait for you, that should be the non-negotiable bottomline. Be bold to be different.'

Experts say that teenagers of warm, caring and supportive parents delay sexual activity. Before we conceptualised and launched a massive HIV awareness programme for the youth in the 80s involving two million university students, we had engaged the Indian Market Research Bureau for a sexual behavior study of the students. The study found out that a large majority of students in the colleges had no experience of penetrative sex. Based on this, messages were designed to reinforce their current behavior and encourage abstinence before relationship as a safer prevention against HIV infection.

To promote the idea of safer and more responsible sex, sometimes we used to integrate into the training, a session on condom demonstration. After attending such a session, a girl returned home and her mother accidentally found out the condom inside her wallet while she was taking out the lunch box. Concluding that the girl was already into casual sex and refusing to listen to her explanations, she made a scene and thrashed the poor girl. The following morning, she reached the school and directly accused the lady principal of encouraging free sex among the students.

An embarrassed principal had to convince the lady that her fears were unfounded as condoms were being used for demonstration only, so that women could insist on safer sexual behavior from the males. With knowledge and skill, risk is replaced by responsibility. And if used correctly and consistently, it is a protection against sexually transmitted infection as well as unwanted pregnancy. The mother confessed that she didn't know all this and actually this daughter was her fourth child born out of such ignorance as she was unaware of contraceptive use to prevent unwanted pregnancy.

Like the mother, her daughter had the impression that holding a boy's hand during menstruation would make her pregnant. Some girls were scared of the periods, thinking it was a sign of cancer. Earlier, in one of our programmes for the adults in villages, a gentleman living with HIV stood up and said he was a regular user of condom and yet got the infection. On further query, we found out that he was actually wearing the condom on his thumb! When he was informed it was not correct, he said the demonstrator was also doing the same during training.

Young minds are always curious and like to explore, investigate and learn by observation, particularly, when the object is one's own body. For quite some time, I was greatly worried about the delay of the appearance of secondary sexual characteristics like hair on my face, armpit and pubic area. When I had my first wet dream, I woke up, sweating with a several stains on my underwear and sticky spots on bed clothes. Was it bed wetting? But I was too old for that. Or maybe, I was seriously sick or something wrong with me. I was in a state of depression, shame and guilt, not knowing what was happening to me and why. Talking to peers didn't help Advised by a quack, claiming to be a doctor, I started taking cold water bath five times every day and practicing yoga, without any result. He told me that it was a disease to cure for which he gave me some very costly medicines made by him. No luck. Years later, I was greatly relieved when a physician told me that it was a very natural thing that happens to every one at this age, when the body releases extra fluids. Girls experience vaginal wetness while getting ready for puberty, reproduction and fertilization.

9

Moon's Mad Boy

The Earth took millions of years for placing itself at the right spot and preparing for the evolution and soft landing of myriad life forms. Personally my landing on earth, particularly the early years, were much harder and harsher. My mother Moon's papilla, a rubber like mouth piece of a baby bottle, got infected soon after my birth, depriving me of natural breast feeding support. Consequently, I survived infant mortality being fed with cow's milk and had a stunted growth. Mom had a family history of breast disease and finally she died of breast cancer, quite early in her life.

That breast feeding with care is beautiful and beneficial, was not known to many. It makes a child feel full and the mother empty and light – and the both satisfied and happy. This most inexpensive life saver of the world is as much healthful to the baby as to the mother. Even doctors in those days were not aware that breast milk contained antibodies that protected babies from common illness such as diarrhea and pneumonia-the two main causes of child mortality world wide. It provides 98 percent protection to mothers from getting pregnant within the first six months of child birth, while reducing obesity and risks of breast and ovarian cancer.

I remember when our second child had an eye infection; Binny cured her with her breast milk by directing the jet repeatedly into the child's swollen eyes. Despite barriers of time, embarrassment and pain, most women continue to breast feed their children. Recently, popular singer and model, Myleena Klass, shocked her fans telling she drinks tea mixed and made from her own breast milk, which she has shared with her friends. Besides enhancing the bond between mother and child, breast fed babies grow up safe and secure with their parents. When my first child was born, milk food lobby and advertisers were telling everyone that mother's milk was not enough. We all believed it, buying packets of milk powder and formula feed from the market at great cost. Mothers were made to feel inadequate. While papilla problem deprived me of mother's milk, propaganda did the same to my children.

A couple of years ago, breast feeding activists had started an awareness campaign called 'Latch on'. Now, many breast feeding women call themselves proudly as 'lactivists', wearing T-shirts that read "I make Milk" and 'I breastfeed', 'Breast against Bottle', telling women how it reduces risk of osteoporosis, breast cancer, gastrointestinal upsets, how it revives the uterus, reduces weight and so on. WHO recommends exclusive breast feeding for infants up to six months followed by complementary food and BF up to two years and beyond. I was not so lucky. Breast and babies are natural friends. During one of my visits to Africa, a Kenyan friend who was in India for three years, asked me, 'Why Indian babies cry so much.' I said, 'Not only in India but babies cry everywhere.' He didn't agree, saying, 'Our babies here don't cry.' Not believing, I cross verified from a couple of sources, including my daughter, who was fresh from a prenatal training. They all said that it was a fact. European babies even cry more. In Western Africa, new born babies are usually very well wrapped, carried in arms most of the time or strapped onto their mother and sometimes father. Even older babies get similar care and attention. So much so, it is difficult to catch a glimpse of the baby's limb, eye or nose. Almost a second womb like situation is created. Very often, babies are kept closer to the breast and are literally cocooned from the outside world into which they have now entered. So, they have no reasons to cry.

My formal schooling in modern education was now interrupted, as father didn't have the minimum resources to send me to a secondary school, about 15 kms away and he had no money to meet my hostel expenses. I made several attempts approaching family friends and relatives but without success. In sheer grief and frustration, I refused to touch food for two days. No one came forward to help. A close cousin, who had promised to lend his old broken bicycle, withdrew at the last moment. In fact, most of our relatives were also not very well off. Dad was a poor priest and a marginal agriculturist. He had hardly any money and no materials which he could sell or barter for a price. He had some water divining skills and knew a bit of astrology that enabled him to earn some money once a while. The family was deprived of the basic standard of wellbeing. It was a condition of ultra poverty, a cheek by jowl existence.

He would start the day with a visit to the village temple sauntering past rows of sleepy houses, singing sacred hymns to wake up the people. Then he would reach the temple premises to perform prayer and purification rites called 'Homa', a Vedic ritual. Once, I had accompanied him to the temple to witness the process that appeared to be very mysterious. I could not understand a word of the mumbo jumbo he was uttering. So, one day, I asked him why is he doing it every day. Without taking offence, he tried to explain how it healed the micro environment outside and the 'Prana' or life force within every one, how it connects us to the cosmos. To perform this, every morning, he would collect dried up cow dung, herbal, medicinal and holy plant stuff and substances from nearby forest and unpolished grains, unbroken rice from home. He would put all of these in a copper container that looked like an inverse pyramid and carry it to the temple.

Then, chanting mantras, a word of which I didn't understand, he would ignite the stuff with a candle and pour clarified cow butter over it, with the help of a small wooden spoon. He would chant 'Swaha' which meant burning mental and physical impurities. He had a firm belief that 'Homa' calms the mind, fortifies immune system, dispels pollutants, purifies and refills air with nutrients and bio-energy. According to him, it also restores ecological equilibrium of the vicinity enriching soil, making plants and animals feel good, as they inhale the flavor of the burnt herbal particles.

He explained to me that the best result would come when all the 108 herbs were offered to the sacrificial fire. He would always put at the entrance to the house, an earthen pot full with water and decorated with turmeric, vermilion, mango leaves and flowers. To his juniors, he would advise to recite the mantras with correct intonation and pitch, as he believed that the ritual power was not in words but in the sound and vibrations it produced. Such vibrations must be in tune with cosmic vibrations to connect with all the five elements i.e. air, water, fire, earth and space.

At the end of this ritual, he would collect the sacred ash and with it smear the foreheads of all those gathered there. Saints in India often smear their whole body with it, believing that it would protect people against radioactivity and infections. The light of fire, sound of mantras and smoke from incense, are believed to banish all negative energy. Then, he would sprinkle the 'spiritually energized' water from the pot on all those assembled, as blessings of the divine. Finally, he would thank all the seers and sages of the past, for all the received wisdom and legacy they have left behind to enrich our lives.

After this, he would distribute the foods called 'Charu' or 'mukam' offered to the 'fire god.' Then, invoking the divine, he would give the first parts of the 'charu' to childless couples expecting a child but not able to conceive as yet. Before this, he would wash their feet with 'holy' water and dry these with a cotton towel. He believed that creative energy entered the body through the feet. I remember, how once he had offered this 'charu' to Manika, his niece, who gave birth to her first child within a year. After this ceremony, all participants would be advised to sit silent, pray and meditate. Aristotle had said that the ultimate value of life depended more upon self awareness and the power of contemplation rather than upon mere survival. Once, I asked father why he was offering foods to his gods who could never eat it. He said he was doing it not to satisfy the God but to sanctify the food. And whenever there was a drought condition, he would go inside a water body, sit in chest deep water and start chanting 'mantras' to invoke the 'water god' for rains. On one occasion, I had actually seen rainfall after the ritual, which I think now, might have been a coincidence. Father was also a 'water diviner.' People in the area, planning to dig a well for water would always consult him for selecting the location having underwater.

He would use a dowsing rod and Y-shaped forked branch from a cactus plant or bush or freshly cut branches from a particular tree known for its rich water content. He would hold both ends on the forked side of the twig, one in each hand with the third, the stem of the "Y" pointing straight ahead touching the soil of the area and he would walk slowly over the places where he suspected signs of underground water. Sometimes, he would also use pendulum of crystal, metal or other materials suspended on a chain to get a sensory cue about the presence of water and its precise direction.

He used to be busy in such pursuits without any regular income to support my study. And for this reason, he put me in a traditional institution to study the ancient language, Sanskrit, so that I could follow his priestly profession. I had just one pair of dress and a towel and had acquired my second pair only after coaching a junior for six months. I didn't have even an ordinary pair of foot wear. The stipend was 15 rupees or 1/4th of a dollar (1955) per month, meant just to subsist and even every day breakfast was a luxury. I didn't have money to buy an important text book and had to save money from the measly stipend by forgoing dinner for one month.

However, study of Sanskrit, now considered world's most computer friendly language, proved to be a real blessing as it enabled me to access the ancient wisdom tradition of India. All the mysterious 'mantras' dad was reciting suddenly appeared meaningful. I suddenly realized how he was actually teaching me many things indirectly as a home educator. It was learning without schooling. The Pundits teaching us were brilliant scholars. On the first day, one young bright Pundit explained to us the meaning of AUM, the primordial sound, which split and created fifty different sounds that converted to syllables, based on which languages developed. Contextualising, he explained why the conch is blown in temples and at home, before worship, before marriage, before battle, after victory and on all auspicious occasions. 'Because when a conch is blown, it produces the primordial sound AUM or Om, chanted by God before creating the universe.'

Then, he explained how each syllable became a mantra or 'creative force' out of which evolved the universe. And all that we see around us are, in essence, wavelengths of the sound AUM. In one session, he lifted our minds to the cosmic level, although at that age it was difficult to stay at that level for long. Exposure to this language and its rich literary and philosophical traditions created in me a new sense of understanding, empathy, emotional intelligence, social skills and a holistic view of life. Every year, soon after the annual exams, a yogi from Uttarkashi in the Himalayan foothills would visit our institute and stay with us for about a month, to train us in various yogic practices. Before the actual practice in early morning, he would make us recite 'AUM' thrice followed by a very short, simple, yet meaningful and motivational song in Sanskrit. Translated, it means : 'Why should I be afraid of any one, when 'patience' is my father, an 'educated conscience' is my teacher and 'forgiveness' is my mother, when 'peace' is my spouse , 'truth' my son and 'service' my daughter, when 'compassion' is my sister and 'self control' my brother, when the earth is my 'bed', 'sky' is my cloth and the nectar of 'knowledge' is my food'. I am a member of that great and real family'. It was so inspiring, I developed a habit of reciting this every night before going to bed feeling immensely relaxed.

At that time, I was just 13 and had a stunted growth with a height of four feet three inches - an unequal stature in comparison to many of my peers in the class. I was feeling vertically inferior. Then, in the next five years I added one full foot and yet still looked smaller than many of my age group. However, I consoled myself when in college, our history teacher told us that Napoleon had a similar complex. Even Adolf Hitler, who was 173 cm, was not comfortable with his height. I had read in my school history book the interesting Shivaji- Afzal khan episode, which was a clever fight between heights, between the small and the tall. One was 4ft 9' small and the other full 7ft tall.

Lucy, was just 1.1m (3ft. 7inch) tall, a small hominid weighing 29kg (64Lb), whose children have grown much taller now. However, not agreeing, some historians say that Nepoleon was mostly seen with his imperial guards who were much taller than him. This contributed to the perception that he was short which he did not like. Or may be it was a factor in his relationships, as a majority of women are reported to be comfortable in relationship with men taller to them by a few inches. It is believed that in a way height helps in the height of romance too.

Supporters cite 6ft 3in, Prince William and 5ft 10 in Princes Kate as an example. However, to a smaller child, everyone looks taller and often daunting. When I was seven years old, an uncle in the village slapped me hard on the face for calling him by his first name. He was a six footer plus. Even if I had wanted to hit back, I could have hardly gone up to his ankles level only. So, I picked up a stone and threw at him and then started running for safety from an unequal adversary.

Height is a great handicap for all children in an adult dominated world. Even shorter adults are subjected to jokes and ridicule. Their only junior companions in this inequality are persons like Jyoti Amge (2ft 6 inch tall), in India, world's shortest woman as per Guinness world record. One is tall or small in relation to another. A 5 foot 8 inches tall, famous Bollywood actor used to feel so awkward to stand with a 5'9" heroine in a reality show that, he would often request her not to come on stage wearing high heels and piling up hair high on her head! Most of the Sikhs in India are of tall frame but look taller by about five inches with their turbaned heads. Husbands in many parts of the world do not like to have wives taller than them. Our driver, Ravi's wife, Prava, was taller than her husband by about two inches and he would always avoid to go with her to any public place. That Ravi was uncomfortable about Prabha's height became obvious when one day he himself shared with me the sorrow and sense of discomfort. The fact was, when he married Prabha, she was just 14 and was full three inches shorter. But in five years time, she gained five more inches! Another unpredictable consequence of early marriage.

In 2008, while in New Ark in USA, I had gone to a nearby Mall to pick up some fruits and vegetables, when I was struck by the sheer height of an Afrcan-American woman, standing near the entrance. Although, I had heard of American Sandy Allen (7ft 7 in) and Indian Siddiqua Parveen, (7ft 8 in.) as world's tallest women, never before had I come face to face with such a huge and tall woman. Inside, I felt like telling her: 'Hey, stop growing.' So deep was the awe, it was difficult to keep my eyes off her frame. Noticing my strange conduct, she now reacted, telling me harshly: 'Hey, Man, why are you repeatedly staring at me? Shall I call the police? Feeling guilty and embarrassed, I apologised and quickly left the place.

Tall girls also have their own problems. Some are considered to be too tall for heels, hairdo and swimsuits, older than they really are. Many smack their heads on roof of small cars, can't borrow friends' clothes and get a spouse matching their heights and so on. Comparatively, sometimes, shorter girls get a better deal. My daughter, Maitri is short, but would always decline an offer of marriage from short boys. One day, she surprised all of us, when a handsome boy, full 12 inches taller than her, proposed to marry her. Subsequently, their children balanced it out with the parents. There are several examples of taller guys falling in love with girls much shorter to them.

The situation had taken the short boy out of the village but failed to take the village out of him. Its baggage continued to weigh heavily on my mind. The familiar flavour of its soil, adventurous bush walks through its dusty dirt tracks winding through wild fruit and nut plants, where we used to play hide and seek games. Its warm comfort, security and magnetic pool, were difficult to forget. I always missed my mutinous friends, the aroma of Mom's open kitchen and cuisine, cooked on fire in an earthen pot and the great care and affection with which she was feeding me. It is now said that feeding with love has more nutritional value than food itself.

In those days, cooking was quite an effort-an exercise full of health hazards. Mom would use a chullah, an oven made of mud, for burning the wood, coal, animal dung cakes, as fuel to heat, boil and bake. To ignite these, she would fix one end of a foot-long bamboo pipe to her mouth and the other end to the chullah puffing and pumping air to fire the fuel with help of a burning charcoal, borrowed from our neighbor. Match boxes were a luxury. If the wood is wet, she would puff and cough inhaling through swathes of billowing smoke. The morning after, she would wash the black dust off the earthen pots with water soiling her saree, face and hands. Household air pollution from burning of solid fuels is a big health risk for women in the poorly ventilated kitchens in rural households. In retrospect, I suspect this might have also contributed to the premature death of many women in my village at early age.

In winter, after the supper, all of us used to sit round the chulla still hot with burnt charcoal. As we dumped into the dying fire twigs and scraps of wood to keep it burning, mom would ask about what we did in the school and then narrate stories from the epics. Dad would explain his struggle, the challenges he faced early in life as an adopted child, the support he got from friends and relatives and the troubled history of the village. Then both of them would discuss family expenditure and accounts, which were of little interest to us. I also pined for my childhood boy and girl friends with whom I was exploring and testing the reality of life. One day, news came about Panchi's sudden death. Her parents had married her off at the age 13. After pregnancy, she died of post natal complications. I was terribly upset but could not go to see even her dead body. I didn't have the needed money nor did any friend come to help out. Before being married off, she used to steal sweetmeats from her house to present me with lots of innocent affection. One day, she was caught in the act and verbally lashed by her mother for this 'crime'. Though very possessive, she was also a forgiving girl and would ignore my teasing, mistakes and indiscretions.

Although we were of the same age group, she was more mature. As she grew up in years, I could see in her both feminine delicacy and maternal love growing stronger. A week before her marriage, she had told me that she had not seen her future husband and had no idea how he looked like. But she was optimistic that he must be good and promised to invite all of us to her new home. After the tragic end of her life, her husband remarried within six weeks.

Life in the hostel was getting difficult for me for want of the little money I needed to survive. Unable to manage further, I quit the studies and took up a job as a junior teacher in a rural school when I was about 15 plus and where most of my students in the school were older and taller. The monthly salary was forty five rupees or about less than one dollar. Food and accommodation was free as I was also made the hostel superintendent, taking care of another 39 boarders. Coming from the farming class, who send their children late to the school, most of them were of my age group and even older. By extra coaching to weaker students, I earned another half a dollar which I was remitting to father every month as support.

Then within six months, repeated pressures came from parents to marry. I was really scared as it would mean the end of my dream of any further study. Early marriage was the prevailing social norm. To break my resistence, dad referred to Gandhi, who, at the age of 13 had married 14 year old Kasturba. I countered by telling him how it was a forced, arranged marriage. No effect. So, to avoid this, I resigned from the job and left the place without informing any one. My aunty, (mother's elder sister) fondly called as Mousi all over India, went round and declared that her sister, Moon's son had gone mad. Because getting a job was so difficult in those days that only mad chaps could think of leaving it. However, this first experience had helped me in two ways. First, in honing my skills and cutting the teeth as a teacher.

Probably, the opportunity of teaching children sowed in me the seed of a desi fire to become a teacher in addition to my own native weakness to spend more time in life with young students, learned teachers and library. So, before I finished my formal education as a student I had become a teacher four times-in a primary school, in a secondary school, in college and university.

Second, I had by now saved some money to pursue higher study, at least for a year, which I completed without much problem. In second year, the principal of the college waived my tuition fee applying a 'merit- cum- poverty' formula. A local lawyer offered two free meals every day. The zamindar (land lord) of my village gave me free shelter in his city transit house in exchange of working as a caretaker. Another teacher offered to meet the cost of my text books. A small business man asked me to do private tution for his school going child for 20 rupees per month (less than half a dollar).

Now, things looked brighter and the struggle tolerable. I became more resilient and life goals appeared to be achievable. Famous historian and thinker Arnold Toynbee had developed a simple formula called 'Mechanism of Challenge-response'. According to this formula, a problem creates a challenge, this challenge leads to a response and eventually the response results in success. Soon, I graduated with honours and distinction and wanted to do my post graduate degree. Father was very concerned. He again wanted me to take up a job and mobilized senior members of the family to dissuade me from pursuing higher studies. It didn't work as I was determined and went ahead without any assured support. It was a high risk decision.

During this period, after going through Swamy Vibekanand's fascinating life story, I was running after a number of Godmen called Baba. Once a Baba, after knowing that I was also visiting another godman, felt very unhappy, said it was wrong and advised me to stop that. When he repeated it couple of times, I respectfully quoted a line from the scripture which meant : 'As a bee goes from flower to flower in search of honey, a real seeker moves from Guru to Guru (spiritual teacher) in search of wisdom'. He didn't like it. However, one great person who impressed me the most was Girinariwant Baba, who had crossed 115 years by the time I met him. Many believed he was 150. He used to live inside a sandy cave like hole on the sea beach in Puri, a temple city, when his followers persuaded him to shift to a small cottage nearby for their convenience. I met him for the second time in this cottage following a group of Pundits (scholars) from a local Sanskrit college where I was studying for some time.

When we reached the place, an older disciple greeted us with a smile and gently led us to an enclosure where we found the Baba sitting cross-legged, closed eyes and naked on a straw mattress in a meditative position. There was absolute silence and a serene aura about him in the faintly lighted place with a stone surface. We waited there for about an hour alongwith the other devotees. Then he opened his eyes and smiled at us. The pundits were introduced. One of them said they have had come with a few questions. 'Ok, go ahead,' said the Baba, in Sanskrit, with another winsome smile. "We wanted to know whether you think there is a God,' asked the second pundit. 'Does he really exist?' The third one asked. 'Is there an afterlife? The fourth one questioned straight away.

Disciples sitting nearby appeared to be embarrassed by such direct questions. They didn't know that these Pundits represented the atheistic tradition of Indian philosophy. Out of the six schools of Indian philosophical thoughts, four are theistic and two, called Samkhya and Mimansa, question the existence of God. They believe that human action or karma itself was enough to create the necessary circumstances to enjoy fruits of action. Mimansa propounds dual existence of nature (prakriti) and spirit (purush), in which there is no place and space for God or Ishwar. Even Rigveda, the oldest of all the Vedas steers clear of creator God and creation universe. There is no idol or image worship in Vedas either.

Another ancient Indian philosopher of the atheist school, Carvaka (600 BCE) rejects outright metaphysical concepts like afterlife, reincarnation, extra corporeal soul and efficacy of religious rites. A Hedonist and materialist, he used to advise his followers to enjoy life to the full even if it meant begging and borrowing. He believed Death was a full stop, once buried or cremated you would never return. All talk of rebirth is nonsense.

Dharmakirti, a famous 7th century Budhist scholar, gives a list of five symptoms of insanity in believers whom he defines as idiots. These are-the one who thinks that the Vedas are holy, divine and the last words of god, one who believes that there is a God- creator for the world, one who bathes in holy water for purity, one who has vanity about his/her caste and the one who performs rituals to be absolved of sins. A popular cinema actor–director, Kamal Hassan puts the debate and the perspectives more succinctly in Dasavataar, the Ten Incarnations of God, by saying: 'I don't say God doesn't exist, I just say that it would be good if God existed.'

Now, back to the Baba. I was really eager to know how and what would be his response to the existential question. Unlike many of us, he seemed to be the least bothered or embarrassed by the question and with half a smile, said: "Dear sirs, let me take up the last question first. There is no such thing as death in real sense. It is an idea that lives in our mind. Like the universe. It exists because of our consciousness of it. Life always returns to bloom again and again in the multiverse.' The pundits looked perplexed but kept quiet. 'As regards God,' he continued 'if you think S(he) exists, then S(he) exists and if you think 'S(he)' does not exist, 'S(he)' does not". In this one sentence, Baba floored every one and synthesized the varied theist, atheist, agnostic and religious traditions and perceptions about God. Einstein had said once that "without science religion becomes lame and without religion and ethics, science becomes blind." I thought Girinarwant was less judgemental and one step ahead of Einstein in this matter. His smart answer generated many more questions for the closed minds. The pundits persisted with the next question: 'But then what about you? Then the Baba said: 'I think and feel that god is within all as well as outside all. The one who sees all things and beings in his own self and his own self in all things and beings, can only realize him. In fact, God does not exist the way you assume or imagine him to be.'

Around 5th century BCE, Xenophanes of Greece had said something similar: 'Mortals mistakenly consider that gods are born and have bodies, clothes and speech like their own.' Predictably, most Indian gods are more or less like imitations of their own men and women. All Ethiopian deities are snub- nosed and black; all Thracian deities have light blue eyes and red hair. Similarly, if a cow or a bull or a tiger or a lamb had the option and capacity to imagine and paint pictures of their own gods, they would paint them just like themselves. French philosopher and writer, Voltaire was right when he said: 'If God created us in his own image, we have more than reciprocated' by creating God in our own image. It is said that the image worshipping Koraish tribe of Mecca had assembled inside a walled compound, hundreds of deities of middle East and India to attract the rich traders to their ancient town. In 629 CE, Prophet Mohammed, after winning Mecca, had put all these images of deities and built a rectangular cube called Kaaba, similar to the Jewish temple of Solomon which contained nothing except the formless living spirit of all the deities..

Years after, I chanced upon the reflections of a Sufi saint which said: 'I searched for God and found only myself. I searched for myself and found only God'. Reflecting the mood ages after, Shery Hostetler, a contemporary Mennonite poet and pastor in her poem instructions, writes: 'Give up the world; give up self; and finally give up God...' However, after listening to Girnar Baba, I stopped running after the monks and the Gurus. Now, I could see and understand the purpose of life more clearly. My spiritual quest was over. I realized that it is a sheer waste of time debating, arguing, and quarrelling endlessly and fruitlessly on the issue. It hardly matters if god existed or not, as long as we go on doing our duties and responsibility to each other, in building a moral world order.

Religion has already played out its role in developing concept of god as an all observing Deity, writing scriptures to interpret His words, building architecture and artistry of divinity, framing moral code of conduct, taming the wild and unruly, establishing social order out of chaos and creating a super state. And, of course, building both bridges and barriers. Struggling for daily survival and security created among humans a craving for supernatural succour. Even, a scientist like Coperenicus, was living in Church to pursue his experiments in relative safety and peace.

Fifty years after meeting Girnar Baba on 4th July, 2012, five thousand scientists, working for ten years, discovered the Higgs-Boson particle, now called the God particle. Physics defines matter as a combination of particles, molecules, atoms and sub atoms. Our physical bodies are made of recycled carbons and hydrogen and virtually balls of concentrated energy. They keep changing. In fact, 65 percent of our DNA is the same as that of a banana and 98 percent, that of a fruit fly. Our mind is a form of this matter, operating at a higher energy level and consciousness is inherent in energy and vibration level. This infinite spiritual substance, say meditation and yoge experts, permeates the entire infinite universe and multiverse.

In positive visualization, one fixes the mind on this energy, mobilizes the resources of the sub conscious to reach the goal. Olympic coaches use it to win medals. The recent discovery of the 'God particle' corroborates this principle. It was the particle that turned the formless into the form, the floating invisible cosmic debris from Big Bang into stars, planets and finally life. In a sense, it was the Bramha, the original 'creating principle' in mythology. Like the water particles inside a glass tumbler absorbing the pieces of chalk and cheese inside it, remaining still invisible. Bhagbat Gita, the ancient Song Divine, describes how only the ignorant are eager to convert the 'formless' into forms through totems, images and a variety of objects.

10

Migrant Seeds, Burnt Certificates

The plane was flying fast over a cloudless sky. I took one more glance down below at mother Earth, our home in space, cloaked in a thin layer of air. It was looking so peaceful and so forgiving, despite so many attacks on it, by mindless maniacs. Coincidentally, the world was observing the 67th anniversary of Hiroshima bombing from an aircraft, in August, 1945, that killed 140,000 people and maimed innumerable. Three days later, another atom bomb was dropped from a military plane on Nagasaki, killing 70,000 more. The two days science turned malign, scientists lost moral authority and politicians, their principles. I'm doubtful whether the lesson has been learnt.

About 35 years ago in 1981, we had launched a massive Green earth programme called 'Youth for Ecology and Peace', involving a million young people from the universities. It was a hot humid day in June and I was sitting in my work station in Utkal University in Eastern India, coordinating the campaign and tying up the loose ends. Then the door opened with a creek and a frail old person with a flowing beard, saintly visage and green head gear, entered the room. He introduced himself: 'I am Sundarlal Bahuguna, have come to meet your volunteers who are doing excellent work in planting trees and saving mother earth.'

I was totally taken aback and humbled by the sudden appearance of this internationally well known promoter of Chipko movement. In the 70s, women were in the forefront of this movement physically hugging the trees from the timber mafia in the Himalayan region. Excited, I called up the vice chancellor's office to fix up an appointment but he had left for lunch, so I contacted his residence and was informed that he was taking his siesta. Sundarlal said: 'Don't bother the VC; rather I would like to talk to children. Can you take me to a school?' Then the VC came on line. I told him: 'Sir, Mr Sundarlal Bahuguna is here and we can meet you if you agree.'

'Who is Sundarlal Bahuguna? He enquired.

'He is the renowned environmentalist, Gandhian and promoter of Chipko movement, sir,' I said.

'What is Chipko?' He asked again. Shocked by his ignorance, I explained to him about it in some detail as to how it has become an international model of eco feminism.

'What is eco feminism? He asked once again and I had to explain in some more details. Sunderlal was overhearing our conversation.

The VC returned to office an hour later and I ushered in Sundarlal to his chamber. A greater shock was in store. The VC neither looked up nor offered him a seat and when I introduced, he asked curtly, 'By the way, what is your qualification Mr. Bahuguna?'

Sundarlal replied with a smile: 'Mr Vice Chancellor, I have burnt all my certificates.'

A shocked VC now looked up and was groping for words for a response. Having spent a life time examining students and now awarding degrees and certificates, he could not imagine how some one could burn his own certificates. The meeting ended in a disaster as he pressed the bell calling the next visitor.

The irony was that a week later, he was selected by the government as the Chairman of a Board that worked for prevention and control of environmental pollution through public awareness and state action! Such things ceased to shock me, particularly after I heard from a senior public works official, about how a Deputy Prime Minister, who was staying in a quarter inside the sprawling estate of the President of India, removed overnight a 200 year old tree to build a cowshed. When he passed away, a nature park was dedicated to his memory!

Later in life, when I was travelling to attend a conference in a university in Garwal, a professor teaching there, narrated how the movement started in the seventies. Popularly called Chipko, which meant 'hugging' in vernacular, it was a women's initiative in the Garwal region of hilly Uttarakhand in India. It followed the Gandhian methods of satyagraha or non-violent resistance, by hugging trees to protect them from being felled by the govt. authorized timber mafia. The landmark event in this struggle took place precisely on March 26, 1974, when a group of peasant women in Reni village, in Chamoli district, led by a forty year old widow Gaura Devi, acted against rapid man-made deforestation. And reclaim their traditional forest rights that were threatened by the contractor system of the state Forest Department.

These brave women demolished the cement bridge used for timber transport, chased away the tree cutters and timber traders and stood there guarding trees for seven days until their men folk returned. Sunderlal was the first to break this story to the world. The innovative method of public protest inspired hundreds of eco activist groups at the grassroots level and spread positive messages about the link between environment and empowerment.

Consequently, this triggered formulation of people-sensitive forest policies and public opinion against open felling of trees in regions as far reaching as Vindhyas and the Western Ghats. Historically, the first recorded Chipko like event however, took place in village Khejarli of Jodhpur district, in 1731, when 363 animal and tree loving Bishnois, led by Amrita Devi had protected green Khejri trees, considered sacred by the community, by hugging them. It is said that they braved the axes of loggers sent by the local ruler by refusing to relent. In the meanwhile Gaura Devi had also passed away in 1991.

These women didn't have certificates or academic degrees. For, knowledge has taught us how to dominate nature, not how to connect with it, not how to love it and save it. Certificates have given social mobility, created professors and officers, brought success and fame but failed connecting science with the sacred, in making the earth habitable and humane. More than certificate holders, what are needed are generations of thoughtful and caring crusaders and true lovers of the earth and its life systems, who have the convictions to be compassionate and work for its restoration. Coming closer to nature is getting closer to the spiritual world.

After the disastrous meeting with the VC that made me feel

ashamed of my university, I gently suggested to Sunderlal if he would also like to meet the new Vice Chancellor, Prof. M.N. Das, designated to succeed the outgoing one. He readily agreed when I mentioned that the new one was a famous historian so when I talked to the successor VC about it, he was extremely happy and came down to my room to meet Sunderlal about whom he said he had heard a lot. Both of them chatted for an hour about the history of the climate change and environment issues.

Then as the meeting was about to end, he asked Sunderlal,

'Do you know when, how and why India and many East Asian countries after that lost their freedom to the British and the Dutch?

'I am exactly not sure. Is it after the Battle of Plassey?' He asked feeling uncertain.

'Yes, you are correct, but do you know how and why?' Sunderlal had no clue and looked blank. Then Das told him – 'It was because of the environment factors and precisely climate change.'

Bahuguna was suddenly excited. 'Tell me Professor, tell me, I didn't know that,' he said eagerly.

The professor now narrated how the real culprit was the unpredictable 'June weather'. The battle had taken place at Palashi in Bengal on 23 June 1757, leading to a decisive British East India Company victory over the Nawab of Bengal and his French allies. This established the Company rule in South Asia, which later on, expanded over much of the South East Asia for the next hundred years. The victory greatly helped in the control of South Asia by the colonial powers. It enabled the British to wield enormous influence over the Nawab's territory and extract large amounts of concession and revenue from trade and commerce. The Company used this revenue to increase its military might and push the other European colonial powers such as the Dutch and the French out of South Asia. This led to further expansion and consolidation of the British Empire in Asia that continued for the next two hundred years.

'This is what is written by the historians. But the real cause was different,' he continued. 'The fact is, the night before the fight, there was a heavy downpour and the entire quantity of gun powder kept carelessly in the open, got spoiled, completely disabling Siraj-ud- daulah's large army as well as that of the conspirators. The month of June heralds monsoon in India, but is also known for its unpredictable behaviour. So, finally it is the weather and water that decided the outcome and sealed the fate of a country for the next two centuries. You can add the rivers and deserts also. The three great rivers, namely Euphrates, Rhine and Danube and the two desert belts of Africa and Arabia preserved the great Roman civilization for a long time. In the 9th century BC, the Mayan and Aztec civilizations had collapsed because of climate change, ie. a long spell of dry weather. Mythological Kingdom of Ayodhya was on the verge of a collapse for the same reasons.'

An overwhelmed Sunderlal now got up from his chair and gave Prof. Das a warm hug for one full minute. It saved my day from another disaster. In the evening, Bahuguna talked to the youth volunteers about deterioration of environment by human intelligence and interference and how the youth are being robbed of their future source of sustenance. Soon after, I arranged another meeting with a well-known environmentalist and pedestrian by choice, Sadhamohan, leading a sugarless Spartan life. Like love at first sight, they had an instant rapport-both being mixture of climate activists and romantics, deeply concerned about an overheated planet. Both in their own ways were fighting the climate ostriches, who believed that exploitation of common property sources was natural and necessary. In The 'Plundered Planet', Paul Collier has stated that if allowed to run by romantics, the world would starve and if run by ostriches it would burn. However, we can lead a normal natural life without starving or burning. An intelligent balance between need and greed can prevent such extreme situations. Sadhamohan and I had started such an experiment long back with encouraging result.

He now explained to Sunderlal about this. Then we met another professor of political history who narrated the story of the origins of the plant world and how in many cases fruits, seeds and plants have also altered the course of life and living of the humans as well their history and culture and drew our attention to the role played by cotton, potato, sugar, tea, quinine and black pepper . How they have caused both wealth and exploitation, power and penury, and in the colonization of the world is worth an epic. A little black seed, pepper that grew in India and the East played a key role in attracting the traders to India. Popularly known as black gold, it was the only spice that made meat edible, as otherwise it used to be heavily salted for preservation. The city of Venice in Italy became prosperous and culturally rich with profits that came from this most sought after seed.

In seventh century, a popular riddle by a learned saint Aldhem of England, asked of the audience:

'I am black on the outside, clad in wrinkled cover, Yet, within I bear a burning marrow. I season delicacies, banquets of kings and luxuries of tables, both the sauces and tenderized meats of the kitchen, But you'll find in me no quality of any worth, Unless your bowels have been rattled by my gleaming marrow, Tell me who am I?'

As the Turks began to way lay the spice trade route, the Italians, the Portuguese and the Spanish looked for alternate routes to reach the East. One of these searches led to the discovery of America and the other to the colonisation of India. Similarly, the discovery of quinine plant was responsible in changing the course of history in three ways. It enabled the white man to set up colonies and expand empires in the tropics in relative safety. Consequently, sugarcane grown in India and the East was brought to the West Indies, America and Europe. The peopling of these countries by the "Black Slaves" was a consequence of the transplantation of sugarcane. Seeds of rubber plant, timber, tobacco and grapes turned out to be green gold and created a moneyed commercial class with profits from wine,opium and cigarettes . Timber shortage led to use of coal and steam power that sustained the industrial revolution. Similarly, the Chinese, who had a virtual monopoly of tea, exchanged it with the British for opium in 18th century, which contributed to the socio-economic decline of China.

It was again tea, which sowed the seeds leading to American War of Independence. Popularly known as Boston Tea Party, it became a rallying point for political protest against the tax policy of the British government and the East India Company that controlled all the tea imported into the colonies. The other black seed was cotton. Originally produced in India, Brazil and the Middle East, it led to the industrial revolution in the West. The popular tuber potato grown in the Andes was responsible in creating social tension and conflicts in England and Ireland as one group exploited the other. Unable to deal with repeated potato famine and seed scarcity between 1840 and 1850, Irish landlords resorted to forced emigration of their tenants, in an effort to 'solve' the problem. In October 1847, the ship 'Lord Ashburton' carried hundreds of Irish emigrants to North America. They were so much poverty stricken that most of them were all but naked for the period of journey. When the ship reached the shore, many of them had to be clothed by charity groups in America, before they could leave the ship. Many had already died of dysentery and fever during the voyage. The survivors re-established their old culture in new America, strengthened by arrival of another million migrants from their home country. They gave America two of its best Presidents-John F. Kennedy and Ronald Reagan.

Like Sunderlal, I had the opportunity of meeting and listening to another great Gandhian plant pathologist of Japan, Mr Masanobu Fukuoka, in the late 80s in Delhi organized by Centre of Science and Environment. He was in India to receive the Desikottam Award by Biswa Bharti University at Shanti Niketan. We were in the midst of a campaign for water conservation and watershed management sending volunteers to Anna Hazare's Ralegaon Siddhi. Earlier, I had already gone through Fukuoka's three thought provoking books: The God Revolution, The One Straw Revolution and The Theory and Practice of Green Philosophy: The Natural Way of Farming. The trilogy had created quite a sensation in the agriculture and farming world. Influenced by his philosophy and practice, a year after his visit, we had set up a Nature Farm called Sambhav, in a remote rural area about three hours drive by road from Bhubneswar in India. Fukuoka was making his experiments like zero tillage agriculture and 'do nothing' farming in a small piece of 3/8th of an acre of rice land in Japan. During the interaction, Fukuoka explained how tilling was killing the soil and how farming should be seen and done as a spiritual approach to life. He was telling through example that sowing was not essential as seeds would always find their soil. Plants out of such seeds in nature go deeper, grow better, and survive longer. Trees in hills don't need watering, while in biomass rich, man-made garden, their roots are starved of oxygen, often because of too much water. Air has 21 percent oxygen, water has only 0.0008 percent. Bamboos in forest first go deeper before going higher. The human civilization survives on the first nine inches of top soil. We have been destroying this outer skin of the planet, our lithosphere, by tilling, digging, mining, roading, damming, deforestation and cutting- earth agriculture and so on. Fukuoka's philosophy was an eye opener for many of us.

In the 4.7 billion history of the earth, for the first time one single species has changed earth's morphology, chemistry and biology! Fukuoka called nature farming without pesticides, fertilizers and agro chemicals as non-violent agriculture. Instead he was using fertilizer harvested from the atmosphere and the millions of bacteria under the top soil as tireless tillers to preserve the productive capacity of earth including its water resource, biodiversity and wild life in a better, safer and sustainable manner, blending love, learning and living. He was not even in favour of milking the cows for human consumption as the calf only has the right over it.

One day, during a discussion following my meeting with Fukuoka, a friend questioned the wisdom behind this principle. I told him, 'Imagine and think for a while, a situation in future, when a superior specie evolves in or appears on earth and orders forcible milking of all lactating women of ours for their children. How would you react? And tell me, who has given us the right to castrate the calves, depriving them of a normal sex life, only to be used as bullocks to till our fields and transport our goods or to make them our meat? He stopped arguing and kept quiet for a while and told me later that indeed he never thought of this angle of the issue.

I had a near similar experience in Indonesia, where, in 1994, I was working as a Consulting Adviser to WHO and helping in preparation of a country plan on youth health and HIV prevention. It was lunch time on the second day of June that I had the first culture shock. The waiter placed on my table a plate of hot rice and red beef in brown gravy. When I told him that I do not eat beef, he took the pieces away leaving the gravy. He couldn't understand when I requested him to change the the plate altogether.

The next day he served me with chicken Biryani telling that this was an Indian delicacy. When I told him that I do not even eat chicken, he took away the plate, removed the chicken pieces from the rice and served it once again. And when once again I told him to change the plate, he was confused. Then I explained to him that I was a vegan and what did it mean. So, this time, he rushed to the kitchen and came back with a plateful of uncut, raw vegetables. Frustrated, I decided to forego the lunch and moved to the Indian embassy in Jakarta the next day.

Before my tenure completed in June, 1995, my Indonesian friends in the Health Ministry and University organized a farewell preceded by a question answer and discussion session. Towards the end it turned personal.

'Why you people in India don't eat beef, it is so tasty,' she asked.

'No, it is not true, only those who believe and consider cow as the second mother avoid beef,' I said.

'How a cow could be your mother? Isn't it ridiculous?' Another asked.

The dialogue was hotting up and the host was now asking the questioner to stop. Indonesia, world's most populous Muslim country and its third largest democracy spread over an archipelago of 17,508 islands, is also home to more than 300 ethnic groups including Hindus, speaking 700 languages. It was inhabited by Austronesians about 1.5 million years ago. In addition to its predominant Muslim population, it also recognizes Christianity, Hinduism, Buddhism and Confucianism.

The liberal and moderate Indonesian society, over past centuries, has assimilated a lot of Hindu-Buddhist culture into its Islamic rituals including Ramayan and Mohabharat epics. Many of them still believe that Rama, the protagonist of ancient epic Ramayan, was born not in India but in Yogyakarta, the modern city whose original name was Ayodhya. Their international and domestic airlines are named after Garuda, the divine bird flying God Vishnu and Sampati, another bird character of Ramayan. Indonesia has preserved all the old temples and stupas as part of its heritage.

So, I didn't find the question offending or embarrassing. I was sure it was more out of curiosity. I said, 'Look, many of us, during infancy, grow up on cow's milk as a supplementary nutritional support to build body and brain. I personally was fully dependent on it during my childhood. She is mother in that sense only. So, how can I eat my mother's flesh? And do you know, even after death she donates every part of her body-her skin, flesh, bones, horns, intestine for our use. She is among the most innocent and gentlest of breathing creatures, tirelessly transforming grass into milk for all of us." The lady seemed to be convinced.

Then another gentleman stood up and asked, 'Then, you have no objection to meat of calf and bullocks?' I said, 'They are my sisters and brothers. We are an agricultural society and our farming is cattle dependent. The bullock helps the farmer like a brother in our labour intensive agro operations. Once we start eating them our agrarian economy will collapse.'

There was a minute's silence before another person stood up asking,

'Then you should have no objection to bull's meat?'

I replied promptly, 'Logically, he is the father, the progenitor of the cattle species. Without him, all your beef will disappear, but then it was probably a religious taboo in those days to preserve the species from extinction. Such taboos are there in many societies.' Every one stood up and clapped.

Then to reinforce the point, I narrated another incident that happened a day before Eid celebrations when I was in Dhaka, the capital city of Bangladesh. The morning news paper had flashed in headline the sinking of a steamer carrying about 200 cattle heads from a neighbouring country.

I asked the hotel manager, "Why do you have to import them?' He said, 'Our cattle population is rapidly vanishing.'

When I asked why was that, he replied with a sense of helplessness, 'Because, we have eaten up all of them.'

I concluded by saying. 'Although I am not in favor of imposing a particular food, I think that humanity, to survive, may have to revisit its food habits someday.'

Another gentleman intervened and asked very gently 'What about other animals?'

I said in all societies including my own, kindness to animals is a casualty. I referred to a sloka (verse) in Yujur Veda, that asks people to abjure all forms of violence and cruelty to animals and plants: "Protect and rear the animals: do not hit and kill the cow: do not hit and kill the goats; nor the sheep; nor any other creature; nor even two legged birds and animals; and you must never injure any loving being." Then

I quoted a line from Anushasan parva of epic Mahabharata in which Bhishma says: "The cow is my mother; the bullock is the father; heaven is my shelter."

Incidentally, many Indonesians are familiar with both Mahabharata and Ramayana stories, episodes and fables. As I was readying to leave the place, a professor of the reputed Gadja Mada University, well known for its research activities, stood up to offer the farewell thanks. He summed up by stating: 'More than you, we thank old India precisely for three important reasons.' I was curious to know and sat down with full attention.

"Number one" he said with emphasis on 'one', "Hinduism came here from your country by the Kalinga merchants and scholars and became a part of our culture. So, in a way, some of us think we are Hindu by culture and Muslim by religion." I had some faint idea about it, but not the details he reeled out to substantiate his view. He referred to the 1st century statue of Ganesha in western Java, the 'thousand temples' in Prambanan, the Jiwa temple in Batujaya and the inscriptions of the Hindu king, Purna Warman.

I was convinced. 'Number two' he announced, 'India gave us Buddhism, the second oldest religion of my country.' It came to Indonesia via maritime silk route. He mentioned how Atisha Dharmapala from India visited his country and how Dharmakirti, born in Sumatra, had visited Nalanda University and taught there. He referred to the Sri Vijay Kingdom and Borobudur and how the Hindu and Buddhist kingdoms had lasted up to 11th century AD.

"Now the third and the most important one for which we are thankful to India"- he paused and I was looking up excitedly: 'Islam-the religion of peace' also came to our country from India,' he said with a lot of satisfaction and pride. To me this information was totally new. The professor explained in greater details how Muslim traders and clerics from Gujrat in India had entered Indonesia in 8th century and consolidated Islam by 13th century.

I thanked the professor for educating me on the subject and told him, 'Look, let me tell you, in India also the word Hindu denotes more a culture and region than religion.'

Before taking the flight, I wanted to have a glimpse of Prambanan, the archeological site of "thousand temples". The original name of this 9th century temple complex was 'Para Brahman' or the 'supreme soul'. As soon as I reached the place, I could realize the truth behind what the professor had told me about the three reasons. I was over awed by the majesty of the three temples dedicated to Trimurti, the three forms of god the creator (Brahma), god the preserver (Vishnu) and god the destroyer (Shiva). The middle one dedicated to Shiva was the highest, i.e. 154 feet.

Pointing at the higher temple of the Trimurti (Trinity), I asked why the middle one was higher than the other two. He explained instantly in half baked broken Sanskrit: "It is simple, Brahma is Deva (a god only), similarly Vishnu is Deva but Shiva is "devanam deva", i.e. Mahadeva (God of all gods). He did not know that I was from India and knew a little bit of Sanskrit. But he had already floored me with his convincing argument. I have not seen a Trimurti temple in India where the statue of a Shiva flanked by Brahma and Vishnu. Similarly, except at one or two places, there is no temple dedicated to Brahma either. Another instance of how the 'created' forget the 'creator'. For want of time, on way back we had just a glimpse of Borobudur, the massive Buddhist stupa, in central Java, which had taken more than 100 years to be completed. By now, the flight attendants were serving a second round of tea, coffee and soft drinks. I had no appetite for these. The internal biological clock of my body had lost its rhythm. I was going through insomnia and fatigue. The plane had crossed several time zones. The world has 24 such zones, one for each hour in the day and each zone is 1600 kilometres wide. A New Yorker arriving in London flies across five time zones. Sleeping time in India becomes working time in America. A tiny part of the brain called the hypothalamus that acts like an alarm clock to activate various body functions such as hunger, thirst, sleep and regulates body temperature, blood pressure, hormones and glucose in the bloodstream, gets confused. The body gets unusual signals.

Doctors in aviation medicine explain that when the eye of an air traveler sees morning or evening appearing long hours earlier or later than usual, the hypothalamus triggers activities that the rest of the body is not ready for. This causes jet lag. Every time I visit USA, my daughter Gayatri would ask me to lie in the sun light for some time to give signal to the body that it is a day. My younger daughter, Niti, was doing a Doctoral course in Virginia Tech in USA and had invited me to visit her University which I did in 2010. She introduced me to one Professor Thurman Lock in the Industrial Engineering and Systems Department whose specialization was Locomotion. They were showing me various devices designed to improve the functioning of the human body and reduce pain.

I told him in jest: 'Professor, you are aware that the source of most of the pain was that nature had not designed the human body to stand and walk on two legs. Nor was it framed to fly in the sky.' Then I drew his attention to physical anthropology and how humans evolved from four-legged to two-legged ones` And since then how they have been carrying the burden of a full body in two instead of original four legs and consequently, how we suffer all the locomotion problems, including joint pains.

Human body contains 29 plus minor and major bones and joints, 123 ligaments, 48 nerves and 30 arteries, in perfect harmony with the muscles and blessed with innumerable motor skills. Its five fingers like five anatomical weapons had enabled and empowered Lucy to grasp branches and jump trees. Nature was not so kind to many other species in this respect, making them perpetually dependent on others for food and survival.

11

Free Thinker in 'Fine City'

As the plane started shaking frequently while descending, a fellow traveler sitting next to me got nervous and started vomiting. He thought the aircraft was going to fall and started praying for his life. When I asked why he was shaking in fear, he said we had all reached the end of our life and must pray for God's mercy now. A minute later, the bumping stopped and the aircraft became steady.

Fear of flying affects a minority of travelers who get panicky. There are chronic cases when such people avoid air travel for going on vacations, visiting friends and relations and attending work related business, always fearing a crash. One of the reasons is many of them do not know how aircrafts fly, how airlines operate, how safety is ensured, how turbulence is a normal experience. While some travelers are given anti anxiety medication, others benefit from behavior therapy.

There was a six hour halt at Changi airport before the next connecting flight. Some started rushing towards a coffin like small glass cabin for a quick smoke. The well organized airport has a place for each activity regulated by law. I saw a middle aged man wearing a tourist T-shirt with a cryptic message: Welcome to the 'Fine city'. Fine for littering $100, Fine for smoking in public place $200, Fine for drinking $300 and so on.

The halt enabled me to make a quick trip to the city to consult a doctor and also visit an old friend living in China Town, in Outram district. I love this City state and disciplined democracy as a development model and cultural melting pot with 'comfortable diversity'. Where a woman can walk in the street dead of night without fear, where in every sixth household lives a self made millionaire, where meritocracy promotes the best and the brightest, regardless of race, religion and socio economic back ground. A country where there is no minerals, no petrol, no gas, not much land, sweet water nor forest resources. And yet the per capita income is one of the highest in the world, where a multi ethnic population lives in harmony and peace, where people do not like to call themselves a nation but a 'society in transition'. It is also one of the least corrupt countries in the world where law breakers are caned for crimes like rape, rioting and vandalism.

Changi is an extremely well designed airport and is one of the best in the world, where 28000 people work day and night to manage over 6100 flights per week, connecting over 220 cities and 60 countries. It has the capacity of of handling 70 million passengers a year. I came out of this huge airport, got inside a radio taxi and proceeded to the city to meet my old friend Jin Ping. During our brief conversation, he repeated one of his concerns about the young Singaporeans who now prefer to stay single despite state incentives to marry and have children. Many have decided not to go in for children. And the decision for child bearing is influenced by cost benefit analysis, personal sacrifice to be made rather than by cultural norms and social expectations. Referring to the westernization of Chinese origin youth, he once again repeated what he had told me a decade ago: "They are like ripe banana, 'yellow' outside and 'white' inside. Globalization has made it worse now. Our five 'C' obsessions have now become 'seven C', he ruminated.

By seven 'C', he was referring to cash, credit card, computer, car, condominium, country- club and companion. The 8th one added recently is 'Career' as the Singaporean youth now place career and cash ahead of family. The attempt of the state to revive Confucian family and culturals values in order to influence social behavior has met with limited success. Spread of materialism and consumer culture are reflected in terms like 'shopping-mall kids', referring to footloose teenagers hanging around downtown streets. I told Jin that this trend was not confined to Singapore alone. While cash, credit card and computers have become an inseparable part of living everywhere, buying a car is difficult in Singapore on account of stringent pollution control measures. Vehicular pollution is now a major environmental and energy issue.

Singapore offers a better and smarter alternative to commuters with an efficient public transport system. But an apartment in a condominium, as against free-standing house, an expensive luxury, is a desire and dream because of the limited space. Unmarried young women usually expect their suitors to have an apartment. Membership in a country club is also difficult and hence a luxury. Young people here love to eat outside, relax, play and spend the evenings in clubs with their companions. So, marrying and raising children has been pushed down as the 9th priority! And those who go in for it are now ridiculed as Kiasu and Kan Cheongs, parents obsessed with breeding superkids, turning children's lives into nightmares, by their anxious, nervous and overstretched efforts to ensure that they don't lose out in life.

They go on signing children simultaneously into music, dance and drama coaching, phonics, mental arithmetic, swimming and athletics in order to make the child more competitive. If the first cousin's second child has a third dog to play with, my child should have fourth one-kind of psychology. I had seen in USA how the Asian parents, particularly the Chinese and Indians are jokingly referred to as tiger mums and eagle dads. Singaporians always aspire world class standards in all that they do. So much so that in 2005, when Singapore port lost its number one position to China's Sanghai, many people thought and reacted in a manner as if their country had been visited by a devastating natural calamity! The tiny city state probably derives its strength and success from such national pride. We were now rushing back to the airport. Deng, the driver, was in full control of the steering, assuring me not to worry. Trying to start a conversation, I asked how he felt about his job. Always focused on their duty, Singaporeans are not great conversationlists but he slowly opened up saying, 'It is very exciting meeting new persons every day. But my focus always is on making each one of them feel safe, reach their destination on time with maximum comfort and minimum cost, and of course to safeguard the reputation of my country.' Now, I asked him about the 'seven C's. He was aware and said, 'We have gone beyond that, our MRT is so efficient that 'car' is no longer a life goal. Similarly, 'country club' membership is no longer special. Our country is now full of community centres with club like facilities.

And I think more than the 'C's, a city's identity should be rooted in its cultural capital, the real 'C'. Impressed, I wanted to continue the conversation and asked, 'Deng, can I ask you some personal questions?'

'Yes sir, no problem,'he replied.

'Are you a Buddhist or Christian? I asked because about 33 percent of Chinese origins in Singapore are Buddhists and a sizable number are Christians.

'No, I am not,' he said, belying my assumption. 'But I like Buddha and Jesus,' he added.

'Then, I guess, you may be a Muslim?' I asked, thinking this time he would answer in the affirmative, Muslims being the second majority.

He said, 'No, I am not, but I appreciate some progressive ideas of the Prophet.'

'You can't be a Hindu either,' I said.

'Yes, you are absolutely correct, but I have read the Gita. It is very enlightening,' he said.

I thought he must be an atheist or agnostic but didn't like to ask. 'Do you belong to any other religious faith?' I asked softly, feeling confused and guilty.

"Sir, I don't wish to shock or disappoint you, but I am a 'Freethinker'. I believe that one doesn't need to follow a particular religion to have peace and happiness. You are finished if you want to see and judge the world through a religious ideology only as you can be chained to an old tree, in the same way you can also be chained to an old idea, to a religion, to a party and to a philosophy. " You are not an atheist I believe' I said. ' No I am not an atheist but I do not need a middleman's help to communicate to God. If God does not like the way I live and believe, I will welcome and appreciate if he talks to me directly, not through you. And if all His prophets left their graves and come to convince me, I would still stick to my own convictions". He finished the statement at one breath, without any discomfiture and now steered the slow moving taxi double speed towards the airport. I really felt foolish and small. This Singaporean taxi driver taught me another important lesson of life, which I had not anticipated at the time of booking the cab. No wonder that about 17 percent of the population in this tiny country of five million people do not have any religious affiliation. Many profess and practice secular humanism.

As the cab halted in front of the Departure lounge, I thanked Deng and apologized for the personal questions. He smiled. Migrating from village, Deng was living in a temporary slum like residency called Hukou near Shanghai. He had five brothers and six sisters, products of Mao's 'human wave policy' aimed at increasing Chinese population. The main job of the residents in Hukou was to service the city. Living separately from city dwellers, they had no property rights nor were they permitted to migrate to other towns or cities in search of better work. Unable to sustain a large family and fearing persecution, Deng's parents had migrated to Malaysia and then to Singapore during the 'Cultural revolution' initiated by Mao in China (1966-76), the movement which tried to strangle free thought.

Freethinking was a logically convincing philosophical viewpoint. It believed that rational human beings should form opinion on the basis of science, logic, reason and self awareness. They should not be influenced by authority, tradition, blind beliefs or other dogmas. Gautam Buddha, himself, was a 'sensible rationalist' and widely revered free thinker of his times and had challenged established dogmas and authorities urging people not to follow anything merely based on tradition or belief or without question. In 'Kalama Sutta', talking to the villagers of Kesaputta, about the virtue of free thinking and a questioning mind, he had advised them not to follow what they had acquired only through repeated hearing, or learned from tradition, gossip and rumor or from scriptures, conjecture, established and accepted principles and not to accept or follow something merely because it was 'agreeable to preconceived notion and belief'. In June, 1987, I was an eye witness to the impact of freethinking process initiated by Mikhail Gorbachev in the then Soviet Union, USSR, although in a different context. We are aware, how free thinkers, with their liberal outlook had contributed greatly for the abolition of slavery in USA and Europe. In the then USSR, 'Perestroika" (restructuring) and "glasnost" (openness), Mikhail Gorbachev's watchwords for the renovation of the Soviet body politic, had played a similar role. The difference was that Gorbachev pursued it as General Secretary of the

Communist Party from 1985 until 1991. I was there in 1987, leading a youth Art and Cultural delegation for the celebration of India Festival in the then Soviet Union. About six years later, in 1993, I had travelled to Berlin to attend the 4th World Conference on STD (6th-11th June) and could see its impact. One afternoon, we visited the site where the infamous Berlin wall was erected in 1961 to prevent East Germans from crossing to the free, democratic Western part of Germany in search of better future and lesser control regime. When the Wall crumbled on November 9, 1991, there were large crowd on both sides, celebrating the event with drums, drinks, trumpets, chocolets and kisses. Such was the excitement that a good many over happy and generous Germans offered the Easterners called 'Ossies' money to go shopping. Before leaving the place, I strolled into a nearby kiosk and bought a small piece of stone of the demolished wall as a memento.

On the first leg of our journey in Soviet Union, we had landed in Tashkent into a grand welcome by warm hearted Uzbekis, led by their Mayor. A helicopter was flying low over our heads dropping flowers and large crowds greeting and cheering us all the way. In the evening, we met a huge audience in the city stadium where I addressed in my working Hindi. I told them three things: 'You have given us a very big sweet fruit, ie, water melon. You have also contributed to our vocabulary, the most important word in any one's life, ie, Mohabbat, which means love. And one of the earliest scholars to have visited India and introduced her to the Muslims outside was also from your country. It was Al Biruni, who, in his landmark Tarikh al-Hind or History of India, had vividly described for the first time, Indian culture and belief systems from an Islamic perspective'. The observation was greeted with wild cheers.

The India festival in the Soviet Union was to be jointly inaugurated by the then Indian Prime Minister, Rajiv Gandhi, and Soviet President, Mikhail Gorbachev, at Kremlin's Cathedral Square. For the Indian delegation, the Soviet organizers had provided a fast running train called Maitri which means friendship. I was travelling in a compartment along with a Russian professor, Pavlov, who understood English. During the journey, he was very appreciative of the Indian Institutes of Technology (IITs) and its highly competitive selection process. He said that in his country, many students were not interested in higher technical education as there was not much incentives in terms of salary. I asked him to tell me about Gorbachev's ideas of Glasnost and Perestroika aimed at promoting free thinking and consultative governance.

Pavlov narrated an interesting story which, according to him, changed the mindset of soviet policy maker and other top comrades. It just happened when a senior polity bureau member was travelling by road and found a group of children playing with an unusual football which had four corners. He asked his driver to stop the vehicle, came out of the car and went up to the children to actually see what this unique four sided object was. And he was shocked to find that it was actually a big sized loaf of bread which the children were using as football. The real footballs being costly, bread was a much cheaper alternative. Pavlov explained that the highly subsidized public distribution system was responsible for this. Many small incidents like this must have made Gorbachev rethink about the prevalent economic system, which he wanted to change.

During my university days, we had started a campaign called 'Hundred percent Sanitation Village' and installed a toilet in each house with generous help from the government. A year later, study by an independent agency found out that none was using the facility and about 90 percent of the households were actually using the small cemented area around the toilet seat for washing clothes because in the mud houses and dirt floors, that was the only cemented area available and many non-users thought it was convenient, comfortable and healthier to relieve in the open. Access to water was the other challenge. We had to overhaul our approach and strategy altogether focusing more on behavior change.

In 1987, Gorbachev had referred to perestroika as a revolution, since the "qualitatively new" and radical changes which the Soviet Union required, constituted a "revolutionary task." Substantively, it meant in the political sphere, the introduction of genuinely contested elections for new political institutions. The process began in 1985 with an anti alcohol campaign, by raising prices of vodka, beer and wine and restricting their sale. Consequently, revenue worth 100 billion roubles was lost. A black market on alcohol flourished.

Glasnost also enabled writers and journalists to push beyond limits that even Gorbachev had not imagined. Inspired by this, people asserted the long suppressed right to freedom of speech and publication. The closed door for banned literature opened, including the the return of the 'Right to read'. Media exposed the past misdeeds, blunders and scandals including hunger, poverty and killings. The horrible Chernobil nuclear disaster and its consequence now appeared on the public domain. Central Asian provinces were shocked to learn how rivers in their region were turned towards cotton plantation converting their farmland into desert and so on.

In promoting glasnost, Gorbachev had assumed that it would enhance perestroika. But as skeletons of truth tumbled out of the cup boards of the past, the country became overwhelmed by the so far hidden ghastly stories of state sponsored terror and torture. One of the best ways to kill a great idea is to convert it into an ideology and then into a dogma that eventually destroys other ideas. This is what happened to communism. In 1917, the year of Communist revolution, Einstein had applied his theory of relativity to the universe calling it static, homogenous and curved and fiercely defended his belief and view. But as soon as it was challenged by the astrophysicists and cosmologists of his generation, with more convincing arguments, he changed his mind and accepted their view that the cosmos was really complex and expanding.

An announcement by the pilot brought me back to the present. The plane was smoothly racing ahead. I noticed some elderly persons slowly walking back and forth to fight the fatigue, while younger ones were glued to the television monitors. Some passengers were busy massaging the leg muscles to improve blood circulation. Some were chewing logenges. A few were looking at the screen to find out arrival time at the destination. A fortunate few were sleeping and snoring wearing eye shades and ear plugs.

Low cabin pressure was a constant irritation to my ear in addition to stomach upset. Doctors always advise to take light meals and avoid alcohol and caffeine. It is also better to avoid frequent air travels for persons with ear, nose, sinus infection and problems with heart, lungs and high blood pressure. Air travel is not a natural activity for humans because of which some people develop flight phobia. In fact, nature has not designed human body for flying.

12

How Big is Small?

As the aircraft was trying to climb above the clouds, my legs were getting tired without walk and work. The short seat had already made me feel cranky and cramped. A direct consequence of airlines competition for more profit. Why not an aviation consumer law as yet? Wondered how the astronauts were going through the rigorous and long training that included weightless flights, isolation and centrifuge tests, in addition to parachute jumps and pilot training in jet fighters.

I had read that the first woman in space, Tereshkova, had to experience a lot of nausea and physical discomfort for much of the flight when she orbited the earth 48 times and spent almost three days in space. With a single flight, she had logged more flight time than the combined times of all American astronauts who had flown before that date. And here I am struggling inside an Airbus-320 to keep my legs alive. Often a wild imagination becomes a thought which slowly transforms into an idea that eventually converts into a strong wish and desire that finally translates into reality. They first appear distant and improbable or at best a dream. And then over a period,the dream slowly makes its way to the drawing board as if spinning out of nothingness. Alex Pentland in his 'Social Physics: How Good Ideas Spread', wonders about the magic that small ideas can play in creating 'cooperative, productive and creative' social structures. Little things, innocuous experiments, small steps have a history of developing into big epoch making events and giant leaps for humankind, like antibiotics and Moon walking. Once thoughts considered crazy soon become 'things' and sometimes things happen overtaking thoughts, making life's journey more exciting.

When Khaled Saeed, a young Egyptian had a custodial death, another young person created a simple facebook page with a message : We are all Khaled Saeed. It went viral leading to a mass movement shaking foundations of many Middle- East. Countries. Seeds of an Arab Spring were shown. Another minor incident on 1st Dec'1955, inside Bus No 2857 in Montgomery, USA led to a mass movement for Civil Rights that created a great leader like Martin Luther King. On that day an African-American woman Rosa Park had refused to stand up and give up her seat to a Whiteman, looking straight at the bus driver, saying No, No, No.

It may sound to be a kiss and tell story, but I was witness to many small things and ordinary steps that, in much lesser measure, eventually became memorable events. One such idea was to reduce the voting age. The United Nations had declared the year 1985 as the International Year of Youth (IYY) and there were hundreds of celebrations all over the world including in India. As a preparatory to this, there was a national consultation in the south Indian city of Bangaluru in 1984. The participants were divided into nine small thematic groups.

In one of these groups, I had proposed to appeal to the Indian Parliament and request the govt. to reduce the minimum voting age from 21 to 18 years, giving eleven reasons in support of the idea. By end of age 18, young people have attained puberty, crossed childhood, completed adolescence, brain and bone growth, finished schooling, entered university, entered the adult world, become eligible for employment and work, to drive and open accounts in the bank and join the military to defend the country. Further, young girls, representing about fifty percent of the population, are also eligible to marry and raise family. Why can't they vote was my argument.

Nobody took it seriously and the idea remained hidden like a seed under the soil for some time. Then, Usha Banerji, a professor in Delhi University, who was present in this meeting, carried the proposal to the then young Prime Minister, Rajiv Gandhi, who was looking for new ideas. He promptly got it included in his party's election manifesto and had a land slide victory. Subsequently in 1988, through the 61st amendment to the Constitution, the minimum age of registration of a voter was brought down to 18 years and became effective from 28th March, 1989. This enabled tens of millions of young people to participate in the decision making process, changing the age profile of the Indian Parliament and state Legislatures for all times to come. I always refer to the International Youth Year as the one 'Year' that reduced three years!

Similarly, in many small group meetings and seminars, I had been pleading that we should dedicate one day every year for 'Voters' the real back bone of Democracy. Again, no one thought it was important. Then in 2010, we heard that the Election Commissioner of India, Dr S Y Quraishi, would be in Bhubneswar to address a small civil society meeting at the Centre for Youth and Social Development. We met and suggested the idea of 'National Voters Day', to welcome the new and young voters and remind the non- voting older ones about the worth of their vote. He jumped at the idea and requested me to immediately prepare an action plan justifying the need, which I did in two days. For me the alphabet 'Q' in Quraishi always stood for 'quick', because I have seen whenever an official wanted to know the deadline for an important task to be done, he would say: My deadline is 'Yesterday'.

So, quick thinking and quicker acting, Quraishi, convinced his colleagues and the Union Cabinet and implemented it in exemplary speed, with the approval of the Prime Minister, almost within one month. Soon, '25th January', the day the Election Commission of India was founded; it was declared as the 'National Voters Day'. On the first NVD, 60 countries participated and close to 800, 000 events were organized throughout the country, leading to massive voter turnout in subsequent elections. The media termed it as 'Participation Revolution' that changed the demography of the Indian democracy forever.

Similarly, in the late nineties, I had developed a concept paper pleading for a 'Youth Development Index (YDI)' to be used as a ranking tool and advocacy document to measure youth development around the world. Initially, the idea did not have any taker. Then, suddenly the Commonwealth Head Quarters in London adopted the concept as one of its new initiatives. It was included in the agenda for the Commonwealth Youth Ministers' meeting and subsequently in the Commonwealth Heads of Government meeting (CHOGM) which appreciated and approved the idea. Soon after, it became a global initiative. There are about two billion young people in the world today and the YDI became the reference and basis for evidence based policy formulation and planning for their development.

In the same way, in another small group discussion, during the International Youth Year celebration, I had suggested to setup a National Institute of Youth Development (NIYD), dedicated to the five hundred million plus young people of the country. A national level experts group, including this writer, was constituted to examine the proposal. We prepared and submitted the report to the then HRD Minister P V Narsimha Rao. As usual, the idea remained in the cold storage for years until Dr. S.Y. Quraishi, who arrived on the scene as a Joint Secretary and Head of the Youth Division, revived the forgotten prposal and pushed it to its logical end. The Prime Minister laid its foundation at Seriperumbudur where Rajiv Gandhi was assassinated. Now, the Indian Parliament has declared it as an 'Institution of National Importance'. There is a side story. Our proposal not to name it after any individual and locate it in central India was shot down by the then HRD Minister, Mr Arjun Singh. I have already narrated how in a small room in Shastri Bhawan, Thomas Abraham discussed with me the idea of making Kottayam, India's first fully literate city. The goal was achieved in six months.

There are many such instances that give one a lot of inspiration and hope and strength for patience to wait for positive things to happen some day. Martin Luther King (Jr)'s famous and inspiring song 'We shall overcome some day' is based on this robust hope. There are books about five, seven, nine best habits of most successful persons and effective leaders. But the only one habit has the potential to be a game changer. That is, an 'incorrigible optimism', a powerful tonic that keeps one's hope alive, despite repeated failures, to the end of life. Otherwise, K. Padmarajan, a 55 year old optimist, hailing from Salem district of Tamilnadu, India, wouldn't have filed his nomination for 165th time (2014) to contest an election after having lost 164 times. He describes himself as the election king of India. A robust faith resting on inner conviction enables one to overcome repeated failure and frustrations. Those who say that an optimist invented aeroplane and a pessimist invented parachute, are not correct, because the parachute was also invented by an optimist to strengthen the faith of those who fly aeroplanes.

Thomas Edison was right while explaining repeated failures of many of his experiments. He said that he had actually not failed but had just found 10,000 ways things didn't work. Through his few innovative devices, he influenced the every day life of the people, more than great thinkers like Karl Marx or Confucious, through their humanistic ideology and high philosophy. From pencillin to discovery of America, failures have produced great successes and have turned many humans into incubators of new ideas, leading to changes in society and civilizations. To generate crazy and audacious ideas, some enterprises even reward people for failing, so that they can take more risks to make new breakthroughs.

Long after, one of the friends narrated to me as to how a small soiled brown bread wrapper which he had noticed on a tray while taking breakfast inside a railway coach proved to be a big break in his career because the very next day, he had to face an interview for a top position in a multinational food processing company. The two piece bread wrapper carried in three factual and small sentences the exact answers to the first three questions that the selection committee had asked of him, ie, about the history of flat and sliced bread.

The actual words printed by the distributing company to impress the consumers were: 'Egyptians were the first to add yeast to bread, transforming it from flat to something softer and lighter. Otto Frederick is called the father of the sliced bread. Around 10,000 B.C, humans first started eating a crude form of flat bread, a baked combination of flour and water.' Once again, I realised the great power of small things in life, including even the throwaways.

Another funny, yet educative incident I was witness to was in a tribal district I was working in 1980s. The then President of India, Gyani Zail Singh, had visited the place during this period. There were thousands of tribal men and women gathered to welcome him. I asked one of them whom was she waiting to see? I was amused when she replied instantly, 'Don't you know, the king of India is coming?' Forty years after independence and after so many general elections, many people in this tribal heartland were not aware that India was a democracy and not a monarchy! Now, as the President was passing through the waiting crowd, a middle aged man with his child advanced to greet him. Gyani asked him 'How are you? Is it your child?' The poor tribal took offence and retorted instantly, 'Any doubt? If not mine, is it yours?' Fortunately, Gyani could not understand the local dialect and a protocol faux pas was avoided. It was a communication gap for both. The man thought that Gyani was questioning his paternity.

A week before this incident, a minister had visited a tribal village to launch some projects where a lot of poor people had gathered to listen to him and present their grievances. Towards the end of his speech, the minister announced pompously that very soon the liquor shop in their village would be closed down and a new post office would be opened. As soon as he finished, the people surrounded him, protesting against his announcement and pressing for cancellation of both the declarations.

The minister was confused and did not know what to say. Then, the village head man came forward and explained that they didn't need a post office as there was not a single person in the village who knew how to read or write and he insisted that the minister couldn't take away the liquor shop as long as they prevented the tribals from producing homemade liquor, a practice banned by the govt. Similarly, long back, in 70s, when I was working in backward Kalahandi, a large group of men had approached me to help set up a 'mahila mandal' or women's collective. I was greatly excited seeing so many 'men' coming together for women's empowerment and that too in a male dominated traditional village. But the excitement was short lived because, soon, I was shocked to find out that their real intention was to get free rice, wheat and edible oil, being distributed by the govt. through women's collectives, as a part of an American food aid scheme. For them, the meaning of 'mahila mandal' was free ration!

However, the post office incident prompted me to undertake a knowledge, behavior, attitude and practice (KABP) study of the villagers. Through a focus group discussion, we found out that most of the residents were daily wage earners. Once the wage work was over, each adult male turned a gentleman of leisure and pleasure. The women went out during the day to collect edible roots, tuber, berry, fruits, seeds, nuts, mushroom and leafy wild vegetables, some of which they sell for a price in the urban market. The burden of managing the household economy is mostly shouldered by women.

Alcoholism was rampant among males and ruining their lives compounded by exploitation. Many of them used to go to forest for collecting fire wood and walk back four hours to the nearest town with head loads and sell it. Then, they would walk back to the village corner liquor shop known as Bhatti, usually run by an outsider vender on contract. They would drink, dance, sing and totally unwind themselves there until midnight, living fully in the present with no baggage, no worry for tomorrow, fully contented and squandering the hard earned amount for the day.

The village had 22 households and the total income per household was about Rs. 1500 ($30 USD) which was enough to sustain a family of three for a month (1985). But none of them had any food in store for the next day. We organized the people and started a brainstorming and sensitized them on the issue. The women, being most affected, came forward to help and we started a literacy program that began with storytelling and ending with song and dance. The time chosen was the same time when the male folk used to visit the country liquor shop.

The idea was to provide an alternative source of edutainment to wean them away from the addiction. Within three months, the impact became visible. Many didn't stop by the liquor shop now. Instead of buying rice for a day, people started buying and storing rice for a week. The example inspired similar initiatives in other districts led primarily by women.

A tall lanky middle aged man named Fagnu was the first convert. He was popularly known as the 'Tiger man' and was almost a folk hero in the area, having rescued a dozen people from tiger attacks in the jungle. His tall frame, full of scars was the silent witness. One day, I asked him whether he was afraid of tigers He laughed, saying tigers are afraid of him. Then, in a serious tone, he said, 'Listen, if ever you come face to face with a tiger in the wild, just stop and stand tall, looking straight into his eyes and the big cat will back off and move away.'

Fagnu's main source of income was selling kitchen utensils made of wood to the fellow tribals. He had lost an eye while fighting with a tiger to rescue a village woman collecting firewood. There were stories about how tigers were scared of him. Once, I had asked him whether these were true.

He smiled and said, 'Partly. The fact is when I encounter a big cat; I look at him straight in the eye. He comes to know that I know he is there. Now, he can't catch and kill me by surprise, so he goes away to capture some other prey to feast on. Tigers are not as brave as they are perceived to be and always prefer to hunt by ambush from behind.'

Our anti-liquor campaign became stronger with Fagnu's support for it. He used to consume five bottles of alcohol a day but had now stopped consuming it. Within one month of his conversion and change of lifestyle, he repaired his old house with the surplus money he had saved. We used him as a role model to convince and motivate others. And within six months, the village was free from liquor addicts except three older people. Women were the most affected by alcoholism among their male counter parts.

Fagnu would tell the men folk in their own idiom about the need for saving, about how a dog buries bones for tomorrow, how squirrels gather nuts as future foods, how wood peckers store food in hollow tree trunks, how bees collect and store honey, how ants carry food stuff and preserve for a rainy day and so on. And the easiest way is to save is not to spend on liquor-he would remind them, just to drive home the point. Then, he would invite them to his half acre rice field and show the new experiments on how the 'rice breeds- fish- breeds- rice-' inter- cropping formula was working as win-win and explain how fish benefits rice plants by fertilizing through its refuse, eating harmful insects, pests and weeds and rice benefits fish by offering shade and reducing water temperature.

Then he would show them the upper part of the field where intercropping of pearl millet with pigeon pea and nitrogen fixing legumes in winter and spring make the soil more productive and his labor more profitable and how it gives him yearlong food security and freedom from indebtedness. He had succeeded in convincing and converting almost half of the villagers by the time I left the place to join the university.

One of the main challenges was the ingrained tribal belief in food communism and disbelief in individual property rights and disinterest in the virtue of saving than sharing. For instance, among the Eskimos, if one has a catch, it will be equally divided and distributed among all members. Sahano Bhunaktu (let us eat together) was an ancient Vedic practice in India. Some social scientists believe that individualism created wealth that led to exploitation and insecurity. Slavery was a byproduct of this process, they say. But I was immensely happy to see bags of paddy stored in the tribal households in place of bottles of liquor. Poverty and property can't live together under the same roof.

The first time I met Fagnu was near the sandy bed of a small river stream. It was noon time and a hot sunny day and he was busy digging the sand with a wooden stick. Coming nearer, I asked him why he was doing so. He first gave me a hard look. I smiled. He now felt relaxed. When I repeated my question, he said, 'I am digging out my food.' I was curiously watching until he pulled out of the sand a covered earthen container and opened it. Lo and behold! It was really hot food! He invited me to share it with him. I readily agreed as I had a second hunger, ie, to know more about it.

Every day in the morning when Fagnu went for work, before crossing the creek, he would bury the covered earthen pot full of rice, lentils and water inside the sand. Six hours later, on way back home; he would dig the pot out and have a hearty meal. The sands capture the heat from the radiant sunlight, lock and store it up underneath, that eventually cook the food materials for Fagnu, the primitive solar scientist. He was single, having lost his wife to malaria. The man, who rescued many women in the forest from tigers, could not save his wife from a tiny insect, the female anopheles!

Small little things change direction of life. Sometimes they may be creating history but also have the potential to ruin great events if not properly taken care of. Rajiv Gandhi, the youthful former Indian Prime Minister, was assassinated on May 21, 1991, at Sriperumbudur, near Chennai in south India. On a sympathy wave, the Congress party won the elections and Sri P.V.Narsimha Rao became the Prime Minister. On his initiative, Rajiv's birthday, 20th August, was declared 'Sadbhabna Divas' or 'Day of Social Harmony' for which he was working hard.

The first Sadbhavna Divas was being celebrated in Indraprastha Indoor Stadium, wherein 25,000 people had gathered. I was the invisible ghost writer and had prepared the speech for him in which there was a declaration for setting up a National Institute of Youth Development.

Narsimha Rao arrived on time and went up to the podium first to garland Rajiv's life size photo, light the lamp and address the audience. Diminutive Rao approached the photo and tried several times to garland it without success. Because someone had made the mistake of fixing the photo of the late Rajeev Gandhi, higher than the hand reaching height of the present Prime Minister.

He was terribly embarrassed in the full glare of media and the large audience, until someone had the commonsense to lift the three step wooden staircase and place it near him to perform the garlanding ritual, to the relief of everyone. But then, a second shock was in store. He also failed several times to light the lamp because the wicks were wet with an overdose of oil and dripping. We often neglect small things that mar big occasions.

The most recent one was the historic oath taking ceremony of India's new Prime Minister, Narendra Modi and his 45 member cabinet, on 26th May'2014, attended by Presidents and Prime ministers of nine neighbouring countries. I had taken an hour off to watch the ceremony. It was a hot afternoon and the event was being held in the sunny open forecourt of the Presidential palace complex with another four thousand dignitaries in attendance. Quite a few of them were ceremonially attired. While cricket captain M. S. Dhoni was with his black bandgala, Pakistan Prime Minister Nawaz Sharif was well dressed with a blue suit and yellow tie. Many Indian guests were wearing thick jackets and silk sarees. As usual, one of the best dressed was Afghan President Hamid Karzai, with his long overcoat and green, purple striped ankle-length cape.

But someone had forgotten a basic thing that the overdressed guests braving the abusive heat would need water for relief. There were parched throats every where and many were using the invitation cards as hand fans to fight the sweat. Unable to bear the heat, the son of a Minister fainted and had to be rushed to a nearby hospital for rehydration. Sensing the discomfort all around, Pranab Mukherjee, the President of India administering the oath, was trying his best to hasten the process. Commandos, deployed for security, were running in different directions in search of water for the thirsty sniper dogs.

As if this was not enough, DD News, India's official news channel, covering the ceremony, now started playing a mournful shehnai, a wrongful choice for the mirthful celebration.

Goof-ups goad event managers and spoil the dignity of important events. Someone somewhere forgets to do his job and consequently, the dignity of the occasion is spoiled. This was going to happen in case of the first swearing in ceremony of independent India's first cabinet. Pundit Nehru, the first Prime Minister of India, had submitted his list of cabinet ministers to the Governor General for swearing in. A little before the ceremony, when he opened the envelope, the small piece of paper carrying the names of people to be sworn in was found to be missing. Then, officials started scratching their heads and scurrying here and there, before the missing list was finally located and the situation saved.

13

Suffering the Stupids

It was a cold winter afternoon on the 10th of December, 2012. Consuming a fresh hot samosa from the Election Commission Canteen, I was chatting with my good friend and colleague Dr Noor Muhammed, a former Secretary to Govt of India and an international expert on election management. Then another colleague, Abhay, an experienced trainer, entered the room with a news paper and drew our attention to an interesting news item. It was about a legal notice by two students, Tanaya and Aditya of Lucknow, served on retired Justice Markandey Katju, Chairperson of Press Council of India. Katju was accused of making a derogatory statement in a seminar that most of the people in India behaved like 'idiots'.

'We are deeply hurt and humiliated by Justice Katju's statement, labelling '90 percent of the people in the country as idiots', they alleged. The statement about the percentage may be exaggerated, but there are innumerable examples of people thought to be rational, judicious and wise, suddenly turning out to be idiots, shocking everyone. In fact, higher the political and positional power they wield, greater is their idiotic damage potential. The Justice had made his point. Long before, popular advice columnist and public speaker, Ann Lander (1918), had made a similar statement in a more humorous way: 'One out of four people in this country (North America) is mentally imbalanced. Now, think of your three close friends.... if all of them seem okay, then you're 'the ONE'. Justice Katju was probably a bit more liberal in his assessment. In ancient Greece, people without basic civic virtue were being called 'idiots' and those repeating the same actions over and over and still expecting different results were called 'Insane'.

Even otherwise, 'glorified' people play idiotic games to abort and demolish new ideas. I had the misfortune of witnessing quite a few such 'idea aborters' and tolerating the absolute irrationality behind their behavior. 'Some believe it all begins in the family itself through hyper parenting, and the encouraging of baseless beliefs and irrational practices. There are stories about gods and goddesses occasionally behaving without any apparent rationality. Otherwise why would a kind hearted Seeta in the epic Ramayana ask Rama to catch and present her with the 'golden deer' and why did wise Rama, who should have known better, believe it and chase a mirage? By the time both realised and regretted the decision, it was already too late. Consequently, both had to undergo terrible suffering. Many Greek gods seem to have been complete idiots. One of them, known as Koalemos, was even worshipped as the 'god of stupidity'. Many led eccentric and weird lives. For instance, Zeus was a womaniser and constantly cheating on his wife. Sisyphus had a stupid habit of murdering his guests and friends. Pan, a shepherd and one of the oldest Greek deities, had the horns of a goat. He had a ravenous sexual hunger and would try to copulate with any animal.

In 1997, Laura Schlessinger, the conscience of 'Talk Radio', addressed the issue of human stupidity in relationships in her two best selling books Ten Stupid Things Men Do To Mess Up Their Lives and Ten Stupid Things Women Do To Mess Up Their Lives. She mentions these as stupid husbanding, stupid parenting, stupid matrimony, stupid sex, stupid ambition, stupid strength etc. But there are millions of things both men and women do together to mess up their habitat, mother earth and ruining its carrying capacity. Twenty percent of them now consume 80% of the world's non-renewable resources, blindly tinkering with the natural evolutionary process. There are innumerable examples of Brains busy destroying brains, repeatedly forgetting the lessons of life and failing to live peacefully with nature and its creators. As economics continue to push out ecology, humans with brains larger than that of any other species in terms of body size have now acquired effective means of their own self destruction. EF Schumacher , in his thought provoking book "Small is Beautiful – Economics as if People Mattered", presents a series of ideas as intelligent alternatives to human stupidity. He blasts the widely held notions that 'big is good and bigger is better'. In reality, we now live in an age wherein 'micro' has proved to be better than small and 'Nano' has now emerged as better than 'micro'. Schumacher concludes that the philosophy of materialism must yield to ideas of justice, self awareness and sustainability. And he finally advises us to work towards ensuring a balance between the four kingdoms, that is, the Mineral kingdom, Plant kingdom, Animal and finally the Human kingdom. The problem is, stupids neither understand nor listen and think that the human kingdom is the only kingdom on Earth and the first three only exist to serve the fourth one. Talk sense to a fool and s(he) calls you foolish – said Euripides.

Stupids always pretend to be clever but are actually uncritical creatures, devoid of perspective as to who and what they are, what they are supposed to do or why they are doing whatever they are doing and how it would affect others. Like wild unreasonable elephants, they often put the life of helpless riders at risk.

Carlo M. Cipolla, (1922-2000), in his famous essay on 'The Basic Laws of Human Stupidity', has asserted that non-stupid people often underestimate the number of stupids in circulation. In fact their number is as high among Nobel Laureates, eminent academicians, civil servants and politicians as among the ordinary, illiterate people. Philosopher Nietzsche in his 'The Anarchist' had claimed that Jesus was an idiot attributing it to his aversion towards the material world. In Indian mythology Lord Shiva also had similar aversion towards wordly life. But they were a different category.

On the other hand, greedy people with profound intellectual disability and acting in self defeating manner are also called idiots in some cultures. There is a story about a scholarly astronomer and weatherman in medieval Europe, whose profession was to forecast weather by looking at the stars movement up in the sky. Neglecting the family and children, he was obsessed with money making by forecasting the weather, sowing and harvesting time. He used to walk fast with his gaze fixed on the stars and one day he fell into a gutter and died on the spot. He had lost touch with the 'ground' reality.

Stupids are also known by different names in India like 'pagal', 'bewakuf', 'baiya' etc. In Northern India, a stupid is called a person who 'Nehin jaanta, nehin sunta, nehin manta' – one who neither understands, nor listens nor follows any advice. The Greek mythology had even a 'god of foolishness and stupidity' called Koelemos. Koelemos's followers are everywhere. The Election Commission of India, a respected constitutional authority had wisely decided to set up an Institute to promote capacity building of 11 million election workers it engages for conducting a general elections and also help young, fledgling democracies. On July 19, 2011, when the US Secretary of State Hillary Clinton and Indian External Affairs Minister S.M Krishna met for a strategic dialogue, both welcomed the initiative. The foundation stone was laid jointly by the Heads of Election Management Bodies of all the 8 SAARC countries in the presence of the Lieutenant Governor of Delhi. The UN and the Commonwealth Parliamentary Forum lauded the initiative and committed support. In fact, the then Commonwealth Secretary General personally visited the site and promised to set up there a democracy resource cenre. I was personally happy as I, as head of a working group had prepared the basic concept framework for setting up this institute. Then a key and senior devotee of Koelemos in the nodal Ministry with a "fertile brain" started working overtime to destroy this venture. An official letter was issued to Delhi Development Authority (DDA) to cancel the land allocated to the ECI Institute. Suspecting foul play, a confused DDA asked the Ministry to consult the Election Commission who had paid for the land. A surprised Election Commission came to know about this game only when it received a blind copy of the mail from the DDA, swiftly swung into action and called the bluff. Idea aborters lost one more plot.

Cipolla defines a stupid as one who causes damage and losses to another person or to a group of persons without deriving any benefit or gain for himself and even sometimes incurring losses He calls them worse than 'bandits' because even bandits follow a pattern of rationality in their behaviour and use reason to guide their actions in advancing self interests. Aristotle believed that ethically desirable behaviour could become one's second nature through training and practice. Sadly, this law does not operate in the kingdom of stupids.

We live in a world often fluctuating between stupids, crazy, serious, frivolous and funny. Once, on my way to USA in 2012, I had halted in London for a few days and stayed with a highly hospitable scholar couple, Sarita and Ravi of Odishan origin. After an early dinner, we were watching TV and I noticed that Ravi was frequently trying to reduce the volume of the television. When I asked him about it, he said that the British law was very strict about this in order to keep the neighborhood peaceful and noise free. Before I had left for London, the Delhi Police had already installed a 24 hour noise pollution helpline, so that anybody trying to keep the neighborhood awake by playing loud music could be prosecuted. Residents could call up and lodge complaints about the decibel overload from temples, religious gatherings, banquet halls or a loud party next door as usual some stupids continued the habit.

Next day, a common friend from the locality visited us. He explained how a couple in London were dragged to the court for indulging in noisy sex with porno music, disturbing the peace in a multi apartment complex. The accused, Jessmina and Kolin, were issued with an order requiring them to refrain from 'screaming loudly, moaning, swearing and raising voices'. They didn't cooperate and following further complaints from neighbours, the couple was charged under the Environmental Protection Act, facing a heavy fine if convicted.

In one of my earlier journeys to Berlin, I saw a religious looking man with a white robe in the front row middle seat busy adjusting the seat belt. Then two lady passengers came there, one assigned to the window seat and the other to the aisle. As soon as the ladies settled into their assigned seats, the man got angry, stood up and moved out, loudly calling the crew. As one of them rushed in, he rudely asked her to either get the two ladies vacate or assign him a new seat where there were no woman seatmates. It was a tall male order as finding a row without a female was quite a drill. Being an unusual seat change request, a bemused and confused crew asked about the reason. The man said proudly that sitting beside a woman, who was not his wife, was against his religion and not even an accidental contact is allowed. I thought, only a full body shield might protect such men from women as they were every where!

There are as many stupids in Air as on earth. On the return trip, I faced a funny incident and bit of a contrast. While feeling the pressure of nature, I went up to the lavatory door in the aircraft and kept on waiting for almost 30 minutes as it was closed from inside with 'occupied' sign on and sounds of banging and squealing were coming intermittently from inside. The door was not locked but was not opening either. Then suddenly a man and woman tumbled out in compromising position, to the embarrassment of everyone standing in the line. Their lip locked heads almost touched my feet. Fools always do things more enthusiastically. In another long flight to Australia, as soon as the lights were off, I had seen a couple in the middle row going flat out snuggling under blankets spread across three empty seats. My seatmate, a frequent air traveler, told me that in an earlier flight, he had also seen how an amorous couple had sneaked off to the lavatory for 'entertainment', putting waiting passengers into great inconvenience. Some high flyers have low habits. It is reported that recently a flight from Newark had to make an unscheduled stop in Istanbul as the vaccum flush system became unserviceable clogged with empty bottles, diapers, tooth brush, tissue papers, condoms and what nots. Many of Lucy's children have long forgotten the sense of place and propriety. I had heard from a friend who had just retired from an airline, about an informal 'Hot coffee and fresh fruit code' used by flight attendants.. It means an 'extremely beautiful and attractive' passenger in a particular seat, whom an FA could 'check out' with special attention in order to break his own flight monotony.

When Binny and I were staying in California, there was an interesting incident relating to a theft where the thief had dragged a resident to court, complaining that he got an electric shock while trying to enter the owner's house through a bathroom window. It was not a safe place for the life of a thief and so violated the human rights of the thief and his right to steal. Thankfully, the lover couple in lavatory have not gone to court against the airline for not providing a sex-safe toilet! In-seat sexual activities underneath the thin blankets are common in passenger planes but not the ones in lavatory. The fact that such scenes were not rare was confirmed by surveys on sexual conduct in the skies. In many a case, travelers feel embarrassed by lacy underwears left on a seat, in flight lap dances on a party trip, men carrying life size female inflatable doll and purchasing an extra seat for it. Once, frightened passengers reported a strange noise in the overhead locker. It was found to be an operating vibrator in a woman's handbag! Through millions of years, Lucy's children have learnt to behave in strange, funny and unimaginable ways.

When I got married at the age of 24, Binny was about 18. As per the custom, the bride and groom were supposed to meet and be together only on the fourth night of the marriage, the first in house traditional honeymoon following the wedding and after sitting through another daylong ritual and fire sacrifice called Homa. During this ritual, the bride and the groom would pray for healthy progeny with pure intellect and right conduct to uphold the family tradition. Then, in the evening , the groom is led to a flower decked conjugal bed room to meet and talk to the new bride leading to their first physical union, to experience their vital 'procreative energy.' The two souls are united in a sacred act of fulfillment. Both of them, expected to be virgins, are now to enjoy what was forbidden before marriage- with no veils, no barrier, nothing hidden, no shameful body parts. They become each other's garment and cover. An experience full of tenderness, intimacy, love and joy. Parents would wait with anxiety to be reassured that everything has gone on well.

The morning after, the couple would wash, go to the temple, seek blessings of God and then bow to the parents and elders for their best wishes. Some conservative, prying mother -in -laws would discreetly watch and inspect the bed spread to find out any blood stain from ruptured hymen- as sign of virginity of the daughter-in-law. I found out from my sister-in-law that my mother was also worried, but for a different reason because she didn't hear any 'love noise' coming out of our bedroom and concluded that probably there was no consummation of the expected union. After hearing this from my Bhabi, (elder brother's wife) Binny and I laughed without knowing what to say. Maybe, in those days, we were not as bold and noisy as Jessmina and Colin. For me, meeting a young beautiful woman in a semi dark chamber with so many excited people in the house was by itself an awkward situation. A close friend had already scared me enough by telling me 'Listen, a young attractive woman is like a speed horse, you can appreciate her beauty but can't touch or sleep with her on the same bed without injury.'

About 25 years ago, I was admitted into a premier medical teaching institution in Delhi for a liver biopsy. The teacher-doctor, bereft of any compassion, was so rude and insensitive; I had to quit the hospital the next day in protest. In fact, most of the doctors are emotionally sick, do not apply head or heart, lack basic etiquette, empathy and listening skills. Some of them even lack common diagnostic sense. For instance, a senior professor of gastroenterology prescribed me to undergo liver biopsy every three months, until I cleared the hepatitis virus. Another doctor told my wife, with a grim expression, to call our family members and relatives as my end was near. I overheard a bio medical technician, while giving the blood report, whispering to his colleague that mine was a 'gone case'. Ten years later, when I mentioned my 'carrier' status casually to a friend who was a professor of pathology, he put his hands on his forehead as a mark of sympathy and sorrow. Scared of infection, another close friend, who used to visit our place quite often, suddenly stopped coming. But today, I am still alive, fit and fine after 27 years of this nonsense and without 100 biopsies they would have otherwise inflicted on my weak liver by now.

A friend once narrated an interesting and instructive story about a doctor and a patient: 'Where were you for such a long time?' A doctor asked his patient. 'I have been trying to reach you for the last one week to personally hand over your lab test result, which carries very bad news.'

'Oh no! What did the result say? The patient asked with great anxiety.

'That you have only 24 hours to live,' replied the doctor.

Feeling greatly relieved, the patient now left the place without a word, laughing all the way! Long ago, Voltaire had said about doctors, who 'pour drugs of which they know little, to cure diseases of which they know less, into human beings of whom they know nothing.'

While in Singapore in 2001, facilitating a conference, I had some nagging pain in my lower abdomen and a little swelling around the testicular area. A local official guided me to a specialist at anearby clinic, who, after examining, asked me to instantly undergo a hernia operation. To convince me, he gave a number of reasons for this instant operation. I was to return to India by the evening flight. He asked me to cancel the ticket or travel at the risk of life. His face was expressionless and he avoided talking to me further and called the next patient. Confused and uncertain and without family and friends around for help, I left the hospital quietly and met another doctor for a second opinion. After examining, he found no sign or symptom of hernia and just prescribed two pain killer tablets. I reached my country safe the same night and my poor abdomen and the nonexistent hernia in the cavity were spared the knives and a forced invasive surgery. It is already 20 years since then.

Thousands of patients are persuaded to undergo ill diagnosed over- medication and surgery that they didn't need. Back home, I talked to an old friend, who was a senior orthopaedic surgeon. He revealed the painful truth about the main reasons why he left a high paid job in a corporate hospital. It was because of the highly unethical system of monthly surgery quota fixed for each surgeon to fetch more revenue. Thus, each incoming patient is perceived as a new opportunity for money making. The business model is to scare and not to share the correct information with the patients. However, the incident taught me the value of a second opinion in decision making. Narrating the incident to my wife, I told her in a lighter vein that as a commoner how luckier I was than King Charles II of England (1630-1685), who had 14 royal and loyal physicians. It is said that in their over enthusiasm to cure the king of sudden epileptic fits, they continued drawing 'impure' blood from different parts of his body including the jugular veins, plastering his bleeding sole with tar and pigeon dung, applying laxatives and enema to drain fluids, blowing poisonous powder into his nostrils to induce sneezing and vomiting and smearing his head with camphors and mustard paste. When he became worse, the priest-medicos took over and subjected his body to all occult therapies to drive away the 'evil spirits'. Finally, an exhausted, bloodless and dehydrated Charles died of ignorant doctors and their useless therapies than of disease and after suffering great agony.

However, without going through such experiences, I wouldn't have realised the value of understanding, empathy and decision making in life. Behavioural scientists say humans are 'pre programmed' to reach out. But then I didn't understand why so many of them are so different and so self centric as if they do not know a third word except 'yes' and 'no' and that too with a paralysed face. Maybe, they have not been taught as students, the therapeutic value of an emotion-rich interaction. Studies on doctor-patient relationship say that patients who feel that their physicians treat them with understanding, respect and fairness and communicate better, are more active in their own health care, now damaged by a passive patient and indifferent doctor syndrome.

About five years before this, I had moved to Bhawanipatna, a sleepy town in a perennially drought prone part of Odisha in Eastern India. About a month later, someone delivered at my residence a flashy card signed by one Mohanty, inviting us to the marriage ceremony of his 'child', Rocky. When I reached the place, about a thousand people had gathered, many with their pets, mostly cats and dogs. The area smelled foul with poop all around. From outside, the arrangement looked lavish and luxurious with a vulgar display of wealth. Pushing towards the well decorated marriage mandap, I found out that Rocky, the groom, was actually a dog wearing a costume-a lion looking Tibetan mastiff with round manes.

These dogs, known for their fierce loyalty, were used by nomadic tribes in central Asia for hunting. Now, they had become status symbols of the wealthy dog owners like Mohanty, who was an irrigation engineer in the corruption ridden public works department. He had two dozen dogs and his wife had another five dozen cats of different breed, in their specially constructed menagerie, much more than Mohabbat Khan, the late Nawab of Junagad in 1947, known for his obsession with dogs. So much so that, when two of Khan's favourite hounds mated after a long wait, he had declared the day as a public holiday in the princely state. 'New Nawab' Mohanty had beaten Mohabat Khan. He went on leave for six months to find out a partner for 'Rocky' before the mating season, spending half a million. The marriage ceremony cost was another five million Indian rupees. More than ten times Khan would have spent on the marriage of his two hounds. The irrigation engineer was busier with his four legged furries than the drought condition in the district.

Recently, I felt disgusted after reading a news about how Zimbabwe President, Robert Mugabe, celebrated his 91st birth day by feeding thousand of his guests with 91 young elephants, buffaloes, cows, lions and crocodiles, spending 100 million dollars in a country with wide spread poverty, 85 percent unemployment and hyper inflation. How would Cipolla define the likes of Mohantys and Mugabes in our society? I quietly left Mohanty's place just before the elaborate dinner was being laid. By then, the number of biped and canine guests had already crossed one thousand. It is difficult to say whether he was a dog owner or dog parent but I am sure the wise animals may be wondering about the height of human stupidity! In Iran, a fraction of such activity, would have earned engineer Mohanty 100 lashes in public, hefty fine and imprisonment.

In late 70s, I was working in another rural district in Eastern India. One day, when I was away from home, an adolescent boy named Bijay from a business family took away my two-wheeler and while driving, hit an old female patient coming out of the local hospital. The police seized the vehicle and apprehended the boy. After making several fruitless visits to the police station, his father, Kishan, approached me with request to use my influence in releasing their son from police custody. I made a feeble attempt without success. They freed my two wheeler but retained the boy. For the corrupt police, it was a big catch to extract money from this rich Marwari businessman. On the third day, Bijay's mother refused to take food. Hearing this, the next day, I, along with Binny, reached their house requesting her to break the fast. Hearing our conversation, the boy's 92 year old grandfather shouted at Kisan, 'You stupid, listen to me, don't further waste time, just throw two crumbs of bread at the 'dogs' and bring back my grandson.'

I was the other stupid, for I couldn't make out what it meant. But Kishan understood the message instantly and rushed to the police station. In half an hour, he was back with his boy. Later on, when I asked him what it meant actually, he whispered to me, 'Look, my old, ailing father is really very wise and it is he who saved my son. He always uses metaphors to convey a message' and then explained that 'dogs' actually meant the corrupt police and 'two crumbs of bread' meant a small bribe of two 'hundred rupee' notes ($4). On further query, he narrated how all businessmen maintained a 'Kutta Khata' or an account book for bribe taking 'dogs' and as and when such a 'kutta' died, they put a one rupee coin on the dead body as final farewell to the corrupt person.

Around the same time, a pundit, named Shyam Sundar had visited us at our residence to discuss his book. Too obsessed with 'purity and pollution', he declined to take any food offered by my wife, not even water. The next week, I met him in his house. He was a widower and living with his recently married daughter but he had a separate kitchnette and would always cook his own food with much difficulty. His daughter complained to me that her old, weak father was not allowing her inside the kitchnette to help him. When I asked Shyam about the reason, he took me aside and said in a hush, hush tone that he could accept food cooked only by an 'akshat yoni' or virgin, whose vaginal wall has not been ruptured and polluted by male contact and now that his daughter was married, she had become 'impure' and hence he couldn't accept food cooked by her! Obstinate Shyam lived and died a stupid. Ancient Greek and the Hebrew were using the word virgin more elastically, as 'people in their first marriage'. To the Romans, a 'virgin husband' was the one who had not married before and a virgin woman was one who could not conceive or has not menstruated.

It was summer of 2006 and at one of the Odissi dance festivals near New Ark residence of my daughter, Gayatri, I happened to meet Dev, a bright young Indian from Benaras, a city older than civilization itself and well known as mother of Sanskrit language studies. He had come all the way here to do a basic course in Sanskrit in an American University. It was like an English man from Britain coming to India to learn English language. Amused, I asked him whether he had heard of Anglo-Welsh orientalist and philologist, Sir William Jones (1746-1794), who, entranced by the Sanskrit language and its rich knowledge tradition, had spent considerable time in India with Sanskrit scholars of Benaras and Calcutta. After studying it in Benaras, India, he had described Sanskrit 'more perfect than the Greek, more copious than the Latin, and more exquisitely refined than either'. He also informed the world how Sanskrit was further related to Gothic, German, Russian and Persian. He used to tell his peers how under every inch of soil in Benaras, (Varanasi) lies buried more than five thousand year old wisdom tradition.

Many believe that this ancient city was the owner of one of the four heads of wise Brahma, the creator god in the Hindu Trinity. The story goes that in a big fight between the destroyer god, Shiva and Brahma, the four headed creator god, the latter lost one of his heads to Shiva. Now, a victorious and dancing Shiva carried this severed head as a trophy wherever he went, to show off his power. Then as time passed, the trophy turned out to be a liability, almost like an albatross round his neck, an ego he couldn't shake off. But as soon as he entered Benaras, the city of great Sanskrit scholars, the severed head dropped off his hand and disappeared, to his great relief. After that, the city of Sanskrit and wisdom became the city of forgiveness. The great Shiva now realized how one's 'ego', born out of power and victory, was an obstruction in the path of self awareness and must be destroyed through knowledge. So, from that day onwards, he decided to live in Benaras permanently. 'You have come from that mother city of Sanskrit,' I reminded him. Dev expressed ignorance and told that his father wanted him to have a degree in Sanskrit from a foreign university!

The next day, I came across a statement by American Indologist, Sheldon Pollock. He was concerned about the steady deterioration of the quality of classical studies in India and said that if Indian education and scholarship continued along their current trajectory, the number of citizens capable of reading and understanding the texts and documents of the country's classical era would very soon approach a statistical zero. And India would become the only major world culture whose literary history, would be in the hands of scholars outside the country. By contrast, in communist China, star scholars like Yi Zhongtian and Yu Dan have successfully rekindled the country's interest in ancient knowledge and classical languages by creative use of electronic media. 'Fast food' best sellers have revived popular interest in Confucius and Tao once again. Modern Indian historians now scratch their heads looking for missing links in history, some of which have now been found in China in translated Buddhist texts taken out of India! Hiuen Tsang (602-664), the scholarly Chinese 'prince of pilgrims', who travelled through India for 16 long years, had alone carried to his country on horse back, 657 volumes of rare manuscripts. So, now an Indian has to travel to China to know more about his own country! This is another kind of social dementia.

Culturally, India also has converted many and then forgotten. One of them is Mark Tully, author and former BBC correspondent. After going through a report 'Megasthenes to Mark Tully' (The Week, 2013), I had met Tully, now an Indian citizen, in May 2014, at his Nizamuddin West residence in Delhi. Wearing a Kurta Pyjama, the towering Tully was talking in chaste Hindi and Urdu spiced with wit and humour, fluently quoting from Indian scriptures and folklore. It reminded me of another visit and meeting long ago in 1986 with Svetoslav Roerich (1904-94), a famous Russian painter, who after marrying the then popular Bollywood actress, Devika Rani, had settled down in India near Bangalore. We were in the city with a Russian delegation, in connection with a Soviet festival in India.

Like Tully's, the walls of Roerich's house in Tataguni estate were fully adorned with paintings and portraits of ancient and contemporary India. Above the entrance door, there was an instructive message written on a canvas: 'Let us beautify our life, let us carry the message of beauty into every heart, and let us make pursuit of beauty our daily prayer.' Roerich devoted his entire life in preservation of ancient Indian art and cultural traditions. When after the meeting, the artist and actor couple came to the gate to see us off, I asked Roerich, 'Tell us one thing that made you stay back in India?' 'Hundred and one things,' he replied enthusiastically. 'Its exoticism, colors, nature and people,' he finished in one breath and then touching his flowing beard and pointing at Devika, he said, 'and, of course, my beautiful Indian wife.' Anything you didn't like? 'Oh, yes, some stupid Indians who know nothing about their own country'. 'Mark Tully comes to mind again. I had sent him three chapters of this book for comments which he misplaced and traced after months. I had kept quiet. Then one day I received an apologetic mail from him which said : You are most tolerant, first tolerating my tardiness and now my 'stupidity'. I was touched by this great new Indian who had the honesty , humility and courage to call himself ' stupid' !

Steve Jobs, the great American pioneer of personal computer revolution, gives another dimension. After living with Indian villagers in the Himalayan foothills for seven months, with his head shaved, wearing cotton robes, studying Indian spiritual traditions, Zen Buddhism and meditating in the mountains, he returned to his country and declared that on return to his own country, he had 'much more of a cultural shock' than in India as in America, he missed the culture of India, the 'power of intuition' and 'experiential wisdom' of ordinary Indian villagers left behind.

Occasionally, attempts are also made to block the mutual conversation and natural journey of cultures and languages. For some time, I was working in Jamnagar House, near India Gate, an office complex on Shahjahan Road, in Delhi, next to the Union Public Service Commission. Here an 'Angrezi Hatao' (Banish English) agitation was going on for months. Around the same time, a part of southern India was hot with 'Banish Hindi' movement. One sunny day in December, during a short walk after lunch, I approached the language zealots near their tent that was pitched over there. Some of the anti English slogans were written in English!

Reaching out, I wished one of them, 'Kalai Vanakam.' There was no response. 'Wunga peru enna?'

Again, there was a blank look.

Switching over from Tamil to English, I said, 'Good morning, may I know your name?'

He understood instantly and replied in English, 'Oh, sorry, I am Ram Avtaar.'

Now, I tried to explain to them that the language against which they were agitating was not a foreign language; it was as much Indian as Hindi, Odia, Urdu, Malayalam, Telugu and Tamil. They gave me an angry look.

Then I asked, 'Did you understand in which language I was greeting you?'

'No idea,' one of them said. 'See, initially I was greeting you in Tamil, which is not my mother tongue. It is an ancient Indian language which you didn't understand. And I had to translate it into English. I think you must first learn the languages of your own country before banishing English. It will enrich your brain and mind power.' By now, more people had gathered overhearing our conversation, so without responding to me, they repeated the old slogans 'Angrezi Hatao'- throw out English.

Holding my ground, I said, 'Listen, I am not a great defender of English, but tell me which of these two words is closer to your Hindi word 'Na'; the English 'No' or Tamil 'ILlai'? I gave a dozen such examples to prove my point, finally telling them how Hindi itself was full of 'foreign' words and terms and has even borrowed its own 'script', how 'foreign' languages have adapted hundreds of Indian words, how languages and speech have evolved through history, how English itself was a pariah in its motherland until 13th century and so on.

Some of them seemed to have understood the logic but blinded by passion, were not willing to accept it, nor ready for any further debate. I left the place as they started shouting at me. Aristotle was right when he said, 'The man asleep, mad or drunk may have knowledge and not use it, and this is the condition of men under the influence of passions.' The irony is that about half of the world today speaks languages including Hindi, Persian, Norwegian and English, whose source is one. In India, there is a highly popular Hindu deity called Saraswati, who is worshipped as Vakdevi, which means the Goddess of all languages and learning of the world. But then, both, Gods and biologists have also fought in vain against human stupidity. Because upright posture helped humans to have a better larynx and pattern of breathing and subtle movement of tongue that enabled them to form vowels and consonants and improve the quality and range of sound and speech.

After the encounter with the language lunatics, I had a first hand yet painful experience of a different kind of self centric half wits. The bizarre incident was a sample about how the so called 'dynamic' Ministers goof up with national honour and image. It relates to a prestigious international youth exchange and friendship programme initiated by the Japanese government called 'Ship of World Youth' (SWY) involving youths from select countries around the world. The participants live together in this ship and while on board and going round the major ports of the world, they study and discuss issues of common concern, from a global perspective. They also organize and participate in various activities that involve multi-cultural and multi- national exchange opportunities like learning each other's language, art and culture, food, life style etc to promote international understanding.

The process of selection being rigorous, we had initiated a national level competition and finally shortlisted 14 highly talented boys and girls from different parts of the country, including the North Eastern states. This process took about twelve weeks. The final list was submitted to the Minister for approval. Simultaneously, we alerted the boys and girls to apply for passports. The file returned in three days. But then, we were shocked to discover that all the selected names had disappeared. And in their place 14 new names have been recommended arbitrarily. The Minister's office also wanted the new names to be forwarded to the Japanese embassy within 24 hours. I met the Permanent Secretary, who said there was no other way, so we forwarded the new names. Then after a week, an official from the embassy informed that this time they were not taking any Indians.

Hearing this, the Minister became furious and wanted to summon the Japanese Ambassador. When he was told that as per protocol, only the Ministry of External Affairs could do that, he lost his cool and wanted us to convey his displeasure to the Japanese. But the meticulous Japanese had done their home work.They told us something more shocking; that all the 14 candidates recommended belonged to one state and to the Minister's parliamentary constituency, that no one fulfilled the eligibility criteria properly, and that the signatures seemed to be doubtful. And worst of all, to the question 'what is your area of interest in Japan', many had left it blank while others filled in the column 'No interest'. Subsequently, the embassy made its own selection.

I felt stunned and stupid. It was another sad day in my life and for my country. We also didn't know what to tell the genuinely selected candidates and I apologized to each one of them as all of them were bright, brilliant and highly talented. I was really angry within but controlled myself. Indonesian poet-writer, Toba Beta, in his book 'Master of Stupidity' says, 'If you are angry at stupid people, you are tempted to join them'. Later on, I was not surprised at all seeing a report in the media (ToI, 22 Oct'13) that three senior pilots and engineers, selected to proceed to Lisbon to receive training and fly back an Embraer Jet, were offloaded and replaced by non technical babus, who knew nothing about flying an aircraft! One compound term and word permanently missing in the dictionary of bureaucracy is 'lessons learnt'. Intelligence without understanding creates more stupids.

The other incident had occurred a year after I left the university to join the Ministry of Education, Youth Affairs and Sports. Youthful Rajiv Gandhi was the Prime Minister and had kept the Youth Department with him. Youth being a huge constituency (400 million at that time), he wanted to connect and address it directly. So, he asked the then Union Youth Secretary, to make a quick video presentation, in fifteen days, about the potential and practice of youth development programs in the country. The secretary called an emergency meeting and asked his joint secretary to quickly produce a video in three days. When the Joint Secy said it could not be done in the suggested time frame, he cut him short by telling 'The PM wants it, we have to have one, find out if any other organization has one.'

So, they scouted the country, sending messages to various networks but failed. The tense bureaucracy was scratching its head in despair. Looking at their condition, I met the joint secretary and told him that there was one which I had produced while in the university. He stood up in excitement saying, 'Great, but where? Get it immediately.'

I said it would be difficult because his Ministry had sent three letters to the university through the state govt, declaring the documentary on youth as a violation of financial guideline.

'Stupid!' He blurted out in anger.

I said it was actually produced by a creative young Indian named Biswaraj at half the market cost.

'Oh, that is really fantastic. The PM will be happy to know it was made by a youth about the youth,' said the JS, sounding more excited.

Then, he instantly called the Undersecretary, the same person who had sent the disapproval letters, asking him to immediately withdraw the letters in question and send post facto approval of the documentary by fax. Next day, an officer flew to Bhubaneswar and brought the documentary to save the day. The rescue operation cost 40.000 rupees ($ 800) while the production cost of the banned video was Rs.30,000, half of which was yet to be paid to the young producer. On 21st Aug'1985, it was to be presented before the Prime Minister in the Parliamentary Consultative Committee meeting that sadly ended with a condolence and prayer as the previous day, Akali Sikh leader, Sant Longowal (1932-1985), had been assassinated by four fanatics at the Gurdwara in village Sherpur for signing an accord with Prime Minister Rajiv Gandhi, to restore peace in Punjab.

The present episode, a development expert shared with me few years back and is about the chief minister (CM) of a poor backward state in India. On a warm afternoon, a team of senior development professionals were making a presentation before the CM with a detailed roadmap for lifting the state above the poverty line. But the CM seemed to have no interest. Every now and then, he would ask his principal secretary about something the presenters failed to guess. They thought it must be some important matter of the state. Then, the CM left the meeting briefly for a smoke. As soon as he returned, the presentation resumed. But within minutes, he started dozing. Trying to wake him up, the presenter suddenly increased the decibel level. On waking up, the CM asked the principal secretary: 'Yes, tell me, what is the latest cricket score ?'

I had the privilege and pain of experiencing different types of stupidity in many international events, particularly in drafting committees. In one such conference of South Asian Association of Regional Cooperation (SAARC), we had to spend an entire night on innocuous words, letters, colon, semi colon, dots and stops. In the Indian delegation led by Minister Mukul Wasnik, S. Y. Quraishi, Prabhakar Parkala and me were the other three members. While all the ministers were taken on a glass boat to witness the marine world, we were busy finalizing the draft SAARC Youth Charter, to be signed by the ministers and declared the next day. A representative of the UN was also present as an Observer.

Then started the verbal duel between Indian and Pakistani delegates on each word of the draft and any new formulation, idea suggested by India was bitterly contested by Pakistan, to the embarrassment as well as amusement of delegates from other countries. It was about 4 am at night and every one was getting restless. Then, the Pakistanis brought in another amendment objecting to some words in the Indian proposal that spoke of 'common history and heritage'. Now, Quraishi stood up and loudly announced: 'India fully supports all amendments and all ideas of the Pakistani delegation and we withdraw our amendments.' There was a moment of sudden and surprised silence. Fully floored by this unexpected gesture, the

Pakistanis didn't know how to respond. The draft was finalized in next ten minutes. We went back to our rooms to steal a few winks of sleep.

Cipolla was correct when he said that stupids were proportionately as numerous among illiterates as among the educated. Whether you live as a virtuous saint in a monastery or 'spend the rest of your life in the company of beautiful and lascivious women' you always have to face same number of stupid people there. Once, we were organizing an international workshop at Barog near Shimla, a popular hill station in India. It was mango season and as desired by the overseas delegates, we had ordered a few dozens to serve them during the breakfast. A few months after, I was shocked to receive an audit objection which said it was not part of the 'approved menu'. The clarification provided was not accepted. The auditor insisted on seeing the seeds of the mangifera Indica to be convinced. We didn't have these. Finally, a senior accounts officer from the London office had to come to resolve the issue. Thankfully, the auditor was changed. The cost of this operation was hundred times more than the cost of mangoes purchased for the guests.

When I narrated the story to an old friend, he smiled and recounted another very interesting story which was worse than my experience. It was like this: After the end of the financial year, a local income tax office sent its inspector to audit the accounts of a Synagogue, a place of worship for the Jewish people. While he was checking the books he turned to the Rabbi, the religious head, and said- "It appears that you buy too many candles. Now, explain what do you do with the candle drippings?" A disturbed Rabbi replied, "We collect and send it back to the candle makers, and every month they send us a free box of candles."

'And what do you do with boxes?

'We burn these for heat in winter,' replied the Rabbi.

The auditor, somewhat disappointed and asked once again in his obnoxious way, "I have found that you people buy a lot of bread and also some knives. What do you do with knives and the bread crumbs?" Realizing that the inspector was once again trying to trap him, he said, "We buy the knives to cut the breads and send the crumbs back to the bread maker.'

'Free?'

'No, they send us a free box of bread wafers once a fortnight." Then the auditor asked, 'Now tell me, what you do with all the leftover foreskins from the circumcisions you perform here? You have shown some expenditure on account of this.'

Disgusted, the Rabbi said, "Here, too, we are extremely careful and do not waste a single piece of flesh. We save all the foreskins and send them to your boss as meat and once a year he sends us a complete prick!"

"And what about the scissor?"

"Your predecessor has taken it away to trim his moustache and genital hair'. Now, fully outwitted, the stupid left for his office double quick without any further fuss.

Another phenomenon in Govt. bureaucracy is to punish the 'performer'with more work and reward the inefficient with no task. It can be called a 'doers curse'. The other thankless task, done by a selected few called 'intellectual donkeys,' is ghost writing; that is no longer a deep, dark secret. Many great speeches and punch lines of greater leaders quoted by scholars and historians are actually written by self effacing small individuals. David Fisher was one of those invisible authors reported to have ghostwritten some 70 books. When I was in USA in 2012, the Wisconsin Governor, Scott Walker was in controversy, as The National Review reported that journalist Marc Thiessen had ghostwritten his book. Marc was also the speechwriter for George W. Bush and Donald Rumsfeld.

I did this many a time for Presidents, Prime Ministers and Cabinet Ministers, some with pleasure and a few with great pain and irritation. On one occasion there were four dignitaries to speak, the Prime Minister, the Minister for Human Resource Development, the Minister of State for Youth and the Deputy Chairman of the Planning Commission. The then Secretary, Youth Affairs asked me to prepare a speech for each one of them. While I was leaving his chamber, he called me back and requested if I could also prepare a draft speech for him also. That was one of the most frustrating experiences in my life because when you write five speeches for five different levels of persons for the same occasion, you have to ensure who speaks what, that they don't repeat each other and the quality and content are to be appropriate to the position each one of them holding. It is a thankless and joyless task.

However, every once in a while, the ghost writer has his rewarding moment and when her ideas and words become policy commitment and even 'quotes', catchwords and slogans. Like 'tryst with destiny', the oft quoted words from Pundit Nehru's midnight address on 14th Aug, 1947, on the eve of India's independence or like the most popular patriotic slogan and salutation 'Jai Hind' of Netaji Subhas Chandra Bose, which was actually coined by Maj. Abid Hasan Zafrani, a Muslim officer of the Azad Hind Fauz. P.N Haksar, a senior diplomat and Prime Minister Indira Gandhi's ghost writer, had successfully projected her as a socialist and secular leader; a positive image that greatly helped her in riding out many political storms.

In my case one such speech and another document resulted in the birth of two great institutions of national and international importance, one for the Youth, another for Democracy. For a long time, I was not aware that quite a few international best sellers were actually written by ghost writers. And history always evaluates the celebrity writers and great leaders based on their words and language written by the invisible, unknown, unrecognised ghosts like me ridiculed as intellectual donkeys!

In New Delhi's posh Safdarjung Enclave, there is an agency called NDMA-an acronym for National Disaster Management Authority, of which the Prime Minister is the Chairman. One day around 2pm, a junior official from the agency rang me up saying, 'Sir, your disaster management guide book for Civil Defence 'Secured Country, Safer Community' is being ceremonially released today at 4pm. Please attend.'

My first instinct was not to go at such short notice. There was a second call half an hour before the event, from my good friend Neel Prusti, Mentor, International Resource Group, who had fully piloted the project. I changed my mind and reached the place. The auditorium was full and I had to share a seat in the last row. Ceremonially releasing the document, the Minister termed it as a unique venture. Soon after, the guests on the dais started speaking eloquently about its merits and relevance. None mentioned about the author or the year long team effort behind this initiative.

After the meeting, I managed to get a copy out of curiosity. Among the missing items was a two page 'Note from the Architect' (me) of the book about how to use the contents. Complete black out of the author in the Foreword, Preface and Messages, no acknowledgement for the artwork and the beautiful cartoons by artist Pradip, who had done it on my personal request while a senior researcher, Sivkumar, a part of the book project, had died of an accident while collecting data. A special mention in his memory had been removed. Sad and shocked, I realized what a real dunce I was and had been taken for a free ride! They had really reduced me to an unnamed 'ghost' writer.

But the worst was yet to come. On 22nd Oct. 2016, while watching the evening news bulletin, I saw a headline announcing that the first World Youth Development Index and Report covering 183 countries had been ceremonially launched by the Commonwealth Secretary General, Patricia Scotland in the presence of a number of Ambassadors, Youth Experts and scholars. It would measure the situation and status of 1.8 billion youth in the world and suggest ways to empower them. I felt very excited as I had floated the idea, developed it in a 40 page long concept framework and done the groundwork for this as early as 1997 while working in the Commonwealth Asia Centre. It was discussed and approved by the Commonwealth Secretariat and then unanimously adopted by the CYMM-Commonwealth Youth Ministers Meeting, Kuala Lumpur, Malaysia in 1998. Soon after- the CHOGM- Commonwealth Heads of Government Meeting also endorsed the concept in full, followed by years of debate in various international forums. So the following day, the first thing I did was to search and access the voluminous document and report. And soon found out that the acknowledgement page had appreciated the contributions of more than two dozen people, except the author of the idea!!

Two competitive feelings struggle to occupy the mind scape of 'ghost writers'- is it foolish to be wise or wise to be foolish? About two decades ago, we had invited late Sri Sharadaprasad, an erudite scholar and information adviser to the then prime minister, as a guest speaker to a national youth camp in Delhi's Bharateeyam Gram near Nizamuddin. He was widely believed to be the 'ghost writer' of the Prime Minister. During tea time, I asked him hesitantly how he felt about it. Smiling, he said, 'Look, it is a special role and relationship, which 30,000 years of human speech has failed to define properly for want of a name. How can a writer be the ghost of another living person? Stupids. Such caps don't fit the wearer.'

In India, the word Babu is believed to have been derived from Baboon, an old world monkey that loves imitating and living in hierarchically ranked groups! Many great institutions led by honest people are severely saddled by such uncritical, blindly imitating souls. Expected to be ordinarily intelligent, many turn out to be stupids. With risk adverse seniors not inclined to push the envelope and break out of cocoon comfort, delaying and damage potential of stupids doubles.

When I was Programme Adviser in the Youth and Sports Ministry. I had forwarded a file recommending supply of audio visual equipments to 15 training centres attached to the Ministry and there were enough funds for it in the budget. Then, I left the ministry on an assignment. Seven years after, when I returned, the concerned file was still making the rounds. There are many such horror stories. CBI, India's premier investigating agency had a little better luck. In one instance, as reported, it had to wait for three years to buy a mobile phone and 100 days to process a proposal to buy a laptop! And 19 years after I left the Govt. the file to fill up the vacancy in my place was still moving from section to section! Finally, when the file was sent to the Department of Personnel, it said since they had managed the work without an officer for 19 years, they don't need this position now!

Bureaucracy is full of such bizarre instances. A junior colleague of mine had to fight 21 years for an annual increment of fifty rupees (one dollar) even after a tribunal had given the verdict in his favour. The Delhi Transport Corporation, a hugely loss making public transport agency, has been fighting a case against its own employee (conductor) for causing a loss of five paise (1/20th part of a rupee), that too for the last 41 years! One can guess how much the corporation has spent by now from the public exchequer in keeping the man, who is now 70, dismissed, harassed and down. Despite the Court verdict in his favour, stupids in bureaucracy have again appealed against the verdict in higher Court, making government the greatest litigant in the country. The new Indian Prime Minister, Modi, while talking to top bureaucrats in June, 2014, struck the nail on the head when he said that while a devout Hindu could attain 'Moksha' (Salvation) by travelling to 'char dham', the four holyr places of pilgrimage, an official file has to travel to 'chalis dham', or forty places, before final clearance.

Both small and tall have fallen victims to stupids. It is reported that Karl Marx's famous book, 'Das Kapital' had missed its deadline for publication by 16 years and that the first royalty cheque arrived at his place 16 years after publication of the book! It was delivered to his children as by that time, both, Marx and his wife, Jenny, were already dead. Constant criticism and controversy about his views made Charles Darwin ill several times. He had to keep his most revolutionary theory of evolution and natural selection under wraps for decades.

Another memory dates back to the 80s when I had encountered an interesting situation while working with the university bureaucracy. I had worked hard for three months in developing a proposal to establish a Continuing Education Centre to be fully supported by the University Grants Commission (UGC). The objective was to engage the universities and colleges in total literacy movement through a campus-community model. The approach was- 'the educated must educate' the illiterate and the method was 'eight months for education of students in campus and four months for literacy by them in the community' because in an academic year, class rooms in colleges and universities remain open for 180 days only. At that time in India, 45 percent of adults were illiterate. The proposal received full support and both technical and financial clearance but got stuck up at the Vice Chancellor's table for six months despite my personal reminders to him once every fortnight.

Then, one day, I was asked to meet him immediately. I rushed and was pleased to see him perusing seriously the pending proposal and file. He looked up and asked me, 'Are there any position of a driver and cook in this project?'

I said: 'Driver, yes but cook, no.'

He was partly pleased. I was disappointed as he didn't ask anything about the academic part of the proposal on which I had worked so hard and consulted so many experts. His focus was on the position of driver and cook who could be used for personal service in his house.

Thanks to the post of driver, the proposal picked up phenomenal speed and was cleared in fifteen minutes!

But I had to quit the university soon after, for failing to follow and satisfy his other wishes. In fact, he made it impossible for me to work, by curtailing all my functional autonomy. Soon, the Union Public Service Commission selected me for a responsibility in the Union Education and Social Welfare Ministry, to look after a study service programme called NSS in 300 universities. So, I moved to Delhi leaving my native state for good 30 years. Indeed, it proved to be a great blessing in disguise and, in retrospect, I now realize how wise was Lord Krishna, when he and his clan decided to quit native Mathura for Dwarka in sea to escape repeated attacks and persecution by his sworn enemies. In western India, Krishna's other name is 'Ranchhodjee', meaning 'the man who ran away from war to live in peace.' A day before quitting the university, I received a post card from my old professor of philosophy, Dr Satyabadi, a student of India's philosopher President, S. Radhakrishnan and grandson of legendary freedom fighter, Gopabandhu Das. It was a hand written short letter, carrying just three loaded sentences. It said, 'I am happy you are out of the cesspool of university politics. Remember, once a while, God in heaven sends stupids down to earth for a practice run, so that he could further improve on their damage potential. You are an accidental victim in God's laboratory.'

Often, stupidity of parents cause irreparable damage to their children in a family based social system. I was a witness to this during my seven years stay in Chandigarh, capital city of Haryana and Punjab states. In 2009 and 2014 general elections in India, unmarried voters in parts of Haryana were demanding 'brides' from contesting candidates as incentives for casting vote in their favor. This otherwise developed state has the lowest sex ratio in the country- precisely 877 women to 1000 men (2011). Many of them are reported to have formed informal groupings of bachelors called 'randa unions' with slogans like 'Bahu dilao, vote pao'- 'get us a bride to get our vote'. We were debating in the Election Commission for quite some time on how to prevent such insidious slogans by voters. Widespread female feticide under pressure from foolish family elders has created acute shortage of girls in this region. Consequently, each of the 7000 odd villages in the state has

150 to 200 males who are unable to marry.

Having worked in different types of organizations from local to global level, I had a close ring side view of bureaucracy of different hues. I categorise them into four types. One type bends over backward to bend rules to favor a person, relation or an agency. The second type bends forward and even crawls to over please the boss and political masters. The third type stands straight without any compromise, with tremendous ability to take knocks on the chin. They also bend the odds but only when it is necessary to change the outcome. The fourth type practices all the previous three types intelligently to serve their interests. I call this category as the 'maximum bureaucrat'.

I had the opportunity of meeting one such bureaucrat, both rigid and flexible depending on situation, brilliant and efficient in work, high in intelligent quotient. Yet he was also hot headed, arrogant, intimidating, and low in interpersonal relationship and social quotient. When in the Youth and Sports Ministry, we were busy mobilizing a million student volunteers to clean the rivers. At the time, this gentleman was already a senior bureaucrat and was invited to address the valedictory session of a National Consultation on the subject. Fifteen minutes before the event, there was a call from his office enquiring who would receive him at the venue?

I said, 'Me.'

What is your job title was the next question.

'Program Adviser,' I replied.

'No, I mean what is your rank, sir? Boss wants that he should only be received by an officer not below the rank of a Secretary to Govt of India and preferably by your secretary, who is junior to him; otherwise, he would not come.'

Three minutes later, he called once again and said, 'Boss also wants to know the seating positions and speaking order as per protocol and whom are you presenting the bouquet first and make sure that a very senior official should offer the vote of thanks.'

Subsequently, the gentleman moved to various key Ministries and then held many important positions but because of his abrasive and aggressive ways and proximity to power centre, he was nicknamed as 'grey wolf', who faithfully served the political masters. Always a go getter and never a push over, he had an elephantine memory. Once

I happened to meet him three years after a Republic Day related ceremony where he was Guest of Honour and asked whether he could recognize me. He not only remembered my longish name but also mentioned the exact date, time and venue of the event where we met! He was more like a rusher driver who loved to zoom past every one cutting across four lanes at a time, screaming at 'slow moving' people around him. While his foot was always on the accelerator, his mind was mostly focussed on his own career advancement. After his retirement, he hobnobbed with politicians of all hues and started running from party to party for a ticket but failed to win a seat. Eventually, the brilliant brain faded away. Yet, today, in retrospect, he was much better in comparision to many low and slow witted babus, in terms of deliverables.

There are several jokes about stupids in bureaucracy. One says, in a bureaucracy, paper work increases as you spend more and more time reporting on less and less you are doing. Einstein thought bureaucracy was the death of all sound work because here procedure was everything and performance was nothing. one goes on and on doing the same thing over and over again and expects different results! The most telling comment was from Franz Kafka, which said that every revolution evaporated and left behind only the slime of a new bureaucracy. It happened to India after independence led by Gandhi and to Russia after the Karl Marx inspired Bolshevik revolution in October, 1917, led by Lenin. One of the witty jokes of humorist, Douglas Adams (1952-2001), says what exactly a stupid bureaucrat always prays for- "Protect me, O Lord, from knowing what I don't need to know. Protect me from even knowing that there are things to know that I don't know. Protect me from knowing that I decided not to know about the things that I decided not to know about. Amen."

In fact, bureaucracy is a big mindless machine run by small men and women, barring a few honourable exceptions. Realizing this, Kautilya's Arthashastra, an ancient Indian treatise on statecraft by Chankya, had spelt out simply and succinctly the primary role of a bureaucracy- 'To honestly defend the interest of the country and its people, to foresee the possibilities of conflicts and calamities and take prevenive steps to avert them before they occur and overcome those which happen, to suppress 'wickedness by foul means' and impartially administer justice, to severely punish sexual exploiters and finally, to work for removing all obstructions to economic activity, in order to prevent loss of revenue to the state.'

But stupids refuse to learn and change and love to repeat the same stupidity time and again. Chinese thinker, Confucious (551 BCE) had said that only the wisest and the stupidest people never change. Long ago, when I was a student and used to visit the Jagannath temple in Puri quite often, I had noticed a middle aged man, who was boxing his ears with both hands and standing up and down repeatedly before the image of the Deity, muttering some words of apology. After observing this for about three months, I wondered why he was repeating the same practice and postures every time. I approached an old priest to enquire about it. He took me aside and said that the man was a rich local trader, notorious for adulterating edible oil for instant profit. He would do it at night and visit the temple in the morning every day, to seek short cut forgiveness from the God. Laughing within, I thought God might be a great neuroscientist but his temple had certainly failed to reform many of his stupid and greedy devotees.

It is said that God gave a drop of water to a microbe; she lived on it happily forever. He now gave half an acre of land to an ant, who built on it hills of prosperity. He gave a full forest to a tiger who built there an empire. He gave the humans the whole universe with all its knowledge, wealth and free will but they turned stupid and converted it into a 'dungeon of dogma', shutting the mind to truth and reasoning.

However, working with stupids reinforced my old faith in the curative properties of laughter. Without stupids, life will be much less interesting. They create amazing and amusing scenes and make one break into loud laughter and feel better and healthier, for there is so much stupidity around the world that some sensible people use these as stress busters. Occasionally, I had made a fool of myself innocently and regreted the folly later on. Like the saying that inside every adult there is a child, probably there is also a stupid lying hidden inside every one of us. Great philosopher, Elbert Hubbard, had once said, 'Every man is a damn stupid for five minutes every day. Wisdom consists in not exceeding that limit.'

One such stupidity I had committed at Tashkent was in 1987,

when we arrived there with a large contingent of young Indian artistes' delegation, as a part of the India festival in USSR. At the reception ceremony, the mayor rose to formally welcome us. Advised by our chief protocol officer, I had also carried a prepared speech in English to respond to him on behalf of our delegation. There was an interpreter ready to translate the speeches from Russian to English and English to Russian but when the mayor started his welcome address, to my utter surprise and shock, it was not in Russian but in Hindi, the national language of my country. For a moment, I didn't know what to do and cursed my sheer stupidity. How could I reply in English when he was addressing us in the language of our country! But my Hindi was also not so good at that time. The Indian and Soviet media were present in full strength and I felt nervous, tense and confused, overpowered by a sense of helplessness, shame and guilt. A lady theatre artist of our team from Hindi speaking Rajastan was standing nearby. I called her and pushed the typed script of my two- page speech in English, requesting her to quickly convert it into a few lines in good Hindi, to save the day and honour of my country. Inside, I was praying for a longer speech by the Mayor to buy time. From that day onwards, everywhere we went, I discharged my ceremonial role with my broken Hindi. I had learnt the lesson.

The ceremony over, I retired to my room in the hotel. The door bell rang and the Mayor entered. There was another embarrassment in store. He said, 'If you and your team don't mind, I would like to make a request.'

'Of course, please tell me, you are such a wonderful host,' I said.

'Our people, who came in thousands to welcome your delegation at the airport and stadium, are slightly disappointed.' Feeling a little awkward, I asked him whether there was any diplomatic faux pas. He said, "No no. It is something else which is not very important for you." I told him to feel free and share frankly.

Then he said hesitantly, 'Our people are very fond of seeing Indian women in 'saree'. They look so graceful, so beautiful and so dignified in that dress. But, sadly, today, at the reception, none of your women delegates was wearing a saree. We have seen plenty of them in Bollywood movies and in fact, my wife was looking for the day to learn how to wear a saree from your ladies. Please forgive me for this feedback.'

I assured him to do my bit in this context in future. Soon after, I called all the delegates and shared my conversation with the mayor, their expectations and the reasons for their disappointment and gently suggested if they could cooperate. All of them readily agreed although some of them had not brought any saree. However, they managed by sharing the extra pieces of their friends. So, from the second day, in all formal and informal occasions during our stay, our ladies came dressed in saree.

The mayor and his people were happy and we had learnt the second lesson. Until now, we were foolishly unaware of the charming power of this eight yard long strip of unstitched colourful cloth that the South Asian women have been draping over their bodies in myriad styles for thousands of years. Flexible as liquid, flowing as fluid and filling as water, this wonderful garment, believed to have been born on the loom of a whimsical weaver, is now the mother of all fashions and grand mother of life style, lending unity to diversity of the female body parts and simultaneously fusing traditional basics with contemporary fashion and style. Soon after, in the evening, Russian and Uzbeki girls started coming to our hotel to learn the skills of wearing a saree from the female Indian artists and our ladies were more than happy to oblige. Some felt a little bit stupid, guilty and ashamed when an outsider had to remind them of their culture and tradition!

According to one of the legends, Bodhidharma, (5th century CE), father of Zen or Dhyan Buddhism and the martial arts Kung Fu, had crossed over to China to spread the ideas of Buddha called as Da Mo in China. He had a strange habit of sitting cross legged facing the wall instead of facing the audience. One day, someone from the audience asked him out of curiosity the reason behind this.

Da Mo's reply was- 'You are no better than the wall. My words bounce back from the wall and my words bounce back from you also in the same way.' In his nine years in China, he could find only three takers of his ideas. So, only individual genius is not enough because ideas can't survive long by floating in the air. They need legs to walk, hands to work on, friends and followers to promote and propagate. And they stand a good chance of being made into 'products' only through connecting and coordinating the people, planning, technology and of course resources. A new challenge for Lucy's ever changing children in the 21st century.

In The Age of Stupids (2008), an award winning film directed by Franny Armstrong, a character living in the devastated future world of 2055, looking back in time asks: 'Why didn't we save the world when we had the chance and when the disastrous results of our stupidity were clearly predictable?' Stupids themselves are a challenge to the survival value of human intelligence. In the Confucian language, when a wise person points a hand at the Moon, the stupids try to examine his fingers.

14

Belief Bazaar & Conversation with Nina

'Have you come here all the way from India to sleep? You have not seen Amsterdam if you have not seen its night life' said Aamir, the lodging house manager, when after a tiring day at the conference I wanted to retire to bed. In early 90s, invited by the World Health Organization (WHO), I had an opportunity to visit Amsterdam, the beautiful city of rivers, canals and gardens. The trip was in connection with the International Congress on HIV and AIDS and Sexually Transmitted Infections (STI).

Aamir, an old acquaintance in the city, now gently pushed me to the street. He was correct. I found out in three hours why some people called it a 'sex city'. One can see here the presence of a large number of brothels and sex shops, offering a variety of products like condoms, sex toys and dolls, enlarger creams, tightening lotions, sex furniture designed for various positions, etc. Prostitution used to be practiced in the city in various forms- 'window' and 'street prostitution', club based prostitution, escort agencies and home-based prostitution, etc, more like the city of Venice, the pleasure capital of Europe in 18th and 19th century, full of gambling women and beautiful courtesans where social vices were tolerated to encourage revenue from tourism. Yet, Amsterdam seemed to be more youthful. In the evening, coffee shops and cannabis clubs are crowded with young men and women smoking marijuana and hashis inn peace and the streets are full with young people freely loitering around.

Earlier, the city used to be one of the top destinations for victims of immoral trafficking. Within Netherlands, victims were often recruited by so called "loverboys" – men who seduce young Dutch women and girls, living separately from their families and later coerce them into commercial sex. After the workshop, in the evening, we visited some streets inhabited by commercial sex workers to study their condition. In India these are called 'Red light streets'. It being the first exposure, I felt very awkward looking at nude women standing inside glass cabins and inviting customers with lewd gestures. I was trying very hard to take my eyes off these women forced into such situation. We were taken inside one of these 'sex shelters' to see and understand the set up, hygiene and preventive measures and found inside, in addition to a double bed, there were clean towels, hot water, contraceptives and condoms of different varieties for safer sex.

It is mandatory for brothel owners in Amsterdam to ensure availability of good lighting and physical examination of clients to detect any visible evidence of sexually transmitted infection before each sexual 'episode' as they called it. All clients must observe safer sex practices. The sex worker can also refuse to oblige where she suspects to be at risk of acquiring infection. Any client with symptoms of an STI is referred to a health centre for medical consultation. Because of these precautions, this country has been able to halt and reverse the spread of HIV.

On the day of the inaugural. I saw a big crowd marching towards the venue, holding posters and placards and shouting slogans like- 'We want vaccine, we want vaccine'. This obviously meant, people were not willing to change their behavior. I was slightly upset because the title of my paper was: 'Awareness: The Best Vaccine'. This can be achieved only through innovative behavior change communication. Earlier, when I was on a WHO assignment in Indonesia, I had met a religious leader and a senior academician in a workshop where both of them gave long lectures stating that their religious values would protect them from the HIV. When my turn came, I gently suggested that neither my values nor their's could protect us from HIV infection if we were not actively aware and careful. For, a simple prick from an unsterilized needle can infect any one with the virus, irrespective of one's position as a pundit, priest, Pope, Prophet or a pathologist.

During this stay, a friend narrated two interesting episodes about how costly communication campaigns failed in another country of the region without proper segmentation of the target audience and without research on their beliefs and perceptions. The first one, aimed at promoting breast feeding, failed because in the targeted community there was a belief that out of the two breasts of a lactating woman, the right one had milk and the left one had only water and left side body parts were unlucky. Influenced by this, new mothers in this community were feeding the children from one breast only, ie, the right breast, resulting in rampant malnutrition.

In a different context, a mythological episode in epic Mahabharat introduces a lactating woman called Putana, both of whose breasts were believed to be full of poison. According to the story, while this evil minded woman wanted to breastfeed infant god Krishna into death, the baby instead killed her by suckling out her life energy. Another version says looking at the infant, her maternal instinct became overactive. Ancient medical texts in India prescribe to worship Putana to protect children from diseases. However, both breasts and babies are a much misunderstood victims of belief.

In the early 90s, I had spent some time in Jhabua, one of the most backward regions of undivided Madhya Pradesh in India. In those days, Jhabua was high on infant and maternal mortality and quite low on contraceptive use. At delivery time the traditional birth attendants used to tie and tighten a thick rope round the belly of the pregnant woman, roll and press it hard to forcibly push out the child. Many women die, often with the unborn baby, being unable to bear the pain. Attitudes and beliefs, often harmful, vary across cultures, race and ethnicity.

In the 'University Talk AIDS' Campaign aimed at student youth, our focus was on behavior change and we had used successfully the social marketing methods that eventually led to rapid reduction in the infection rate. Social marketing uses all the methods of commercial marketing like product, price, place and promotion, to sell positive behavior. In fact it sells life while commercial marketing often sells death. One sells goods and services while the other sells 'behavior change' like someone promoting milk, and the other promoting liquor. The aim is to make the target audience voluntarily reject an old behavior like smoking, drinking, unsafe sex and accept and adopt the new behavior of withdrawing from these old habits.

The males did not know how to and from where to obtain a condom and how to use it to avoid unwanted pregnancy. There were instances when some innocent, ignorant persons were using it in the fingers believing it could protect from infection and conception. Here the challenge was first to change the belief and attitude of the target audience with knowledge and skills transfer and then change the behavior and practice.

In Middle Ages, in many parts of Europe, the main rival of the science of medicine were astrology, theology and quackery. Astrologers were being consulted even for the best times for battle and bloodletting. They were predicting the events of tomorrow by looking at the heavens of today. During Louis XIV's rule in France and parts of Europe many people used to take bath only once or twice in a year. They thought water created disease by penetrating the pores of the skin and thereby infecting the blood. In order to combat the resultant body odour, they used to douse the body with powder and perfumes. It was supported by another strange belief that a thick, grimy layer of filth would keep one strong and healthy.

In our neighboring village, there was a lady called Pali, who was a divorcee and a widow and didn't have any fixed source of income for survival. One day, she went into a trance and started shaking her head violently, uttering words and sounds that no one understood. People flocked to her to find out what was happening when someone declared that she had been possessed by an evil spirit. Then, confusion converted into awe and people started asking her favor to solve their everyday problems. This continued for a month when another destitute woman of the area also went into a fit for a minute and then declared herself as a superior spirit more powerful than Pali. In fact, she rushed to Pali's place and gave her a big slap on the face. Pali came back to her senses and fled, ditching her devotees for good.

Subsequently, it was found out that Pali was actually sick and her behavior was an outward symptom of hookworm infections. The belief in influence of 'evil spirits' on human affairs is cross cutting and unshakable. Like India, it is widespread in South-East Asia, known by different names. In Myanmar, these are called 'Nats', in Vietnam 'Ba', in Indonesia 'Tujul', in Brunei 'Hantu', in Cambodia 'Nak Ta' and 'Bomo' or black magic in Malaysia. Now, doctors are incorporating a patient's beliefs and behavior into the treatment plan to find out the causes of their mental and physical disorder. In human life, the dividing line between natural and supernatural sources is very thin. We crave for supernatural when the natural forces fail to explain a particular phenomenon.

Rare birds and animals have met threats from beliefs. One of them is houbara, intensive pursuit of which occupies a romantic place in the Bedouine's Arab culture for its supposed sex enhancing properties of doubtful scientific evidence. Princes, kings, royalty and the wealthy from the Middle East and Persian Gulf regions flock to Baluchistan with their hunting falcons to kill the white- plumed, beautiful houbara. Sex was a gift of nature to create life with pleasure and not to destroy creation by cruelty.

And strangely 'baseless beliefs' are stronger in many rationalistic communist countries like China and Vietnam! Even after living 75 years in a rationalist, communist regime, Russians witnessed a collective mass psychosis when in a town east of Moscow, panicked citizens vulnerable to mystical belief, stripped their shelves of matches, kerosene and candles, influenced by the rumors that the world would end on December 21, 2012. The source was a report about the impending 'doomsday' at the end of a 5,125 year cycle known as the 'long count' in the Mayan Calendar. The prophecy turned out to be a big business. An entrepreneur in the Siberian city of Tomask made a fortune by selling emergency kits containing vodka, buckwheat, matches, candles, soap and ropes - stockpiling all essentials to survive the Armageddon.

In parts of India, there is a belief that when you are in deep trouble, feed a male goat sumptuously and sacrifice it before the local female deity to overcome the crisis. Recently a cricket captain in India and a Railway Minister in crisis followed this practice. Instead of coming out of the crisis, one lost the match and the other, his Ministry. When awareness loses control, irrationality influences human life and behaviour as a standard value. Once, I had stopped over in Sydney on way to Solomon Islands. A co-passenger in the waiting lounge narrated how in parts of Australia, people used to blame a particular tree with dark flowers for causing student suicide. In India, it was the flowering season for mangoes. Subsequently, it was found out that the cause was not the tree or flowers but the stressful examination season. Kabir (1440-1518), a widely respected Sufi and Bhakti saint used to say: If by worshiping stones you can find the God then I will worship the stony mountain itself. It is better to worship the grindstone. Referring to Muslims in the same manner, he would say: You collect the stones and build a Mosque and on it stands the Mullah and recites his prayers loudly, is the Khuda hard of hearing? Kabir's poetry is replete with such pithy, earthy imagery. A weaver by profession, he spent his entire life battling social discrimination, economic exploitation and religious superstition. Incidentally, in Arabic, al- Kabir means the Great, which is the 37th name of God in Islam.Thus changing sexual, cultural, social and faith based behavior is a very challenging task even among educated people.

How customs and practices vary from place to place, I witnessed in course of my travels to more than sixty countries in five continents. Malays in south-East Asia love to joke around including raw ones, make fun of themselves and laugh a lot while in some other cultures people take jokes as offence. Elderly Indians don't like to be addressed by first names by their juniors; teachers would just be horrified to be called in such manner by students. On the other hand, Americans and Europeans would insist to be called by first names only.

During my last visit to a Middle East country, a guide had cautioned me not to add salt to the food offered as it offends the host. But in the neighboring country, the dining table had three bottles full of a variety of table salts for different types of foods. The French don't like you to eat their fries with tomato ketchup that they think destroy their cuisine and food culture. Nor do they appreciate their children to turn vegetarian. The Americans love to express affection by hugging; the French are just not into it. There were different views and advisory for travellers about greeting with a kiss, about how many kisses should one give. Should one's lips touch the cheek or graze the air, should there be a kissey sound and so on. In Indonesia, the Javanese convention of courtesy requires social inferiors to show respect by kissing the feet, knees and hands of their seniors according to rank. In the highly hierarchical Japanese society one bows more deeply to a superior than to an inferior and stay down in that position longer than the superior. In the Kobe conference on HIV prevention, I had a glimpse of it. I was amused to see two Japanese officials bowing and staying down for a longer period until someone reminded one of them that he was superior to the other. Each of them had assumed the other person to be superior.

So, every time we think, speak, behave or act in a particular manner, a message goes out carrying different meaning for and interpretation by others. Therefore a sensitive awareness to the feelings of others helps in avoiding unpleasant situations and reactions.

On 5th November 2013, I was watching, with great interest, India's first Mars Mission. A day before the launch of PSLV-C 25, when a thousand plus space scientists were busy checking every parameter at Sriharikota launching venue, the leader of the team and Chairman, Indian Space Research Organisation was in Tirupati Venkateswar Temple, about 100 Kms. away from the launch pad, for, he was busy participating in rituals and offering prayers for the success of the Mars mission. Interestingly, the launch date was also decided to be 'Tuesday' called Mangalbar, the day of the Mars called Mangal in Indian astrology. As the Mangalyan rose to the sky with a roar drowning loud cheers, I was a bit amused looking at the tango of the rocket science and religious practices. Subsequently, I found out that his predecessor, another great scientist, had also gone through similar rituals in the same temple for the safety and success of the mission.

Most of these prejudices are acquired in family during growing up years. Some are fond beliefs carried through old wife's tales like when a lady's brassier falls off, it means her husband remembers when you bite your tongue, you will have a delicious meal, when a bird sings in the court yard, friends are likely to visit you etc. Personally, it took years for me to shake off these. The challenge of distinguishing science from snake oil is formidable.

After having a glimpse of nightlife I rushed back. Next day, after a poster presentation on "Awareness: the Best Vaccine', I returned home. A couple of years after, I was again in Amsterdam. This time I travelled by train to Hague, to meet an old friend. Hague is the third largest city of the Netherlands, after Amsterdam and Rotterdam and about 150 international organizations are located in this small city of roughly half a million people, including the International Court of Justice and the International Criminal Court. This has made The Hague one of the most important cities of the world, hosting a large number of U.N organizations and competing with bigger international cities like New York, Geneva, Vienna, Paris, Tokyo and Nairobi.

As the train left the station, a young lady, appearing to be in her early thirties, came and sat beside me on the vacant seat. With golden hairs falling over and cascading down both her right and left shoulders in curled waves, she was looking more like a Barbie. The skin- tight cat suit flaunted her firm curves, showing off vital parts. It was winter and hence I was a bit surprised. She touched the cross dangling over her chest, closed her eyes for a moment before settling down. What followed was a sweet- sour- conversation, the memory of which remains etched in my mind till today.

After subjecting me to a visual X-ray, she greeted me with a smile and said, 'Hi, I am Nina. What about you?' And without waiting for my reply, she said, 'I guess you must be from India?' 'Yes, you are absolutely correct,' I said. I was wearing a typical Indian jacket.

'And what about you, certainly not from the East?' I asked.

'You are correct, I am British, my mother is Dutch and father fromUK, and I am studying in the university here,' she said.

'Interesting, where are your parents now?' I asked, now entering into deeper conversation. Much later I came to know that people in the west feel offended by invasive personal questions.

Seemingly surprised, she said, 'You mean my biological parents?'

'Yes, yes,' I said, feeling a little awkward and unable to swallow her emphasis on 'biological'. Though true, in a way it was a sort of culture shock.

'No, they are divorced long back; I don't know much about them, they must be pretty old by now. But when I was in school, Papa used to tell me interesting stories about your country. He was working in India as a police officer during the latter part of the British rule,' she replied.

'Oh, that sounds really interesting! In fact, the police were the real rulers in those days,' I said.

'But the more interesting fact is, he was in charge of your Gandhi's security.'

'Oh, really? But as far as I know, Gandhi never wanted any security. Was your father sure that Gandhi was aware of his role?' I quipped.

'No, Gandhi didn't know about it. In fact, my father had two sorrows in life. The first one was that although he was in charge of Gandhi's security, he had orders to keep his own identity a secret and was forbidden from talking to Gandhi. He thought he was deprived of once in life time opportunity of interacting with the Millennium Man. His second sorrow was that, as soon as the British withdrew, the new Indian government failed to protect Gandhi.'

She had touched a raw nerve in me. 'Yes, I agree, it is extremely unfortunate. We will carry the burden of this guilt forever', I confessed and said, 'You must know that Tom Reiner, the man who first overpowered Gandhi's assassin, was also from Lancaster in your country. He was there to attend the prayer meeting out of curiosity. He wanted to meet the 'man of peace' who had been fasting and praying for five days to restore communal harmony.'

Now she looked directly at me and seemed pleased to hear this. Personally, I have been frying my brain often asking a question to myself- Did Gandhi survive in British India because England was a democracy? Would a dictator or an autocrat have allowed a bitter opponent like him to live? Resuming, I said, 'I'd love to meet your father some day. You must find out where is he now. And what about other members of your family?' I asked, trying indirectly to find out her marital status. Our conversation was getting personal.

'No, I am single,' she announced confidently with a smile and then added with a mischievous twinkle in the eye, 'But don't worry, I have another 250 million singles with me around the world.'

'And where is your wife?' She now asked me more directly and said,

'Sorry, but your women are an interesting lot.'

'She is back in India. I think women everywhere are an interesting lot. I had come here to attend a World Conference on Family,' I said.

'Oh, that is exciting. Can I ask you a personal question, if you don't mind?'

'It's okay, go ahead,' I said.

'Good, tell me, for how long have you been married?' She asked, now more directly.

'Ummm, that's a good question. We are together for the last 31years,' I said.

She slammed the note book down and glared at me for a few seconds and said, 'No… I mean, you are living with one and the same woman for the last 31 years?'

'Yeah, yeah,' I said, feeling my answer didn't go down well with her.

'Impossible. I can't believe.' She appeared to be clearly shocked.

Assuring her, I said, 'Madam, maybe another 31 years or more and most likely until death separates us. We are now looking forward to celebrate our Golden Jubilee. In India we are married for life.'

Grudgingly recognizing the fact and turning the conversation on its head, she said. 'Married for life? Funny! But why? Is it compulsory in your culture? Now, I think what I had heard was correct.' I could sense an undisguised disdain in her tone.

'What was that you had heard?' I asked gently, clearing my throat.

'That you people marry without love and force your women to live with you in life time bondage. Now, I can see why people say yours is a male dominated society. And by the way, what is this 'arranged marriage' I hear so often? Isn't it absurd and atrocious! It is really a human rights issue.' Swallowing the bombshell, I could sense she was almost cribbing and was in a combative mood after throwing a loose ball. I was not prepared for this. Years after such perception persists as is evident from the article by writer – photographer Rachel Rueckert titled 21 American Habits Which I lost in India. Here she confesses how, many of her assumptions about India were wrong including arranged marriages which in many cases blossom into positive and successful relationships.

About Nina's unkind comments, I had two options now- to miss it or hit it.

I decided to explain and clarify, saying, 'That is more a perception than reality. I believe it is a relationship issue and not individual 'Rights' issue. We are not disconnected individuals but part of a collective culture. We live in family and in community, we fight, love, accommodate and adjust to each other and do a bit of sacrifice to stay together, to care and share, for our own harmony and happiness. Many of our marriages blossom into positive and lifetime relationships over a period of time. Otherwise India is home to a wide variety of wedding systems. Mutual consent based on mutual attraction is one of them. Historical Vedic religion favoured it. Subsequently during the period of classical Hinduism, self arranged marriage changed to arranged marriage. But now it has become more elastic, particularly in urban, educated India and can't happen without mutual consent.

'Hope you are not defending the system' she said.

Reminding her gingerly, gently and mixing an element of jest, I said, 'Why should I ? In this matter, some of our people just follow your royal tradition, I mean the way the British and Dutch Princes marry. And all of you celebrate this 'arranged marriage', including your Parliament!' 'No, I can't accept that,' She said now more emphatically and angrily surprised. 'Then you must study and find out for yourself. In your country, the royal parents and government also engage, arrange and approve the marriage. The only difference is, we do not send emissaries and doctors to test virginity and fertility to confirm the bride's 'venereal cleanliness' and ability to conceive.' Fully flummoxed, she demanded, 'Are you sure?'

I said, "Do you know how Princess Diana's uncle, Lord Fermoy, had to make a public statement to assure people and the paparazi that she was a bonafide virgin? And knowing fully well that broken hymen of an unmarried girl is not always caused by premarital sex. Historically, even Joan Arc, who was declared a saint of the Church and daughter of God, was subjected to a virginity test by king Charles of France. She was burnt to death by king of England on charges of sorcery and witch craft.'

'I am really not aware of this,' she confessed with a disgustedly surprised look.

I said, 'Look, arranged marriage, no longer popular, used to be a consultative process, an old value of an agricultural society and will not disappear as long as parents think they have a stake in the future of their children. Over the years, old generation parents have only been replaced by new generation parents, like Internet dating service providers, who now grill potential partners about their attitude, intention, habits, income, age, weight, body shape, whether skinny or curvy, astrological sign etc, more than what traditional parents used to do earlier.'

'And as regards male domination, do you know how disappointed were Diana's parents, when she was born?' 'No idea,' she said.

'That was because they were hoping for a male heir to carry on the Spencer family title. And do you also know that when Catherine de' Vinci (1519-1584), the future queen of France, was born in Florence, Italy, her parents declared they were 'as pleased as if it had been a boy'! King Henry II, her husband, neglected her as she could not produce a male heir for the French throne, during the first ten years of their marriage. On the otherhand, when Queen Elizabeth II first delivered a male child, Richard Coleville, Press Secretary of the palace excitedly declared that he knew she would not let down the country. It is reported that hearing the news of the birth a male heir to the throne, Prime Minister Clement Attlee and opposition leader Winston Churchill were equally overjoyed alongwith many courtiers and ministers. Interestingly, Sir John Weir, the official physician of the royal family confided to Elizabeth's Private Secretary, Maj. Thomas that he had never been so pleased seeing a male organ in life!'

Stumped by the hard facts, Nina was feeling uncomfortable. I paused for a while thinking I was probably getting argumentative. 'You have not answered the Rights issue I had raised.' She was now trying to provoke me.

I said, 'Do you know that in India and south-east Asia, all men and women were given equal voting rights soon after Independence, whereas in the 19th century 'democratic' Britain less than 3 percent of the population had this right? And women didn't have this right until 1918, after which only women above thirty, with minimum property, were allowed to vote. Only after the Representation of People Act in 1928, voting franchise was extended to all women'. O, really? I didn't know that, I have not even voted once,'she said non-seriously.

'That is your choice but in USA, another great democracy, women had to agitate and wait for long 144 years after independence to get this right. In fact, the process was completed in respect of black women in 1964 only, when the Civil Rights Act was made into law, almost 200 years after the American Independence in 1776.'

Nina looked at me with big eyes. 'Wow, super! You know so much about us which even I do not know.' I said, 'No, not much really. Being a student of social history, I am an admirer of many positive qualities in your culture, particularly the gender- just way the head of the monarchy is selected. Otherwise, I am sorry if I have hurt your feelings.'

'There are many good and bad things in the society of yours and mine. A thoughtful study of human history only can remove many of our perceptions and prejudices. When Spaniards reached Philippines, they were baffled to discover women there were never the property of men as they fondly believed earlier. The second shock was to see the easy divorce procedures. In Sumatra Island, men were regarded evanescent figures like ashes and were buried in their maternal family graveyard. In old Cambodia, Vietnam, Thailand, Burma and Tribal India, women were in charge of market, money changing, buying, selling, and trading and wealth management. An outsider marrying a local girl was not allowed to leave the country and was obliged to live with his in-laws. In India many Hindus, firm believers in theory of 'rebirth', think that once married means the bride and groom are destined to be man and wife for the next seven lives.'

'It is interesting, but don't you think that is pretty long, uncertain and unrealistic?' She asked.

'Yah, but that is the belief, probably to serve a purpose. And in order to reinforce that belief, the priest makes the bride and groom go round the 'sacred fire' seven times, called Saptapadi, making seven marital commitments to each other'.

'Yes, I have seen some such colorful scenes in Bollywood movies, but what exactly are these commitments? Are they practical and doable?' She seemed curious.

I said, 'Colours, fun, festivity, foods, music and dance apart, each commitment has deep meaning and great message. But, lately, it has been reduced to a minor ritual only, much like marriage vows in other cultures and faiths. 'But then I am really interested to know, if you don't mind,' she insisted.

'I am not a priest nor an expert but let me tell you what I know of and remember. In the first round, the groom tells the bride: 'With our first step together, our bond has become stronger. As our home maker, you will look after food and finance; I will embrace you and work for the welfare and happiness of our family'. In another round, the bride asks of the groom a more significant commitment- 'You shall love no other woman but me as your wife'. The groom now responds positively: 'Yes, I shall love you with all my heart and shall look upon all other women as my sisters.' 'Aha, that is the real commitment'-she exclaimed excitedly.

With cold comfort, I said, 'Yes, but it has to be mutual to survive. So, the bride in turn declares, 'I too will love you with single minded devotion and treat all other men as my brothers.' 'Wonderful, but impractical, what is the next one? She asked.

After this the groom announces: 'I offer my life to you. Now, we have attained spiritual union, our love and marriage will be forever, we shall pray for pure food and prosperity and for virtuous, noble, healthy and brave children'. 'And then? 'Then both of them recite the mantra that means: 'We will be truthful to each other in all matters and love each other for ever.' These commitments are made publicly in the presence of every one- family and clan elders of the bride and the groom, friends, relations, parents, priests and above all the 'sacred fire'. A relationship, to be life long, needs understanding and support of every one concerned.

So when there is a crisis in a relationship, there is a pressure from both the extended family networks of the bride and the groom, who come forward to help disinfect the relation of pollutants and prevent a potential break up. Although legally there is always an exit door, a majority do not exercise that option. By breaking up, one may have the pleasure and freedom of several liaisons and yet it gives hardly any time to settle down in life. Many so called 'love marriages' repeatedly fail as they are high on expectations and low on efforts to sustain it. High pillars bonded by low quality materials break and collapse under pressure and tension. Saptapadi is one of the many marriage cementing mental materials to save the family, the seed bed of civilization and the smallest welfare state of the world'. Nina looked to be in a reflective mood and said, 'I agree, your Saptapadi is a great idea and I could see some merits in it'.

I said, 'Of late, things are changing in my country also and parents' role and influence has been weakening. The practice of arranged marriage involving all stake holders, is not always hunky dory and is slowly dying out increasingly replaced by mutually agreed relationships'. 'Oh really?' She said feeling confused.

Then trying to tickle a bit of her funny bone, I said- 'But then, we also often wonder why in some cultures, where boys and girls date for years, chase each other , fall madly in love, live- in for long and marry, are witnessing rapid divorce and breakups. When you have no parental involvement and all the freedom to choose your suitors, why do you fall apart so often, at so short periods? Is it because of an overdose of individualism or an allergy to long term commitment? Nina appeared a bit unsure and said: 'I am really not sure and have not thought of it seriously. Maybe the context has changed and the values are outdated.' I told her- "Like you, I had also read a report about a study of dating websites in the 'Daily Mail', which said that now the minimum qualification of a person to be a perfect sex partner is that he or she should have had atleast 10 lovers in the past. Is it true?

She said, 'There are different reports and all these are not always true.'

Then I asked her in a lighter vein, 'Tell me, is it true that a spouse here goes to the family court for divorce on petty issues like farting and snoring?'

Happily disgusted, Nina first collapsed into a fit of giggles and then biting her lips to keep from laughing further, said, "What is wrong in it? Everyone has a right to a good night's sleep. We also forgive many of men's relationship errors including cheating and infidelity. I hope you would appreciate that annoying bedtime habits like sleep talking, profuse sweating; passing wind, fidgeting, hugging the duvet, and sleeping naked are quite irritating. That is why you must live- in with your partner before marriage, just to find out whether he has any such irksome habits. I would rather share my bed with a pet than with such a partner.'

Half convinced, I said, 'Don't you think it would be wiser to seek medical assistance than legal remedy? Incidentally, do you know that people who fart frequently have less high blood pressure and hypertension? Are you aware that flatulence is one of the sure signs of an active stomach? Gastroenterologists say that hydrogen sulphide, a toxic gas, generated by bacteria living in the human gut, is very natural.' At that time, the present British company 'Shreddies' was nowhere and had not developed its new range of underwears with foul gas killing carbon filter pads to help thousands of people suffering from irritable bowel syndrome and their suffering, tolerant spouses. It is said that smelling a big market, an enterprising couple of Colorado, US, tested the product on themselves. And became famous overnight by releasing to media a picture showing a male model sniffing and kissing anal area and butt of a female model. American spouses had laughed to their heart's content. However, not feeling comfortable and willing to be dragged into a debate and still giggling, Nina now changed the subject saying, "I have also read you people practice something called caste system, untouchability and follow a social hierarchy. This is very unfair. Why don't you do something about it?" I told her, 'Yes, I agree and this is unfortunate. In fact it is a relic of the proto-Indo-European society, which was divided into three orders ie, a clerical class, warrior class and herder-cultivators, called flamines, (Brahmin) milites (Kshyatriya) and squirites (Sudras) in ancient Rome. Later on the 'slaves' formed the fourth category. For each category Romans had prescribed a color code for clothing-white for priests, red for warriors and blue and black for others. The French revolution (1789) was a direct consequence of this inequality and exploitation.

As regards India, its constitution has banned untouchability and made caste or social class based- based discrimination punishable. Actually, the system degenerated when inter- marrying stopped across groups of migrants constantly on the move, about 2000 years ago. The recombination and remixing of paternal and maternal genetic materials stopped. Manusmriti, a book on moral code of conduct, written around 100 BC, rationalized the practice by prescribing professional tasks to social classes. Slowly, it got stratified, when manual work was considered inferior to the mental. Consequently, the Indus Valley civilization also lost its soul and started waning.'

'Frankly, no one has told me this side of the story and history,' said Nina.

'It is to some extent similar to your upper class, the most privileged ones, the middle class and the most deprived working class, without upward social mobility. The most privileged have high level of economic, cultural and social capitals. The phenomena is already losing its hold and lingering mostly in rural pockets. Two persons most worried about this were Gandhi and Ambedkar. One led India into freedom and the other, rising from the oppressed class, helped writing of the country's constitution that banned untouchability for ever.

In fact, during his frequent meetings with villagers, Gandhi used to point out to the five fingers in his left hand, one by one, representing five ways to fight for freedom, ie, removal of caste based discrimination and untouchability, spinning for self reliance, empowering women, abstinence from alcohol and drugs and social harmony. Then he would point to his wrist, the base of the five fingers and say: Together, this is non-violence. He sacrificed his life for upholding these values.' Nina seemed to be listening with attention. I continued- 'But I have also read something about your country, tell me how far it is correct.' 'Yes, tell me,' she said. I quoted from memory a famous couplet of Froissart, a medieval chronicle writer, historian and court poet about the prevalent class division in England:

'When Adam delved and Eve span, Who was then the gentleman?'

This implied, when Adam was ploughing the earth and Eve plied the loom, were there any class division in the Eden? Why is it so now on earth? Why do we have Lords, Nobles, Aristocrats, Barons, along with beggars, bonded workers and vassals in the same society? In fact, in England, feudal land owners had petitioned King Richards-II to forbid a serf from sending his son to school without his Lord's consent (1391). Seven centuries after Froissart's question, the practice still continues'. Nina didn't say anything.

Continuing, I asked, 'Is it true that in your country, the royal protocol approved by queen Elizabeth-II, has demoted the future queen 'Kate' in royal ranking because she was a commoner? How true is the report that the blood princesses, those born royal like Princess Beatrice and Eugenie, are given higher protocol preferences in public and private?

Is it correct that this order of precedence has been drawn after Prince Charles married Camilla, the commoner? I also saw a report that Camilla had to wait in the rain outside Guards Chapel Windsor, for the arrival of Princess Anne at a memorial service in 2006 because Charles had not accompanied her!'

I could see a sense of consternation in her face and she looked further confused and replied softly: "Yes, I faintly remember such a thing happened and if true, it was not fair."

I reminded her that nobody understood the lower, upper middle class system better than George Orwell. In one memorable passage, he recollects how children of his youth days had been taught that the 'lower classes always smell'. We have to fight such trends and mindset together irrespective of our racial and national identities.

She nodded her head in approval and then, wearing a mischievous smile said- "It seems you have an unusual interest in our princesses."

I said they were very popular in my country, including your present queen. The most popular was of course Diana and we were so saddened by her death. I still remember how an economist was simplifying the complex issue of globalization referring to the manner of Diana's accidental death.

He would narrate - 'A British princess, fond of Indian chicken tikka and Chinese hakka noodles, ran away from a Paris hotel with an Egyptian boyfriend, in a German car with a Dutch engine driven by a Belgian driver drinking Scotch whiskey, closely followed by Italian paperazi on Japanese motorcycles. The car crashed in a French tunnel and the victims were treated by an American doctor using Brazilian medicine bought from a Russian chemist wearing an African hat that failed to save their lives.'

Then he would smile and tell his students that, jokes apart, globalization, if chased without sufficient and thoughtful preparation, might have disastrous consequences full of discontents. It can be a virus without visa. Nina was now listening more attentively. In the meanwhile, the train came to a halt. She stood up and thanking me profusely said- It was great talking to you, convey my regards to your wife.' I said, 'I will, and hopefully we shall meet again.' 'But how?' She insisted. 'We now live in a smaller world, let us keep in touch, we have already broken the ice.' I gave her my business card before she left.

I thought I had made my point without making an enemy. Living long inside a room, some people think there is nothing higher than the roof. Similarly, people in some countries continue to have strange notions about other societies.

Breaking my chain of thoughts the train screeched to a halt at The Hague, known as the city of museums and the14th largest city of the European Union with a number of world heritage sites. My friend drove me straight to the historic. The Hague castle after which he led me to a restaurant in the eating street. And lo and behold! I found Nina there serving food to the tourists. Seeing me, she rushed to our table and warmly greeted us.

Observing some sense of surprise on my face, she explained that every day she worked in the restaurant for two hours to support her study expenses in the university and that many university students take up part time work like this. I said that back home, I would give your example to the students in my country. Earning to support learning is a great idea. I had done it myself at age 16. Nina said she would like to buy a book to study further about the intricate caste system and religious practices in India.

'Wait a minute,' she said and rushed back to the open kitchen in the restaurant corner and came back with a plateful of foods. On one side of the plate there was a full sausage doused in curry ketchup and on the other side, a Turkish donar kebab with French fries, onion and sauce. Thanking her, I asked whether I could have some serials and vegetables instead. She quickly understood and replaced the plate with another having deep fried patty made from ground chick peas and fava beans in addition to massed potatos and egg plants blended with olive oil, lemon juice, salt and garlic. She called it Hummus. We had some quick bites and left the place after giving her a book which contained several of my articles on Gandhi for Nina's father.

Nina's reference and inference about 'caste' revived some old memories of my university days. We had started a small campaign in early 80s for dropping caste indicating surnames. I did it in a court through an affidavit. There was instant disapproval from my clan and caste. Father thought I have converted to another faith. Some friends ridiculed. However hundreds followed this and publicly dropped their caste surnames. Many threw away their caste indicating 'sacred threads', cut off pigtails and other such high caste markers. We met the then Odisha state Chief Minister, Janki Ballav 'Patnaik, in 1983.

He had given us appointment at 12:30 midnight. Popularly known as JB, he was a great scholar.

We made two requests; one, that he should set an example and drop his upper caste indicating surname 'Patnaik'. Now he looked serious. Continuing, we said he should talk to the education minister and issue a circular to the education department asking them to prohibit mention of surnames of any student at the time of their first admission into the school.

In support, we cited a number of examples stating that none of the saints and sages, writers and scholars like Plato, Aristotle, Socrates, Bashisth, Biswamitra and none of the kings, monarchs and emperors like Dasarath, Dhritarastra, Janaka, Ashoka, Nepoleone, Alexander, none of the gods and goddesses, prophets, sons and daughters of god in history and mythology had any caste surname. In fact, in India, many men even didn't have their own name and were known by the name of their wives and mothers. Like Ram was addressed as Seeta pati (Seeta's husband), Krishna was called Devki Nandan (Mother Devkee's son) and so on. However, the argument failed to cut ice.

So the practice continues as is evident in the matrimonial advts columns of so many 'progressive' news papers of 21st century India, seeking brides and grooms from a particular caste, sub-caste, clan, gotra, area, colour and surname! One advt. proudly asks for a fair, Maithili brahmin, Shandilya gotra girl. Another seeks a match for a mangalik, kshatri, aurora, mahajan boy and so on. To many, living in the pigeonholes of artificial, inherited and enforced identity, these markers and beliefs of purity and superiority provide a zone of comfort and psychological security.

15

Shengnan, Shengu and Six 'T's

Why was Nina not willing to believe that a marriage could last for 31 years and beyond? In this context, it will be relevant to share an educative experience in Kuala Lumpur, Malaysia, where I had met a gentleman named Chou, from Honkong, on the occasion of an international seminar on 'Family Life Education' (FLE). After several small conversations, we became friendly and our light and casual interactions now moved slowly into personal territory. He was 42 and still a single. Today, number of singles has increased manifold and it is feared that 21st century was probably going to end as the 'century of singles'.

'So, you are the most eligible bachelor in our group here,' I told him in a lighter vein pointing towards some female delegate.

'Not by choice,' he replied, still smiling.

'No issue. You have great companions like Isaac Newton, Voltaire, Beethoven, Leonardo da Vinci, who were alone without feeling lonely. We have many great saints, philosophers and leaders who remained single by choice,' I added.

He reflected for a moment, and said, 'Jokes apart, I really wanted to marry, but no luck. Seriously I think your social system and customs are still better in this matter.'

Partly pleased and curious, I quipped, 'What makes you think so?'

'Because I have seen proactive Indian parents in Hongkong. They don't allow their young people to remain outside wedlock for long and take the initiative and facilitate matrimony through continuous groom and bride hunting. Whereas in our case, I have to chase the girl and if she doesn't agree, I have no choice. Then, sometimes, even if I am interested in someone, I am not sure whether that 'one' is marriage material. Then, often you long to marry but unable to catch attention.'

'Don't your girls also chase the boys?' I asked.

'Yes, some of them do, but most of our girls have become very smart and choosy now. Our social protocol dictates that men wishing to date and flirt should approach the women first. You don't know that I am a very shy guy and often feel horrified at the prospect of rejection. In the process, I have wasted the entire third and fourth decade of my life in this fruitless auto romantic enterprise. Then there are some social values and expectations.'

'For example?' I asked. 'That, in a relationship the males must be higher than females in everything, ie, in age, in height, in education, in income. I have now given up. I can't marry a girl of or above my status nor can she marry some one below her. So, you can call me a Shengnan.'

What is that? I asked feeling curious.

'Oh sorry, it means 'left over', men unable to marry for reasons beyond their control. In our language, they are referred to as 'Shengnan' and for women unable to marry for the same reason, the term is 'Shengu'.

I told him there was a third category in my country. Wedded to social causes, mission and or spiritual quest, some strong minded persons consider matrimony as a distraction and try to avoid it.

After carefully listening, Chou agreed but explained he had no such mission and said how after a day's work, he latchkeys into the empty small flat and switches on the internet and music system until feeling sleepy. His last shock was from a smart girl he was dating for about two months. When he proposed, she asked him some questions that put him off. These were: How religious was he, whether he used condom before sex and had he tested for HIV or any sexually transmitted infections? The last one was whether he would mind if after marriage she decided not to have a child.

I agreed with him that these were hard questions but there was nothing wrong because before entering into a long term relationship, each partner needs to have clarity about where the other partner stands on certain sensitive issues. I reminded him about former British Prime Minister, Winston Churchill's confessions that his most brilliant achievement in life was not winning the Second World War but the success in persuading Clementine to marry him. 'So, don't abandon the chase. Birds, beasts even insects do it better than us. Snails, squids, crickets, bed bugs, butterflies chase their females in style. A male Sarus crane begins courtship with loud trumpeting calls. Blue whales chase their non receptive females with pleasing songs. And among male Cicades, the one whose love call is louder, deeper, longer and more frequent finally wins the female attention. So my dear, switch off the cell phone, computer and music systems and go out and propose to the girl you like, without hesitation or fear of rejection,' I insisted. He just smiled shyly, still diffident.

Next day, he came to my room. In order to convince him further, I quoted some studies that said a man and woman living together lived longer. How couples in long term and stable marriages were more content than those who were not married and stayed single, how sharing a bed has multiple benefits. It leads to healthier and happier life. Sleeping next to a loved one also helps lower the stress hormone cortisol, creating a sense of security and reassurance. It also lowers the level of protein that triggers heart attack and boosts oxitocine, the love hormone. Further, the psychical benefit and emotional value of a happy union is immense and even a nagging spouse keeps one physically and socially active. And finally you can share with your new girlfriend the latest research finding that having children makes a mother safer and live longer in old age.

Getting interested, Chou said- 'If all that you said is correct, I would make one more attempt. In fact, I often fail to muster courage to frankly express feelings. But if I ever succeed some day in my chase, tell me how to make the relationship durable? I can't restart chasing girls all over once again.' 'There is no single answer nor am I a highly successful person in this. It is an invisible chemical attraction that draws a woman and man together. We must surely step out and make an effort. Often singles like you comfort and console themselves that they are much better off without getting hitched of hooked. Some of them set too high standards that become self limiting. Some others wait endlessly hoping that one day the right person would appear knocking their door and ringing the bell. These don't happen,' I said. I explained how my brief exposure to family life education had saved my own marriage. And about how experts had identified four essential components which they call FTF, ie, "Four T Formula". That is - Trust, Time, Talk and Touch. I always add two more- Tango andTransparency. The fifth 'T' or Tango is a popular Latin-American dance and music with dramatic stylized body positions where both partners take a long step and then pause before the next move. Tango is also a bicycle with two seats, one behind the other, to enable both the riders to jointly pedal to have the joy of moving together. In the ball room of life, a relationship sustains when both the partners strive to nurture it, when two minds, two hearts think together and eventually become two soul mates, while complementing, respecting each other's views, preferences and limitations but still maintaining their individual identities.

'Trust' comes from 'transparency' in relationships, a reliance on the truthfulness of the spouse, from a mutually faithful relationship based on an expectation that the other one won't cheat on you. And hence to be trusted is as important as to be loved. Equally important is 'Time', a critical resource to nurture a relationship. The more time one invests on it, the better would be the rewards. Similarly, 'Talking' between spouses works as a tonic that promotes better understanding. Even claptrap or empty talks also helps. Talking together in bed at night is known to be a great booster in reinforcing marital ties. Studies say that most couples converse meaningfully for an average of nine minutes each day. There is a worldwide hunger to be heard. Reversely, use of words filthy and foul, interrupting and not allowing people to speak have caused innumerable and avoidable conflicts and even wars, both at domestic and international sphere. Our friends and enemies live in the mouth and vocal cord. May be, realizing this nature has taken care to keep the tongue inside the teeth!

Similarly, talking through technology and gadgets is no substitute for direct, face to face, interpersonal communication. Einstein had feared that, the day technology would surpass our human interaction; the world would have a generation of idiots. Personally, when Binny was angry with me, she would stop talking to me for a while. This would make me feel as if she had inflicted upon me a cruel punishment. My mother used the same weapon to pressurize her husband into submission. It is said that famous Italian sculptor Michaelangelo used to see a living and talking angel in each piece of marble and would continue carving until it is set free to fly. After years of carving, he completed the incredibly expressive and life like statue of Moses and looked at his creation for a moment in silence, expecting it would now talk to him. And when it did'nt, he violently hit the knee of the silent statue with a hammer, angrily shouting, Hey, Moses, why don't you talk to me? Talking animals dislike long silence. Some talk to themselves for want of a receiver.

Like talk, 'Touch' often injects fresh life and a new zing into relationships, provides intimacy and reassurance, and conveys care, concern and a feeling that one is not alone. It is a part of our mammalian biology traced to maternal nursing, when a mother holds the head of her child in her chest and carries it in her arms. Hugging helps both in sorrow and happiness, in victory and defeat. It is also equally popular in animal world. When an elephant is found to be in distress, other elephants come closer to her, touch and caress her trunk, tail and genital areas, as a mark of affection, solidarity and support. Partners spending too much time with other friends and too little between themselves and living without comforting body contacts, are among the top bugbears in relationships. Like a stitch in time, a touchy kiss in time can prevent nine potential fights and break ups. The French don't say 'I love you' but 'Bisou, bisou'- which is a mixture of soft words with a little kiss. And what is that critical time for a spouse? Experts vary. Some say it is before going to sleep and others prescribe it before getting up from bed or upon parting from a person whose company one truly enjoys.

"Actually, I am not sure whether I could give so much time and follow all that you said to keep a girl in good humor and maintain the relationship," reacted Chou with a helpless look. I reassured him that it was actually not that difficult if one compared the benefits. Many women dump their men, who do not like to spend a little time in talking to them. My wife, Binny, is always very fond of talking and I used to take her out for a stroll twice everyday for about 20 minutes so that we could talk to each other freely in privacy. Both of us felt very relaxed after this.

An old teacher of mine in the university had a habit of hugging his wife in public whenever they met outside their home. When I asked his wife, who also happened to be a personal friend, about her feelings, she explained that she was not embarrassed at all but felt happy, particularly when her spirits were low. A good, tight bear hug that I occasionally give my grand children dissolves all my work related tension. During my last trip to New York City on way to Virginia, I was struck by a strange advt, which said: 'Hug and Earn'. 'Hug hungry people', come here and pay generously for a few moment of hugging and cuddling, feel happy and go back to work.' Spending exclusive time together as spouse, friend and lover, hugging and cuddling together before sleep, repairs bruised and broken hearts, makes the marital ties stronger. In fact, seven of the 'Ten Commandments' deal with relationships only!

It is reported that when President Reagan was recuperating in the hospital after an assassination attempt on him, wife Nancy slept nearby, wearing one of his shirts, to be comforted by its scent. When my wife was away in my home town to look after my ailing father, I used to spread her saree on the bed every night and sleep on it to feel her presence and also to drive away negative thoughts. Recent research says hugging and complementing the spouse is the best way to sustain a relationship. When we have time to hug pets, why not partners? Even in the midst of an intense election campaign President Barack Obama didn't forget to send a romantic message to wife Michelle that stated- '20 years ago I married the love of my life and my best friend. Happy Anniversary! And when he visited Africa, the continent of his ancestors, he felt amazed and excited while meeting the original ancestor Lucy's fossil in Ethiopia and became emotional after touching a vertebra from her torso.

A Bisou-bisou or small kiss and touch often triggers a big affairs that helps partners stick around and stay together. Many men are not aware how much a woman in relationship values it. Similarly, an affectionate pat, hand holding, hug, warm words and humour strengthen the intimacy between two individuals and keep the relationship healthy. By giving and receiving love we exchange and acquire new energy, new interest in life. And much like fine wine, it gets better with time.

The power of 'touch' turns sworn enemies into friends. Internationally, the most talked about peace making touch was a hand shake between American President Ronald Reagan and the then Soviet President Gorbachev. With this, began the end of cold war. Similarly, the world became more peaceful, when Richard Nixon and Mao Zedong shook hands, when Israeli Prime Minister Menachem Begin and Egyptian President Anwar Sadat touched each other and when Palestine leader Yasser Arafat and Israeli leader Yitzhak Robin clasped hands for the first time and signed a peace treaty. Once again, the peace warriors touched their hearts with great relief, when in the Summit of the Americas; US President had a historic handshake with the hostile Cuban President Raul Castro, in the sidelines of Panama City. This thawed the two countries 'decades' old frozen relationship, opening a new door for dialogue. Serious Castro turned humorous in the summit, claiming six times more 'talking time' as compensation, as his country had been excluded from five earlier summits. While political opponents 'talk after the touch', lovers 'talk before the touch'. Either way, touch and talk add value to each other.

In 2002, I was staying briefly in a hotel opening to a street called 'Little India' in Singapore. It was Saturday and I had overslept after a long session followed by late lunch. About six in the evening a strange mix of humming and buzzing sound woke me up. For a while I could not make out what it was and peeped down through the windows to find out a mass of men and women excitedly talking to each other. I came out of the hotel to the street which was full and found almost everyone was talking to someone. As if each one had a story to talk about and share. It looked like a huge talking society. I moved forward, mingled with the crowd and spoke to some of them and discovered that most were migrant workers; predominantly males from Bangladesh. They assemble in this street and adjoining bylanes every Saturday evening only to talk to each other. Being away from family and home, talking in their own language to their own people was like a therapy and gave them lot of satisfaction and happiness. Like talk therapy, touch therapy is equally effective. Among lovers, touch powers the passion into action.

Many doctors earn patients' trust through the power of talk and touch. Holding a patient's hand or feeling their pulse, while discussing their medical situation, provides reassurance and makes a clear statement of empathy. It has great therapeutic value. It is also the number one bed side manner. Millions of people are starved of 'touch' and wander in search of it. I heard about a recently opened new shop in Japan's Akihibara district called 'co-sleeping speciality shop' offering for a price, touch and talk oriented services like cuddling, foot massage, affectionate pats, intimate talks etc. Women were paid to sit with men, listen to them, fill their glasses and light their cigarettes.

One may be the most successful and famous person in the world and simultaneously could be a total failure in personal and marital life without understanding the basic principles of living together. Instances are legion. Renowned physicist Stephen Hawking's marriage failed twice. According to his first wife Jane Wide, it was the wave of fame and fortune that 'engulfed' the relationship and then 'swept it away' into the 'black hole of despair'. Then he married a 'wonderful woman' he loved, named Elaine Mason, who also left him quietly. Nelson Mandela, another living legend of his time, fell in love and married thrice, first to Evelyn, second time to Winnie and third time to Graca, Mozambic President Samora Machelle's widow. The first two broke up in divorce. Finally, he found peace in the third, when he was already 80 and old. American President Barack Obama's father Sr. Obama and mother Dunham fell in love and got married against stiff oppositiom from both the families. The marriage collapsed in three years with a divorce. Both of them again fell in love and married to persons of their choice, which again ended in divorce. Barack was mostly raised by his grand parents.

World famous comedy icon Charlie Chaplin (1889-1977), who entertained millions of cine goers, failed miserably and repeatedly, in saving his marriages and relationships. His first love and marriage with a 17 year old actress Mildred Harris ended in two years, as he discovered it was 'irreconcilably mismate'. The second marriage with another teenager Lita Grey, again failed with a bitter divorce with Lita accusing him of 'perverted sexual desire'. The third relationship with Panlette Goddard, also met with similar fate after which he married Joan Barry that ended with a paternity suit by her. His last marriage was with a teenager Oona O'Neill, a girl 36 years younger to him.

Fame and popularity in public life has often proved to be a failed cement to bind people together at personal level.

The first moon walker, Neil Armstrong, could not understand why his first wife Janet divorced him. He went into depression for a long time and became reclusive. It was probably a conflict between fame and family or may be lack of attention. It is said that JK Rowling, unable to cope with the fame after the roaring success of Harry Potter books, had sought psychiatric therapy. As regards Armstrong, the reluctant, reticent hero, he was never wearing his fame on the shirt sleeve nor bothered about it ever. Similarly, world's first outer space walker Valentina Tereskova and her Cosmonaut husband Andrian Nikolaev married after intense love but failed to live together and divorced. Philipa was feeling very lonely and depressed as Christopher Columbus, being mostly on sea, had hardly any 'time' for his wife. She died young. Albert Einstein had married twice after intense love but failed to keep the family together.

Personally, Binny and I were so different, opposite and ideologically distant from each other, like South and North poles, that thoughts of breaking the relationship had crossed my mind a couple of times. But probably, I was not as bold as these greats. Then, Binny would often blackmail me emotionally with a threat to end her life if ever I did what I said. Or thought. So, in a way it was she who saved the marriage. Fear of its negative impact on the children was the other positive factor.

In another biography, titled 'Love and Capital', Mary Gabriel describes in detail about the frequent drinking episodes of Karl Marx, revolutionary socialist and father of Communism (1818-1883) and how Engels, his best friend and alter ego, saved Marx and Jenny's marriage from a certain disaster. While wife, Jenny, was away seeking financial support for her family and children from her relatives, Marx is reported to have had sexual relationship with Lenchen, the family house keeper and had an illegitimate male child. However, before Jenny could smell it on return, Engels swiftly claimed parenthood of the new born baby. As the story goes, famous writer and thinker George Bernard Shaw was known for his numerous affairs with married women, including wife of great poet W.B Yeats and daughter of Karl Marx. He was instrumental in destroying a couple of marriages and at last his own late marriage to Charlotte Payn-Townsend, a lady with a romantic past, could not be consummated for various reasons. Famous English playwright William Shakespeare is reported to have had affairs with a number of persons including a 'dark lady'. In his last will before death in April 23, 1616, he had bequested his 'second best bed' to wife Anne Hathaway stating: 'I give unto my wife my second best -bed with the furniture'. Critics considered this as a slight to Anne by an indifferent, unfaithful, cold hearted husband. Great poet Rupert Brooke (1887) whose most popular poem ' The Great Lovers' had made waves failed in his own love life three times and had a mental breakdown after the third break up.

India's first woman Prime Minister, strong willed Indira Gandhi's famous marriage with Feroz Gandhi failed partly because of power dynamics and partly on account of mutual distrust. Many power couples face such problems, particularly where a husband has to play a subordinate and self effacing role. God Zeus and his consort Hera, the queen of heavens in Greek mythology were such a power couple. Stories of their frequent domestic quarrels and confrontations are well known. Hera was short tempered and too proud of her beauty. So much so that when two women namely, Side and Gerana claimed to be fairer than her, she cast one into a dungeon and changed the other one into a crane.

Strangely, most relationships begin with high commitment and end in bitter complaint. A Chinese proverb says, 'govern a family as carefully as you would cook small fish. Find out if someone is not listening'. About three years after my last meeting with Chou, he had sent me a mail. writing: I am no longer a shengnan and have found my soul mate. Do you know why we have chosen to live together? Because we had no expectations from each other! Yes, we have decided to follow the 'T' principles!

16

Long Living Weaklings

I had neither anticipated nor realized it. When our first child, Gayatri, was born, it was immediately followed by at least a dozen new 'births' in the family. In Binny, a mother and in me a father was born. Then her and my parents suddenly became grannies and grandpas and declared their new incarnation with pride and jubilation. Her two unmarried sisters suddenly became 'Mousi' (maternal auntie). My brother became a Kaka (paternal uncle) and Binny's brother a Mama (maternal uncle). Infact a host of new relationships were born each with a new social role, as if extending the umbilical cord to its end. A protective social ring was formed around the new born. Eventually, it turned out to be a kind of family co-operative. Like in the wild, baby elephants are reared by all the female elephants in the herd and are weaned until they are 10 years old; the mother elephant's sister playing a special role. In my case, four years later, when our second child was born, the family members completely took charge of the first one and from time to time, made me conscious of my own deficiency as a self disciplined parent.

Such support system is disappearing. Yet children are born to live. Although death, destiny and doctors had snatched away from mother, seven of my siblings, nature otherwise has blessed the humans with not only variety and diversity, but also with a fairly long life span. Maternal instinct and family support have also played a crucial role in ensuring longevity of children. Otherwise humans are so vulnerable that even a tiny five milimetre female mosquito could kill a hundred kg six footer human in seconds.

Over the ages, from living fast and dying young, humans have started living long and growing old, with care and support around them. Whenever elders visited us, they would always bless me with words, 'Live long up to old age, live for 108 years' a form of blessing born out of prevalent concerns about premature deaths. Because when Shakespeare was writing plays in England and Meera Bai was singing devotional songs in India, only one in three children lived beyond 21 years. Humans are designed to be born fully formed but they develop slowly. They have a longer lactation and infant dependency, followed by slow moving life stages. And over millions of years, each succeeding generation has added years of life to its children by providing better care and nutrition. Thus, when mortality was controlled by care, longevity became the consequence. A clear example from the animal world is that of baboons, whose normal life span of 30 years in the wild increases to 45 years, with assured food supply and care in a sanctuary.

But without proper planning and management of longevity, a major part of this fairly long life is wasted in non-productive activities, ie, in disease, disability, frustration, fear and fights. Tiger cubs are completely blind for the first week after birth and stand on their own soon afterwards. Similarly, the puppies, born both blind and deaf, soon overcome their handicap and emerge as one of the most agile, adaptive and the happiest. Their mother quickly gets them out of her womb unto the ground, to be able to run and catch the prey faster. Just a few days after birth, the mother birds shove their young ones out of the nest, escort them up in the sky and drop them in an attempt to train the chics to try their new wings and then fly on their own. They wait and watch for a while, ready to rescue, in case there is a danger of free fall to death. Then let them go and take charge of their own lives. Rabbits run and rapidly reproduce multiple babies within months of their birth. A mosquito becomes an adult in just 11 days ready to reproduce. By contrast, in case of humans the ability to stand up takes more than a year. The day my daughter, Gayatri, stood up after falling down five dozen times, we had celebrated the occasion with a big feast. And when she started walking, taking faltering baby steps, Binny called me out loudly and excitedly to watch the event, as if it was a 'miracle'. The next exciting event comes when the child utters a full sentence answering questions of 'why' and how'. We had a lot of worries when our second child Maitri took a longer period to do this. Her son is now 11 years and still bedwets.

Thus from toilet habits to formal education and training at primary, secondary and tertiary levels now takes away 18 to 25 years for preparing a child to face the world of work. Almost a third of life span.

This long life span of the humans is now getting longer. Consequently, many age old social institutions are already under pressure. Quite a number of them developed over three millennia would now require realignment and overhaul to cope with this rapidly changing socio demographic scenario. To survive the new and unknown challenges, one would need conscious and careful 'life-span- planning', well in advance. The first attribute of any planning is the ability to foresee the unforeseen. One must know where to go and what to do when, why and how. If you don't have a plan, your life is spent implementing some body else's plan. You can plan better when both time and imagination are on your side. Birds and beasts also believe in meticulous planning. For instance, before undertaking a long distance journey to warmer regions, migratory birds first shed their older wings and regrow new ones. They eat plenty of foods to give them the needed weight and energy to withstand the long trip, in addition to training their children for the purpose. Insect species have better survival instincts. Wasps and bees love to live in colonies and organize themselves to optimize their resources to meet future needs. Cockroches, whom we always want to kill, form a congenial society and manage it by consultation and consensus, practicing a very simple form of democracy sharing resources like food and shelter. In case of certain male and female species, the relationship does'nt end after mating and laying eggs and fertilizing. The responsible male returns to protect the eggs from predators. Trees store their memories, learning and exchange nutrients and information through soil, fungi and roots about whether water was available, whether pests were in the air and so on, behaving in one way as a super organized community for survival.

Humans are one of the longest living animals on earth. They think, reflect, learn and grow. The huge, cold blooded Galapogos tortoise lives for 177 years, almost double the age of humans and yet has remained where it was millions of years ago. On the other hand, the omnipresent and the oldest life form bacteria live for 20+ minutes only. In between, the human's life journey has advanced, enriching itself progressively, endlessly towards evershifting goal posts. Assuming a normal life span to be 100 years, it can be divided into ten overlapping stairs, one progressively leading to the next over ten decades. Now, only one in 11,000 people's lives beyond their tenth decade and this ratio continues to rise. Mahatma Gandhi was following a planned life style to live for 120 years and he would have made it but for his assassination. During this long life span one undergoes many stressful life events like marriage, pregnancy divorce, death of a spouse, parent, close family member or friend, personal injury, accidents and illness, job loss, jail and retirement etc. Educational institutions do not prepare students to face and deal with these, nor do family and societies take any active interest. Unfamiliar events overtake ill prepared individuals almost every day. Prince Gautama (Buddha) was prevented from seeing these real life events, fearing these might change his outlook and attitude to life. Since most of these are predictable, they can be dealt with effectively with advance preparation and planning. Why a prince Gautama or anybody should be shocked? In order to overcome the surprise element, Jainism identifies five important and auspicious life events in order of priority, to prepare for. These are: garvadharan or descent into mother's womb, janma or birth, diksha or initiation into education, keval jnana or attainment of wisdom and nirvana or final emancipation.

It was an exciting moment when in my village I saw for the first time, a cow giving birth to a calf. After pushing it out, she first licked her clean, was fiercely protective and did not allow any one to come nearer her child. But then within an hour, the calf started moving. It didn't have to wait to grow up to walk and run. In two months time, the infant langurs acquire quadrupedal locomotion and start walking, running and jumping. Similarly within days, the mother bird takes the chic for a few flying runs and then lets it be on its own. A camel is still luckier. It is born with rows of long eyelashes to protect against blowing sand and hot sun in a desert, with nostrils that can be closed to keep out dust and with a large hump that can store fat to survive long periods without food and water. It is also blessed with long, strong legs to carry heavy loads over long distances and with broad, flat, leathery pads to prevent its legs from sinking into sands. This is not so in case of humans.

During my first visit to Zimbabwe in Africa, I had the opportunity of witnessing a Giraffe delivering its baby. Soonafter, she started nudging and kicking the newborn repeatedly until it was able to stand up on its own and walk. Many animals and plants are blessed by nature with special characteristics to survive in their habitat. A camel is born with two rows of eye lashes to protect itself from blowing sand and hot sun in a desert. It has huge humps to store fats to survive long periods of starvation. And it has broad, flat, leathery pads at the bottom of its hooves to prevent the legs from sinking into sands. Birds like penguins have airs trapped under the feathers to absorb body heat and withstand extreme cold weather. Many plants have special capacities to self repair and replace body parts in fluctuating temperatures and so on.

By contrast, in case of humans, their first decade in life ie, age 0 to 9, is virtually an 'age of dependency and helplessness'. As soon as a baby is pushed out into an unknown, alien world, it screams aloud, not knowing how and where to relocate. The mother feeds, cleans and helps it learn to walk and talk. From mother's womb to the family womb is a 280 days long journey. A few years later it starts going to another womb, the school, where it stays more than a decade. The first day in school is also the day that separates the child from the warm parental care and security, after surviving the day one, month one, year one and year five. In our neighborhood school the grandmother of a child would sit close to the classroom to assure that she was there. Otherwise the child would cry. In epic Mahabharat all the seven siblings of Lord Krishna born before him, could not survive the 'day one' and were killed by the agents of their uncle, King Kamsa. A Biblical episode describes how King Herod, worried about the birth of a 'new King' to dethrone him, ordered that all the infants in his kingdom under two and living in Bethlehem, must be killed. Kamsa also had issued such orders. A similar thing happened to Bhisma's siblings in the epic Mahabharat. His mother had thrown all her new born babies, one after the other, to the river Ganges until she was prevented by her husband that led to their separation.

Archeologists have found that in pre Columbian Mexico, at one place, 42 children were sacrificed to one god of Aztecs. Holy Quran documents how pagan Arabs were sacrificing their children to the idols. Genesis 22 describes how God tested Abraham by asking him to present his young child Isac as sacrifice on Mount Moriah. In the middle ages, children were the victims of wars among tribes in New Zealand. In the long running wars between Ngati Maniapoto and Taranaki supporters, children were being taken as prisoners and eaten by the warriors when there was shortage of ration during the war. In some male preferred cultures, as a girl child, the fact of your very birth indicates you have survived the sex selective test and abortion. There is a Jesuit saying: 'You give me a child until it is seven and I will give you the man'. When one is young, she or he creates a picture of the future watching others, ie. Parents, teachers and adults.

Despite my repeated attempts to push it back, it continues to haunt me. The Second Decade, i.e., age 10 to 19. A period of transition towards adulthood, known for rapid physical growth and discovery of self identity. The sexually active period full of risks arrives through puberty with a bloody, fluid farewell to early childhood. Post pubertal changes like enlargement of penis, sperm production, pubic hair, and increase in size of vagina, clitoris, and uterus keep teens body focused. At around age 13, there is a sudden surge of hormones, and oestrogen that awaken 'awareness of and interest in the opposite sex'. The cause for infatuation for the opposite is more chemical than cordial. Giving a poetic expression to this physical attraction, Nobel Laureate for literature, Tagore (1861-1941) had written in Deher Milan: 'Each part and particle of my body cries to meet each part of yours.' Nature has taken millions of years to create in male and female the drive for sex and love and union and bless them with erogenous spots and patch of sensitive tissues to enjoy the experience.

This is also the period children prepare for leaving the family, choosing career, selecting friends and partner, adjusting to social norms and adopting citizenship roles. These are to be addressed now with understanding and imagination. Adolescence to adulthood is a decade long transitional phase full of restless vitality. Referring to the storm and stress of this period, when someone asked an old lady for an opinion, pat came her reply: 'If I had the choice, I would bury them at 18 and dig them up at 80!'.

I had many bumps and bruises during this period particularly when I became sexually aware. Every girl suddenly seemed good looking, more attractive and I felt happier, energetic and body conscious in their presence. During this phase, often the primal impulses come in conflict with family and social norms, creating tension. It does not spare even the gods. The most turbulent period in Krishna's eventful life was during the second decade of his life. Now, new research by prestigious Massachusetts Institute of Technology says that presence of opposite gender in organizations boosts productivity of its workers.

Looking back now I understand how idiotic I was during this period spending long hours excitedly talking to young girls, most of which was meaningless sweet nothings. A slight disapproval from parents met with an instant rebellion. Some one has rightly said that the cause of political struggle was rooted in the conflict between parents and children, born in two different time zones and generations. Some like Malala Yusafzai turn to be social rebels. At age 17 this gritty girl asked teachers, preachers and politicians some fundamental questions: why is it that it is easier to give guns and difficult to give books? Why is it that it is easier to make tanks but difficult to build schools? Moti, a teenage girl in our neighborhood, always under tight control of her mother, went into a secret relationship and got pregnant just to show her defiance and assert her independence. During the long drawn Vietnamese war, a large number of young Americans under 20 had resorted to smoking, alcohol, drug and sex as a way of registering their protest against the war. Gandhi was just 19 when he left India on September 4, 1988 to study law in London's Inner Temple and returned to India in June, 1891. He has confessed in his autobiography how he had to face intense storm and stress including peer pressures to visit brothels. When Greek philosopher Aristotle was asked to share the experience of his adolescence, declining to comment, he had said he wished to forget that turbulent period of wild infatuation and blind excitement in life. In several cases, it lingers on to adult years.

Plenty of instances show such excitements are not confined to a particular age group and spill over to adult years.. It is reported how a hurriedly arranged meeting between highly attractive Hollywood actress Angie Dickinson and Indian Prime Minister, Nehru, scheduled for a couple of minutes for want of time, lasted for two long hours and how a dull meeting between Nehru and Kennedy had suddenly brightened up after Jaqueline, the first lady, came in.When asked about it, an amused Kennedy is said to have commented that it was the problem with all his 'distinguished visitors.' Both Kennedy and Clinton were also vulnerable to such influence.

Socially, the first life choice about career, curricular and extra-curricular priorities is made during this time. It is a double struggle young people go through. At 18, they also become eligible to vote, to drive, to work and to marry (in case of girls). It's a fertile period for dreams and aspirations. The other big event comes through opening the academic door for higher studies, a second door for higher autonomy. Now young people tend to be more adventurous and fearless. Young David was a teenager when he dared, defeated and killed the legendary, powerful Goliath. Krishna of Gita fame was hardly eleven years young when he killed Kansa, the ferocious king who had killed all his siblings. Similarly, Ram, the Epic hero of Ramayana, had won Seeta's hand against many powerful suitors by breaking the unbreakable divine bow, when he was hardly 20. He defeated and killed the demon king Raavan, not only because of his supernatural powers but by the sheer energy and determination of youth. Raavan was already a grandfather by the time he faced the young energetic, Ram. Later in life, the same Ram was defeated by his young twins, Lov and Kush, when they were in their early teens.

Among the long tailed, black faced Langur Hanumans, the famous South-East Asian primate, the younger have the higher social rank than the older. Here, the physically stronger and younger male langur drives out the weaker and older ones, to mate the female. He even kills the infants sired by others. The younger people have always an edge over the older.

During the first half of the third decade, formal education comes to an end followed by a sense of autonomy. People like to live on their own in privacy. Some start looking for a boyfriend or a girlfriend, whom they can marry to eventually settle down. They also learn political beliefs and behaviour from socializing groups and people around them. Three critical life events that mostly happen during this phase are, the end of formal education, beginning of work life and looking for a partner to live with. It can be called the decade of hope and happiness. Many young people fall in love during this period. The excitement of first love and its memory lasts a lifetime.

Not every one marries, some avoid and a few are afraid, many do not like to be trapped into a relationship. A few do not want restriction on sexual freedom and responsibility of raising children. But those who do, marriage are preceded by a lot of excitement, anticipation and apprehension. In addition to channelizing one's sexual energy, it is also the first testing ground to perform duty as a house holder, to trip, fall, rise, learn and grow. By this time parents and teachers become remote. But education has not trained one for choosing a compatible partner and starting a family and for lack of skills; young people are uncertain and nervous about partner selection which has a life altering impact.

Like oil and water, some marital choices do not mix or match and end in disaster. Some love privacy and like to be lonely- seen both in human and animal world. A few years ago, I had visited the Delhi Zoo. An official guide led me to the tiger enclosure and showed me a tiger named Naresh with a missing tooth. I was told he was a lone ranger and had been consistently dodging both female company and fatherhood. Young beautiful tigresses introduced to the big cat one after the other, not only failed to attract him but were invariably attacked and chased away by him. A friend of mine who had set up a matrimonial match making firm, would always repeat that 'marriages are made in heaven' to convince his clients and persuade them to accept his advice.

Once, I confronted him by telling him that 'If all match making and marriages are madein heaven and blessed by God, why do they break up'? Why couples run from fat weddings to big fights, crying and cribbing? And rush from bedroom to court room, losing both money and 'heart'? And if God decides everything why don't you wind up your match making company? He argued that heaven was also occasionally visited by thunder and lightening. So, help of heaven is not always fool proof. Selection of a right partner is a skill that every young person has to learn. The sentiment and lack of confidence is captured by a popular musical 'Fiddler on the Roof':

'Matchmaker, Matchmaker, make me a match;

Find me a find, catch me a catch.'

The Fourth Decade, covering age 30 to 39, is considered by many as the prime of life. Physically, by 35 most humans have fully grown wisdom teeth and the third molar bones fully fused. This is also the period when one has seen and tested the world, the family and challenges of parenthood and understood how they work. It can also be called the 'age of happiness' and final years of youth hood, with a settled family, close circle of friends and stable career, that makes one a provider to those one loves and lives with.

For many career couples, this is also the time to go off contraception in preparation for pregnancy. There are occasional problems in personal and sexual life. A close colleague of mine would repeatedly complain to me about how his wife refused to have sex with him and resist whenever he attempted to disrobe her. Subsequently it was found out that she knew nothing about sexual relationships and considered it unnatural and sinful. Her perception changed only after counselling by a psychiatrist. Another woman in her late 30s and obsessed with her looks, kept on postponing marriage and maternity, fearing a bloated belly, misshapen breasts and rolls of excess fat.

An IT engineer couple, living in front of our Delhi flat, used to disappear from our colony for about ten days almost every month. Their envious friends would light heartedly compare this absence as monthly honeymoon trips. Then the trips stopped when the young lady became pregnant, about five years after their marriage. The gossips stopped. The fact was, they were trying for a baby and the days most likely to be helpful were from 10th to 18th of one's regular monthly cycle. During this period, they wanted to spend more time together, undisturbed. As advised by my wife, they had refrained from taking tea, coffee, soft drinks, smoking and alcohol well before that. Now, with arrival of the first child, planning for future begins. The first child makes parents break out of self centric, sex centric singlehood.

Young parents get connected with a new person in life and develop a sense of duty. Children also work as ice breakers, warmers and glue in bonding the relationship and preventing break ups. How many millions of marriages children save every year have not yet been estimated? My own marriage was one of these. When our first child arrived, the fragrant flowers in our bed room slowly made way for baby powder, huggies and milk bottles. The bathroom looked like a domestic war zone. Responsibility and romance now engaged in friendly fights for their rightful space in life. I am not sure whether the new baby increased marital satisfaction but new responsibility certainly decreased personal autonomy.

In terms of marital happiness, each successive child produced diminishing returns and increasing concerns. When our second child had a habit of going into bouts of yelling, crying, breaking things, Binny would first try to bribe her into silence, failing which she would also lose her temper. The result used to be a duel, leading to disproportionate and recurrent temper outbursts by the child. Unskilled as we were, we didn't know how to handle such behavior.

When our youngest daughter, Niti, who had delivered a baby boy, stopped calling us for a long time, we were worried and rang up her husband, Ashis. He told us that Niti didn't have proper sleep since the baby was born and was feeling extremely irritated and tired. The baby wakes up and cries frequently in the night to be breast fed, a problem common to most of the mothers. I asked a professor of paediatrics, who had just returned from an international research seminar. What he told was revealing and beyond my imagination. According to him, it was a perfect and thoughtful evolutionary response to protect the mother and the child. Frequent crying for breast feeding at night, according to him, delays resumption of mother's ovulation to prevent the birth of a sibling, with whom the baby has to compete for care and attention. Birth of siblings without spacing is linked to increased mortality of infants as well as the mother. So, the crying baby actually helps both- itself and the mother! Apparently, many of our so called 'problems' are actually solutions, once the plan of nature is understood.

Occasionally, unexpected death of a child or spouse becomes traumatic, abruptly changing the tide of good fortune and direction of life, creating great emotional storm and stress. The unforgettable loss of the loved one is borne as a silent cross throughout life. The hardest to heal is the loss of your own child. My brother, Manab's first child, whom I had christened as Nitya Nutan, a budding young cricketer and an extremely lovable boy, suddenly died in a road accident, when we were in the midst of a marriage ceremony. The bridal turned into funeral.

Life for his heart- broken parents in their late 30s, turned upside down as the coping mechanism collapsed. They responded to the tragedy with wailing, anger, grief, denial and a feeling of great betrayal by god and refused to accept the fact and come to terms with the reality and swallow the shock. They carried on the survivors' guilt for a long time and kept on insisting that one day the boy would return. Wailing with anguish and anger, the boy's mother would be asking everyone-'I have not harmed anybody in my life. Tell me why did this happen to me? Why, why, why?' She would wail and then faint.

The other major challenge is how to cope with the new situation without the deceased, on whom one was totally dependent. This happened to one of my cousin sisters, Rani, who lost her husband about six years after her marriage and after delivering three children in quick succession. She was 20 years of age and had been married off at 14. This sudden widowhood after an intense reproductive life, with three little children around to look after, disabled her further from an emotional relocation, replacement and in starting life once again with a new person though widow marriage, in any case, was a social taboo.

Thus, the tragic incident forced her to rearrange, restructure and redefine her life to replace the roles of her deceased husband. We all rallied around her, trying to revive her inner strength and reminding her about the children, who were her future hope. Being convinced about 'why' to live for, she slowly learnt 'how' to live and from 'where' to get 'what' that was needed to move forward in life. This needed a lifetime of commitment and struggle focusing on here and now. Her roster of friends also quietly atrophied, forcing her further to fend for herself. As if her cup full of woes were not enough to deal with, in the midst of the struggle, she was struck by a terminal illness that slowly ate away her remaining energy. Despite this, she had never forgotten her natural affection for life. Pushing away the dark clouds of unmitigated sorrow, she would show up like a shining moon and join us in all our happy moments. However, the emotional vacuum and the existential need for readjustment and coming to terms with the new situation took its toll. Unable to bear the stress and deteriorating health, she died prematurely, about thirty years before the expected time of her departure from the world and I lost a loving sister.

Unfortunate and unexpected life events, like sudden death by accident, infidelity, divorce, loss of job, do not refuse to be determined by cause and effect, nor can they be fully prevented and controlled. One has to try and train the brain to deal with it. Life, the greatest show on earth, always carries with it, pleasure and pain, light and darkness. In Spain, people rationalise and react to such situation by saying 'Que sera sera', which meant 'whatever will be, will be'. Even great and emotionally mature men and women have not been able to overcome personal tragedies. When a friend tried to commiserate and comfort Karl Marx, the father of Communism, at the funeral of his eight year old child Edgar, he had shouted back in anger and anguish, saying- 'You can't give me back my boy'. When Abraham Lincoln lost his only son Willie, his tall frame convulsed continuously with profound grief and intense emotion as he watched with pain, Willie's dead body being washed and dressed for the burial. Confucious, one of the wisest ever born in the world, died of frustration, shock and sadness (479 BCE) when his only son passed away and his most favourite disciple was killed. In epic Mahabharat, Dronacharya, the wise teacher and invincible Kuru Commander-in-Chief, fainted after wrongly hearing that his warrior son, Ashwathama, had been killed. Even after recovering, he lost all will to fight again, abandoned the defensive armour and was slain in battle that very day. It takes a moment to love some one, but a lifetime to forget the loss. Particularly, when a flower falls off or plucked before turning into a fruit and ripens.

Similar things happen in case of divorce, when the one time lovers have to deal with complex feelings of failure, pain, rejection and betrayal. And the great heroes are those who not only face the tragedy but fight and overcome it with greater courage. 'He who overcomes, I'll make him a pillar in the temple of my God and he shall go out no more', Jesus had said (Revelation: 3:12).

Neil Armstrong's sister, June, recollects how her brother was doting deeply on his two year old little daughter, nicknamed Muffle, who was diagnosed with a malignant brain tumor. She died of pneumonia which emotionally broke Armstrong. The personal tragedy made him and his wife quiet for months, like an earth quake quietening many other quakes. June feared her brother would have a heart break. Yet, the death propelled him to invest his energies into something very positive and challenging. He became a daredevil astronaut and landed on Moon seven years after the personal tragedy. Christopher Columbus (1451-1506), was 34, when he lost his wife, Filipa Moniz, who died at the age of 29 years only. A shattered Columbus decided not to marry again despite pressures from friends and relations.

Pregnancy on the wrong side of 30 often becomes high risk for women, as I had found in case of my mother. One of the reasons is that the growth hormones start plummeting after 35. Mumtaz Mahal, in whose fond memory Mughal emperor Sahjahan had built the world famous architectural marvel, Taj Mahal, at Agra, on the bank of river Yamuna, died of postnatal complications caused by frequent pregnancies. The end came at the young age of 38, after she delivered the 14th child in the 19th year of her marriage. Out of the 14, only sixsurvived- four boys and two girls. Seven died at birth.

I had lightly told the guide, who was excitedly narrating the story to us inside the monument- 'Listen, if Mumtaz had access to contraceptives, there would not have been a Taj Mahal here, to construct which 20 thousand workers had to struggle for long 22 years. Nor there would have been an Aurangzeb to imprison his father emperor Sahjahan in Agra fort, nor a guide like you to narrate to us the romantic tragedy. Looking mystified, he asked 'How?' 'Because, Mumtaz would not have 14 pregnancies that killed her, she would have convinced her loving husband to limit it to one or two. Aurangzeb was the sixth,' I said.

The third and fourth decade together is also very important in the sense that they bring out the best in many people. All men and women went to space before forty. Alexander the Great, born in 356 BC in Macedonia, became the most powerful military leader during this period. Before he turned 30, he had an empire stretching over 3,000 miles from Greece to India. Swami Vivekanand, a revolutionary monk, was 29 years old when he mesmerized the distinguished audience at 'World Parliament of Religions' at Chicago. Jesus was 33 when he was crucified and before that he had influenced millions of minds with his message of love and compassion.

Buddha had decided to leave his palace pleasures and comfort zone for good at the age of 29 once he came face to face with the painful reality of the world. After years of spiritual quest, and finally after a 49 days of meditation, he is said to have attained Enlightenment at the age of 35, Aadi Shankaracharya, the famous spiritual thinker of the East and interpreter of the Vedas had dazzled the world with his brilliance before leaving his body at the age of 32 only. Prophet Mohammad was at the peak of his religious best around 40. Srinivas Ramanujan, (22 December 1887–26 April 1920) an Indian mathematical genius, with almost no formal training in pure mathematics, made extraordinary contributions to mathematical analysis, number theory, infinite series and continued fractions, before age 30. This extra ordinary young man's birthday, 22nd December, is observed as National Mathematics Day in India. Albert Einstein (1879 to 1955) propagated the theory of gravitation and published the famous paper on the general theory of relativity in 1916 when he was 37. Valentina Vladimirovna Tereshkova (born 6 March 1937) was the first woman to have flown in space, having been selected from more than four hundred applicants and five finalists to pilot Vostok. She was 26 years young at the time. WL Bragg was 25 and Malala Yusafzai was 18, when they bagged the prestigious Nobel Prize against the average winning age of 62. Malala was the youngest Nobel Prize winner.

Why and how was it that young leaders were so famous in the past? The fact is that in most part of the history, the ancestors of humans didn't live beyond their teens or twenties. Anthropologists say mother of humanity 'Lucy' died when she was a young adult. So, it was the youth, who were in charge of wars, power, authority and public affairs. Babur (1483-1530), who established Moghul dynasty in India, was 15 when he had started his conquests. Asoka (304-232 BCE), another great emperor, was in his 30s when he had expanded the Mauryan empire. Thus, over a long period, the youth developed a genetic predisposition to lead, that turned many of them into early achievers. So, in a way, younger people looking for new opportunities to lead, is more a natural instinct than a conscious effort.

The Fifth Decade.ie, age 40 to 49 called 'middle age', begins with end of cell renewal in the body. One doesn't feel old but has to be careful to maintain health to improve chances of living to twice this age. During this period, some are possessed by a feeling of 'let go' and eventually end up flaunting their pumpkin bellies. Careless women frequently change size of the body wear on account of obesity. While working in Indonesia during President Suharto's regime, I had seen how he had made it compulsory for all officials to undergo physical exercise during office hours as he didn't like pot bellied officials. When I was in Kobe, Japan, the land of chubby Sumos, a friend informed that they had a 'Metabo law', an euphemism for obesity, which declares men above 33.5 inches waistline as falling foul of law and at risk. It gives a two- inch additional concession for women!

When I met my favourite teacher, Padmacharan, for the first time, he was in his late 40s, slim and still childless. His rough and tough exterior hid a soft loving heart inside. He would always walk to his office covering a distance of 3km. Every day, he would wash and clean the house, climb the stairs to his room, wash and press the laundry and eat his lunch walking around. Whenever a colleague visited him for discussion, he would instead take him for a 'walk and talk' session outside. If he had to talk to a friend, he would walk to the friend's house instead of using the phone. In the morning, he would go to the sea shore, walk 3 minutes, jog 2 minutes and run 1 minute, repeating the cycle five times. Before going to bed, he would press and massage his mother's legs and wife's head for five minutes. He believed that human body has been designed to move, not to sit.

An eleven year old daughter of my friend, Pravas, was one day found missing. After a two days frantic search, she was found to be with a boy of her age in a restaurant. Wayward children bring additional grief during middle years. You suddenly realise how correct were your parents in disciplining you when your children start thinking how wrong you are! The generation gap turns full circle.

Safety of grown up girls in an unequal society, sex stimulating environment and fear of children being misguided into high risk behaviour, keep parents on tenterhooks. Children with hands on parents have better coping and social skills, better self esteem and self control and inter personal relationships.

In our colony in Dwarka, a struggling widow in her 40s was constantly worried about the poor academic performance of her 16 year old boy. He was hooked to the smart mobile phone most of the time, telling his mother that he was actually busy accessing educational information to face exams. One day, the gullible mother accidentally accessed his Facebook to find out strange codes and acronyms which she failed to understand. Intrigued, she called another boy older to her son, to explain to her what these actually meant.

Under pressure, the boy reluctantly explained that 'MIR-TTYI' meant

'Mother in room, talk to you later'.

'What is 'TDTM'? She asked, now more worried.

The boy explained hesitantly, 'It meant 'talk dirty to me'.

'Oh, no' She reacted. 'And 'GYPO' and 'IWS WYN'?'

'Ma'm, excuse me, I can't,' said the boy.

'No, no, you have to tell me, I want to know,' she insisted obstinately. Quite unwillingly, the boy said-'GYPO meant 'get your pants off' and 'IWS WYN' meant 'I want sex with you now'. The mother was shocked out of sense and remained in a state of depression for months. She was finally taken to a psychiatrist.

Midlife offers a menu of pain and pleasure. I had to change my job twice during this period. First time, because I didn't like the boss and second time, when I felt as if I was on a treadmill all the time. Now, researchers have discovered that it was partly genetic. As in humans, chimpanzees and orangutans also face midlife crisis and undergo a 'U' shape. Behaviour scientists confirm that our level of happiness declines after childhood until middle age and then gradually we feel more content again. People with everyday high career pressure like beating traffic, meeting deadlines and demands of multitasking and fast paced life, suffer a different kind of menopause symptoms called andropause. These are reflected in low energy, higher stress, low sex drive and lower level of male hormone testosterone. In many developed countries, male managers have been fighting this trend for quite some time. Now, there are a number of cases where women in their 20s and 30s are having menopause as a result of stressful living.

Elsewhere, to counter the negative impact of a fast life, a 'Go Slow' movement is catching up in faster cities of Europe. Inspired by popular actor Mae West's words- 'Anything worth doing is worth doing slowly', there are small movements promoting slow food, slow car, slow city, slow street, slow traffic, slow noise and slow crowds. The most recent one is the 'slow love', movement which says if you want to make it last, take it slow, avoid 'no rule, no criteria relationships' and don't jump to sex until you have expressed mutual feeling of true love. Decades ago, the spirit was captured in an old pop song by The Supremes: 'You can't hurry love-you just have to wait, Love don't come easy-It's a game of give and take'.

Gandhi used to say- 'There is more to life than increasing its speed'. When we cross certain age and still chase our love for the speed, we are cautioned to slow down, not by the police but by the doctor! Naturopaths say that the three things that negatively affect our health are: hurry, worry and curry. We often neglect the fact that some times the wheel of life also needs a first gear. And also a reverse gear once a while. It is said god is never in a hurry and his plans are never rushed under pressure. Without advance learning about and preparation for life events, one gets confused and uncertain about the priority.

Is it wise to make the 'best of life' or the 'most of life' and how to? I learnt my first serious lesson from an unconventional and upright bureaucrat, Sahabuddin Yaqub Quraishi, the man who has left his imprint anywhere he worked. In the early 90s, one day I saw him a little upset and gently asked for the reason. He was as reluctant as I was persistent. The fact was, he had received a message from a batch mate, alerting him to get ready to move to the Prime Minister's Office. Any bureaucrat would have jumped to grab this position of immense power and influence to make the most of his career with a sure finger on every pie, but not Quraishi. He almost lobbied to get it cancelled. Many of his friends, well wishers and batch mates advised him against such a move. Yet, he withstood the temptation and stuck to his stand.

He feared that power and authority would kill many of his personal interests, creative pursuits, relationships and values in life. He didn't like getting sucked into a process over which he would have no control. So, he chose not to miss out on the 'best of life' in mad pursuit of 'the most', and eventually rose to be India's most innovative and effective Chief Election Commissioner, who made India the global gold standard in zero error and zero violence election with large voter participation and dared the high and mighty risking his future. He was a non directive, human relation oriented leader with dash as well as vision.

As a forest dweller always loves to return to his habitat, I returned to my native place after completion of my tenure at the Commonwealth Asia Centre. One day, when I was in the midst of a civil society meeting, a short cryptic SMS flashed in my mobile with a tingle. It read- 'Doctor Sahab, my NACO orders have come, you pack your baggage.' He had been appointed as Director General of the National AIDS Control Organisation, with a mandate to halt, prevent and reverse the spread of HIV in India. I could not say no, again because of his high trust and high relationship style.

We worked together, developed an effective strategy preceded by extensive consultations with the stake holders that eventually reversed the spread. Then, he became Union Secretary, Youth and Sports Ministry and I joined him as Senior Adviser with a monthly salary of one rupee, again on account of high relationship. I went back to my village as soon as he moved to the Election Commission. When he became the Chief Election Commissioner of the country, we had invited him and the other two Election Commissioners, Mr V.S Sampath and Mr H.S. Bramha, to our state civil society convention. There, I made a presentation on how to involve the country's 500 million youth in promoting and strengthening democracy through ten strategic steps called YUVA- an acronym for Youth Unite for Voter Awareness. The strategy began with a slogan coined by me:

'Wake up, you are eighteen, Sit up, you are an elector, Stand up, you are a citizen, Walk up, it is voting time.'

During the presentation, I mentioned passingly, how I had worked for three months in developing this strategic framework. Now, when his turn came to address, he shocked all of us by his first sentence- 'Dr Bhagbanprakash said he had taken three months in developing this plan. I don't believe him. He is telling a lie.' There was a moment of shocked silence and embarrassment after this bombshell.

Then, smiling, he said- 'I know him for a quarter century, he can do this in three days! There was a big applause, as tears welled up in my eyes. This was his style. The capacity to recognize, appreciate and admire in public.

Once, President Bill Clinton was in Delhi after his second and final term, when Dr. Quraishi had also shocked him and all of us present there in a similar way. He was chairing the meeting and in his concluding remarks stated- 'Mr Clinton, now that you are free, we can offer you a job.'Clinton was initially clueless and felt awkward in the full glare of the media and senior diplomats. An Indian offering a job to a former US President was a bit difficult material to digest but he laughed heartily when Quraishi, with a mischievous smile, said- 'We offer you the position of Honorary Adviser of our Life Skills campaign to drive out HIV from the world.' Clinton stood up and embraced him. They established an instant rapport with each other. From that day onwards I was introducing him as the man who offered ajob to Bill Clinton!

On 25th April, 2014, his book 'Undocumented Wonder' was to be released at ITC Maurya, in Delhi, followed by a panel discussion. On the dais were eminent media leaders Vinod Mehta, Siddharth Varadrajan and veteran film personality Kabir Bedi. The hall was full with who's who in the capital city, with many standing on the side for want of space. After effortlessly handling critical and often embarrassing questions on Indian elections from the audience for almost two hours, he stood up and said with a smile- 'If I tell you everything about what I have written, then who will buy my book?' Everyone present broke into loud laughter. Continuing, he said- 'But I would tell you about the man who was the key person in this endeavour, motivated and chased me to write this book. He is here and sitting in the last row behind all of you'. He had already spotted me and now called me to stand up. There was another round of applause. The gesture became my reward.

Humour and humanity, laced with wit, warmth and depth made Quraishi unique among his peers. All big bosses with swollen heads disappear from mind while mentors like Quraishi sit fixed in the memory permanently. He often reminds me of popular Japanese monk and spiritualist, Soko Morianaga Roshi (1925-1995), who had the unique trait of answering abstruse philosophical questions through raw yet enlightening humour. Soko had travelled to many countries including India, Myanmar and Srilanka, talking at seminars and workshops regaling audience with his inimitable witticisms. In one such seminar, he was to talk about the experience of enlightenment, so he began by asking the participants whether they had 'urinated' in the last one hour, making every one split into laughter. Then, he explained by telling that as he 'can't urinate for them, he can't wear clothes, eat, shit for them and can't carry their body and live their lives. Similarly enlightenment is a purely personal experience, unique to the individual.'

Unlike Quraishi, there are many who do not believe in the relationship dimension of a meaningful living. Life span education can enable them to prepare for it. To take the best out of the best, in order to make the best of life. Learning about and from life is an endless continuum. Even very late in life, we learn how to ask for help, how to overcome fears, how to adjust and accommodate, how to love, be loved and overcome loss, when to be tough and when to be soft, how to discover self and how to lose it and many such lessons. The book of life is full of important lessons and wild diversity.

One of this bewildering variety was a talkative fast walking, middle aged lady in our neighborhood, named Nanda and nick named as CCB- 'chirpy chatter box'. Non-stop talker, Nanda was lucky to have an equally tireless listener in her husband, who would tolerate her nonsense for about an hour and then react saying, 'Oh, stop it, please.' Nanda would stop for just half a minute before reopening the CCB. She had a habit of saying something about everything understanding nothing. Fond of twaddle, she was an unsolicited adviser, uninvited intruder, perennial grumbler and always in a hurry. Whenever you met her, she would open the conversation narrating how busy she was, and would go on and on, taking the harried listeners round and round the mulberry bush. Almost like a talking machine. She was both a megaphone and chatterbox and would often start a high decibel argument and pick up a fight with her husband every now and then on petty issues, screaming choicest expletives. Once a while, the noise spilled over, disturbing the neighborhood. Whenever her poor husband, suffering from hypertension, tried to make past her to escape the gaali and further tension, she would block his way and shut the door. There is a belief that a domestic quarrel will die an instant death if one of the spouses refuses to participate in it. In case of Nanda's husband, this strategy didn't work. One day, to get rid of the endless verbal abuse, he disappeared from home and never returned.

Recently, I came to know that a 45 year old man, after a verbal thrashing by his wife, jumped into the enclosure of lions in the Nandan Kanan sanctuary, near Bhubaneswar in India and got seriously mauled.

A few months ago, I saw a report in the media about a police man, who, after a bitter argument with his wife in a restaurant, pulled out his pistol and shot himself in the head before his wife and children. My parents used to fight once a while but when it was going to turn ugly, father would invariably step back and go away, depriving her of the pleasure of a win. In later years, I found this attitude and strategy immensely helpful. Thus, whenever I see my wife turning aggressive and unreasonably argumentative, I change the topic or leave the place quietly to buy peace for both. It is said that great boxers often duck to divert the punching power of the adversary. I am greatly convinced about its efficacy in marital fights. It is also good commonsense, to allow once in a while the sharpnels to sail past. There is no urgent need to put bat to every ball.

During the 40s, conjugal life tends to be more stressful and children start departing for higher education. If the family is strong, it makes easier for children to sail away from the safe harbour to explore their dreams and aspirations. When my daughter was selected for a B. Tech course in Bio-medical engineering, I had accompanied her to distant Coimbatore and returned home alone crying all the way. Now, when I miss my children, I hold and press their old garments to my chest for instant relief.

Thoughts of divorce and changing partners occasionally visit the mind and in some cases actual divorce and remarriage take place because there is still time to restart life once again. In well- knit families, worry about living away from old parents bothers and providing care for the loved ones from long distance becomes an anxiety. Over all, the 40s that begin with lesser cells and sights end with more insights and hindsight, often followed by unexpected emotional upheavals. Some symptoms overlap decadal boundaries, like the peri menopausal period, spanning from 39 to 53, is a good time for willing acceptance of the inevitable life changes.

17

Second Fifty: 'Blues', Silver and Golden

Fifty plus Vidya, a close relative of ours and mother of two, while visiting our house, would regularly sit at a place nearer to the wash room and would rush to the loo every now and then during our conversation. She was a good badminton player in her school but would now refrain from physical activities and would sit cross legged most of the time. She would not even laugh freely. One day, I asked her whether she had a problem. She replied in three words- 'Your wife knows.' I found out that the problem was that she would 'leak' when laughing, sneezing or coughing or doing small sports activity like skipping rope. While going out, she would always carry a lot of pads in her shoulder bag. Because of this problem, she had stopped playing for a long time. She became doubly conscious when on one occasion, there was high pressure on her overactive bladder and urethra and being unable to control the urge, she 'splashed', embarrassing everyone present there.

Age related muscle loss or weak muscle in the pelvic floor is the real culprit but many women do not report this fact to the doctor out of shame. In those days, there was no rubber device to lift the bladder and keep the urethra shut. The gel like injection and ointments to thicken the vaginal wall and other low tech solutions were unheard of. When I took her to a lady doctor, the first remedy she suggested was to stop consuming multiple cups of tea and other liquids like cola and start regular physiotherapy.

I was half shocked and half surprised one morning, discovering in front of the mirror, the first strand of white hair inside the thin moustache. I was 51. So, I pulled out the unwanted guest forcibly and pretended as if it was not there. Denial! Next week, there were two at another part on the head. By end of the month, three more sprung up above the upper lip. I shaved off the entire patch. Again denial! Then it became a punishing morning routine. Because when you pull out one, five come out from different corners as if to join the funeral of their friend. In between, black and grey, white looks wise and pretty for a while, as a silver line. Slowly and reluctantly, you accept the losing battle and forget it when others start respecting the 'white reality'. An old friend advised me to accept and respect the 'white', because in the life's long journey, when all colours leave you behind, it is white that remains a loyal companion. Classical Indian poet and playwright, Kalidas, has described a similar incident in Raghuvansa as to how a few white strands had helped King Dasarath in taking a decision to peacefully transfer state power to prince Rama. Already in his late fifties, one morning, he suddenly discovered a grey hair on his temple and decided to step down and retire from public affairs. It was probably life's first warning signal to slow down.

At personal level, the fifty plus begins with a mixed bag. For many, like forty plus, a new phase of life also begins at fifty plus as they overcome financial pressures like children's education, marriage having their own home, financial security, etc. Others go through a series of mid-life blues, both mentaland physical. Fear of nearing retirement and being left on the shelf haunts a few. The journey towards the existential certainty of death gets faster now-often unnoticed. Age 50 to 59, the Sixth Decade, is also known as the –'Age of biological decline'. Some call it 'silver years' as loss and greying of hair becomes more visible now.

However, discipline in the 'first fifty' years makes living through the 'second fifty' relatively less painful. People become more aware of the need for keeping fit, modifying food habits and life style. Optimists do not accept age as a mere number because evidence shows that a greying old person of 72 can have an anatomy of 42- with discipline. However, many people wish to avoid an intense work life. A fitness conscious colleague of mine used to miss from his room every half an hour irritating his boss. To break the sitting time before computer, he would stand up, move around and go out for a short walk.

The hormonal storm that had overtaken one with puberty at the onset of the second decade ends its reproductive journey with menopause and decreased libido for both women and men. The body and mind often hijacked by sex hormones in the previous decades, start returning home. The instinctive obsession of the body with survival, pleasure and procreation needs weakens, giving a sense of liberation, freeing the fifty plus to focus on more important matters of life. Although the symptoms of menopause in most cases last until mid 50s, some women experience them for the rest of their lives. The most common symptoms are hot flashes, night sweats, irregular periods, loss of libido, vaginal dryness, mood swings and irritability. Some suspect Indian Prime Minister, Ms. Indira Gandhi, was going through this difficult period when her 100 year old political party split and her frequent, fickle and impulsive decisions alienated many of her close colleagues.

It was also reported to be one of the stormiest periods in England's first woman Prime Minister, Margaret Thatcher's life, (1973-1980) whom Russians had termed as 'iron lady'. Her post menopause moods and words created enemies, she fell out with senior party leaders and thought of resigning and leaving politics. Golda Meir (1898-1978) was in a denial mode. True to her style she declared- 'I must govern the biological clock, not be governed by it.' She went into an overdrive mobilizing huge resources for strengthening the state of Israel. Yet many fail to govern the clock and resort to antidepressants. A few succumb. Back home, when I heard and read about Indian Minister Shashi Tharoor's third wife, socialite Puskar's sudden suicide (Jan. 2014), after publicly professing her love for Shashi, I first wanted to find out her age than the autopsy report. She was 51 plus and could not handle the stress aggravated by a relationship issue. Instances galore about post-menopausal women making great waves as well as meeting tragic ends.

When my spouse Binny was going through this period, I actually didn't know how to handle this problem. She had just crossed 49. Unable to sleep and rolling on the bed, she would often cry without reason and go into spasms, making me nervous. I had no idea about this phenomenon and I am sure she also didn't know. Women, who marry late and close to menopause, have to give up hope of having a baby now. But it also finally liberates women from the Eve's curse, from contraceptives and from the anxiety of child bearing. Amanda Redman, famous actress of BBC detective series 'New Tricks', had nine miscarriages before menopause and tried for a baby after it for umpteen times, without success. She was heartbroken without knowing that in this matter nature intervenes in favour of women only because beyond 50, child bearing could be more complicated and fatal.

After this defining life event, the body gives signal of ageing in form of wrinkles in skin, obesity, grey and falling hair, and joint pain. The dreaded 'R' word looms large as people start worrying about retirement and loss of income. A time for stock taking for facing the end- of- job- life and competitive post retirement world. Those who are already connected to social causes, organisations and networks while still in job, find it easier to adjust to the impending transition than those who wake up late after the power quotient has vanished. Some people become more religious and spiritual. Grown up children get married and bring happiness as well as unrest. Joint families undergo stress.

I happened to witness an interesting event during my short stay in Japan where the students were celebrating their teacher's birth day at 60, with a big party to which all his children and close friends were invited. The teacher was dressed in red garments which symbolizes a return to dependence and care of children and a time to pass on the household to the next generation. In Japan, Red is a color reserved for the young. This Celebration of 60 is repeated at 77, 88 and 99. Similarly in Chinese society, filial support to the old and retired is a cherished family value. Society looks down upon children whose parents live in Old Age Homes. For native Americans, it is a time to pass down learnings to younger family members. Old Indians continue to be recognised and respected as the head of the household. In ancient Rome, the elderly used to get this status by virtuous living. One works for decades to reach this stage and age. In many cases, there is a subdued reluctance to separate from the 'work group' and everyday colleagues. Lack of experience to socialise for leisure suddenly becomes an issue. There are interesting stories about this important pot retirement life event Different people react to retirement differently. A retiree in India's Central Secretariat, whom we gave a grand farewell, wanted to break the bridge with the past work life completely. He piled up all his career memories, ie, appointment letter, promotion orders, personal file, curriculum vitae, rule books, business cards, office entry pass, appreciation certificates, photos with boss and colleagues and finally his 30 year old wrist watch and neck tie and made a bonfire of these, dancing around it with joy of liberation from the routine. Then he opened his laptop and deleted and deactivated all the sentimental materials from it, including official correspondence, Facebook, Twitter, other social networks and email accounts of many. And finally heaved a sigh of great relief and relaxed. The day after he claimed that 35 years after, he had an undisturbed, restful sleep for the first time.

He started walking in the parks, volunteering for community work, participating in social occasions, visiting old friends, reviving lost relationships, and travelling places with his spouse. He would always advise old and retired people to be closer to their companions as one of them would leave the world earlier and sometimes without notice. In order to avoid internal loneliness, he tuned to Yoga and meditation. Once, he told me with a lot of happiness that he had willed his wealth to the children and charities, surrendered his body to the doctors and his mind to the God and was now free from all ambitions, fears and regrets.

I was old enough to remember a ceremony that I had watched long ago in the holy city of Puri and close to Kriyayog Ashram on the beach. In Hindu spiritual tradition, it is called initiation to Sannyas or renunciation when one breaks completely with the old way of life. The spiritual master or guru asks the devotee first to forget his past, deleting all memories of the material world, shave off the head, throw away the old garments and take seven dips in the sea, completely naked. Then the guru gives him a new name, new yellow-red coloured dress and a staff called danda to lead a new life of inner purification, selfless service and spiritual practice. S(he) vows to get rid of all the worldly desires, and work to spread light and truth. The ceremony ends with a havan or fire worship followed by blessings from senior sannyasis (Monks).

Pradeep, another colleague of mine was no sannyasi. Having repeatedly postponed marriage, he suddenly felt lonely after retirement and now started looking for a 'retiree' bride as a companion. He even gave an ad in the matrimonial column. A lady came, stayed with him for about a month and then left, complaining of incompatibility. Another childless couple who had married to their office and work suddenly discovered they had time and means now to adopt a child and started scouting the orphanages. Some empty nesters, whose children have left, also consider this option worth trying.

Some people, unable to reconcile to loss of money, power, authority and identity, get a rude shock. Many die of it. Some go under depression. On 11th Oct. 2012, a retired colonel, M L Mohajan, jumped to his death from the fourth floor of a Noida Mall, leaving a suicide note that said- 'Because of my depression, I am unable to do anything, Please forgive me.' His Hongkong counterpart was worse and didn't leave any clue. This 68 year old retiree jumped from his flat to death holding his 13 month young baby grandson. Was it a murder, suicide or revenge? Neglect, madness, depression, drug or drinks? No one knows.

In a posh New Delhi residential colony where I was living in late 90s, a 67yr old man was found to be living with the dead body of his 94 yr old mother for days until the neighbors noticed it and called the cops. The man, separated from his wife for 18yrs, was too close to his mother and feared to be too lonely without even her dead body. Obviously, the surrounding society had failed to build an emotional connect with this urban loner. Some get a pet just to have a feeling that there is some one around. During our regular morning walks, an old friend and widower showed me and Binny a small item inside a news paper with tearful eyes. It was about a Canadian couple living together for sixty two years in an Elderly Home and Assisted Living Centre. The picture showed both of them weeping inconsolably as the Centre asked one of them to vacate as it didn't have space for two. I couldn't suppress my tears.

Although freedom from compulsory work may sometimes show a small bounce in health, in many cases it increases the chance of suffering both from clinical depression and physical conditions. One of the reasons why some people don't want to retire early is this. Another very honest bureaucrat and widower friend of mine ended his life for a different reason. Half the day, he was spending on news papers and the other half, watching news channels. His nights were mostly restless and sleepless as he was feeling greatly depressed thinking about negative news of rape, murder, incest, corruption, inflation, pollution, adulteration and degeneration of social and political values. Then, he started reading the sports news only until a report about match fixing by one of his favourite cricketers shocked him further.

When the media highlighted a barbarous case of gang rape and murderous attempt by the rapists by insertion of rods and pulling out internal organs, he was under terrible depression for days. The last straw on his back was when he saw a report in the media about a teacher exploiting visually handicapped minor girls in a school for the blind. The same night he committed suicide. For some people, all round negativity drains out the desire to live, taking away 'meaning' from life. Even political retirements often prove to be fatal if not planned well. After such a retirement, former South Korean President, Roh Moo-Hyun, under great depression, committed suicide on 23 May 2009, jumping from a 45-meter mountain cliff. He was 63. He had left a suicide note on his computer apologizing for making "too many people suffer". "I can't begin to fathom the countless agonies down the road. The rest of my life would only be a burden for others…" he had written.

Famous Oscar winning comic genius, Robin Williams (1951-2014), a cool, disciplined character actor, entertaining millions for decades and subjecting Presidents and Prime Ministers to irreverent mimickry, suddenly ended his life by first cutting his wrist and then hanging himself with a belt in his home in SanFrancisco, shocking and baffling the entire world. He was 63. Nobody could guess immediately whether the cause was age or agony. Subsequently, it was found out that he was under severe depression while battling with Parkingson's, an incurable and debilitating nervous disorder. There are several instances like this of sad, suffering people making others laugh while covering up their inner sorrow.

My old friend and classmate, Shivnath, had a different attitude and was a bit strange. Once, he confided to me how happy he felt when he lost contact and became irrelevant to his friends and how withdrawal from outward activities gave him more time to go inward, more opportunity to watch, reflect and wonder about the mystery of life. Although I had visited him five times, he never made a return visit. And ten years after, when he started losing memory, vision and hearing, he thought these were god's blessings because now he felt less attached to the world and didn't have to search for a silent, undisturbed place for meditation and prayer. Spiritualist Gudrun Hille was correct when she said- 'Treat your wrinkles as badges of honour that you have received in the battlefield of life, not scars.' Famous Italian artist and sculptor Michelangelo was one of them. Although prolonged hammering and chiselling had accelerated degenerative arthritis in his hands, intense work kept these in shape. Defying the loss of dexterity in old age, he continued to hammer and create one masterpiece after another until his death in 1564.

When the secretary of the ministry where I was working, retired, a grand farewell was organized in his honour. A week after that he was to leave the city. Having worked with him for years, I wanted to see him off at the airport. On way, a senior colleague stopped me and wanted to know where I was going. On being told, he started laughing and said- 'You are a fool. No one rushes like you to meet and see off a 'setting sun'. You must go back and greet the rising sun, our new Boss, who has just arrived. I had told him that in my culture, early evening prayer or Sandhya Aarti to the 'setting sun' was considered holy.' In fact, in India, more people offer prayers to the setting sun than to the rising one. These rituals at Dasaswamedh ghat in Benaras and at Ganga riverside in Haridwar (India) draw hundreds of tourists from all over the world.

When I decided to decline an extension and leave Commonwealth Asia Centre, colleagues had organized a farewell and had pasted a message at the gate which read- 'A Big Thank You for giving us an Opportunity to Work with you.' Although embarrassing, till today I remember these words as the best reward for all my hard work for seven years in this great organization.

'What are your future plans?' They had asked me in the meeting.

'To be a full time husband to my wife,' I had said in a lighter vein'.

'And with half the salary,' my wife quipped, sending the audience into loud laughter. For no-nonsense wives, it is a double whammy that makes many retirees go scurrying to look for work once again.

'Give us a message,' they insisted.

I said- 'Forget me, sooner the better.'

A few days before this event, a senior retired friend had alerted me saying, 'Look, I am telling from experience, post retirement, the love and loyalty of your former colleagues do not last more than 72 hours. So, it is always wise not to be in delusion and to look forward as looking backward brings more grief.' In one instance, it lasted 24 hours only.

The day after I left the Election Commission of India, I found in my mobile nine missed calls from the professor of an agriculture university seeking an appointment to come down personally to invite me to be the chief guest and address a national seminar. In the evening, he reached my residence with two other colleagues to persuade me to agree. But when I incidentally mentioned that I had just left my position in the Election Commission of India, he cleverly changed the subject and all of them left the place in five minutes without mentioning a word about the national seminar. There are examples galore about colleagues not returning calls, the buddy network suddenly declining, favourites forgetting and so on.

Broadly, power is of three types - the first one is called personal power (capability, morality, truth, love, integrity, intelligence), the second is professional power (skills, expertise, knowledge, innovation, creativity) and the third one is positional power (position, authority). For obvious reasons, self seekers always run after the third category and turn their back double quick as soon as the 'powerful' boss is out. However, people in the first and second category do not face such problems as these are integral to one's character. Always on short supply, they don't retire or go away.

Dr Biren Mohanty, a learned professor in my university had just retired. One day, he felt so happy and proud hearing the news about one of his favorite students becoming the chief secretary of the State, he wanted to meet him immediately and congratulate personally. Alas! He was made to wait for three months for an appointment, after that three hours in the waiting chamber and their meeting was over in three minutes as the 'favorite student' failed to recognize his learned teacher. Crestfallen, old Biren had a heart attack. Seven years later, his 'student' also retired. The fellow had a swollen head and an exaggerated opinion about himself. With plenty of time, he would now spend it only by boasting about his past. Always clinging to the trappings of power and authority, having never helped any one or done an honest day's work in his long career, he faded away without a friend. So, I tell my retiring friends- 'When your 'favourites' forget to remember you, you must remember to forget them for your personal peace and tranquility.'

I knew a very senior professional, whom we lovingly called Nimbu da, a person I always admired for his wisdom, commitment and personal integrity. He was a well-known social work practitioner and institution builder with strong spiritual and moral fiber. And headed an institution near Kolkata (India) that he had built brick by brick, working almost sixteen hours a day. He was so obsessed with the institute that it almost became an extended part of his self, like a body of his soul. In this obsession, he had forgotten that one day he had to leave it.

One fine morning, the Chairperson of the Management body informed him that shortly he would cross sixty five and had to retire. It came to him as a rude reminder and shock. How could he live without the institute, he thought and wanted an extension. In order to help him overcome the attachment, he was given an extension for two more years. Still he was not ready to quit. Another three extensions were given before he crossed 70. In the meanwhile, his wife also expired. They were childless Yet, Nimbu da didn't give any sign of leaving.

Now, once again he was gently reminded by the management to hang up the shoes and yet again he ignored it and kept on coming to the institute, until one day he was physically prevented from entering the campus by the security, who were recruited by him. A shocked Nimbuda was still not prepared to accept the reality and give up. Every day at 9 in the morning, he would come dutifully and stand outside the closed gate waiting to be allowed to his dear institute. The gate would not open. This continued until Nimbuda was fully frustrated and lost all hopes of ever returning to work. But finally one day the gate opened. Not exactly for him, but for his dead body, for, Nimbuda had passed away the previous night after a heart attack. The staff of the institute, including the management were there in full strength near the gate, with flowers to pay their last homage to the person who had given the best part of his life in building a great institution.

Being an admirer of him, I am still at a loss to understand why wise Nimbu da behaved in this manner. Didn't he know how the great builder of monuments and institution Moghul Emperor Shahjahan was dethroned and put in jail by his own son? Yes, sometimes an institution becomes the lengthening shadow of an individual but then, a sensitive person should not overstay his welcome. In the epic, Mahabhrata, the Pandav brothers had made this blunder against Krishna's advice. They lost all their five children by deciding to overstay at the battle field, Kurukshetra, just by one more day after their final victory. A surviving adversary, Aswathama, killed their sleeping children in the darkness of night, mistakenly thinking he was killing their parents.

In Indonesia, both, President Sukarno and his successor, Suharto, were removed from power unceremoniously because of overstaying their welcome. Sukarno was a national hero and had united the country of islands by developing a common identity and common language called Bahasa Indonesia with the help of linguists and by eliminating complications in tense and verbs. In less than 20 years, the 350 language speaking country started speaking one language. But he was not willing to part with power. A few years before Suharto's ouster, I was in Indonesia for six months and had an inkling of popular anger against him but he seemed to have decided to ignore it.

The disease is not limited to dictatorships alone. Instances of driving out unwilling rulers galore and still lessons are not learnt. Wiser ones pass on the baton with all its attendant power and authority to the next generation before they claim and snatch it away from the elders. Kicking away before being kicked out is always a soul satisfying experience. Biologically, during this period, the fire in the groin starts flickering with lower sex drive, moving towards slow extinction in the 8th decade and in many cases even before that. To delay this, some go in for testosterone replacement, thinking life without sex as meaningless. For them death of a spouse becomes a kind of sexual bereavement. But for some, growing older together, the sexless relationship becomes more intense as they start living now as real companions and soul mates with platonic interdependence. A few feel happy getting rid of the passion. Like Gloria Steinem, (1934), American feminist and political activist, who on her 80th birth day declared what a 'terrific advantage' it was to have a dwindling libido that freed the brain cells to do all kinds of great things! Instead of fudging the age, she was always eager to celebrate ageing publicly and defiantly, telling the world about its benefits. At 40, she organised a fund raising ceremony called 'This is what 40 looks like' and donated it to a magazine and used to repeat it every ten years after. On turning 80, she declared it was time for celebrating mortality and not ageing and wanted her funeral to be used as a fundraising event for a worthy cause. Like her, wise, lucky and good life event planners can now start leading a tension free life. For, longer one lives, still longer one is likely to live. Precisely because, one has survived critical life threatening periods like infant and child mortality, suffering a bad boss in office and many killer diseases.

This is also the time when grand children arrive; years after one's own children have left the nest. Holding them in arms adds new meaning and new hope, reviving old feelings of parenthood for the second time. When my daughter, Gaytri, had her first baby, a friend from Rajsthan rang me up and wished good luck for climbing up the 'golden ladder'. For some time, I couldn't understand what it exactly meant until another friend explained to me that it was a metaphorical reminder that you have stepped into the third generation. In parts ofIndia, people congratulate new grandparents for climbing one more step upward in the 'golden staircase', a step that begins your golden journey towards heaven.

Many married women now become widow, as women live longer than men and are mostly younger to their spouses. Most of those who had married men older to them also meet the same fate. Many live- in relationships do not survive up to this age making men and women companionless and lonelier. Some widowers look for new companions. For some, children have left but old parents are still around to be taken care of. So the 'younger old' and the 'older old' now live together. In our colony near Andrewsgunj in Delhi, we were greatly disturbed witnessing a daily fight between the 'younger old' son and his 'older old' father on trivial issues. Both of them were retired. The first fight started when the son removed the name plate of his father replacing it with his own. The father couldn't swallow the insult as the house belonged to him. After retirement, both had lost their official identity and now started fighting for personal identity markers at home.

Long before this incident, I had been subjected to continuous ridicule by my friends, when I had hung a name plate at the entry of my newly built house with names firstly of my wife and children and mine below that. My father used to visit us once a while but would not agree to live with us permanently. Once I asked him why. He avoided a straight answer for some time. When I repeated the question, he said- 'My dear, I always love living with you and your wife takes care of me so much. But I have no identity here and no name. People address me as 'so and so's father whereas I am well known in my own home town and every one calls me by name with respect.' I could realise it only after a decade when I visited my daughter in USA and stayed with her for a few months. At a public function, where I was a guest speaker, the master of ceremony announced-'Now, with great pleasure, we invite Gayatri's parent to deliver his speech.'

I had a strange feeling, more like Ziauddin Yousafzai, Malala's father, when his teen ager daughter won the Nobel. In her book 'I am Malala', the sensitive daughter writes, about how odd her 'Abba', who groomed her to be a brave fighter for justice and women's equality, must be feeling in the altered reality- "I used to be known as his daughter; now he's known as my father."

In our colony, my friend Mathew, already 62, bought two apartments near each other, the bigger one for him and the smaller one for his parents because his parents wanted to have their own space in order to maintain their own routine, pursue their interests, without disturbing the children. But for support in emergency, they wanted to live in close proximity but at an 'intimate distance', as old neighbours of a new age joint family.

The eighth decade, from age 70 to 79 – is the 'age of decreased mobility'. But then, there are exceptions in case of people who are highly disciplined. Gandhi had led the 'Quit India' movement in 1942 to independence in 1947 when he was in his seventies. During this period, the little pains of younger years reappear. Hearing and vision become weaker, visits to doctors become more frequent, some ailments need surgery and post operative care and recovery takes a longer time. There is a lighter joke popular among older people, which they share with each other sitting in a park that goes like this...

An elderly person requested the spouse saying- 'Honey, let us go upstairs, clean the bed and make love.'

To this the other spouse replies, 'Sorry, darling, I can't do all the three, I am too old to be so bold now.' It reminds one of the sad story of an old, one-horned rhinocerous from Guwahati, named 'Shiva', who refused to cooperate with the breeding programme of the zoo by repeatedly avoiding to mate with the two young female rhinos 'Maheswari'(18) and 'Anjuga'(8), already in heat. Soon, it was found out that in addition to old age, Shiva had a painful illness and was in great agony. He would frequently rub and bang his snout on the enclosure walls to get rid of the pain. Eventually, he died putting an end to the breeding hopes of the zoo manager. Rhinos are an endangered species now.

When some one referred to old age as a disaster and massacre, Mark Twain had remarked that age was an issue of mind over matter and if you don't mind, it doesn't matter. It is okay as a motivational comment. Age, environment and social values have an impact on ability. A very close friend, already 75 plus, confided to me how he wanted occasionally to have sex with his wife but found it difficult as there was no privacy and also because often his wife loved to sleep with her grand children. His second inhibition was the prevalent perception that sexual feelings in old age were weird, abnormal and shameful and that 'oldies' were supposed to be religious and not sexual. He was confused and I had no answer. So, he now met his personal physician who reassured him that sex once a while was not only normal but important for keeping his prostate healthy. And for women it can reduce dryness, loss of elasticity and thinning of vaginal walls and help in maintaining good sexual and mental health. Many Widows miss the loving touch of cuddling and fondling and an occasional desire to be desired.

In old age, interplay of matter, mass and mind determine behavior. Golda Meir had once said- 'My dear, old age is like an airplane flying in a storm. Once you're in it, there's nothing you can do. You can't stop a plane, you can't stop a storm and you can't stop time. So, you might as well take it easy, with wisdom..."

When my father-in-law crossed 80, his grand daughter presented him with a video game for children, which he could play in an adaptive mode. Although every one laughed at the idea and thought such a gift was improper and useless, playing it revived both his working memory and motor skills to a great extent in six weeks. His dementia slowed down. The greatest enemy of old age is mental inactivity and lack of stimulation. As the grey cells stop ticking, experimental actions forces it to learn new things and rewire.

One of the persisting problems among many in old age is physical movement. It is said you are as young or as old as your joints. Then, the circle of friends and age group mates starts to dwindle as they start to die. Once a while, one gets a cruel shock to discover that a very close schoolmate is already dead and gone ten years ago, a dear colleague has left the world before you are aware of it. Heart attacks, strokes, and cancer also take their toll. If one has survived this critical phase, one enters the golden years, the ninth decade, i.e., age 80 to 89. - the 'age of assisted living'. During this period, some people are active and can still take care of themselves, while a majority may need somebody to help them in daily routine. It is a period in life when one's energy runs out before one's money. One stands alone defenceless, facing punches and pushes of everyday living.

For some, unable to bear the sheer loneliness, with children living abroad or faraway, neglect and indifference of near and dear ones or the insecure environment, it is time for shifting to old age homes. A feeling of isolation enhances stress hormone increasing the risk of premature death of elderly. Tripathy, an old family friend and retiree from Indian Foreign Service, had big plans to start a senior citizens home for the poor and the abandoned but he could not sleep properly at night after shifting to his new house in an isolated, unfamiliar locality. He came under acute depression and felt as if something was creeping through his bones. His blood pressure rose rapidly, leading to a stroke and then death. Social and physical isolation is as potent a cause of death as alcoholism, chain smoking and obesity. All relationships are illusions one needs to overcome. Attachments lead to bondage and suffering- thought Buddha. The ancient Vedanta calls the phenomenon as Maya.

The other day I read about internationally acclaimed film director, Richard Attenborough, maker of the famous film Gandhi, moving into a care home in a wheel chair, after selling off his ancestral London house. Richard's famous film, Gandhi, had won eight Oscars in 1983. Earlier, his 90 year old wife, Sheila, had shifted to the care home, after being diagnosed with senile dementia. Their daughter Jane and grand daughter, Lucy, had been killed in the tsunami that blasted Thailand in 2004.Late Margaret Thatcher had to shift to a hotel as she could not climb the stairs in her house. This is the time when one needs 'care givers', who can personally 'be with' than 'doing to' the patients. Impersonal and too cold care kills people faster. Unable to bear pain, some wish to die. The mother of one of my close friends was bedridden with paralysis. Whenever I visited their house, she would ask me with folded hands and tearful eyes to kill her by giving poison. Loneliness itself is another big killer. Figures released by different studies indicate that nearly half of senior citizens in the urban world live away from their children.

For many, without a spouse, it is a solo unassisted living and for them, 'longevity', a defining marker of development, becomes a liability! Dementia or loss of memory and alzhimers is very normal at this age. Virtually, this period is like a 'second childhood' when the elderly behave like small children in many respects. Some lose muscle control and may become incontinent, frequently visiting the washroom. Some have to wear adult diapers and quite a few lose their mind control. The wheel of life turning full circle, it is a time when parents themselves are in need of parenting by their children. As memory fails, strong instincts and weaknesses in respect of food and sex, under control by stronger discipline for decades, reappear and take control of the mind. An 89 year old, widely respected person near my village, with a strong moral character, would now embrace any woman that came nearer him and start touching her breasts until the shocked, embarrassed lady extricated herself from this unexpected situation. Family members didn't know how to handle this incidence. When the old man was asked about it, he would say he didn't remember what he did. So, finally, females outside the family, including girls, were not allowed to go near him.

Memory also plays truant, with data overload, stored over a life time. Like the hard drive of a computer, overcrowding of the brain with experience, information and knowledge of the past, slows down its function. With increased difficulties in recall, people forget names of their own children, spouse and acquaintances. Ronald Reagan could not recognize his wife Nancy after living with her for half a century. Old Margaret Thatcher would repeatedly call out her late husband, Denis, as if he was still alive. 'With Denis there, I was never alone,'she had written in her memoir 'Downing Street Years', paying tribute to her late husband. And then the memory forgot the 'memoir'.

Every morning, my father, who was 87, would ask of my wife to tell him how many children he had and what their names were. He would repeat the same question and keep alternating between past and present. Once, he went for a walk and forgot the return path to the house. He continued searching our house for an hour and getting exhausted, sat under a tree on the footpath. Many passersby mistook him to be a street beggar and some of them started putting coins in his hands as alms. Worried about the delay in his return, Binny went out and finally traced him sitting under a tree and both his palms full of small coins. Furious, she led him back to the temple premises and ensured that he gave back the amount to the really poor sitting there. One morning, hearing my two daughters giggling loudly, I came out and found father standing stark naked in the balcony in front of them without any sense of shame. Earlier when he started bedwetting and taking off his clothes, Binny had made him to wear a pyjama. But he would often forget to tie it properly and seek her help to untie it.

Another lady in our colony would not recognize any one, including her husband. Yet the man would spend two hours every day playing with her a 'count the coins' game, hoping to revive her memory. Once I asked him how he played with a person who didn't recognize him. He became emotional and said- 'It is so painful. But I do it thinking that one day, she would recognize me and smile, and that will be my reward. In fact, had I known that the most important person in my life would suddenly stop recognizing me, I would have spent more quality time with her.' A very late realization. A year later, his wife passed away. Soon, he himself developed neurological disabilities that numbed his reflex. And then he had a fall in the bedroom while tripping over an object left carelessly on the floor. It fractured his hip and leg that eventually immobilized him. With the genetic fountainhead of youth far behind, the wounds failed to heal. Confined to the bed, he used to spend the whole day looking at the picture of his wife on the wall and closing eyes in between to think about her. And one morning, the eyes closed forever. The other day I was shocked to read a report about a South African couple Wilf Russel (93) and Vera (91) who were married for 71years. Wilf, battling dementia stopped recognizing wife Vera and passed away. Vera, who had become ill after her husband stopped remembering her, died four minutes after Wilf. When one life stops, another life goes.

Dementia and Alzheimer have no cure and it worsens as it progresses. In the early stages the most common system is difficulty in remembering recent events followed by long term memory loss. Most persons die within seven years. President Ronald Reagan survived for ten years after having been diagnosed of Alzheimer's. Mental stimulation, exercise and balance diet help in prolonging the life span.

Sometime ago, in an art museum, I had seen an interesting picture by a self taught artist, Bruce Camahan, in which he had feelingly depicted how an elderly woman was struggling from her bed to reach the wash room. As she haltingly saunteres, the back of her gown opens, exposing a 'tattoo' on her bare, wrinkled, right buttock, a strong sexual statement, boldly announcing her 'love'. It was so real that it looked like as if the artist had painted it by dipping his brush into the blood in his heart. Art, like a microscope, reveals deeper secrets of life innovatively in simple lines. Long ago, may be during her adolescence, she must have been a rebellious, wild and passionate lover. The tattoo captures and tells it all. The passion has gone, the pain persists. Many tattoos are permanent markers, loud and proud declarations of lifelong commitment. As relationships break down, they become an inseparable burden of the body, often bearing bad memories of sad endings.

Some older people like astronaut Armstrong become reclusive and withdraw from everything, even from people who visit them to pay regards. Incidentally, it is said that Armstrong was so withdrawn that during his life time, he had given only two or three TV interviews. When he passed away on 25th August, 2012, at the age of 82, his family members posted a simple yet significant request for those who wanted to attend his funeral and pay tribute: "Honor his example of service, accomplishment and modesty and the next time you walk outside on a clear night and see the moon smiling down at you, think of Neil Armstrong, and give him a wink."

Probably, nature prepares older people to slowly forget, so that the link with the present and the past becomes weaker, making the departure easier. During this period, pre-existing health problems resurface and become more severe. Loss of denture in many cases leads to indigestion and in some cases loss of memory. Fear of impending death pops up and haunts now and then. Severely depressed people attempt suicide Ancient Indian scriptures advise older people to spend this period in life in 'Vanprasth', ie, in solitude of the forest, freed from attachment to past events, places and people. They are expected to overcome the snare of all desires, cut off their worldly ties and proceed to live a quiet secluded spiritual life, as a preparatory to the final departure from the world. Almost like an old eagle, for, when an eagle becomes old and feels that its feathers are weakened, it retires to a lonely quiet place. Sitting on a rock, it plucks out each and every feather from the body until it is fully unburdened and bare. It is like shedding old memories, habits and weaknesses to make the final flying out of body lighter, quicker and simpler. More like the upward journey of a rocket when it leaves behind the excess weight to break the pull of gravity in order to reach its final destination faster.

Celebate Vinoba Bhabe, one of Gandhi's most learned and favorite followers and father of Land Gift movement (Bhudaan) had a cardiac problem in his late 80s. Soon after, he decided to "leave his body before his body left him". He stopped taking food, water and medicine, declining all requests to reverse his decision including a personal appeal from the then Prime Minister, Indira Gandhi. All attempts to force feed him also failed, as he refused to cooperate. Doctors told, his body was not ready to die and might revolt. But he didn't listen. And died peacefully on November 15, 1982, at age 87. Earlier, after reaching 75, he had withdrawn gradually from all social and political activities, spending time on reflection, meditation and prayer.

Adi Sankara, the monk who wrote Vedanta, interpreting the

Vedas, stressing that there was only one God and tried his best to free religion from ritualistic practices, had stressed a four fold practice in life. Vinoba followed these in letter and spirit. These are: Viveka or power of conscience or discrimination, Vairagya or detachment, Sat-sampatti or moral code and Moksha or liberation from cycle of birth and death, the final farewell.

For some people, bitten by viveka, this is the time for making amends, admission and confession, of thoughts and actions considered morally wrong or sinful and kept hidden as personal secrets during previous decades. An 87 year old lady in my village, on death bed, called her daughter in law and pulling her close, whispered into her ear- 'Thank you so much for being my rock, for all the care, nursing and support in my old age and forgive me for being rude and unjust to you so many times in the past.' Next day, she breathed her last, maybe, after being freed from the sense of guilt. At age 89, N D Tiwari, a former chief minister, governor and veteran leader in India, ended a six year old paternity suit, finally admitting to having an affair and fathered 34- year- old Rohit Sekhar, declaring him as his biological son. All three felt greatly relieved and lighter. The Catholic Church has a tradition of sacramental confession. It requires three "acts" on the part of the penitent: 'contrition' which means sorrow of the soul for the sins committed. The second part is called 'disclosure of the sins' known as the 'confession' of the actual guilt. The third and last part is 'satisfaction', popularly known as 'penance', ie, by doing something to make amends for the sins.

During my college days in the coastal town of Puri, I used to visit a saint named Pranavanand, whose ashram was raided twice by the intelligence people who took away all his old photographs. The reason was he exactly resembled Subhash Chandra Bose, an extremely popular freedom fighter and leader, who had militarily challenged the British Empire in India during the Second World War, taking help from the Nazis and the Japanese. Although he was reported to have died in a plane crash, there were strong rumours that he was alive.

A few years after this incident, Pranavanand called all of us to his ashram and pointing at his body, said: 'Look, this body has become old and weak. I have decided to quit it. When I am gone, pack it in a wooden coffin and consign it into the river Ganga.' He passed away the day after, sitting cross legged in a meditative pose, listening to and respecting the signal and siren of the body. In some parts of India, there is a popular tradition called 'Santhara', when an older person, wishing to take farewell from the world, meets his/her spiritual guru. And with his permission and guidance, prepares to leave the body. The five Pandav brothers, after winning the Mahabharata war and enjoying all the glory of power, authority and fame, decided to go on a 'journey to the high hills', renouncing the material world and finally disappeared into oblivion.

Towards the end of epic, Ramayan, there is an interesting episode about an encounter between an ageing Ram and Mahakal, the 'Lord of Time'. Disturbed by seeing the elderly Ram over busy with the worldly affairs of his kingdom, Mahakal met him to remind that his 'Time' or 'kaal' was up. Ram was shaken out of sense and immediately decided to call it a day and started preparing for the final journey. The fact is, most people do not survive this decade. G.K.Chesterton captures the mood in this period of life in 'A Second Childhood':

> "When all my days are ending
> And I have no song to sing,
> I think that I shall not be too old
> To stare at everything........."

Then, arrives the most critical phase, the tenth decade, i.e., age 90 to 99, the, 'pre-centenarian period'. Some prefer to call it the 'golden years', when the wise stop worrying about what might have been, what they could have done and not done. Any one, who has entered this chamber and is still kicking, must have led a disciplined lifestyle or inherited good genes and good family support. If one is mentally and physically active, one may live to be a centenarian. Socio-demographers say that the life expectancy at age 90 is 3.8 years and by age 99 it drops to 2.1 years. It is the last page in the book of life. To many, each day becomes a struggle for survival. On any given day, there can be multiple health problems to deal with. Unable or unwilling to bear the burden of an ailing body, some nonagerians desire to die. Physically challenged famous physicist Stephen Hawking has confessed how, wishing to exit with dignity, he had briefly tried to commit suicide by not breathing but failed, as the reflex to breathe was too strong. Yet many resist the temptation and still hang on to the hope of a still longer life.

A rare few are not afraid. One of them was noted scholar, journalist and jester, Khuswant Singh (1915-2014), who thought spending long time in prayer and worship in old age was conceding defeat. He passed away in sleep at 99 on 20th March when I was writing this chapter. True to his unconventional style, he had left his own self written epitaph, full of wit, humour celebrating his own death. It reads: 'Here lies one who spared neither man nor God. Waste not your tears on him, he was a sod, writing nasty things he regarded as great fun. Thank the Lord he is dead, this son of a gun.' Many super centenarians, i.e. a person who has lived to the age of 110 or more, linger on by sheer strength of hope, ready to die and yet active enough to live on. About one in 1,000 centenarians achieve this stage. A Scottish investment firm and office of National statistics (2012) reported in Daily Mail says, one in three babies born now will live to be 100, marry 8 years later than their grand parents and work until the age of 70. Bio medical gerontologist and longevity researchers predict that the first person who would live to see 150th birthday has already been born and the first person to live 1000 years could be less than 30 years younger to the first one. These people would be visiting hospitals in future fo stem cell therapy and immune stimulation to maintain a long life through medical control of health and well being.

Old age is perceived negatively in some cultures. Words and adjectives like senile, geriatric, superannuated, debilitation and dementia are freely used to describe the old. For old women frequently used words are hag, old maid, witch etc. Even in highly elder friendly Japanese society, it is not uncommon to use terms like 'Kaigo-jigoku'- which means caregiving hell. In some parts of the world, there are very cruel inhuman practices to get rid of the elderly particularly after they cross the 8th and 9th decade. For instance in a small community in Tamil Nadu in Southern India, there is a traditional practice called Thalaikoothal, which literally means showering or senicide, killing of the elderly. It is a form of involuntary euthanasia, by the old person's own family members. In this practice, the elderly person is given an extensive oil-bath early in the morning and subsequently made to drink glasses of tender coconut water which results in renal failure, high fever, fits, and eventually death within a day or two. The practice is illegal and banned in India Thalaikoothal has, for a long time, received covert social acceptance, and in some case the family even inform their relatives before performing it and invite them to attend the rituals following this tragic event. This shocking practice made news in early 2010, when an 80- year old man escaped after coming to know of his fate, overhearing his family members discussing how they were going to "share" his lands after performing Thalaikoothal. He ran away and took refuge in a relative's house. People in the area seldom report to the police about it. In such cases, shifting to a senior citizens' home is safer than living in one's own home with own children. A gray tsunami is going to take over the world in the coming decades and it is time for serious conversation on planning for the life span and end of life preparation. Like art of living, it is important to prepare people in the art of dying also, so that we walk into the night with grace and without regrets.

During my tenure as a senior Consulting Advisor with the Help Age India International, an elderly man attending a workshop stood up and asked me to include 'Assisted Dying' as a recommendation to end the artificially prolonged 'Assisted living' of the terminally ill. And those who have no possibility of leading life in a meaningful way, who struggle with loss of autonomous living, mobility and unable to put up with loneliness, fatigue and loss of loved ones.

'Would you allow your dog to suffer like this? Right to live also implies right to die,' he argued.

Supporting the view, another octogenarian said- 'When life is not worth living, why can't I decide to die with dignity?'

A third one asked-'Why the law and the doctors can't allow me to have my choicest glass of wine and a pleasing pill to get rid of my incurable pain and bid goodnight for good? Why someone else would determine the method and manner of my death?' French philosopher Albert Camus had said what could be good reasons for living could also be good reasons for dying. It is in a way completing one's journey of life through haps and mishaps, reaching the ultimate goal post. And then drop off freely like a seagull! Quantum physicists corroborate what spiritualists have been telling for ages that it is a transition of energy, spirit, consciousness and soul. Nature recycles everything and all of us. At sub atomic levels, all raw materials, including the organic human body, are non- materials, particles like protons, electrons, and bosons are impulses of energy and information. Thus, the essence of 'me' in 'me' is actually 'purified energy' that makes one feel, walk, run, cry, laugh and talk. That energy doesn't die or disappear. And that is immortality.

Asserting oneness of the supreme self, about three thousand years ago, Isa Upanishad had declared, nothing dies, nothing is lost: 'That is whole. This is whole. Wholeness emerges from wholeness. Take wholeness from wholeness, what still remains is wholeness.' But then, living a lifetime in and with a body that grew up in time and space, experiencing the world through its five senses, makes it difficult to accept its end and transition. An extension of that energy which me and Binny created, has now reached far away California, another part is growing in Delhi and the third particle in Singapore. And they have already united with their partners and created their own children, the new energy forms and fields, expanding our biological immortality.

So what we leave behind is the legacy, the memories in the minds of others that connect the present to the future, giving life to the dead and gone. Lucy's incredible children have built great dynasties, huge monuments and large empires hoping to live and last forever and have developed innumerable technology and tools to protect and push civilizations forward. They have invented an intricate variety of hammer and nails to fix, delay, enjoy and consume time. Without realizing that it is the 'Time' that ultimately consumes them! Ages ago, in an early Indian epic, Mahabharata, Yaksha, a semi-divine character, describes it through familiar metaphors: 'With help of earth as the pot, the sky as the covering lid, the sun as the fire, day and night as faggots, the seasons and months as stirring ladle, the Time cooks all beings.'

18

From Obituary to 'Woven Mat'

Lost in thoughts, the announcement by the captain and the clicking of fastening seat belts all over, were enough to alert me. The caring cabin crew came rushing to help passengers. I thanked them for all the attention. The plane now started descending. We were informed about the local time and temperature at the destination point, as well as time left until arrival. The cabin staff became overactive, checking seat backs and tray tables. Pulling out the half read news paper, to quickly glance through the rest of it, I chanced upon the mostly ignored obituary page, where time stands still for a moment. There were seven photos of departed people of all ages staring at you, with touching obituary by their near and dear ones. One was about a 14 year young boy, who died of accident in 2011. It began like this: 'God accepts only what is good- thus spoke Prophet Mohammad. Yours was a short unfinished life and tragic end. Yet you displayed exemplary courage in adversity. You are an innocent soul and our hero forever'.

The next obituary stated: 'Papa, eleven years have passed since you were reduced to a few grams of ash, we now realize, love is stronger than death. No matter how hard death tries, it can't separate people from love and it can't take away our sweet memories of you either. In the end, life is stronger than death'. In another corner, a son wrote, in an unusual style: 'Hey Dad, you were a great guy. I miss you so much.' Under another photo, three children remember their mother, quoting her last words on the death bed: 'Mama, remember you had said -

'Miss me, but let me go. The sun has set for me. Don't cry for a soul set free.' Yet, this is to let you know that despite all that you said, we shall wait for you at home forever'.

Children of a departed air force Commodore, looking smart in his uniform, wrote: 'Our father has taken his last flight into the blue yonder, his body gone six feet under the ground'.

Another short, touching obituary from an emotional daughter says:

'Mom, I still wear the pullover you knitted for me.' It was an expression of finest human emotions and I couldn't help controlling my tears. The next one, a bit formal, was that of an 88 year old William Duran, born on 12th June 1924. It was the longest obituary. The gist of it was:

'William Duran has passed away peacefully on Wednesday morning, July 18, 2012. He was the only child of his parents. During the Second World War, he served in the Navy for two years. William married four times during the course of his life: he had six children with his first wife and another eight through the other three. He was estranged from his last wife at the ripe old age of 86 and while the process of a divorce was on, he passed away. He loved to spoil his wives with multiple gifts of jewellery and even indulged for himself in expensive watches and diamond rings... He shifted to the Senior Citizens Home for a long time. He is survived by his fourteen children and twenty seven grand children. We, the family members would in particular like to thank William's caregivers at the Senior Citizens Home for all their services including funeral and burial. We were not able to come personally. 'Also thank you, Dad, for providing for us, even in death, through your just and generous will. Thank you for the sacrifices you made for us and most of all, thank you for your love for us and our children and every one of us.' Immersed in thought, I was wondering why a loving and generous grandfather like William, with fourteen children and umpteen grand kids, had to move to a Senior Citizens Home in the 9th decade of his life and why none of his children was with him when he breathed his last and even during funeral. Was it his destiny? There is no easy answer.

The final test and measure of a civilized society is how it treats its elderly. William's children have failed this test. Humans are called not only rational but also social individuals, driven as much by economic incentives as by need for human and social relationships. Concern, care, companion and community- are considered to be the four pillars older people look forward to for support before leaving the world.

The three institutions which can hand down or transfer the quintessence of this social capital to our children are – the family, the community and the school. We live in social units which satisfies our social and associational needs. An individual is socially helpless if left to oneself. It is said that human life is a game of five juggling balls in air- ie, family, friends, health, spirit and work. Among these five balls of life, 'work', the last one, is one ball which bounces back if you drop it. But not others, as they need continuous care, culture and nurture. Some clothes need deep immersion in the washing machine, some others need dry cleaning. What we need is a society for all ages. 2600 years ago, one of the four life events that had caused a deep metaphysical anguish in young Siddharth, the Prince of Sakyas, was old age. Societies respond to it differently.

During my short transit at Auckland airport in New Zealand, I happened to meet a Maori teacher named Hika. She was returning home from an education seminar on inter-generational education and understanding. During our brief conversation, she narrated how programmes were organized by schools to recognize and emphasize the mutually supportive relationships between young and old. This innovative curriculum is called 'Te Wharki', a word used by the aborigine Maori tribe which means the 'woven mat'. Te Wharki weaves individuals into family and community through continuous relationships between people and their habitat. It integrates children with the cultural, social and linguistic knowledge traditions of the locality.

It is basically an 'ecological model' that educates the child about their context, that includes their families, communities and other factors that determine a child's well being, sense of belonging, communication, value discovery, contributions and support to the society and responsibility to the elderly. For Maories, who live in small groups of 12 to 20, like many tribals in India, the family is the central structure of the society, to enrich which generations collectively create and provide the environment and exposure. For, each new generation needs an enabling environment to grow with the collective knowledge tradition. In this 'woven mat', the oldest generation, ie, the grand parents, pass on knowledge, information, codes of behavior, cultural traditions, beliefs and values to the youngest generation, ie, grand children. In Whariki curriculum module, family and community are integral, children and elderly are both contributors and beneficiaries of family and community resources. It recognizes that each member of the family and the community, whether young or old, .learns through reciprocal relationships with people, places and things. Thus 'Te whariki' connects one with the community's faith and culture, provides meaningful connections between all generations through bonding and social capital formation and values the significance of both ends of the life cycle and their inter dependence. Every person learns how to contribute to others' well being.

In many traditional and tribal societies elaborate rituals are performed to promote acculturation and integration. Many Hindus perform puja and prayer before and after a woman's pregnancy followed by a series of ceremonies after the child birth that goes on until marriage and adulthood. In some Pacific North West societies girls and boys are first named after flowers and carnivores respectively and then are given extra names when the child laughs for the first time, when it utters the first word, when it goes for the first hair cut and learns the first letter and so on. The biggest ceremony is reserved for the day when a child does the first economic function such as collecting nuts and berries. Interestingly, in some societies men are recognised as full adults only after becoming grandparent followed by another ritual. This helps the families to remain together. In human history, families have successfully moderated barbarous impulse of its members by imposing social and moral codes. That is how the rationalist inside the mind subdues the rapist. When life itself becomes a universe of learning and everything that happens to us comes as a lesson. Picking up these in the utility tool kit, Lucy's children have moved forward.

While life goes on, the obituary connects one to characters in contemporary history and samples of conversation between the living and the dead, while reminding one about the ultimate and inevitable event of life. Once a while one discovers that everything written in a long obituary may not be always true but it is the most truthful page in any news paper. Sheila Ebert, a Sri Lankan colleague of mine in the Commonwealth Secretariat, had narrated to me once, a personal experience. In Colombo, she had a very wealthy friend named Gunaratne, who had never bothered about his father who was 96 years old and living lonely and without help. But when the old man passed away, Gunaratnes had hired a funeral service company, ordered for a gold plated coffin and customized silver coated chariot to carry the dead body to the burial site. The company fixed black flags and flex boards and hired a local politician and crowd of mourners with badges and banners. The elaborate funeral was followed by a grand feast. He arranged to publish a full page obituary in the newspapers, in memory of his father. Just to wash his sense of guilt and ingratitude. Like many devout Hindus' belief that one ritual dip in 'Holy Ganges' would wash away all their accumulated sins. Significantly, one of the Ten Commandments asks of children: 'Honour thy father and thy mother that thy days may be long upon the land.'

As children become cleverer, parents also are becoming more practical. In our locality, there is a middle aged entrepreneur, who has even made an elaborate planning for his own death ceremony, signing a contract with a funeral service providing company, alongwith a wish list of how it is to be performed. He also ensured similar arrangement for his wife, as all their three children, two daughters and one son, live at far away places. 'I would not like to give them any additional burden and worry,' he said. He even selected the inscriptions to be engraved on his and his wife's head stone, when they died. For his own head stone, he showed me the inscription which he got engraved: 'I have now left this beautiful world without regrets and without burden to any one. I am grateful to my God, who has always blessed me.'

In retrospect, we learn lessons from life's myriad events and experiences. Virtuous Yudhistir, the eldest Pandav in epic Mahabharata, meets Yaksha, the Guardian Spirit to answer some basic questions of life in exchange of the life of his brothers.

"Who is truly happy?" was the first question from Guardian Spirit. "He who has no debts," answers Yudhistir in five words to the four worded question.

'What is the greatest wonder and lesson of this world?' was the next question.

Answering, he says, "Day after day, countless people die and yet after seeing this, the living still wish to live on forever." Satisfied, the Spirit revives the dead brothers as a reward for Yudhistir's wisdom. Something similar happened to Greek hero Oedipus when he arrived at Thebes. Sphinx, a winged monster blocks his way until he solves a riddle: 'Who walks on four legs in the morning, two legs at mid day and three in the evening?'

'Humans,' replies Oedipus, 'because an infant crawls on all four during morning of its life, walks on two legs after standing up and uses a crutch as a third leg in twilight years.'

One four legged animal whom Chankya called a life teacher is the dog, which our ancestors tamed, fed and spread, about 15000 years ago. A familiar saying about the dogs is- 'no matter how far they roam, they can always return home.' I recollect, during my first visit to San Francisco, I had met a journalist who was working in the strife torn Yugoslavia when it broke up. I wanted to know from him what the image of Indians in California was. He had given me a matter of fact, yet meaningful reply in four words- 'They always return home.' I said, 'Yes, it is an old habit. In fact, for about 90 percent Indians, including the young metropolitans, night life begins and ends at home with family, children and of course the home theatre. In a way, we are more like Amur Falcons.' He didn't understand. I explained how Amur Falcons travel a long flying distance of 22000 km every year at a stretch, from Mongolia to South Africa and back via India, but never once forget to return home. A good lesson from a bird.

Centuries ago, Chanakya (c.370–283 BCE) a famous Indian teacher, philosopher and royal advisor, teaching in Taxila, world's first university, had advised students to learn six lessons of life from a dog. A dog who never complains about life, about food and shelter, instantly goes into deep sleep but ever alert, is absolutely loyal to the master and fearlessly brave. For, while tigers attack something that is smaller than them, the dog is not afraid of even challenging a tiger and even a jumbo.

A few years ago, I had read about an Argentinean dog who had spent long six years near his master's grave as a mark of loyalty and love for the man it loved. This dog, named Captain, a German Shepherd, had disappeared from his home in Villa Carlos Paz, following the death of his owner in March, 2006. 'Captain' had a richer heart than Commander in Chief Alexander the Great, who understood the meaning of life only in front of certain death. And only after conquering many kingdoms and killing millions. The famous story says that helplessly waiting to breathe his last, he had called his generals and instructed them to ensure that his physicians alone must carry his coffin. That was obviously to show to the world that doctors can't give life to anybody and hence life should not be taken for granted. But then, Alexander learnt these new lessons too late in life, just when he was dying (June, 13, 323 BC) after taking lives of so many. Had he realised it early in life much suffering,loot, pillage and plunder could have been avoided. The Indian emperor Ashoka (304-232) also learnt the lesson from another only after inflicting massive death and destruction, killing more than 100,000 people and deporting about 150,000, including many innocent women and children in the bloody Kalinga war (about 260 BCE). 'Oh my, what have I done?' He now asked himself, after seeing rivers of blood, burnt houses and scattered dead bodies. But it was too late.

Why did Alexander behave the way he did? He was the favorite student of a great legendary Greek scholar, philosopher and teacher, Aristotle (384BC – 322 BC), himself a student of Plato. It is said that it was Aristotle who was continuously encouraging his student Alexander towards Eastern conquest. His attitude towards Persia and Asian regions was unabashedly ethnocentric. In one famous example, he counsels Alexander to be "a leader to the Greeks and a despot to all 'non Greek barbarians', to look after the former as after friends and relatives and to deal with the latter as with beasts or plants." To him all non-Greeks were slaves by natural selection. In Mahabharata, another scholar and royal teacher, Dronacharya, had used his students to settle personal score with his opponents. He had agreed to Bhisma's request to teach the Kauravas and Pandavas on the condition that they later help him in defeating and teaching his opponents led by Drupada, a lesson. Like Aristotle, he probably didn't have any sense of detachment, a primary requirement for being an educator. Hitler's history teacher Poetsch was another example. The 'great' teacher captivated the minds of his young students, with heroic tales from

German history and the racial superiority of the Aryans, focussing on the need for uniting all German speaking people against Slavs, Jews, Gypsies, and other minorities, telling his students to exterminate all of them as the "Final Solution".

In the battle between wisdom and power, between principles, prejudice and ambition, why such great teachers sided with the latter? If the heart of education is education of the heart, no teacher seems to have taught Alexander, Hitler and Asoka, this basic lesson. .Another emperor and poet, Bahadur Shah Zafar, the last Mughal, was not as lucky as Alexander. For, his one last wish to be buried in his own country, India, remained unfulfilled. He even had marked a spot for himself wishing to be buried there. Banished to Myanmar as British captive, at age 82, he had written down his feelings before death, in form of a ghazal, full of pathos:

"Kitna hai badnaseeb Zafar dafn ke liye,
Do gaz zameen bhi na mili koo-e-yaar mein"

'How unlucky is Zafar, to not even find two yards to be buried in the land of his beloved country.' He died on November 7, 1862 still in exile. Unlike Alexander, he had neither the generals nor the jewels, nor even the doctors to carry his coffin.

There are a lot many stories and fables about sacrifice, life and death, which my father used to narrate to me on way to our temple visits on Thursdays. Those were mostly episodes from Rigveda and the Upanishads. The one that remained in my mind till now was about a dialogue between Yama, the lord of Death and the underworld and an inquisitive child named Nachiketa. Whose angry father had sent him away to the 'house of death' for questioning his sincerity and motive in giving up wealth and possessions? He was in the habit of gifting away old and used things of little utility value including dry and old cows. Bhagbat Gita describes three types of 'Giving', ie, tamasik, rajsik and sattwik, ie, for selfish reason, for ego and fame and for love, joy and compassion, when you give up things you liked the most. The real motive behind giving defines the character of the giver. There is a saying that one should never brag about giving and in fact when giving in right hand, the left hand should not know about it. The best principle and practice may be to forget after giving and remember to return what you have received. In 1983, an old student of mine had met me after ten years and handed over a sealed packet. On opening it, I was surprised to find inside two 500 rupee notes ($20). 'Why are you giving me this money?' I asked.

'Sir, it is indeed your money, not mine, which you had given me ten years ago when I didn't have money to pay for my admission fee', he said and continued. 'Now I am well settled in life and am grateful to you for the timely help.' I returned the packet to him telling this was not the best way one should return a debt to his teacher. He didn't understand and apologized profusely for the long delay in repayment. I assured him it was not the reason and told him that the best way for him to return the money was by helping other students in similar difficulty and financial distress.

My friend, Abraham, had once told me a story in the New Testment, wherein Jesus had advised a young ruler that, in order to overcome death he must give away entirely what he had, to the poor and come alongwith him. But the greedy, power hungry ruler was not mentally ready. Similarly, when a follower publicly declared undying love for Prophet Muhammad, he had replied saying: 'Be ready for poverty if you really want to be my true follower'. It is said that no silver or gold coin remained overnight in his house as he would not sleep peacefully as long as he had not given it away to someone in need. The best Islam to him was to feed the hungry, to spread peace and conquer ego through relentless jehad against the self-centredness. Like Muhammad, Buddha didn't believe in having personal property and was living by begging every day. He would politely decline if a giver offered alms for more than one day. In Buddhism, a begging bowl or 'Alms bowl' has rich symbolic significance. It stands for non-attachment. A legend says when he was meditating beneath the Bodhi tree for enlightenment, a young woman, believing Buddha to be a divine incarnation of the tree, offered him a golden bowl filled with rice. Buddha divided the rice into 49 parts, one part for each day of meditation and threw the precious gold bowl into the nearby river. Thus the joy of daily begging of food and the virtuous pleasure of alms giving to monks was a part of spiritual tradition in many Asian societies.

In 2001, while celebrating the International Year of the Volunteers in Delhi, the Asia Centre had invited eminent social workers and activists from different parts of the world. Famous anti corruption crusader Anna Hazare and Nanaji Desmukh were present.It was a three day event. On the final day we gave to each participant a closed envelope with a cheque inside towards their honorarium for attending the event. A week later Anna returned the envelope addressed to me. There was a hand written letter inside, alongwith the cheque stating that it could not be encashed as he had no bank account! He explained: 'When you gave me the envelope I had no idea that it carried a cheque in my name.

Anna is bachelor, leading a simple Spartan life in a ten by eight ft. small room in the corner of a temple compound, without any property or bank account. In 2011, the Foreign Policy Magazine had named him as one of the 100 top thinkers of the present day world.

Long back, Prof. Luxman Mohapatra, a retired vice chancellor and close friend, admitted into All India Institute of Medical Science in Delhi for immediate operation, sent an SOS to me for help in finding a blood donor of a rare group. A day after, his wife informed me that a young man came to the hospital and donated the required blood. But by the time they came to know about it and wanted to meet and thank him, he had already disappeared. Giving is more like a noiseless excercise, in which one's body loses weight and soul gains strength. And givers, like fruit bearing trees, have made the world a haven of hopes. In 'Ants, Galeleo and Gandhi' the author presents several such examples that sustains the world.

Coming back to young Nachiketa, he waited for three nights without food and water as the Lord of Death, was out on tour of the living worlds. On return, he felt bad, seeing a child from the Earth waiting for him for three nights. He wanted to make amends for not being there by granting Nachiketa three boons, one for each night of waiting. Using the first boon, he requested Yamaraj to pacify the anger of his father. Against the second boon, he requested Yamaraj to show him the fire sacrifice and all the rituals and ceremonies that went with cremation. Yama granted both instantly. About the last boon, Nachiketa said, 'Oh Angel of Death, if you really like me, tell me the mystery of life and death. There is no better teacher than you to explain it.' The Angel of Death said- 'I will fulfill all other desires of yours if you withdraw this particular request. Nachiketa declined all allurements. Seeing his determination, the 'Death God' finally revealed the secret and ended by saying that life and death are one, as the river and sea, seed and fruit are one. There is nothing in death. All beings sprout and grow like grain and die again to sprout again. By mere reading of scriptures or joining intellectual debate, one can't realize the 'self'.

In 2007, I had visited Kobe and then Tokyo in Japan for the second time. While travelling, a message written on most of the Japanese bus stops that caught my attention was, "Only buses will stop here – Not your time, so keep walking towards your goal." Walking through life's complex, zig zag lanes and bylanes becomes simpler without an internal jury always out to judge others. Some one had once asked Mother Teresa to tell what she felt about her critics. She had replied saying that God had sent her to serve people; she had no time to judge them.

In 2002, I was in Ladakh, leading a multinational delegation of Change Agents. It was the traditional two day Hemis Festival time, preceded by a week long prayer and worship. A great religious show, where young Chham monks, draped in wine-red and marigold robes, captivated the audience with their ritual, swirling delicately on their toes, to the tune of traditional musical instruments. Falling on the fifth Tibetan Lunar month, the occasion was the birth day of Guru Padma Sambhav, who was a famous preacher of tantric Buddhism and had carried it to Tibet in 8th century. Coincidentally, Tibetan spiritual leader and Nobel Laureate for Peace, Dalai Lama also happened to be there in Leh, the capital city, standing on a rugged terrain. Our Ladakhi coordinator, Stanzin Dawa, had fixed an appointment with him. We called on him in his monastery and after paying respects, gently requested to address the delegates. He readily obliged and talked to us for an hour during which he made some very significant statements, without mentioning the name of god even once. The essence of what he said was that 'true love was absence of judgement' and one should cultivate a state of 'no mind' free from past thoughts and emotions and be present in the 'now'. Answering a question from one of the delegates, he counselled, 'whenever you feel that you were too small to make a difference, try sleeping with a mosquito.' He explained about the beauty and wisdom of various spiritual traditions. Concluding with an optimistic note, he explained how 20th century was the century of violence with two World Wars and a lot of killings. He advised to develop 'holy and healthy' envy for the other person's faith and work together for a peaceful 21st century and explained how science and religions were partners and friends, telling the same story in two different languages and trying to discover the same truth in different ways. Similarly, all faiths teach the same things- ie, the beauty of kindness over cruelty, creation over destruction, love over hate and giving over taking. He didn't utter a word against China nor for Tibet. This is the stuff great leaders are made of.

Once, while travelling by train, I happened to meet an old inmate of Seva Gram, an ashram set up by Gandhi that became a nursery of freedom fighters.

What was the main strength of Gandhi?' I asked him. 'Many,' he said and narrated a story. 'Gandhi had many illustrious 'followers', who actually were not following some of his principles in practice. Many of them were frequent visitors to the Ashram though. For instance, in the strategy group meetings with Bapu, Pundit Nehru used to go out after every 20 minutes for a smoke. Sardar Patel would listen to Bapu attentively but would comment afterwards that Gandhi's ideology was more ideal than practical. Maulana Azad, an erudite scholar, would come to the meeting after taking a peg. Rajendra Prasad, who became independent India's first President, would always come with an upper cast cook, scrupulously avoiding the ashram food. Acharya Kriplani, a professor turned socialist politician and chronic late riser, would mostly miss the 'All faith' early Morning Prayer sessions. Md. Ali Jinna, who later on deserted Gandhi to spearhead the movement for Pakistan, had scant regard for any ashram ritual and would never squat on the ground with others,. Nor would he wear Khadi, the coarse and humble hand spun freedom fabric that symbolized the fierce fire of nationalism and self reliance. Sarojini Naidu, another admirer, would call Gandhi a 'Micky Mouse' and laugh at his Spartan style of living in self imposed poverty, which she considered expensive. Netaji Subhas had great doubts about the efficacy of Gandhian methods. And so on. So, one day an old worried follower asked Gandhi- 'Bapu, aren't you aware how each one of your great followers is violating the norms and principles of your ashram and some even your ideology? And still you tolerate them?' Wearing his ever winsome smile, Gandhi said- 'Mere bhai, deshki azadi ke liye sabko sath me leke chalna hai- 'My dear, we need to take every one with us to reach the larger goal of liberating the motherland. Where is the time to find fault and judge these great leaders now?'In the ashram, he had a separate kitchen called 'Bapu ki rasoi', as he did not like to impose his healthy yet 'tasteless' food fads on others. A political pragmatist to the core, he never allowed his uncompromising personal ideology to cloud interpersonal relationships with people, who had otherwise high dedication and rich leadership qualities. Finding fault is a job best done by a gutter inspector.

I had a colleague named Harry, who was always over critical and had the habit of picking holes in every coat. And like a monday morning quarterback, he would offer unsolicited, uncharitable judgements on people and events. One day, we were chatting in my drawing room when he suddenly looked up and found my photos with some celebrities including Dalai Lama, Bill Clinton and popular Indian President, Abdul Kalam, and other presidents as well as eminent social activists. Then, he started reeling out juicy and scandalous stories about almost each one of the celebrity to convince me about how imperfect they were until I discreetly changed the topic of discussion, diverting his attention to some other issues.

Once, A V Swamy, a member of Indian Parliament and an old friend of mine, had forwarded to me a mail he had received from an old student of mine, insinuating that my academic and research degrees were spurious. The insult went down to my memory and remained there undigested for months, until Sheila Ebert, a Buddhist friend from Sri Lanka, narrated to me a real life incident, that finally healed my hurt ego and pride. It was about a monk whose monastery was always full with spiritual learners. One day, one of his disciples came running and told him:

'Master, people in the city are telling that you have an illicit relationship with a married woman, living in the monastery'. The monk said: 'Oh, really?' And continued his teaching, unconcerned. After a month, the same disciple reappeared and whispered into his ear- 'Sir, I am really shocked to learn that people in the city are now telling that the woman has become pregnant and you are the father of the child she is bearing'. The monk once again replied: 'Oh, really?' And continued doing his work.

Two months after, his old disciple came back once again and said excitedly- 'Sir, I have great news for you.' The monk asked, 'What is that?' The disciple said- 'Sir, now the same people are telling that whatever they said about you were all lies.' The monk smiled and said: 'Oh, really?'

On being asked by his close followers as to how could he be so indifferent and forgiving to people abusing his character, he replied:

'If you do not accept the abuse, it returns to the abuser. I have a mental filter that retains positive thoughts only.'

Tell me Sir, how can I be like you?

No, you needn't be. Rather be your own self . But calm your mind like space in which birds fly, clouds float, planets move and stars twinkle, yet the space remains silent.

There is a saying that life is ten percent of what happens to you and ninety percent of how you react to it. Nothing is easier than fault finding, rumour mongering and creating ill feelings. The main objective of people prone to this habit is to damage and destroy the targeted person's credibility and respectability without enhancing their own. Such people have an internal jury that loves to sit in judgment on everyone and everything. I had the bitter experience of being subjected to this several times. Whispers have large wings while truth is a slow walking pedestrian. The more the whispered words pass around, the more distortion and dilution they generate.

Negative emotions like this, dump high levels of adrenaline in the blood that constrict its supply line to the heart and slow down movement of white blood cells that fight disease. On the other hand positive attitude and emotions release endomorphins, happy hormones that strengthen body's basic immunity. They work as natural pain killers.The Monk, obviously, was rich in this. He had a firm faith in a positive and optimistic view of life. He didn't need the standard gossip and rumour management practice of seeking feedback, cross verification with reporting managers, colleagues and other workers to modify behaviour.

Two friends were travelling in a boat. One of them looked down under the blue water and discovered muddy dirt; the other one looked up into the blue skies and found bright stars! We are often chained to habits that are too light to be felt and too heavy to drop off. An old legend about life of Jesus says, soon after Resurrection, he straight walked into the heaven, carrying all our sins. And in his right hand he was holding the sins of people whose only hobby in life was to harm and hurt others. Rest of the sins he held in his left hand. Observing his overfull right hand, Archangel Michael said, 'Now, I realize why you had advised your apostles to forgive seventy times seven!

As I was lost in thought, the captain came on line and announced, like a drill instructor on obstacle course: "Flight attendants, prepare for landing please, cabin crew, please take your seats for landing. Ladies and gentlemen, fasten your seatbelt. We have just been cleared to land. Your journey is over.' My journey reached its last leg. As soon as the captain announced the landing information, people started getting up and the moment the first wheels touched the tarmac, they started walking and crowding the narrow path way. Then, they started opening the baggage cabins, looking towards the exit door with the impatience of a premature baby, trying to push its way out of the mother's womb, before the pregnant aircraft was ready for it.

With people closing in, competing and gesturing to move forward, I could feel the elbow push, butt brush and breast knocks on my back from a lady hurrying up behind me. There was no space for me to move. Bags were dangling out of the overhead lofts, threatening to tumble down and hit heads. Another air bag touched my ass and pushed, followed by a trolly striking my lower calf. Another person was prodding me to push up, close in the gap and occupy the small polite distance I was trying to maintain in front in order to avoid an intrusion. Suddenly, one realizes how important is the need for personal space and feels so claustrophobic, so lonely and anonymous, in a jostling crowd. Everyone is talking to someone outside but not to anyone inside, each for himself, trying to walk fast past the other, in the distasteful horse race of life. When I shared the experience with a sporting coach, he laughed saying how such behaviour would have disqualified a skater. There is a 'forearm rule' regarding skater's mobility, which stipulates that a player will be expelled from the game, if he or she made a conscious attempt at pushing, punching, grabbing, shoving and even touching the forearms of an opponent for more than three seconds .

An African proverb says: "If you want to walk quick, walk alone, and if you want to walk far, walk together." I was not able to do either. There was no semblance of order. Every one trying to arrive early overtaking the other, saving in the process not more than a few seconds. No different from the behaviour of the people we observe at busy railway counters, bus terminals, airport check-in queues, crowded temples, ration shops, buffet dinner lines and ticket sales outlets at cinema halls. Even birds and beasts display better behaviour and respect socially important rules in matters of basic needs. They neither push nor rush. One of the many examples is, about their water use discipline, to quench thirst, a basic survival need. In this matter, they follow scrupulously certain routine, order and sequence. For instance, monkeys, birds, peacocks, wildfowl and the like, make it a point to arrive first near the water point, just before the sunset. They are followed soon after by wild boars. Then sambars, deers and cheetals arrive. The last to reach the spot are carnivores, like tigers and lions. And this order is just reversed before the dawn, with carnivores arriving first, followed by herbivores and so on. This sequence is repeated everyday without fail. Each species follows its own time and space. Each waits for the other with patience. It helps everyone. In fact many of the unwritten social and moral codes of the humans like monogamy, fidelity, social discipline and courtesy to females were shaped by species like Sarus crane, bald eagles Gibbon apes and angel fish that came well before us. Cultural and lifestyle revolutions have overtaken and overwhelmed the biological markers, making Lucy's children change both their natural drinking and eating habits. Yet, chimpanzees continue to eat their best fruits, raw roots and vegetables and are satisfied, following a time tested lifestyle, in compatible with the environmental evolution. Socrates, one of Lucy's wise descendants, had probably foreseen this restless behaviour of humans, when he said: 'Contentment is natural wealth, luxury is artificial poverty'.

The aircraft had landed with a thud, a hard landing caused by a sudden change in wind speed. It was a rude reminder of another return to the earth and for one more check of the ground reality. The big shaking bird was settling itself through rain clouds, readying to receive the staircase, baggage trolley and signals, before opening the doors to its familiar old world. In minutes we will be descending down to earth to be with Lucy's children, now a little cleverer, a little wiser and a little more foolish. Lucy's spine, wisdom teeth, upright walk as well as ability to evade, lie and prevaricate, continue to define them even today. Her descendants have now fine tuned the 'art' of playing tricks and telling lies in bewildering ways. Some of them have become great artists, poets, play wrights and painters recreating lies into imaginative stories and portraying magnificently the inexact pictures of the real world. 'Telling lies?' 'No Papa'- Parents are still testing the lying skills of their smart children. In fact, linguists vouchsafe, deception is at the root of the development of human language. Doctors use it as a medicine to sustain patients' hope in hopeless medical condition. For lawyers and lovers, it is an assured source of survival and success. Pandav and Kaurav brothers in epic Mahabharata were using it generously to cut each other's throat. On at least one occasion, it was done with Lord Krishna's knowledge. Later on, 'lies' received moral sanction and support from royal adviser and medieval Indian scholar Chanakya, when he said it was not a sin to lie, flatter or exaggerate on five occasions. Namely, while praising people, pleasing women, negotiating matrimony, protecting property and saving life. He reinforced it further by advising people never to be too simple and straight forward and substantiated his views by stating that a straight tree and a simple person are the first ones to be axed and screwed.

Neuro-scientists have discovered that people who tell small, self-serving lies slowly progress into bigger falsehood and over a time the brain starts adapting to such dishonesty. Lucy's Children who have become wayward politicians, corrupt financiers, profit obsessed business persons, unfaithful spouses and self-glorifying egotists have a tremendous love for lying. Consequently, the brain also becomes desensitized to lying. For, everyone lies once in a while to make a friend, to please the boss, to feel better or in self-defense and denial. In relationships, a lover invariably tells the beloved that she is the most beautiful woman on earth. Superlatives are laden with lies that falsely generate a sense of feelgood.

Long live Lucy! The socio biological marker continues to give her children a new high, a new lift, a new sense of power, pleasure and superiority over others. Their power of imagination has now become the new reality. Despite walking erect with the inherited pelvis and leg bones, the competition for more imaginative, efficient tricks, deceit and dishonesty for dominance is on in a kind of counter Darwinism. Honesty and truth, continue to battle for survival, against the entertainment value of lies. Evolution has taken new direction with new tools. Yet, the silver line and flickering hope is that her smart, lying children have also invented smarter devices to detect their own lies. And are racing fast forward to meet the end of the millions of years of natural selection and survival story, likely to change their basic biological structure. A few small and large planes, still hissing, were waiting on the tarmac, like boats coming from different directions and waiting to reconnect to the mother ship. Now, I could hear the pitter patter of rain drops, falling on the large wings of the plane and kissing clean its silky skin. The eternal June has returned once again to welcome us outside the arrival lounge. It was time for fastening the real seat belt of life on earth, to face its events, excitements and challenges and once again to feel its breeze, smell its flowers, taste its fruits, hear its music and put up with its madness. One finally realizes how short is a long life, to feel its wonders and to learn its lessons!!! Were Lucy to return to her planet today, she would exclaim like Miranda in Shakespeare's The Tempest, (Act. V), yelling full throat:

'O wonder! How many goodly creatures are there here!
How beauteous humankind is!
O brave new world, that has such people in it'.

And then, looking around once again, she would be stunned to find her habitat devastated by dams, raped and run over by roads and railways and its belly pulled out by timber, mine, oil and gas merchants. Overcoming the shock, feeling lost, lonely and angry, and unable to recognize her own descendants, she would shout- 'But where are my children?'

Index

A
Agni–the Fire God p10,
Afro-Asian p11,
Artemis p44,
Arabian Desert p97,
Ahalya & Gautam p116,
Arnold Toynbee p137,
Anna Hazare p294,
Aadi Shankar p28,
Angelou, Maya p29,
Angel of Death p38,
Abu Barakat p64,
Apollo, Housewives and
Flush latrine p74,
Asia Centre p91,
APJ Abdul Kalam p90,
Adolf Hitler p133,
Arranged Marriage p215,
Aristotle p287,
Alexander p287,
Anna Hazare p290,
Arnold Toynbee p137

B
Brahma p18,
Bodhi, Baobab p18,
Buckingham Palace p6,
Bunking Class p21,
Brihad Aaranyak p24,
Bill Gates p27,
Binny's Kitchen p58,

Banyan & Peepal p66,
Beethoven's Teacher p90
Bill of Rights p70,
Bharat Ratna p95,
Bollywood films p102,
Breast feeding, Bhagbat Gita p41,
Burnt Certificates p142,
Belief Bazaar p205,
Bisou Bisou p230,
Bill Clinton p253,
Baba p139,

C
California p16,
Charlie Chaplin p18,
Caged Parrots, Confucious p20,
Casanova, Giocomo p29,
Chilka Lake p36,
C-Section baby p54,
College to village p-94,
Century Ago p111,
Chipco Movement p142,
Confucianism p150,
Cipolla p192,
Cultural Revolution p296,
Commonwealth -166

D
Dingo p11,
Diana Spencer p6,
Dunce Cap p28 ,

David's Carrot p105,
Dharmakirti p139,

E
Elnino p1,
Emerald Budha, Einstein p39,
Egyptian Religion p125,

F
Forty Niners p16,
Flower thief p6,
Food Medicine p71,
Focus Magazine p76,
Free Thinker in Fine city p155,
Fifty plus Vidya p257,

G
Gandhi's, Genghis Khan p11,
Genetic Streams p12,
Great Forces of Knowledge p22,
Ganesha p67,
Gotra p67,
Geeta and Samosa p83,
Grand Canyon p89,
Girnar Baba, god particle p140,
Gorbachev, Glasnost p160,
Golda Meir p259,

H
Himalayan Peaks p2,
Harvard School p27,
Hindukush p9,
Himalayas p9,
Henry p5,
in England p36,
Hippo and Monkey p101,
Hiuen Tsang p10
Hiranya Garbh p18,
Henry Kissinger p31,
Homo Sapiens p6,
Hindu Trinity p44,
How cooking make us huma p60,
Hindu Vaishnavism p68,
Honiara Reception p108,
Height handicap p134,

I
Indra p7,
Indian Mythology p123,

J
Janani p7,
June p1,
Jesus Christ p19,

K
King Solomon and Buddha p45,
Kabir p6,
King Cadmus p9,
Kali Paahari p4,
King Zamorin p17,
Karl Marx p14,
Kingdom Manuel p17,
Kurukshetra p65,
Kapil Kaul and donga fights p79,
King of Kindne,ss p80,
Kalama –sutta p159,
Kuala Lumpur p225,
Khushwant Singh p277,
Kalinga War p287

L
Lord Krishna p7,
Long living weaklings p235,
Land of Babel p19,

M
Mala p2,
Mao Zedong p46,
Manica – the 'Agony aunt' p85,
Menopause p118,
Mahisasur p123,
Moon's Mad boy p128,
Mysterious Mantras p132,
Migrant Seeds p142,
Mangalyan p210,
Mokshya p275,
Maori Teacher p283,
Mere Bhai p293,
Mental Filter p294,
Malala p259

Mekong River p2,
Milky Way p8,
Mead Margaret p24,
Mandan Misra p28,
Mahabharat p34,
Museum of Menstruation p5,
Men of Gold p18,
Museum of Natural history p5,
Meghasthenes p10,
Methuselah p18,
Martin Luther King p34,
Mad and blind guide p30,
Margaret Thatcher p60,
Millennium Survey p76,
Mao Zedong's death p46,
Mark Tully p187,

N
Neuro Scientists p29,
Nicolas Copernicus p82,
Neanderthals p6,
Nandini p9,
Nanima's Child husband p56,
Neil Armstrong p233,
Netaji Subhash p293,
Nirvana p64,
Narsimha Rao p172,
Nimbuda p267,
Naturre Recycles p279

O
Obsession with Gold p17,
Obituary to woven mat p281,
Oedipus p4 and p286,

P
Push Girl Push p55,
Pedagogy of the oppressed p78,
Protect me O'Lord p200,
Parsi p9,
Prince Harry, Prince William p6,
Purva Mimansa p28,
Padma Sambhav p31,
Protective Mother Bird p43,
Padmacharan's three worries p44,

Pythagoras and Isaac Newton p45,
Pushed out to unknown world p57,
Public display of affection p107,
Plato p287,

Q
Quraishi . S.Y and Quick p165,
queues p41,

R
Rainbow race p18,
Raavan Samhita p33,
R.N. Tagore p42,
Rights to Animals p42,
Raza, Rani, Panchi and Dena p103,
Resurrection p295,
Robert's question p105,
Rajiv Gandhi p190,

S
Shiva p8,
Sven Daughters of Eve p11,
Sri Lanka p18,
Shakespeare's Tempest p298,
Seven Marital Commitments p217,
Six 'Ts p228,
South Africa p16,
Story of Civilization p40,
SAARC Minister's Conference p63,
Sunita Williams in space p83,
Sita's Lap p55,
Sexual Freedom p116,
Swayamvar p118,
Sunderlal p144,
Shengnan, Shengu p225,
Seven 'Cs' p157,
Suffering the Stupids p175,
Sukarno, Suharto p267,
Second Decade p240,

T
Thomas Abraham p27,
Tenjiku p27,
Transcendence p98,
Tashkent p202,

Te Whariki p283,
The Tempest p298,
Tigerman p169,

U
Upside-down bottle p18,

V
Vishnu p8,
Vishwamitra p9,
Vasco's Fleet p17,
Vladimir Putin p3,
Vasistha p9,
Vedic Drink p10,
Victoria Falls p18,
Vice Chancellor p149,
Varuna – the Water God p10,
Venus p15,
Value of time p75,
Valentine Terescova p73,
Virtue of Selfishness p92,
Vedic rituals p130,
Voltaire p140,
Vedanta p275,
Vinoba Bhave p275,
Vairagya-detachment p275,

W
Washington DC p16,
Wooden Millstone p30,
White House p6,
Winston Churchill p227,
Waterpoint p29,
Waits, Worries and Wise Women p38,
Will Durant p40,
Why not God the Mother? p44,
Where are the Powerful? p73,
White Revolution p90
Wendy Doniger p120,
Western Africa p128,
Why should I be afraid p133,
Water point p296,

X
Xenophanes of Greece p139,

Y
Yinduren p64,
Yuri Gagarin and God p74,
youth Development Index p165,
Yuva p253,

Z
Zeus p7, p116,
Zakir Hussain p18,